MR. PIZZA

J. F. PANDOLFI

ISBN: 978-1-7325445-1-2 - Paperback

ISBN: 978-1-7325445-0-5 - Ebook

For Pop

1

Maybe he was a jerk. Who wears a wool pea cap in eighty-four-degree heat, in a room with no air conditioning? Of course, he could merely have been eccentric. Or perhaps the cap was a defiant slap at conformity. Then again—maybe he was just a jerk.

As Tony Piza sat at his book-laden dorm desk, a sheet of paper stared at him from a worn Smith-Corona typewriter. Other than April 22, 1973 in the upper right-hand corner, the page was blank, and had been for an hour. He looked relaxed, in a tee-shirt and cut-offs. But there were things on his mind.

The open window on his left revealed a vast, manicured lawn, one of the features that made the campus an oasis in the cluttered, brick-and-concrete landscape of the Bronx. Removing the cap to scratch his head freed the wavy brown hair. A muted yawn surfaced as he stretched his slender body and watched less-burdened students toss Frisbees, read under trees, or lie sprawled on a blanket. He would miss Fordham.

Reaching across his desk, he grabbed the open Jack Daniel's

bottle and took a swig. It loosened the grip of nostalgia, aided by the arrival of his roommate, who swan-dived his six-three frame onto Piza's bed. He'd miss Jack Morrow too.

"Feels like July out there," Morrow said as he sat up. "Why are all these books on your desk? You're a senior. I could have you incarcerated."

"I have a paper due."

"When?"

"Tomorrow afternoon. Now stop with the twenty questions."

"I refuse. How far along are you?"

"I have the topic. Kind of."

"This is fun. What's the kind-of topic?"

A slight eye roll. "Anything concerning Leibniz's theory of the monads."

"Hmm. Can't help you there. Now, if we were talking about *go*nads. . ."

Piza smiled as he handed him the Jack Daniel's. "Getting a jump on your med school humor?"

"Not really. My legendary wit just seized the moment. So, do you have any idea what you're doing?"

"Of course not. It's the key to my success as a philosophy major. The Jesuits love abstract thinking, so I concoct theories that are so ridiculously abstract they think I'm brilliant."

"As opposed to full of shit."

"Exactly."

Morrow shrugged, took a slug from the bottle, then placed it back on the desk. "Okay, if you say so. But I think four years of this stuff has—"

"Guys. Guys? Are you here?" a shrill voice called out.

Piza groaned, and Morrow lay down, emitting an "Oh God".

The doorway was instantly filled with the presence of Manfred Linkmeister. A bona fide prodigy, he was a senior at age eighteen—academically brilliant but well behind the curve socially. He was of average height, but at first blush appeared squat, the result of being overweight and having legs so short they had to have been an afterthought.

"Can I come in?" Linkmeister waddled into the room and plopped onto Morrow's bed, an open jar of petroleum jelly in his left hand. "Guys, I need help."

"I hear Lourdes is nice this time of year," Piza offered.

Linkmeister stuck out his tongue, and was rewarded with a thumbs-up from Morrow. "Good comeback, Manny."

Linkmeister ignored him. "I'm serious. I was having an argument with Phillips over in 2C. I maintain that when you stick your finger in this stuff"—holding up the jar—"it feels just like a girl's, um, you-know-what. Phillips says I'm crazy. But honestly, I don't think he's had much experience, so he probably wouldn't know it if he fell into it, if you get my drift."

Morrow, who'd been making a visible effort to keep a straight face, couldn't stifle the laughter and covered his head with his roommate's pillow.

Piza stepped in before Linkmeister could react. "Um, okay, Manny. Let's make sure we understand the premise here. Let's define our terms, okay?"

"Okay."

Morrow re-emerged as Piza continued. "Now, what exactly is the 'girl's you-know-what' you believe the contents of that jar feels like?"

Linkmeister blushed. "C'mon. You know what I'm talking about."

Piza expelled an exaggerated sigh. "Manny, Manny. We're seniors in college. We're men. So let's talk like men, okay? In order to make the comparison, you obviously did something with a girl. What exactly did you do, Manny?"

Linkmeister was now perspiring. Having been on the receiving end of Piza's barbs before, you'd have thought he would simply walk away. But he continued to sit there, now methodically inserting his right index finger in the jar, then removing it, as if subconsciously keeping time to a metronome.

"C'mon," he all but pleaded. "You know what I mean."

Piza leaned back in his chair. "Manny, I've gotta tell ya, I'm a little disappointed. Clearly, you engaged in an act of passion, and now, for whatever reason, you're afraid to admit it. Well, tell you what, I'll do it for you. Here goes. You were with a girl. First, a little kissy-face. Then, gradually, your hands wandered into the glorious hill country. The heat intensified, building and building and building, and then suddenly, as the two of you were catapulted into lustful abandon, you thrust your finger into . . . what? Her nose? Her ear? Her—"

"Stop it!" Linkmeister shouted, face flushed. "You're a goddamn perverted shit, Tony."

Piza looked askance at him. "I'm perverted? Excuse me, Manfred, but you're the one sitting on my roommate's bed, defiling a jar of ointment. And by the way, for whatever it's worth, that's the wrong finger."

"You suck," Linkmeister spat out, yanking the finger from the jar, then pointing it at Piza. "I, I come in here in good faith and, and all I get for my trouble is your bullshit."

Piza was about to respond, but Morrow intervened. "Look, Manny, why don't you just go. Tony's trying to finish a paper, so this isn't the best time to discuss the sexual attributes of skin moisturizer."

Linkmeister puffed out a breath of frustration, got up, and walked out—his index finger once again immersed in the jar.

Morrow sat up. "What the hell was that? Don't you think that was over the top, even for you? Ya know, you can occasionally be a bit of a dick, but—"

"It's part of my charm," Piza interrupted.

"I know. What I was going to say is that you're usually a good-natured dick."

"I think that may be an oxymoron."

"Pretty much everyone likes you," Morrow continued, disregarding the remark. "They take your wisecracks with a grain of salt. But with Linkmeister, I don't get it. You've always flipped zingers at the guy, but that performance was borderline vicious. What the hell is it with you and him?"

"I don't know," Piza answered, a hint of guilt in his voice. "It's just that— I mean how can someone so smart be so clueless? And look, I get that maybe he can't help it, and I should just accept it. But for whatever reason, it makes me nuts, and I guess he just showed up at the wrong time." He attempted to lighten the mood. "I beg you, sir, help me mend my ways."

"I'll enroll you in Scumbags Anonymous tomorrow."

"Thank you. Anyway, I'm pretty sure in the grand scheme of things old Manny probably won't even remember this. But you know what I can't get past? The idea of him going into the same profession as me. How can I be a lawyer if he's gonna be a lawyer? How can I enjoy something he's gonna enjoy? I dunno. I may have to rethink the whole master plan here."

Morrow's eyes widened. "Whoa! Is this your way of telling me you're thinking of ditching law school? Holy shit."

"Don't go freaking out. It's only a thought."

"Yeah, right. Christ, this is probably the biggest decision you've ever had to make in your life. And do I have to remind you what going to law school means to your family? . . . Don't shrug at me, you asshole. If you were conflicted why the hell didn't you say something sooner? And don't make like this is no big deal either, because I think that scene you just played out with Linkmeister was a lot more about you than it was about him. God you piss me off sometimes."

"Well, that was healthy. Nothing like a good old-fashioned catharsis."

"Which catharsis, mine or yours?"

"Oh, bite me," Piza replied as he reached for the liquor.

An hour later, the drained Jack Daniel's bottle teetered at the edge of Piza's desk. Morrow was lying sideways on Piza's bed, his feet high up the wall, his head resting by the side. Piza was lying on the floor, surrounded by an unbroken circle of philosophy books. Both of them looked comatose, but then Morrow spoke.

"So now that we've determined you're gonna postpone law school, what are you gonna do for a year?"

"I wanna do nothing for a year," Piza mumbled, eyes still closed.

"What'll you do for money?"

"I wanna do nothing for a year and get paid for it."

"How about welfare fraud?"

"With my luck, I'd get caught."

Silence returned. Morrow suddenly sat up, then immediately lay back down. "God, why did I do that?" A momentary pause. "Anyway, listen to me. I've got it."

"Got what?"

"The answer to your dilemma, pal. The next best thing to welfare fraud. Teaching."

"You do realize I have no teaching credentials, right?"

"So what? Teach in a Catholic school. You don't need a teaching certificate. My brother did it for a year."

Piza forced himself to sit up. "What were his qualifications?"

"Um, let's see. As best I can recall, he was free of venereal disease and could recite the alphabet without breaking into song."

A grin managed to surface. "Why are they so selective?"

"Why? Because the pay sucks and you have to spend every day hanging around women who drape themselves in black even when they're happy."

"Gee, that's enticing."

"Hey, you wanted an option to law school for a year, and I gave you one. My work here is done."

Piza lay back down. "I'll consider this when the feeling returns to my extremities."

He closed his eyes. But shutting out the world didn't translate into shutting down his brain, which raced with the excitement and anxiety of lurching off a career path that, until that moment, had been set in stone.

2

As he scrambled up the smooth, white concrete steps, a minute late for his appointment at the convent of Our Lady of Perpetual Tears, Piza questioned for the thousandth time whether he was making the right decision.

Since eighth grade, the assumption was that he would go to law school. That was when the school principal, Mother Christina, told his mother that with his inquisitive mind and feisty spirit, he would make an excellent lawyer. Her seemingly positive message couldn't quite conceal her true sentiment, which was that he was a stubborn pain-in-the-ass. But the devoutly Catholic Mrs. Piza completely missed the sarcastic undertone, and saw the nun's comments as a divine proclamation for her son's future.

Angelo and Mary Piza had emigrated from Sicily in 1950, while in their early thirties. A year later, Tony was born. They'd learned English by watching television and interacting with co-workers and customers at a Bronx delicatessen, which they later bought when the owner retired. Now, if it weren't for a slight accent, you'd have thought they were born here. They'd sacrificed major luxuries in their life to ensure there was enough money put away for their son to fulfill the destiny the Almighty had chosen for him.

Given that, the idea of delaying law school took on proportions no less monumental than spitting in God's eye, undoubtedly a mortal sin although, technically, it's not listed. Yet, despite the prospect of eternal char-broiling, Piza had decided to postpone his legal education. The schools at which he'd been accepted had agreed to hold a place for him for three years. More importantly, his parents had given him their unqualified blessing.

"Anthony, we want you to know that, however we may feel about this, you should do what makes you happy," his father had declared. And with that, his mother fainted.

Our Lady of Perpetual Tears was in the New York City borough of Staten Island. The school was located in a neighborhood populated primarily by blue-collar Italians and Irish, with a growing Jewish contingent, and small communities of African-Americans and Eastern Europeans. One of the Jesuits at Fordham had relatives in the parish, and had gotten Piza an interview. If he got the job, he'd commute from his parents' home in Carteret, New Jersey.

Reaching the large double-door, he adjusted his tie and, with just a twinge of hesitation, pressed the doorbell. He hadn't heard it ring, and after at least a minute, he began to wonder if it was broken. He was about to give the large brass knocker a go when the door opened with no apparent human intervention. An angelic face, encased in what appeared to be pristine white cardboard, poked out from behind it.

"Oh, good afternoon," the face uttered with a demure smile. "You must be Mother John's one o'clock. Please, come in."

He returned the smile. "Thank you."

As the face emerged from behind the door, he could see the cardboard was enshrouded by a black veil, which blended with a floor-length black habit. The nun was quite petite and seemed like an over-sized doll as she glided across the polished wood floor.

Crossing the threshold to follow her, Piza caught the scent of incense and detergent. He was instantly a young schoolboy again, where one whiff of that blend of the sacred and the profane invariably triggered an intense feeling of unworthiness, followed by a compelling need to confess his sins, even if he couldn't think of any.

"Mother will be with you shortly," the delicate voice announced, nudging him back to the present.

"Thank you." He had to stop himself from bowing. "Thank you very much."

The nun nodded pleasantly and floated down a hall. The room was spacious, with ten-foot ceilings, large frosted windows inlaid with metal, and walls covered with rich cherry wood paneling. He was actually a little nervous, and decided to tour the area rather than sit in one of the expensive-looking red velvet Victorian chairs.

The room was populated with glass-encased, life-sized statues of saints whose names he remembered, but whose stories he'd long forgotten. He visited each, reading the brief biography at the base of each enclosure.

As he approached one, a chill shot through him. He instantly recognized the image of Saint Lucy, and there, on a silver plate she held in front of her, were two very realistic eyeballs staring at him. He didn't have to read anything; he knew this story by heart.

His introduction to the saint had come in first grade, when Sister Sophia took the class on a tour of their church. As they approached Saint Lucy's statue, the kindly nun told them that many years before, Saint Lucy had been a young girl who'd devoted her life to God and had also taken a vow of chastity. Of course, no one in the class had any idea what chastity was, but if Saint Lucy was doing it, it had to be good.

One day Saint Lucy learned that her family had arranged for her to marry a pagan prince. As far as she was concerned, marrying *anyone* was out of the question, never mind a pagan. None of the kids knew what a pagan was either, but if Saint Lucy didn't like it, it had to be bad. So, in an effort to make herself less attractive to this heathen, she made the perfectly rational decision to pluck out her eyes.

This revelation was traumatic enough, causing some random sniffling within the group. But when they reached the statue and got a look at those detached peepers, three of the little ones flew shrieking toward the exit. The frantic nun rounded up the escapees and reunited them with their now sobbing classmates.

She tried to undo the damage by breathlessly pointing out that the face on the statue *had eyes*. God, she desperately explained, had let Saint Lucy's eyes grow back to reward her for remaining pure. Small consolation to a bunch of horrified six-year-olds, what with the old headlights still resting comfortably on the serving tray.

"I hope when God was rewarding you, he threw in a few years of therapy," he murmured to the stone figure.

"Did you say something?" a melodic voice asked from behind him.

Piza whirled around, and almost gasped.

"I apologize if I startled you," the nun said. "I'm Mother John, the principal of Our Lady of Perpetual Tears. And you must be Mr.— I'm sorry, is it pronounced 'pizza', like the food?"

He didn't answer immediately. He was too shocked by the bulbous nose that, at first blush, appeared to occupy most of the woman's face. He did manage to discover small blue eyes and a tiny, thin-lipped mouth, but he wasn't sure if they were actually small or just seemed so in the shadow of that mammoth beak.

"No, actually it's a long 'I'," he explained through a smile he hoped masked his shock.

Further assessment revealed Mother John to be a large

woman, perhaps in her fifties. "I'm very happy to meet you," he continued. "Father Janicek at Fordham had nothing but good things to say about you and your school," he lied, the Jesuit having never mentioned her.

"I don't know Father Janicek. Your interview was arranged through our pastor."

Geez, you couldn't just accept the compliment? Nailed on his first suck-up, he struggled to recover. "I guess he was telling me so much about the school's wonderful reputation that I just assumed you knew each other personally." If he smiled any harder he'd have fractured his cheekbones.

She looked wary. "Well, I'm glad he holds us in such high regard. I look forward to meeting him someday."

Piza nodded, the overblown smile still in place. After a brief —yet endless—pause, she motioned for him to follow her. "Let's sit down, shall we?" It was an order, not an invitation.

He dutifully fell into step as she led him to a small alcove, where they sat in austere wooden chairs separated by a nondescript glass coffee table. *This must be the area reserved for interrogations.*

"So," she opened, "you want to teach."

"Yes, ma'am."

"I reviewed your résumé, and your educational background is impressive. But you majored in philosophy, not education. And you don't have a teaching certification."

He'd anticipated this line of questioning. Leaning forward, elbows resting on his knees, hands clasped, he began to weave his tale.

"To be truthful, Mother John, I only recently became aware of my desire to teach. For as long as I can remember, I envisioned going to law school, but—"

"Sorry, I don't mean to interrupt you, but if I recall, don't most pre-law students major in political science?"

It seemed an innocent question, but he was disturbed she'd broken his rhythm. "Uh, they do, actually. And I did take several poli-sci courses. But for me, philosophy seemed to make more sense."

"Hmm, interesting. Anyway, you were saying . . . about law school?"

"Right. Yes, law school, that was the plan. Until last month." He looked down.

"What happened last month?" she asked with seemingly genuine interest.

He raised his head and tried to look past her nose directly into her eyes. "That's when my roommate died." Not wanting to jinx his friend, he'd cleared this ruse with Morrow before using it.

The nun's hand shot to her chest. "Oh, my goodness. How terrible. What happened?"

Gotcha. "Well, Jack—that was his name—went home for spring break. One day he was walking to a store to get some milk for his mom. A car ran a stop sign and. . ."

Making the sign of the cross, she said, "I'm so sorry for your loss, Mr. Piza. To lose a friend at such a tender age."

"Thank you."

A quizzical look appeared. "But I don't understand how that led to your desire to teach."

"Well, after all this, I did quite a bit of soul-searching. Re-assessing my priorities, I guess." He stood and began to pace. "One day, it struck me—was being a lawyer the best way for me to spend my life? I mean, you hear these stories of deceit and manipulation. That's not me."

"But surely you can't condemn an entire profession for—"

"No, no, don't get me wrong. I don't doubt there are plenty of upstanding lawyers out there. But for me, that path didn't make sense anymore. I decided my life would be better spent teaching children the basic values of honesty and decency. If I can provide them with that foundation, maybe it will lead to a better world."

As soon as he unleashed that last line, he realized it had probably been too much. He scrambled for damage control. "I know it may seem kind of pie-in-the-sky when I talk like this, but it's something I've grown to feel very strongly about."

Her lack of immediate response or expression was unnerving. "I admire your idealism," she finally said, a hint of skepticism in her voice. "But talking about it is different than doing it. How do you know—and how do *I* know—you can manage twenty-five or more children of different intelligence levels and personalities?"

After a slight pause, he replied, "Well, I was a camp counselor in high school, and I had a wonderful time. So did the kids, from what their parents told me. And yes, I realize this isn't summer camp, but I think it proves I have the ability to work with children."

He *had* been a camp counselor. But, it had been for two weeks one summer, since he joyously jumped ship when offered a slightly higher-paying job at a golf course.

The principal stared at him for a couple of moments. "Mr. Piza, as I mentioned before, you were highly recommended. And although I think you may be a little naive about teaching, I'm willing to take a chance with you."

He grinned, more out of relief than joy. "That's great. Any idea what grade I'll be teaching?"

"Actually, I've already hired another teacher, Mr. James Bauer. You and he are the first male teachers we've ever had here, by the way. I gave him a choice between second grade and sixth grade. Whichever one he chooses, you'll get the other."

"That'll be fine," he said, elated there would be another male teacher around, yet mortified at the possibility of having to deal with seven-year-olds.

"Do you have a preference, in case it doesn't make a difference to Mr. Bauer?"

He restrained himself from falling to his knees. "Well, if it really doesn't matter to him, I think I'd like sixth."

"Okay, then. Are you aware of the salary?"

"Um, not really. I know you don't pay as much as the public schools, though."

"It's forty-five hundred dollars . . . for the year."

Holy crap. Oh, well. "Uh, that's fine. I'm okay with that."

"Good. We'll mail you a contract. There'll be a teacher orientation on August eighteenth, and you'll get your syllabus and books then. School begins on Wednesday, September fifth. It's been a pleasure meeting you."

She rose; he followed her lead. "It's been a pleasure meeting you too. I'm looking forward to this new challenge."

"It will be that," she responded as she led him to the door. "And since you've never done this before, let me give you some advice. Aim the level of your teaching at the average students. That way you won't completely lose the slower ones, or completely bore the smarter ones. And since you're new, they'll test you. So you might want to consider not smiling for a while."

"Um, okay. How long is 'a while'?"

"My suggestion? Christmas." She didn't appear to be kidding.

"I'll remember that," he said, wondering if he'd just signed on to be a teacher or a prison guard. Either way, he thought, nothing I can't handle.

As he descended the front steps, he loosened his tie and congratulated himself. He'd deflected Mother John's obvious doubts—if not outright mistrust—and marched to victory. What he didn't know was that, barring his showing up dressed as Satan and smelling of sulfur, the job was his the moment he arrived. Mother John had had no choice. No one else had applied.

3

Piza's black 1967 Pontiac Firebird pulled into the parking lot of Our Lady of Perpetual Tears church. Despite the fact he was late, he sat there for a minute, hoping to quell the stomach discomfort he blamed on the breakfast sausages he'd consumed an hour before. Attributing it to nerves would be ludicrous, he reasoned, since there was no rational basis for being nervous about babysitting a gaggle of eleven-year-olds.

The orientation in August had gone reasonably well. Jim Bauer seemed like a nice guy, if a bit serious. Although he'd also just graduated, with a degree in education, he was two years older than Piza, having gone to school at night. He was just shy of Piza's 5'10", but his barrel chest and protruding stomach made him look shorter than that, and a receding hairline and streaks of premature gray added ten years to his appearance.

Married, with a four-month-old daughter, he'd have preferred a job in a public school, where there were benefits and better pay. But jobs in the public sector were tight. It was either teach in a parochial school or not teach at all, and the latter wasn't an acceptable alternative.

There were two sixth-grade teachers that year, Piza and a nun, Sister Theresa, whom he'd gauged to be about his age. At orientation, she'd been very sweet, with an energy level he remembered experiencing only once in his life when, at fourteen, he mistook one of his mother's diet pills for an aspirin.

In contrast to the traditional dress of the older nuns, she wore a modified habit—a small headpiece and short veil covering the back of her head, white collared blouse, black hip-length vest, and matching ankle-length skirt.

He'd also met a fifth-grade teacher, Colleen O'Brien, who looked to be twenty-six or twenty-seven. She was stunning, with penetrating dark green eyes and straight black hair that fell halfway down her back. The remnants of a Brooklyn accent delightfully complemented her looks.

He'd made a zealous attempt to dazzle her. He was a decent-looking guy, not jaw-droppingly handsome, yet enough to hold a girl's attention while he unleashed the charm. But his effort with O'Brien had been too forced. He'd come off as smarmy rather than engaging, causing her to end their conversation with a thin excuse. Undaunted, he'd vowed to resume his quest when school began.

An opening day mass was being said for the success of the school year. Exiting his car, he wrestled his way into his jacket and speed-walked to the church. As he approached the entrance, he almost felt like a trespasser. Despite having attended Catholic schools all his life, his only appearances at church the previous couple of years had been for weddings and funerals.

His study of philosophy and theology at Fordham had triggered a fierce spiritual upheaval, resulting in a bare-boned conclusion that no one has a clue why we're here or where we're going. The perfection of the universe led him to concede the possibility of a higher power, but he'd decided that whoever, or whatever, it was probably couldn't be bothered with the human race. Yet, he always felt a trace of anxiety whenever he entered a church. He chose to attribute his uneasiness to the conflict between his current beliefs and his rejected surroundings, rather than the notion that his newfound freedom wasn't quite as uncluttered as he imagined.

When he entered the cavernous building, the mass had already begun. The place was a sea of fidgety uniformed children, nuns, and lay teachers. He noticed Bauer leaning against the wall abutting the right aisle, near the rear, and moved to join him as inconspicuously as possible.

"Hey, buddy," he whispered as he came up behind him.

Bauer seemed genuinely glad to see him. "This is it," he whispered back, extending his hand. "I've gotta tell ya, I'm really excited. Nervous too. How about you?"

"Excited, yes. Nervous, no," Piza replied, ignoring his stomach.

Bauer smiled. "Then you're a better man than me."

Piza noticed Mother John frowning at him from the front of the church. He waved faintly, to which she responded with a telling glance at her watch that caused him to shrug and flash a disarming grin. She appeared unmoved.

He continued surveying the area and spotted O'Brien toward the front on the left. To his disappointment, she seemed immersed in prayer. *Ugh. She's one of them.*

"Any idea where our kids are?" he asked Bauer. "I'd like to see what the little brats look like."

"Not a clue," Bauer said, speaking louder to be heard above the choir and resounding pipe organ that had launched into a hymn. "I think they're going to pair us up with them when the mass is over. I've been—"

He was interrupted by an absolutely seismic fart emanating from a row of boys a few feet behind them. This was instantly followed by groans and an attempted evacuation of the toxic area. Before any of the victims managed to escape, a wiry, middle-aged nun stemmed the exodus.

"How dare you engage in such disgusting behavior in the Lord's house. Is this what you do in your own homes?"

Some of the boys giggled. One looked like he was about to answer, but apparently thought better of it.

"Which one of you passed wind? I demand to know immediately."

No one replied, and she began to tap her foot. "Fine. I'll see this whole row in my classroom after school. We'll uncover the responsible party then. We have ways of finding out, you know."

As she left, Piza chuckled. He leaned close to Bauer. "'We have ways of finding out, you know.' What's she gonna do, check their butt holes for gunshot residue?"

Bauer instantly buried his face in the crook of his arm, in a failed effort to stifle a laugh. When he settled down, he lightly coughed, as if purging the remnants of mirth, then let go a deep sigh.

The choir finished its song, and the priest celebrating the mass asked everyone to stand and recite the Lord's Prayer. This and the Hail Mary were the only prayers Piza remembered intact. He had no desire to participate, even for show, but decided he'd better.

The prayer came to an end as the congregation declared "and lead us not into temptation, but deliver us from evil. Amen." Everyone fell silent. Except Bauer.

"For Thine is the kingdom and the power and—" He abruptly stopped, chagrin spreading across his reddening face. He nonchalantly cleared his throat. He'd been speaking only above a whisper, and it appeared no other teachers had heard him. Then, Piza tapped his shoulder.

"Um, pardon me. The ending to that Our Father rendition you just offered . . . um, what was that?"

Beads of perspiration formed on Bauer's forehead. "Can you keep a secret? And I'm serious."

"I'd go to my grave before betraying a trust."

Bauer lightly tugged at his shirt collar. "Okay, but you have to promise you'll keep this to yourself."

"I already told you I'd die before blabbing, what more do you want?" Piza was enjoying this, especially since he knew the answer.

"I'm not Catholic. I'm Protestant." He had now graduated to a full sweat.

"Go on! You *sly* dog." Then his expression turned serious. "I can't believe you lied to Mother John."

"Gimme a break, will ya? First of all, I didn't lie to her. She didn't ask if I was Catholic, and I didn't happen to mention I wasn't." He was becoming more visibly upset. "You know what? If you think this is such a crime, then go and tell her, okay? If you wanna ruin my—" He must have realized the tartness of his reply, because he immediately apologized. "I'm sorry, Tony. I didn't mean to go off like that." He hardly knew this guy, and his job probably depended on the man's silence.

Piza, however, was delighted that the only other male teacher in the school apparently had a touch of larceny in him. "I was just busting your chops. Your secret's safe with me, and I would never hold it over you."

Bauer was patently relieved. "Thanks. I'm not comfortable with the charade, it's just that I really need this job, ya know?"

"I understand completely. Oh, by the way, did I mention how dirty my car is?"

Bauer smiled and looked to the front.

A short time later the mass ended, and Mother John strode to the center aisle. "Pay attention, everyone," she bellowed. "When you hear your names, form a line in front of me. Your teacher will then take you to your classroom. Remember that you're still in church, so I don't expect to hear a single sound out of your mouths. Understood? Oh, yes, and welcome back."

Piza whispered to Bauer, "Feel the love."

"I'll say."

"Kind of makes you glad you're not Catholic, I bet."

"Please don't do that," Bauer pleaded. "I'm nervous enough about this as it is, okay?"

"Kidding, kidding. I promise I'll be good."

Bauer didn't appear reassured.

Mother John began to read lists of names, pairing teachers and students. After a few minutes, "All right, you second-graders whose names I just called, your teacher is Mr. Bauer." She motioned to him. "Mr. Bauer, if you'll come up, please, and take your class."

He glanced at Piza. "It's game time. See you later."

"You'll be great," Piza reassured him, patting him on the back. "And as for your secret. . ." He mimed locking his lips.

Bauer blanched, then tentatively walked away.

Piza turned his attention to finding O'Brien. He saw her engaged in what appeared to be a hushed, yet animated, conversation with Sister Theresa, and decided to join them.

"Mr. Piza, it's so nice to see you again," the nun gushed. "I think this is going to be a terrific year, don't you?"

Piza was already exhausted by her enthusiasm. "I do, indeed," he responded with a too-wide grin. "And please, call me Tony. All my friends do."

"There's a short list, I bet," from O'Brien. Her smile was as phony as his had been.

"Colleen," Sister Theresa said, emitting a nervous chuckle and brushing aside unruly wisps of exposed blonde hair, "play nice."

"Aw, I was only kiddin'. Mr. Piza—or should I say Tony—and I started ribbin' each other when we met at orientation."

The nun seemed placated. "Well, that's good to hear. Had me going there for a minute."

"Sixth-graders, pay attention." The booming voice echoed through the church.

The haphazard sequence bothered Piza. "How did we go from second grade to sixth?"

"What difference does it make?" O'Brien asked.

"It was just a question," he shot back.

O'Brien shook her head. "I dunno, sounds kind of anal to me."

Before he could offer a comeback, Sister Theresa placed her hands on their shoulders. "Come on now, kids, you can finish your little game later. The other children are waiting for us."

Her class was called first. Then Mother John told the remaining sixth-graders to line up, and announced Piza as their teacher. Aside from a few sneers, the children's expressions ranged from concerned to terrified. Relieved that they seemed more ill-at-ease than him, Piza was on the verge of a grin, but caught himself as he recalled the principal's warning that a premature smile might launch Armageddon. He wasn't inclined to attribute value to anything a nun might have to say, but this was foreign territory to him. Besides, maintaining discipline—and distance—suited the spirit in which he'd taken the job.

His students formed two misshapen lines: girls in one, boys in the other. A scowl from him straightened the queues. Satisfied his troops were in order, he led the rigid band of twenty-seven into the new school year.

4

Our Lady of Perpetual Tears school, built in the mid-1920s, was an imposing brick-and-stone structure that conveyed solemnity and grandeur. But the well-preserved facade belied a battle-scarred interior.

When Piza attended orientation, the barren, faded-yellow tile walls, cracked white ceilings, and scuffed linoleum floors of the hallways had been instantly depressing. As his group now traversed those halls, the walls were adorned with a variety of colorful "Welcome Back" signs and motivational clichés. The ceiling was untouched, but the floors had a semblance of a shine. From Piza's perspective, the token embellishments only emphasized the underlying dreariness.

The classrooms were a bit cheerier, thanks to the large, unshaded windows that ushered in volumes of natural light. As his entourage passed by them, glimpses into each revealed an assortment of colored banners, posters, maps, and pictures. It was obvious other teachers had gone to some pains to brighten their little domains, and Piza fought to deflect guilt for not having done the same.

His classroom was at the far end of the hall on the second floor. When his group reached its destination, the children's reaction to the desolation aggravated his discomfort. Frowns mingled with a vocal, though discreet, undercurrent of displeasure. Piza noticed some smirks, which he saw as hostility—a sentiment he was more comfortable dealing with than disappointment.

"Okay, listen up," he commanded, before anyone could sit. "Please form a line around the perimeter of the classroom, assuming you know what a perimeter is." The clearly befuddled youngsters made their way around the desks. "My name is Mr. Piza. That's P-I-Z-A. Note the one 'z' and long 'i'."

A thin, lightly-freckled girl with short blonde hair raised her hand.

"Yes, what's your name?"

Without appearing to take a breath, the girl answered, "My name is Suzanne K. McDermott but everybody calls me Sukie which is okay because I like that name better."

"Yeah, that's Sukie, like in pukie," a hefty, sweating boy joked.

"Very funny, Matt Majinsky," she shot back, blue eyes blazing. "That's Matt, like in fat."

The others oooo'd at the comeback.

"That's enough of that," Piza warned. As the class quieted, he continued. "Now, Miss McDermott, what would you like to know?"

The girl was surprisingly undaunted. "What I want to know is why the blackboard says your name is 'Mr. Pizza', if it's really 'Mr. Piza'?"

Someone had misspelled his name on the board, in very neat print. The children nervously laughed as he all but ran to the error and, in nearly one motion, erased the name and printed the correct spelling in large block letters. The quiet returned as soon as he turned back.

"As you're aware, this is my first year here, and someone obviously made a mistake. Since I've had this name for as much of my life as I can remember, you'll have to take my word for it that it's Piza. And if any of your devious little brains are scrambling to concoct witty pizza jokes, I've heard them all. Any other questions?" His glare didn't invite a response. "Good. Now, when I call your name, take a seat starting with the first desk of the first row to my left. That's *this* hand," he added in a mocking tone as he raised and waved the hand. "Work your way to the back of the row, then start the second row, and so on."

He sat behind his desk and removed a piece of paper from the center drawer. It was the first indication the desk wasn't deserted. As he read the names, the children dutifully took their seats and settled in.

He had jotted down some hastily prepared remarks the night before, so he'd have something to bolster the illusion he knew what he was doing. He unearthed the notes from an inside jacket pocket.

As he was about to begin, a lanky boy with mousy brown hair partially covering his eyes casually came forward from the back of the room. Some of the children grinned as he strolled up; others wore looks of uncomfortable anticipation. The boy came around Piza's desk, slapped him on the back, and extended his hand.

"How ya doin', Mr. Pizza?" The ridicule in his voice made his smile irrelevant. "I'm Kevin Davis, and the class elected me to give you an official OLPT welcome. That's Our Lady of Perpetual Tears, in case you didn't know."

A smattering of laughter.

Piza looked at the still-extended hand, then shifted his gaze to the boy's humorless gray eyes. He was surprised at being tested this soon.

"Thank you . . . Mr. Davis was it? You can take your seat."

The boy withdrew his hand, shrugged, and sauntered back. Piza casually surveyed the class, taking his time, conscious of the building tension. Then he spoke. "You know, first impressions are so important. It can take only seconds to make a bad impression. But trying to change that? Well, that can take quite a while."

There was a trace of smugness on Davis's face, but everyone else's expression was either blank or worried.

"Mr. Davis here has made a bad first impression. Now, of course, I won't let that affect how he does in this class. But if something goes wrong in here, like, oh, I don't know, like if when I wasn't looking, someone threw a spitball at the blackboard; or purposely dropped a book; or coughed too loud, my inclination would be to suspect Mr. Davis. And maybe that's not really fair but hey, it's only natural. He seems to think he's a hotshot, but my first impression of him is that he's just a disrespectful clown." There was a collective gulp. "I noticed a number of you seemed to be amused by Mr. Davis's showboating."

The children shook their heads in vehement denial, and some tossed mumbled epithets at the glowering Davis. Piza marveled at the control he wielded over this brood in such a brief time. He let them twist for a bit, then continued.

"No? Okay, let's play it by ear then, shall we? Now, getting back to the way things are going to be this year"—he skimmed the sheet of paper in his hand—"I don't know what you're used to, and, frankly, I don't really care. My belief is that people your age have been spoon-fed for too long. So I expect a lot more from you than you're probably used to. Bottom line, you're going to work harder than ever before."

There was no effort to muffle the groans.

"Remember first impressions," he spat out, and quiet returned. "If any of you have problems with the work, tell me during class and I'll see what I can do to help. I don't believe in staying after school and, truth be told, they don't pay me enough to do that anyway. You get homework every night—"

Resigned frowns.

"—but not on weekends, unless you really tick me off."

Smiles all around.

"You'll get tests periodically, and I'll tell you *exactly* what the tests will be on. I don't believe in throwing in things we haven't studied, like some other teachers might do."

In preparing his remarks, he'd thought back to teachers in his past who'd done just that. He'd never seen a basis for it other than stupidity or sadism, neither of which had been an acceptable reason for making his life miserable. And although he found no particular joy in the prospect of standing in front of this group for the next ten months, he had no desire to bring any unhappiness into their lives.

He glanced at his notes. "Well, that wraps up what I have to say, and I think it was clear enough for you not to have any questions. So what I'd like you to do now is get out some paper and give me four pages on how you spent your summer."

More groans.

"I realize it isn't very novel, but giving this assignment fulfills a life-long dream for me. So stop whining like kindergartners. It's a little after ten now. Dismissal's at noon today. So that should give you plenty of time to get it done. If you happen to finish early, take out your history book and read the first chapter."

A petite girl with light-brown hair worn in pigtails, tentatively raised her hand.

"Yes, ma'am, what's your name?"

The question seemed to intimidate her.

"I'm going to find out eventually," he said without sarcasm.

"I'm Laura Perotta," she answered, her voice barely audible.

"Speak up, Miss Perotta. I assure you I don't bite unless absolutely provoked."

The class tittered, and the child blushed.

"I just wanted to know, is this paper going to count?"

The question caught Piza off-guard, as he hadn't given any real thought to day-to-day procedures. Yet, after a moment, he found himself talking.

"The answer to your question is 'yes' and 'no', Miss Perotta.

No, it won't count as a grade. Yes, it will count in giving me some indication of your writing skills. And one more thing—and this goes for all of you—I want you to be less concerned with grades, and more concerned with learning."

He was instantly amazed by what he'd said, because he realized he believed it. He'd just become aware that he was mildly interested in seeing how well these kids could write. And he was equally struck by the statement that learning was more important than grades, since he'd chosen the reverse priority in *his* scholastic life. He valued learning, but not at the expense of reality.

A bit unnerved by these revelations, he curtly ordered the children to begin their assignment. As they reluctantly obeyed, he removed *The Prophet*, by Khalil Gibran, from a desk drawer. For some time he'd been meaning to investigate the allure of this poet, who was idolized by many a "flower child". He planned to use his year off for a lot of catch-up reading.

The clanging dismissal bell unceremoniously roused him from his sojourn in the world of peace and love, and he instinctively held his right hand to his heart. His shock caused unrestrained laughter from his audience. "Man," he said with a fleeting smile, "*that's* a coronary waiting to happen."

As he stood, his transition to stone-face was instantly mirrored by the children.

"Okay, people. Tomorrow, playtime is over, so be prepared to begin in earnest. In other words, don't leave your brains on the pillow."

"Ha, ha," from an anonymous male voice.

Piza couldn't tell who said it, so he decided to drive home a point. "What was that, Mr. Davis?" he asked, staring at the boy despite the fact the comment had come from a different area of the room.

"I didn't say it," Davis almost shouted. "Whaddya blamin' *me* for?"

"Because I'm not exactly sure who the big-mouth is. Therefore, I'm assuming it's you."

"Oh, man, that's not fair. This sucks."

"Hey, pal, first impressions," Piza hurled back, deciding not to call him on his language. "If you didn't say it, who did?"

Davis glanced across the room, but quickly looked straight ahead again. "I don't know who said it."

Piza's patience was already wearing thin. "I think you do." He sat on the edge of his desk, not taking his eyes off the boy. "And we're all gonna sit here until you tell me. How's that sound?"

Moans from the rest of the class turned to gasps as Davis, fists clenched at his side, began walking toward the front of the room.

The teacher realized he'd pushed too far, and frantically searched for a way to save face and yet not hurt the boy. When Davis was ten feet away, Piza fought the impulse to stand, which he saw as an invitation to a physical confrontation.

"Something I can do for you, Mr. Davis?" he asked with forced calm.

The kid stopped, his face flushed. "Yeah. You— You can get offa my case." He stepped forward, and Piza rose.

"You know what, Mr. Davis," he said, his eyes narrowing, "why don't—"

Heads snapped in unison as the front classroom door banged open. Mother John strode to the front of the room.

"Is there a problem here, Mr. Piza? The dismissal bell rang. These children should be in the hall."

Piza's immediate reaction was to give Davis up, but then he paused. He drew a deep breath as inconspicuously as possible, noting he was about to be judged by every other person in the room.

"No problem at all, Mother John. We were discussing how the children spent their summer, and Mr. Davis here volunteered to share his experiences with us. I wanted to give him a chance to finish."

Davis's attempt to mask his relief was transparent at best.

Mother John raised an eyebrow. "Kevin Davis volunteered? That's a first, Mr. Piza. Congratulations."

The child's face reddened. The principal's look dared him to challenge her.

"Well, I guess I'm either a very gifted teacher, or Mr. Davis was just trying to make me look good on my first day," Piza said with a smile, attempting to break the standoff.

She faced him. "From now on have your children in the hall on time, Mr. Piza. We have rules for a reason." There was dead silence as she left.

"Okay, people," Piza said after a brief pause, "into the hall, please. Leave your paper on your desk. And remember, tomorrow it's for real." He glanced at Davis, who avoided eye contact.

As the children filed out, a tall, handsome boy who'd been seated in the second row approached. With his impeccably styled dark brown hair and neatly pressed school uniform, he looked like a candidate for a fashion photo shoot.

"I'd like to apologize for the class, sir," he said. A condescending air betrayed the appearance of sincerity.

Piza stared at him. "And your name is. . ."

"Robert Giacobbi."

He immediately disliked this kid. "Are you the one who made the comment?"

The boy looked genuinely shocked, and raised his hands in front of him. "Oh, no, no, no. I just think the behavior of the class—especially Kevin Davis—was completely inappropriate, and I felt someone should tell you that."

"I don't really have a problem with the class," Piza replied with seeming nonchalance. "I just don't care for wiseguys."

"I don't blame you."

"Yep," Piza continued, "wiseguys. And, of course, brown-nosers. Can't stand brown-nosers. How do you feel about brown-nosers, Mr. Giacobbi?"

The boy's face flushed. "I'm, I'm not sure what you mean by a brown-noser, sir."

"You know," Piza pressed on, "a brown-noser. A sycophant. Toady? Butt-kisser? Stop me when you get my drift."

The boy's eyes narrowed. "I get it." He walked out.

As Giacobbi exited, Piza sat at his desk, drained. The intensity of the morning's confrontations rammed home the realization that his plan for a year of unencumbered rest and relaxation might have been a gross miscalculation.

"Maybe welfare fraud would've been worth the risk," he muttered.

5

Most of the OLPT students on Bus 5 seemed upbeat, as they headed to their first full day of school. The exceptions were a few of Piza's kids, who'd congregated in the back. They didn't necessarily look dejected, just more subdued than the others.

Sukie McDermott was struggling to defend their new teacher. "In my opinion—"

"We don't want your opinion," Matt Majinsky interrupted, fumbling to undress a Nestlé's chocolate bar.

"Shut up, Matt," she said. "This is America and I have a constitutional right to say what I think."

"Yeah," Majinsky replied between the two bites it took him to finish the candy, "but that doesn't mean we have to listen to it."

Sukie ignored him. "Anyway, I think he was a little nervous because it was his first day and all. And I also think he's gonna be nicer, and a really good teacher. Um, maybe not today, but, ya know, soon."

"I hope so," Laura Perotta said. "He's kind of scary."

"He *was* a little weird," Majinsky chimed in as he scoured his lunch bag for more goodies. "But ya gotta admit, he didn't squeal on you, Kevin, when The Nose invaded."

Davis barely looked up from his comic book. "He's an asshole."

"You'd better stop talking like that, Kevin," Laura warned. "And besides, you deserved it."

His face reddening, the boy said, "I was just goofin' on him a little! Ya think I robbed a damn bank or something."

"Yeah," Majinsky agreed. "Kevin didn't rob a bank. He's saving that for high school."

A crooked smile from Davis accompanied, "Screw you."

"He *was* kind of funny when the bell rang, though," Laura said with a giggle.

Sukie responded with an enthusiastic nod. "That's right, that's right. He definitely has a sense of humor. You'll see. Why, I bet—"

"Whoa, man!" Majinsky was gaping out the window as the bus pulled into the school parking lot. "Get a load of the new wheels Giacobbi's mom's driving. Jaaguaaar, baby. Oh yeah, baby. Hot car and hot mother."

Laura looked repulsed. "That's disgusting. It's his *mother*. Ew."

"I don't care if she's his mother or not," Majinsky argued. "She's still a certifiable babe."

"Leave him alone," Davis piped in. "It's the only thing that keeps him from eating."

"I still think he's a pervert," Laura said, her voice firm.

"I'm *not* a *perv*!" Majinsky shouted. As the surrounding inquisitive heads went back to their business, he mumbled, "I mean, it's not like I'm looking at my own mom or nothin'."

"Will everybody please be quiet," Sukie said. "You're giving me a headache."

"Okay, kids. Everybody off the bus," the elderly driver intoned. "Slowly, please. I don't want to end my days by being trampled to death."

"What does he think we are, buffaloes?" Majinsky protested.

"Whaddya mean, we?" Davis joked. "Anyway, kiddies, I hope none of you left your brains on the pillow, 'cause it's time to see the Pizza Man."

"You'll see," Sukie uttered, gathering her book bag. "You'll see I'm right about him."

Laura sighed. "I hope so."

Piza had slept through his alarm, the result of a mid-week celebration of life with some friends the night before. Upon awakening, he instantly shifted from stupefied to panicked. If there were a world record for dragging an electric razor over your face, combing your hair, gargling, and dressing, he'd have broken it that morning.

His mother had refrained from checking on him to that point, but was now making her way up the stairs, the look on her face: "Please, God, let him be alive."

Her concern was rewarded by almost being bowled over as her son, clutching his jacket, flung his beer-wracked body down the steps. "Sorry, Ma."

He was almost at the front door when a voice from the kitchen yelled, "Hey, where is my kiss, big brother?"

He could have kicked himself. "Get your head out of your ass, Tony," he murmured as he raced into the kitchen. He pulled up behind the girl, who was carefully extracting an overflowing Minnie Mouse spoon from a pink plastic bowl of Frosted Flakes. He placed his hands on her shoulders, kissed the top of her head, and ruffled the short black hair. Deepening his voice, he said, "See ya later, Peppermint Patty."

She grinned and mimicked him. "I am not a candy bar." Her speech was slightly garbled, which is common with Down syndrome.

"Are too," he yelled as he bolted. "Don't give Mom a heart attack today."

"Okay," she shouted back.

His mother reached the front porch in time to see him jump the four brick steps, wrench open the car door, and heave himself into the driver's seat. "Be careful, you're gonna kill yourself," she called out. "And you didn't have breakfast. You could faint, Anthony. Plus your shirt's wrinkled. Is that the same one you had on. . ." The rest of her words trailed off as he raced away, waving from the open car window.

Patricia Piza pushed herself away from the breakfast table and quietly began making her way to her bedroom.

"And where do you think you're going, young lady?" came the voice from the front hall. "Did you put your dish in the sink?"

"Um, I think I'm going to the bathroom, because my tummy hurts," came an uncertain reply as the girl kept moving.

"Isn't it amazin' how your stomach hurts whenever you have to clean the table. I think I should take you to the doctor, with all these stomach aches, Patricia."

Patty stopped in her tracks. "Um, guess what? I think maybe it's better now. I'm gonna get my dish. Oh, and my spoon too."

"Praise God, it's a miracle," her mother declared, her arms raised to the heavens. "I'm gonna be a very rich lady. I found a cure for bellyaches."

"You're funny, Ma," Patty said, grinning as she retrieved her bowl and spoon.

"I know. I'm hilarious. Now go get washed up. The bus is gonna be here soon."

Children with Down syndrome weren't integrated into the regular school system, so Patty attended a special school, with other developmentally disabled kids. She had the mental capacity of a seven-year-old, and could only handle the most basic reading and writing; even that was hit or miss. But her disability couldn't impede an outgoing personality, sense of humor, and love of music. Any member of the family would tell you that if you put her anywhere near a dance floor, you'd have to tackle all 4'7" of her to keep her away.

Patty was seventeen. When she was born, her diagnosis had shocked the family, since there was no history of Down on either side. Public thinking on the subject bordered on the medieval. On the day after Patty's birth, Angelo's sister, Rose—after saying how sorry she was—asked whether they were going to "put her away." From her hospital bed, Mary glared at her. "This was God's will. She's our little girl, and she stays with us no matter what. You got it?"

It was never a topic of conversation again.

"C'mon, Patricia. The bus is here. Chop, chop."

"I'm comin', Ma. Make them wait for me, okay?"

By the time he reached school, Piza's eyes were transitioning back to olive green from Gothic bloodshot, and the throbbing in his head was now only marginally incapacitating. However, his appearance was not lost on his students as they filtered into the classroom.

When they were seated, Sukie raised her hand. Piza reluctantly acknowledged her. "What can I do for you, Miss McDermott?"

"Do you feel okay? You look very pale. Can I get you something from the nurse's office?"

"Oh, please," Majinsky groaned.

"Shut up," she snapped.

Piza was too depleted to take offense at the question, or referee the battle. "Enough," he said with barely mustered authority. "Stop the wisecracks, Mr. Majinsky, and I'm fine, Miss McDermott. But thank you for your concern." He wasn't insincere. "Listen, people, I had planned to begin our regular schedule of subjects today." This was true. "But I read your essays last night," he lied, "and it's clear your writing skills leave a lot to be desired. So this morning, you're going to rewrite the essays."

The kids were visibly distressed. Piza was equally upset. He saw their reaction as a loss of face on his part, adding to the growing awareness that he'd trapped himself in a commitment that was becoming less tolerable by the minute.

"This isn't fair," a small boy mildly protested from the back of the room.

The remark provided the catalyst Piza needed to regroup. "Isn't fair?" he flung back, suddenly rising and slamming his hand on the pile of unread work on his desk. "And what's your name, pal?" He pointed at the overtly petrified student.

"Um, uh, I'm sorry. I didn't mean it," the boy replied, cowering in his seat.

"That's a mighty-long name."

"I— I'm really sorry. My, uh, my name is William Reilly. I'm sorry."

Piza's hangover wasn't moved by the boy's anxiety. "Okay, Billy boy, let's see here." He leafed through the essays. "Ah, yes. Here's your masterpiece." He held up the unread paper. "Of all the crappy essays I had to endure, yours was one of the crappiest. Congratulations. So I think that, under the circumstances, you should be the last one to complain about a re-write." He glowered at the student.

The previous day's episode with Kevin Davis had implanted in Piza the belief that defiance was the normal reaction of a sixth-grade boy to a teacher's exercise of authority. So he was completely taken aback when the child began to cry.

There were no heaving sobs, only random, delicate rivulets betraying the boy as they escaped onto his cheeks from behind the barrier of his black, horn-rimmed glasses. It was evident he was trying his best to fight it, but the tears were apparently as unsympathetic to his plight as Piza had been.

The total silence that had prevailed to that point was briefly violated by some giggles at the boy's expense and a muffled comment about his manhood. Other than those insensitive few who'd enjoyed Piza's assault, the remainder of the class appeared revolted. Their visible disgust smacked him to his senses.

He'd just acted like the teachers he'd despised when he was in school. And now, these kids despised *him*. It filled the room. He felt an overwhelming desire to defend his humanity, to let them in on the joke, to apologize. What emerged instead was a flaccid order. "Okay, people, enough snickering. I can assure you Mr. Reilly's paper wasn't really the worst one I read, so get to work on the re-writes."

He sat down, engulfed by the dejected silence, and took out *The Prophet*. He read four pages in the next two and a half hours.

The bell jarred him with only slightly less impact than the day before. This time, his students didn't react to his body's minor spasm. A white-sashed eighth-grade "safety" appeared at his door to escort the kids to lunch. They somberly filed out, a handful casting a glance in his direction.

Sitting at his desk, he fought the guilt pecking at him for what he'd done to William Reilly. But he knew it ran deeper than that. Post-inebriation malaise notwithstanding, it was his first full day and he'd made no attempt to engage his students. Although his being there was a charade, he'd intended to do his job, albeit at a level least inconvenient to himself.

Enter logic to ease his discomfort, as he reasoned there was no benefit in berating himself over his ill-advised evening or the morning's events. *What's done is done.* That settled, he decided to start fresh the next day. He'd fill the looming void in the afternoon session by having the student authors read aloud their revised essays, saving him the trouble of having to review them that evening.

He considered going to the teachers' lounge, but the thought of being amusing in his condition nixed that notion. He put his feet up on his desk, closed his eyes, and awaited the return of the disenchanted.

6

The following morning, Piza was wearing a starched, powder-blue shirt, charcoal-gray slacks, blue blazer, and striped tie. "You look nice, Tony," Patty had said when he kissed her goodbye.

Eat your heart out, Giacobbi. God, that kid irked him.

Despite his students' evident dismay the previous afternoon on learning they'd be reading their essays, his more relaxed manner had made for an almost pleasant three hours. He'd occasionally forgotten Mother John's warning, catching himself smiling at some of the more amusing stories. It hadn't resulted in mayhem, and he'd decided her advice, although probably well-intentioned, wasn't ironclad.

He planned to begin the day with world history. From perusing the textbook at orientation, he was aware that the year's course began with the travels of Christopher Columbus. He hadn't looked at the book since then, reasoning that since he'd minored in history, a quick perusal of the text, in class, would trigger the neural chain-reaction necessary to bring him up to speed.

He pulled into the parking lot five minutes early, and was almost looking forward to the day as he entered the building. "Mr. Piza," the already unmistakable voice barked, as he passed the main office. "May I see you, please?"

Geez. I'm barely here two days, lady. What now?

He turned toward Mother John, who was in the doorway of the waiting area, motioning for him to follow.

"Good morning to ya," he said as he approached her.

She turned without response, made her way to her office, and stood behind the maple desk.

He started to sit, but was cut off in mid-squat. "Don't bother to sit down, Mr. Piza, this won't take long."

"Ooookay."

"A parent called me, yesterday. She was extremely upset. She claims you humiliated her son—"

That little bastard Giacobbi. What an actor.

"—and I told her I'd speak with you and get your side of the story."

He had no problem handling this one. His behavior with the boy had been perfectly justifiable. Besides, it was time the little twerp got his comeuppance.

"Mother John, this child was arrogant and disrespectful. And, frankly, I don't know how he could have been humiliated, since he and I were the only ones in the classroom."

"Mr. Piza, I have great difficulty believing William Reilly was disrespectful, never mind arrogant."

"Who?"

"*William Reilly*. Small? Thick glasses? Pokey black hair?"

Oh shit, that *kid.* His embarrassment at not immediately remembering the boy was instantly surpassed by the need to cover himself.

"William Reilly. Of course." He hoped his fabricated nonchalance was convincing. "Yes, he refused to rewrite an essay I had the children compose the day before. It didn't seem like they'd given much thought to what they'd written, and I felt I had to send a message that a half-hearted effort wasn't acceptable. Mr. Reilly made it clear he wasn't going to do it."

"You're telling me William Reilly spoke to you like that."

"Yes, ma'am, he did."

"What exactly did you say to him?"

"I told him his essay was one of the worst I'd read, so he should be the last one to object. Now, that wasn't really true. There were plenty that were worse. But I was being tested, and I felt I had to make a point."

"Did you curse at him?"

"I beg your pardon?"

"She said you cursed at him."

"I most certainly did not." Now he was angry. He'd used the word "crappy," but that didn't come close to cursing at the kid.

"No, no, I misspoke," the nun said, shaking her head. "I'm sorry. She didn't say you cursed *at* him. She just said you cursed."

So much for his righteous indignation defense. "I have no idea what she's talking about." That insipid response provided the few seconds he needed to conjure up an escape. "No, wait," he added, holding up his hand. "I think I know what she means. In describing his paper, I didn't say 'worst'. I said it was one of the 'cruddiest'. Probably not the most eloquent way to describe it, but I'd hardly consider it a curse word."

"Mr. Piza, I'm a bit skeptical that a sixth-grade boy would mistake the word you used for a curse word." She paused. "But it *is* William, and it's conceivable he might think that way. But according to *your* story, he apparently turned into Al Capone over the summer."

Piza was growing tired of this game, so he gambled. "Mother," he practically sighed, "I told you what happened. If I'm going to have to go through this every time I reprimand a student, this isn't going to work. And I don't mean any disrespect, but if you won't believe me, then I shouldn't be teaching here." You'd have sworn he really meant it.

She waited until it was clear he'd finished. "Mr. Piza, I'm not sure exactly what occurred in your classroom. But I had an obligation to bring the complaint to your attention. Maybe William has changed. More likely, he was simply having a bad day. At any rate, let's put this behind us for now. And in the future, try not to use slang. Okay?"

He nodded. Nothing else was said as he left the office, his step lacking the bounce it had enjoyed just minutes before.

Piza sat at his desk, lost in thought. The previous evening, he'd decided to preserve yesterday afternoon's lighter atmosphere, tempered with caution. He was outgoing by nature, and the gloom-and-doom approach was as disagreeable to him as it obviously was to the kids. But this morning's meeting with Mother John weighed on him. The faint sound of children in the hall nudged him to alertness.

As his class filed in, the best he could muster was a noncommittal smile. Muted groans met his announcement that the children would take turns reading from the history textbook. A glare stopped the discontent cold.

Despite his subdued state, he couldn't refrain from expanding on some of the book's content, much of which he found bland; some, outright wrong. *Columbus came to America to convert the Indians to Christianity? He was looking for loot, numbnuts. Who wrote this?*

The history lesson, which Piza also conveniently viewed as a reading lesson, segued into having the children write an essay about what they'd just learned. That neat little trick took them to their lunch break.

He once again chose not to venture into the faculty lounge,

opting to stay in his room, read, and tackle the massive meatball hero his mother had prepared. Lunch and recess duty was handled by volunteers—mostly mothers of the students—so the teachers actually had an hour to themselves.

After reading for about fifteen minutes, noise from outside drew his attention. He went to the window, which offered a view of the playground. The scene below was exactly what you'd imagine for recess on a beautiful end-of-summer day: older kids milling around; younger ones running helter-skelter, only momentarily heeding admonitions to slow down. Some of the boys in his class were throwing a football.

He noticed Sister Theresa leaning against a basketball pole, smiling as usual, playing a guitar. She was surrounded by about twenty children from various grades. O'Brien was engaged in conversation with several students. The possibility of reconnecting with her, after their thinly-veiled sarcastic exchange in church on the first day of school, was enough to lure him from the tranquility of his classroom.

He meandered onto the playground, his copy of *The Prophet* in hand, and sat at a remote, vacant picnic table. He got an enthusiastic wave from Sister Theresa, which he returned merely by raising his arm. Unfortunately for him, O'Brien was now actively engaged in a game of kickball with a group of girls.

His presence caused a collective look of shock from his students, after which most of them came running toward him. Even Kevin Davis sauntered over, lingering on the outer edge of the group.

"Hey, Mr. Piza, what are you doing here?" Majinsky shouted as he approached.

"I work here, Mr. Majinsky. And I wanted to get some fresh air and read a bit. Am I not allowed to be out here?"

"No, no, sure you are. Absolutely you are. Absolutely."

"What are you reading, Mr. Piza?" Laura meekly asked. "Is it a novel?"

"Actually, it's not," he answered, tickled that one of his urchins might have an interest in reading. "It's called *The Prophet*, and it was written by a Lebanese writer named Khalil Gibran. It's basically a collection of philosophical essays and prose poetry."

"Oh, that sounds very interesting." Her blank expression was replicated in the face of every other child standing there.

Piza shook off the initial pleasure of realizing how impressive he must appear to these kids, and opted to continue the discussion. "Lebanese are people who come from Lebanon, which is a country in the Middle East."

"Oh, that's where they have all the deserts and oil wells," Laura interjected, her face awash in excitement.

"Very good, Miss Perotta."

Sukie inserted herself in the front of the group. "But what about that other thing you said? You know, about some kind of essays."

"Philosophical essays. 'Philosophical' comes from the word 'philosophy', which means—"

"I think it means something that deals with life," came a voice from the back of the group. "Kind of why things are the way they are?"

"Shut up, Reilly," came from an unseen source. "Nobody asked you."

"Hey, back off," Piza warned the phantom speaker. "Mr. Reilly, come up here."

"I'm sorry, Mr. Piza," the boy said. "I just thought that. . ."

"There's nothing to be sorry for. You were absolutely correct." The child emerged from the pack. "As I said, you were right. I wanted to tell you to your face."

"Oh, well, that was, um, very kind of you, sir," Reilly replied, not making full eye contact.

Piza realized he must have really traumatized this kid the day before. "Not a problem, Mr. Reilly. But if you ever call me 'sir' again, you're getting detention."

The boy's face dropped.

"I think he's kidding, William," Sukie comforted.

"I knew he was kidding," another boy, Vinny Pinto, bragged, his words followed by innumerable "me too's" from the rest.

Every school class has a kid who's the class "something". Reilly was the class brain. Sukie, the class busybody. Vinny Pinto was the class athlete, taller than all the other boys and good at every sport he'd ever tried.

He held up a worn football he'd been twirling in his hands. "Hey, Mr. Piza, wanna throw the ball around?"

No one could have reasonably interpreted the boy's question as sinister or disrespectful; nor did Piza. But the other children's eyes were riveted on their teacher, making him wonder if they'd seen their classmate's proposal as a subtle challenge. A quick analysis was in order.

How would this impact his plan to *slightly* diminish the distance between him and them? If he said yes, would the dividing line be blurred forever? If he answered no, would they possibly conclude he couldn't throw a football? It didn't occur to him that weighing his students' perception of his athletic ability against the nature of his relationship with them was inherently obnoxious.

In the seconds it actually took him to dissect the perceived problem, he decided on what seemed to him a Solomon-like solution. "Let's see that pigskin," he said to the boy.

His kids were clearly surprised and delighted. Pinto tossed him the ball.

"Okay, go long," Piza instructed. "Let's see what you've got."

With that, Pinto took off across the macadam. Piza watched him pick up speed, then launched a perfect spiral the boy caught without breaking stride. The dumbfounded look on the children's faces was followed by whoops and hollers.

"Whoa, Mr. Piza. Nice throw," the panting child said as he rejoined the group.

"Good hands," Piza said. "You're fast."

Before Pinto could respond, some of the other boys raised their hands and began clamoring for a chance to retrieve a pass.

"No, no," the teacher declared, smiling and waving his arms. "You know, people pay big bucks to see me toss a football. You guys are lucky you got a freebie today." He'd executed his plan, and that was that.

His response devoured every particle of joy born in the past couple of minutes. The intensity of the children's disappointment caught him off-guard. "Uh, maybe some other time," he blurted. He forced a grin. "I think I may have thrown out my arm with that massive heave."

The feeble humor fell flat, and the children abandoned him, muttering among themselves. A few glanced back at the source of their letdown as they walked off.

"What a schmuck."

Piza whirled around to find O'Brien sitting at the picnic table he'd vacated. The reality of what had just happened made resentment pointless. "Yeah, I probably could have handled that one better."

"And the understatement of the year goes to. . . You know, I don't get you. Why are you even here?"

"Excuse me?"

"It wasn't that difficult a question, but let me see if I can help you out. When you were hittin' on me at orientation—"

"Whoa! Boy, did *you* misread my intentions, lady."

"Come off it, Piza. When we were talkin', you wasted no time lettin' me know you went to Fordham, and that you were a philosophy major. And I get it. Let's make sure everyone knows how impressive I am. 'Wow, philosophy. He must be deep.' Chalk it up to insecurity or nerves or whatever. That didn't really bother me, but—"

"Please, spare me the dime store psychoanalysis. I've got better things—"

"Wait a minute. Hear me out. You wanted to know why I asked the question, and I'm tellin' you. What really pissed me off was that you made it a point to say you hadn't taken *any* education courses. Not even that you hadn't majored in education, but that you hadn't taken one course. Like you were proud of it. So I have to ask myself why someone like that is teachin'."

He folded his arms. "You done now?"

"Yeah, pretty much."

"Good. First of all, you don't know anything about me. Second, I have nothing against education majors, which I'm assuming you were. And, frankly, *you* seem kind of defensive about it, so maybe you're the one with the issues. And third, believe it or not, I took this job to help kids. Maybe change their lives for the better in some small way."

She paused. "I had no idea."

"In that case, I won't demand an apology," he said with playful smugness.

"No, I mean I had no idea how full of it you are. Every teacher's goal is to connect with their kids. You just had that opportunity handed to you on a silver platter, and you blew it to smithereens. And it wasn't like you had a brain cramp or something. You purposely chose to do it."

"That's not true," he protested. "I—"

"Oh, come on. It was written all over your face. What is it? Image? Ego? Are you just too cool to be a teacher? You wanna change their lives for the better? Please. I don't know exactly what your game is, but do me a favor and peddle that line of crap somewhere else."

She might as well have kicked him in the gut. His glib tongue deserted him, and the only response he could think of was, "Like I said, save it for someone else."

"Whatever, Piza." She got up, started to walk away, then

stopped and turned around. "And by the way, that little psychological profile wasn't from a five-and-ten. You didn't bother to ask at orientation, but I have a masters in psych from Boston College. And I'm takin' night courses at *your* alma mater for my masters in education." He looked like he was about to speak, but she cut him off. "And there are plenty of teachers here with really good academic backgrounds. We just don't feel compelled to walk around with it tattooed on our foreheads."

Watching her leave, he couldn't remember ever having felt so small.

7

Throughout the following week, the fallout from Friday's playground disaster subsided. Piza had arranged each day's activities with an eye to gradually persuading his students that he wasn't really the aloof fool who'd refused some innocent requests to toss around a football. There was a little more interaction, in bits and pieces. But he hadn't gone so far as to venture outside at lunch again.

He'd occasionally seen O'Brien, but she'd kept her distance. As much as that annoyed him, he'd decided she was someone to whom you gave a wide berth until time worked its healing magic. Hopefully.

What disturbed him most from that miserable schoolyard incident was that Sister Theresa had witnessed it. He'd found out on Monday, when they were sitting in the back of the spacious school library, as both their classes were being treated to a spellbinding presentation on the Dewey Decimal System by the librarian, Mrs. Fitzsimmons. The woman was hard-of-hearing, and attempted to compensate by speaking at decibel levels rivaling a snowblower. Although deafening for the children, it provided sufficient cover to allow the two teachers to speak at close to normal volume.

"I saw what happened Friday," the nun said without judgment in her tone. "With the children."

"Oh. You did? I, uh, thought you were, you know, across the playground. Playing your guitar?"

"I was. But when I saw the crowd around you. . ." A slight shrug accompanied a guilty smile. "Sometimes curiosity gets the best of me. But anyway, with the children, it will all be fine. I really do believe that."

Despite her unsolicited reassurance, he thought he detected a wisp of disappointment. At orientation, he'd concluded she was one of those rare effortlessly genuine people. Now, the idea that he may have somehow let her down disturbed him.

He greeted Friday's arrival with a profound sense of relief. The pot was sweetened by the fact that there was a teachers' conference that afternoon, which meant the kids were only in until twelve thirty.

The school held its faculty meetings in the cafeteria. He sat behind the other attendees, having no desire to be anywhere near the center of the action. Jim Bauer joined him, milk carton in hand. Piza tightened his lips and shook his head. "When are you gonna grow a pair and make the big boy switch to chocolate milk?"

Bauer flashed a fake sneer and took a sip. Within a minute, O'Brien and Sister Theresa came in and sat at the table in front of theirs. The nun warmly greeted them. O'Brien did the same to Bauer, but scarcely acknowledged Piza.

While they waited for the meeting to begin, Piza surveyed the faculty spread out in front of him—mostly nuns, with a small contingent of lay teachers who seemed to range in age from forty to seventy. One nun stood out, not only because she was the only person there with a notebook and pen in front of her, but also because she appeared to be a hundred and fifty years old. Piza leaned forward to get Sister Theresa's attention.

"Hey, who's the nun with the pen and paper? The one who looks like a prune."

"Shame on you," she admonished, albeit with a grin. "That's Sister Immaculata. She's been retired for years, but she still likes to attend these meetings."

"Wow," Bauer said. "How old is she?"

Before she could answer, Piza remarked, "I don't know, but I saw a painting of George Washington's wedding once, and I'm pretty sure she was the maid of honor."

Bauer yanked a handkerchief from his jacket pocket to stem the flow of milk from his nose. And though neither Sister Theresa nor O'Brien turned around, their bouncing shoulders gave them away. *So maybe I'm no longer on the shit list, eh, O'Brien?* At that moment, Mother John rose to address the assembly, bringing any frivolity to a halt.

She gave some preliminary remarks and then yielded the floor to the assistant principal, Mrs. Florino, a well-groomed woman who looked around sixty and always sounded like she was annoyed. As she yammered on about curriculum changes and new school policies, Piza felt himself slipping into a stupor. The words "sixth-grade field trip" jolted him back to full consciousness.

"This is the annual sixth-grade trip," Mrs. Florino intoned, "and it will be on Tuesday, October sixteenth, to the Museum of Natural History in Manhattan. Buses will be provided."

Sister Theresa turned toward Piza, her face as radiant as if the Pope himself had spritzed her with holy water. "This is so amazing," she whispered. "What fun."

He managed a listless thumbs-up as his mind raced with the myriad of disaster scenarios his neurons were transmitting. Before he could transition to full-panic mode, Mother John once again took center stage.

"At this time, I'd like to turn the floor over to our pastor, Monsignor Lombardo."

The man was nowhere to be seen, but then strutted through the doors. Although the monsignor was the one who'd arranged his job interview, Piza had never met him. He'd meant to visit the church rectory to introduce himself and thank him for the opportunity, but hadn't followed up. Eventually, he reasoned too much time had elapsed to fulfill the marginal obligation.

Despite his dim view of Catholicism, he had nothing against priests, and in fact had shared a beer more than once with some of the younger Jesuits at Fordham. But he was skeptical of the ones designated monsignors, considering them politicians in clerical clothing.

He did have to admit, though, that Monsignor Lombardo cut a striking figure. He was a handsome man, slim, with manicured silver hair, and he wore his black cassock and purple sash well. Rimless glasses conveyed the suggestion of intellectual depth. Many of the women had preened when he entered, including some of the nuns.

The priest reminded Piza of the television personality Bishop Fulton Sheen, whose show his mother never missed when it aired in the 1950s. The bishop had a powerful, melodic voice, and was a bona fide Catholic superstar. The comparison to Bishop Sheen hit a wall as soon as Monsignor Lombardo began to speak.

"Thank you, Mother John," he rasped.

Holy crap! It's Vito Corleone in disguise.

He would later learn the priest's gravelly delivery was the result of years of chain-smoking unfiltered cigarettes, a vice allegedly on equal footing with his partiality to single malt scotch.

"It's a pleasure to be here with all of you today," the Godfather said. "It's my sincere hope that we will once again have a successful year here at OLPT." Enthusiastic applause. "As you're aware, one of the major problems in every parish today is money.

Running a parish is a costly proposition, with expenses increasing every year."

Piza leaned toward Bauer. "You can bet your ass teacher salaries don't fall into the 'increasing expenses' category." Bauer gave him an imploring look that said, Please be quiet, I'd like to keep my job.

"With that in mind," the monsignor continued, "I'm directing each of you to instruct your students to speak with their parents about increasing their weekly contributions at mass. And that means less jingling."

It was obvious some of the teachers didn't get his meaning, because they looked to their neighbors with anxious expressions of confusion. The priest appeared to pick up on it. He slowly accentuated each word. "More paper, less coins." The barely masked derision in his voice sealed his fate as far as Piza's opinion of him. "Well, that's really all I have for now. So, again, have a great year, and remember. . ." He rubbed his right thumb against his forefinger and middle finger, then strode out of the room.

Mother John broke the uncomfortable silence. "Please remember Monsignor Lombardo's instructions," she said, "and pass along that message. Now, there's one more thing to discuss before adjourning. I believe I made it clear at orientation that the children are not to talk when lined up in the halls. Many of you have been lax in enforcing that policy, particularly Mrs. DeFazio, Mrs. Kowalski, and Mr. Piza."

The faces of all three of the accused reddened—Mrs. DeFazio's and Mrs. Kowalski's in apparent humiliation, Piza's in anger. *Talk about bush-league. You couldn't take us aside and tell us?* He was also perturbed because it made no sense to him that children had to be quiet just because they were in a line.

"My God, they're kids," he murmured. The sight of heads snapping around to face him told him his pithy comment hadn't been as hushed as he'd thought.

Mother John crossed her arms. "Something you want to share with us, Mr. Piza?"

He raced to calculate the possible responses, and the pros and cons of each. As usual, practicality prevailed. "No, not really, Mother. It's nothing."

"Oh, but I think it's *something*, Mr. Piza. I'm sure I heard you say . . . something."

"I, um, said they're kids," he reluctantly responded. "I guess what I meant was that I don't understand why they have to be quiet in the hall, especially at dismissal. As long as they're orderly, of course." *Don't want her to think I'm advocating anarchy.*

"It's called discipline, Mr. Piza," she replied. "They're children now, but someday they'll be adults. And if we don't exercise discipline as adults, well. . . Don't you agree?"

Anyone expecting a knock-down-drag-out fight, or even a genuine debate on the issue, was going to be disappointed, because Piza had already concluded a standoff wasn't worth the risk. All he wanted was to put the week behind him. Thus, his complete surrender: "I see what you're saying, Mother John. And looking at it that way, yes, I do agree. Point taken."

"Good," she said. It almost seemed she was disappointed, perhaps sensing a missed opportunity to put him in his place more forcefully. "I think that does it for today. So you're dismissed. Have a nice weekend."

Some of the teachers stole quick looks at Piza as they left the room. Bauer said, "That could've been worse," and patted him on the back. Sister Theresa gave a wave and followed Bauer out.

A smirking O'Brien stayed behind. "Geez, you kept your mouth shut," she said. "That's a novelty, I'll bet. You really agree with her?"

"*No*, I don't *agree* with her."

"Well, the good news is you actually showed signs of understandin' a little about kids. Hope springs eternal, Piza. See ya Monday."

"Yeah. You too," he managed.

He waited until he was relatively sure the parking lot would be empty. He was already questioning his decision not to challenge Mother John on her discipline theory. As he saw it, his self-anointed status as the resident nonconformist of OLPT had taken a hit.

But by the time he pulled into his parents' driveway, he'd completely justified his position. Besides, now there was this museum thing to worry about.

8

In the two weeks leading up to the museum trip, not much changed in Piza's domain. He did lower the wall between him and his students a bit more, because ultimately it was impossible for him not to let his sense of humor show. He'd ventured outside at lunch a few times, always carrying a book. Apparently, the kids viewed that as a signal, and there had been no requests to toss a football. Nor had he offered.

The day of the museum trip was gorgeous: sunny, with an expected temperature of seventy-five. Piza coasted into the school parking lot, hoping the weather foreshadowed a trouble-free day. But his tempered optimism hit a snag when a school bus carrying some of his students overheated on its way in, costing them time.

He was already anxious about the trip, and this wasn't helping. Jack Morrow had once called him a walking contradiction. "Sometimes you can be laid back to the point of being almost comatose. But if something doesn't go exactly as planned, you turn into a mutated nerve ending. You're a weird guy."

The truth was that Piza was calm when he had virtually complete control of a situation. But when there were outside influences at play, his comfort level sank. Broken-down school buses fell into that latter category.

Pacing in his classroom, he looked out the window for the tenth time, when he saw the bus pulling into the lot. One of the eighth-grade safeties corralled the occupants and escorted them into the school.

In light of the daylong trip, all that was necessary that morning was to take attendance and collect some outstanding permission slips and trip money. He was about to launch into a last-minute lecture on expected behavior, when Sister Theresa appeared at his front classroom door, urgently motioning to him. Raising his index finger to his class, he hustled into the hall.

"What's wrong?"

"It's Sean Malarkey," she said, near-panic in her voice. "He's got his permission slip, but no money. I'm not sure what to do. Why are you grinning?"

"That name. Malarkey." He was practically giggling. "You know, full of malarkey. Kind of like the Italian name Bologna. Baloney?"

"Stop being an infant," she snapped. "It's a good solid Irish name. Now help me figure this out."

He'd never seen her quite so feisty. "Look, if he doesn't have the money, he can't go, right? I mean how is this *your* problem? It's on his parents, not you."

"That's unacceptable. Assuming *your* children are set, he's— *Are* all your students paid up?"

"Yes, amazingly."

"Then Sean will be the only sixth-grader not going. How's he going to feel? Why should he be punished for something his parents did?"

"I get that, but what's the alternative? Let him go without paying? How's that fair to all the kids who did pay?"

"I know," she answered, more subdued. "I'm just trying to figure a way around this."

"Why can't the school lend him the money for today, and then get it back from his parents?"

"It's against policy. Plus the school doesn't have any money."

He was getting aggravated. "It's five stinking dollars. The school can't spring for five bucks? No offense, Sister, but we're talking about the Catholic Church here. It could *buy* the Museum of Natural History."

Dejection was beginning to show. "I don't care about the Church or its money right now, I care about my student. And this is going to crush him."

A slight sigh from Piza. "Tell you what," he said, touched yet again by her decency, "I'll pay for it."

Rather than look relieved, she appeared more concerned. "No. I can't let you do that. I know you don't get paid a lot, and this isn't why I asked for your help. You know that, right?"

"Of course I do. It never crossed my mind. It's fine. But don't tell him where it came from. I know it's not in your nature to be deceitful, but take one for the team and make something up." He reached into his side pants pocket and retrieved a faded money clip. Smiling, he handed her a five-dollar bill. "Now, go and lie for the greater good."

"Thank you for this," she said, lightly touching his arm. "You're a good person."

He re-entered the classroom, calmer than when he left. He was finishing his brief behavior speech when the loudspeaker screeched to life. "Sixth-grade classes, report to the parking lot," Mrs. Florino commanded. "Stay in line, no talking, listen to your teachers on the buses and at the museum, don't misbehave in any manner at any point during the day, don't touch anything, and enjoy your trip."

"Wow," Laura Perotta said. "I think she told us not to do even more things than you told us not to do, Mr. Piza."

"Well, either way, you all get the point, right?" A sprinkling of "right" could be heard. "I said *right*?" he repeated, clapping his hands. "Right!" they shouted in unison.

"That's what I wanna hear. Now, let's go learn something!" *Oh, God, did I just say that? I'm going insane.*

As Piza's kids boarded their bus, he could see Sister Theresa speaking with Sean Malarkey. She was doing the talking and he was nodding vigorously. Seconds later, she patted him on the back, and he got on the second bus, still nodding. She gave Piza a discreet okay sign. He smiled and returned the gesture.

Piza sat toward the front of the bus, while the class mother, Florence Schaeffer, sat in the back. He'd only met her that morning, but she appeared to be quite pleasant.

On the ride into the city, something occurred that Piza found enlightening. A ruptured water main forced them to detour through side streets. Several homeless people were gathered on one of them, next to an alley and a rundown building. With traffic stop-and-go, the kids were able to get a good look. One of them pointed out a row of cardboard boxes in the alley. To Piza's surprise, they seemed to have no idea what to make of it.

If he'd known them better, he'd have understood. They didn't read newspapers. The standard one television in the house was usually tuned to variety shows, sitcoms, or cartoons. These solidly middle-class children had had virtually no exposure to the squalid conditions that were so many people's daily environment. Sukie asked why they were so dirty.

"Because they don't have access to showers or baths," he told her. "See those cardboard boxes in the alley there? That's where they live."

"Why would they live there?" another girl, Rebecca Schaeffer, asked. "Why don't they just go home? I don't—"

"Don't you get what he's sayin'?" Kevin Davis interrupted. "That *is* their home."

Piza resisted the urge to intervene, choosing to let it play out despite the fact Rebecca's mom was sitting in the back. Mrs. Schaeffer didn't seem disturbed in the least.

"You're so full of it, Kevin," Majinsky said. "Mr. Piza, tell him he's full of it."

"He's not, Mr. Majinsky."

"My father says poor people are like that because they're too lazy to find a job," Robert Giacobbi observed with apparent innocence.

"Is that true, Mr. Piza?" Laura asked.

"No, it's not, Miss Perotta," he answered, looking at Giacobbi. The child adjusted himself in his seat, his eyes not meeting his teacher's. "Mr. Giacobbi isn't completely wrong, though." The boy's head popped up. "There *are* lazy people in the world. There's no denying that. But most of the people you see on the street out there are the way they are for a lot of different reasons. Some might be down on their luck. Some are addicted to alcohol or drugs."

"Like marijuana," William Reilly offered.

"Worse than that, Mr. Reilly. And some are mentally ill."

"Wackos!" Majinsky hollered, eliciting a laugh from the others.

"There's nothing funny about mental illness, Mr. Majinsky. It can happen to anyone. There may even be people you know who have it, but it's just not obvious. You don't have to be a raving lunatic to be mentally ill. At any rate, if you learn anything from this, remember that there are plenty of people who are less fortunate than you. And believe me, it's not by choice."

Not so much as a casual clearing of the throat disturbed the resulting silence. *Way to go, Tony. And the award for the world's biggest killjoy goes to. . . You know what, screw that. I'm their teacher, and they just got a life lesson. Welcome to reality, kids.*

He did try to lighten the atmosphere a bit by pointing out some local landmarks. But a subdued mood ruled the bus. He hoped it would be gone by the time they reached the museum.

9

The American Museum of Natural History is a marvel. Located on Manhattan's upper west side, the main entrance is an impressive granite facade with a large entry arch bordered by two giant columns on each side, and the words Truth, Knowledge, Vision etched above it. In front of the arch stands a large bronze statue of Theodore Roosevelt on horseback. The country's twenty-sixth president was probably the museum's most famous and passionate supporter.

Individual tour guides had been assigned for Piza's group and Sister Theresa's. The plan was for them to start in different locations, then meet at eleven forty-five for lunch in the cafeteria. After that, they would all head to the Hayden Planetarium—which is part of the museum—for an exhibition about Mars and Saturn.

The guide for Piza's class was named Carter. Pencil thin, with close-cropped hair and rimless glasses, he appeared to be in his mid-twenties. Piza's instant conclusion, and concern, was that he was a bit of a nerd. But when he introduced himself, his voice was deep and resonant, and he was just exuberant enough to be entertaining but not appear deranged. Piza breathed easier knowing he probably wouldn't have to worry about any of his brood trying to score a laugh by mocking the young man.

The tour began on the fourth floor, which housed the primitive and advanced mammals. More significantly, at least in terms of sheer star power, it was home to the dinosaur exhibit.

Piza had been to the museum twice as a kid, and the wonder that had coursed through him when he first saw those gargantuan bones remained fresh in his memory. He'd been surprised to learn that none of his students had visited the museum before, and he found himself looking forward to the awe on their faces when they got their first glimpse of the prehistoric buffet awaiting them.

One step inside the hall was all it took. There wasn't one child whose eyes didn't widen, and whose mouth didn't gape. Carter was a fount of tantalizing information, and knew exactly what gory, T-rex meat-eater details would keep the children enthralled.

The tour continued, and although all the exhibits were well done, it wasn't until they reached the Hall of Ocean Life on the first floor that they had another *wow*! moment. This was the site of the Blue Whale, a ninety-four-foot long, twenty-one-thousand-pound fiberglass reproduction dramatically suspended from the ceiling. As the children entered the hall, they were visibly awestruck.

"Are they extinct too? Like the dinosaurs?" a seemingly mesmerized Laura Perotta asked.

"Oh, no," Carter replied. "There's not as many as there used to be, but they're still around."

"It's hard to believe something alive today can be . . . that big," William Reilly observed.

"Did you know that blue whales can hear each other's groaning sounds from several hundred miles away?" Carter said.

"No way," Matt Majinsky scoffed.

Carter raised his right hand. "I swear, it's absolutely true."

"Wow, imagine what would happen if it sneezed," Giacobbi joked, drawing laughter from his classmates.

I don't believe it. The Stepford kid may have a sense of humor. "Okay," Piza announced, "I think that's a great way to end our tour. Let's all give Carter a big round of applause for a terrific job."

The children clapped enthusiastically, to which Carter responded with a deep bow. "You guys were great," he said. "Enjoy the planetarium this afternoon."

"All right, everybody, line it up," the teacher ordered. "We're meeting Sister Theresa's class in the cafeteria for lunch."

The kids formed two perfectly straight lines.

"Mr. Piza," inquired Laura, "are we allowed to talk in line?"

"We're not in school, Miss Perotta. Talk if you'd like. But not too loud."

They started animatedly discussing everything they'd seen. Piza was pleasantly surprised to see Kevin Davis involved in the conversation. *I need to figure this kid out.*

Where the tour had been calm and structured, the cafeteria was outright mayhem. There was another school visiting the museum that day, and many of its students were running around hurling food at each other. A few harried chaperones were making an unsuccessful effort to rein them in, while the other adults sat, chatting.

Piza turned to face his class, ready to warn them against any attempt to join the fray. It wasn't necessary; they looked appalled at what they were witnessing.

Through the chaos, Mrs. Schaeffer caught Piza's eye and motioned toward Sister Theresa, who had saved two tables for him.

He looked bewildered when he reached the nun. "Where are these other kids from? Our Lady of Alcatraz?"

"They *are* kind of unruly."

"Kind of? I just missed getting laid out by an airborne hotdog."

"Okay, maybe more than 'kind of'. Anyway, I wanted to wait for you before taking the children up."

Getting the food merely entailed going to a counter and picking up an everything-included boxed lunch. The teachers stationed themselves at the counter and handed out the boxes.

On her way back to her table, Sukie passed two older-looking boys from the other school, who were fighting for control of a can of soda. One of them pulled away from the other, elbowing the girl in the face. She dropped her lunch and reached for her cheekbone. Piza saw it and immediately moved toward her, but not before Kevin Davis handed off his lunch to the girl behind him and grabbed the offender by the front of his shirt.

"See what you did, asshole," he screamed at the boy, who was struggling to loosen Davis's grip. "She's my friend, and you hit her in the face."

Piza reached them just in time to stop the confrontation from escalating. "Let go of him, Mr. Davis," he ordered. The child didn't oblige. "Now." Davis finally released his grip. "Get your lunch and go to the table. I'll handle this." Davis glowered at the other boy, as he retrieved his meal and walked away.

"I'm sorry. I didn't mean it," the boy said, looking from Piza to Sukie and back.

Piza stared at him, then, "Fine. Go back with your group." He turned to Sukie. "Are you okay, Miss McDermott? Do you want some ice to put on it?" He had to check the impulse to put a consoling hand on her shoulder.

"I'm okay," she replied, wiping her eyes with her sleeve.

"Next time maybe we'll take a trip to the zoo," he said. "The lion's den might actually be safer than this place."

She smiled. "It's nice when you're nice."

The innocence of the remark touched him, and he returned the smile. "Let's get you some food and head for safer ground."

When they returned to the group, Sukie's friends doted on her, demanding details of what happened. She thanked Davis for helping her.

"No problem," he responded. "But the Pizza Man should've let me deck that guy. Did he get in his face?"

"Not really. The kid apologized, and Mr. Piza told him to go back with his friends."

"It was hard to see with all those other kids in the way, but it looked like Mr. Piza was talking to you," Laura said.

"Yeah. He just wanted to make sure I was okay. He was really kind of sweet."

Giacobbi rolled his eyes. "Oh, please."

"Back off, Giacobbi," Davis warned. "Leave her alone."

"I'm just saying," Giacobbi answered. "*Sweet* is probably the last word I'd use to describe that guy." He went back to eating.

Within ten minutes, the children from the other school left the cafeteria. Piza sat down at an empty table and motioned to Davis. "Mr. Davis, a word, please."

"Crap," the boy muttered. "I'm not apologizing," he told Piza as he sat down across from him. "That jerk could've really hurt her. And I don't care if you wanna report me to The No— I mean, Mother John."

"Nobody said anything about apologizing, Mr. Davis. And I'm not going to rat you out to Mother John. I wanted to tell you that I understand why you did what you did. I had to stop you, obviously, but considering that kid was bigger than you, you were pretty brave."

"Oh," Davis said, clearly caught off guard by the compliment. "Uh, thanks. I wasn't scared or nothin', either."

"I wasn't scared or *anything*," his teacher corrected. "And what

I was going to say was that standing up for Miss McDermott like that was downright chivalrous."

"Whaddya mean?" the boy asked, his eyes narrowing.

The change in demeanor threw Piza off. "What's with the—"

"You sayin' I been drinkin'?"

"Huh?"

"You said something about Chivas. That's liquor."

Piza had to tap into his self-restraint reserve not to burst out laughing. "No, no. 'Chivalrous'," he said, enunciating the word. "It means you acted with honor, defending someone smaller and weaker than you."

"Oh, okay. I get it now. Thanks."

"You're welcome. Um, not for anything, but how do you know about Chivas Regal?"

"My old man used to get sloshed on the stuff, before he took off on me and my mom." He paused. "Actually, he had one bottle, and he used to refill it with cheap stuff. He said Chivas was too expensive, but this way he could still impress his friends. I guess they were too stupid to know he was connin' them."

Piza was surprised the kid had opened up so easily. But his tone was more bluster than melancholy. Maybe he saw surviving a father who was a drunk as a badge of honor. "When did he leave, if you don't mind my asking?"

"1970. November twenty-third. Monday before Thanksgiving. No biggie, though. Me and my mom are fine without him."

Piza was so taken aback by the specificity of the answer, he suppressed the urge to once again correct Davis's grammar. The kid had to have been what, eight or nine back then? He had the feeling if he asked the boy the exact time of day his father had abandoned them, he'd know that too. Apparently, the bravado was all show.

"Well, I'm glad you and your mom are doing okay," Piza said, not wanting to turn the conversation into an interrogation. "Why don't you get back to your friends."

Davis nodded and rejoined his group.

"Are you in trouble?" a worried-looking Sukie asked.

"No. We just talked about what happened. He was pretty cool about it."

Giacobbi countered with a snide, "I thought you hated the guy."

"I don't hate him. I— I dunno."

"Let's go," Sister Theresa announced. "Mars and Saturn await."

Their time at the planetarium was exciting and, after the cafeteria fiasco, refreshingly uneventful. The children marveled at touching a real asteroid. Stepping on scales to see how much they'd weigh on different planets resulted in lots of laughter and good-natured taunts. The Mars and Saturn show itself was awe-inspiring, with extraordinary special effects. The fact that the narrator sounded like the often-imagined voice of God only added to the surreal atmosphere.

At the end, the dazzled yet tired children filed out, forming lines understandably less rigid than usual. After the museum staff distributed bags of souvenirs, the kids dawdled in groups as the teachers and chaperones consulted on any additional items to be addressed. They all agreed that a pre-return bathroom stop was a must.

The boys and girls separated and queued up in front of their respective restrooms, with one adult waiting by the door and another keeping watch at the back of the line. As the last of the children emerged, an unexplained apprehension that had been nagging Piza for the past few minutes suddenly ratcheted up. "Is William Reilly here?" he shouted to the group. "Where's William Reilly?"

He scanned the area. The children shrugged nonchalantly,

seemingly oblivious to the panic that blanched every adult's face. Piza instinctively shifted into crisis mode. He had the ability, in times of severe stress, to take a virtual deep breath and will himself to calm down.

"All my kids. Here. Now." They immediately gathered around him. "Has anyone seen Mr. Reilly?"

"I was talking to him after the planetarium," another boy, Ralph Restivo, said. "But then I went to line up for the bathroom, and I don't know where he was after that."

Other than Restivo, no one recalled having seen Reilly. Piza called over one of the museum staff and explained the situation. The staffer said they had a protocol, which included sending people to each floor of the building, monitoring the doors, and making an announcement over the speaker system.

As much as Piza appreciated the game plan, he wasn't about to wait around. He told a visibly shaken Sister Theresa to keep all the children together while he conducted his own search.

"I don't fucking believe this," he muttered as he traveled the halls. "If anyone hurt that kid, I swear to God. . ." As he approached the entrance to the Hall of Ocean Life, he abruptly stopped. There was Carter, leaving the exhibit hall. Next to him was Reilly, head down, arms limp at his sides.

"I thought I might find him in there," Carter announced with a smile as he reached Piza. "Something about that whale really connected with him. I could see it. I'll let everyone know the mystery's solved."

Piza was torn between relief and anger. He thanked Carter and ordered Reilly to stay put when the boy tried to follow the guide. As soon as Carter was out of earshot, he said, "What the —What were you thinking? Do you have any idea—"

"I don't care if I get in trouble, I had to see it again," the boy blurted out. "It was the most amazing thing I've ever seen in my life."

The teacher was stunned by the response. The kid had to

know he was wrong, but his passion for science had unleashed an unexpected defiance. Although Piza couldn't relate to it—having never been truly passionate about anything—he understood it.

"Listen, I get it," Piza said, locking eyes with the child. "I get how important this was to you. But you have to realize I'm responsible for your safety."

"But I would have been right back. I just wanted one more look."

"God, Mr. Reilly, for a smart kid, I swear. . . How was I supposed to know you'd be right back? How was I supposed to have a *clue* where you were? Everybody was worried sick that something had happened to you."

"I— I didn't think of that. I didn't want to make anyone worry. I'm sorry. I really am."

"I believe you," Piza said, his anger and anxiety dissipating. "Just promise me you'll never pull a stunt like that again, okay?"

"I promise. Cross my heart." After a brief hesitation, he said, "Uh, Mr. Piza, am I going to get in trouble? At school?"

"Well, I'll talk to Sister Theresa, but I don't think anyone else needs to know."

His student's eyes brightened. "Thank you."

Piza and Sister Theresa had a brief discussion and agreed there was no need to inform Mother John of the boy's rogue behavior. If she found out, they'd worry about it then.

The children filed out to board the buses, heading back with what had to feel like more than a day's worth of adventures to rehash on the way home and beyond.

The trip impacted Piza as well. It didn't take long for him to realize just how much.

10

The children's mood seemed deflated for the rest of the week after the trip. A natural reaction, Piza reasoned, after a much-anticipated adventure that had lived up to the hype. By Friday, he was schooled-out himself and looking forward to meeting Jack Morrow in Manhattan that evening. They'd talked a couple of times during the summer, but hadn't seen each other since graduation.

Morrow was attending Cornell University Medical College, on the city's east side. They'd agreed to meet for dinner at six o'clock at O'Neals' Balloon across from Lincoln Center. Piza had been there before, when he and some other friends visited Fordham Law School, across the street.

Flustered, as usual, by his failure to be on time for virtually anything, he reached O'Neals' front door at six fifteen. Morrow was waiting for him.

"Sorry I'm late, Jack," Piza said, embracing him. "How long've you been waiting?"

"About a minute. I geared my arrival to Piza time."

"What if I'd been here for six?"

"Then you'd have gotten a taste of your own medicine. Either way, a win on my end."

Piza began walking away. "Hey, it's been good seeing ya. Gotta run."

"Okay. Let's make this a regular six-month thing," Morrow yelled.

I really miss this guy, Piza thought, rejoining his friend. A window table opened up as they entered. A waitress quickly brought menus.

"I don't think we really need these," Morrow told her. He looked at Piza. "Cheeseburger medium, fries, and a Heineken?"

"You remembered," Piza gushed. "Aren't you just the best ever."

"Finally. Recognition." Then, to the waitress, "I'll have the same."

She returned with the brews in record time.

"So, not to get all mushy on ya," Piza said, "but you look like shit."

Morrow's eyelashes fluttered. "Six months apart from each other, and in less than five minutes you've managed to touch my soul. It leaves me weak."

Piza laughed and said, "Glad to see med school hasn't dulled your wit. But kidding aside, you do look a little frazzled. You okay?"

"Yeah, I'm fine. It's just that med school is like college to the tenth power. I mean, all I do is go to class and study. I actually feel guilty being here."

"You should have said something. We could've done this some other time."

"Nah. It's not gonna change anytime soon. Plus I really needed to clear my head."

"You needed to clear your head, and you thought of *me*? Now I'm really worried about you."

Morrow grinned. "So, anyway, what's going on with you? How are your mom and dad?"

"They're fine. Pop's still putting in twelve-hour days at the deli. I'm afraid he's gonna morph into a chunk of provolone."

"The man enjoys his work. Leave him be. What's up with Patty?"

"Still getting in trouble, and charming her way out of it. Most of the time, anyway."

"Good for her. Glad she hasn't lost her gift for mischief."

"And *your* folks?" Piza asked.

"Healthy . . . and still driving each other crazy."

"Happy to hear it. There's something to be said for consistency."

Morrow smiled. "I guess." After a sip of beer, he said, "So tell me, is your year off with pay everything you'd hoped for and more?"

"I can best answer that by saying, 'What the hell was I thinking?'"

"That bad?"

"Please. The principal is the Wicked Witch of the West—before Weight Watchers. The pastor's a money-grubbing reprobate, and I'm virtually positive he's head of one of the Five Families."

"That's it? A walk in the park for a Bronx kid like you."

"Yeah, right. Plus it's killing me because I have to toe the line, at least to some degree. I'm gonna have to put this job on a résumé someday, and a bad reference could really hurt."

"No, I get it," Morrow said. "But there are no positives at all? Other lay teachers? Seductive nuns?"

"Actually, there is a nun who's a real sweetheart. She teaches the other sixth grade. Sister Theresa."

Morrow's eyebrows shot up. "I was kidding about the seductive nuns, but tell me more."

"No, no it's nothing like that, smartass. She's just a really good person. Cares about people."

"Innate goodness can be very sexy," Morrow persisted. "Is she attractive?"

"Enough about the nun."

"Ah, the infamous Piza 'back off' face. Fine. Any other lay teachers there?"

"Yeah. I really don't interact with them much. There's another male teacher. Good guy. A little serious, but he's got a baby and all, so I guess that's understandable."

Morrow tilted his head. "And?"

"And what?"

"God, if I wanted to pull teeth, I'd have been a dentist. No babes?"

"Babes? What are we, in high school?"

"Listen, my friend, I'll have you know that according to the *Playboy Forum*, 'babes' transcends age . . . and possibly time and space. Plus, you're avoiding the question."

"*Playboy*, eh? Does that count as 'studying'?"

"Hmm. I could take the easy out here and tell you it's extra-curricular anatomy research. But I respect you too much for that. So let's just say a man has needs and leave it there. But you still haven't answered my question."

With a roll of the eyes, Piza responded, "Fine, you relentless bastard. There's a fifth-grade teacher who's twenty-seven or so, and yes, she's a 'babe'. Jet black hair, green eyes. . ."

"Oh God, I love that," Morrow said. "I'm visualizing as we speak." He closed his eyes. "Don't panic if the table starts rising."

The waitress returned, food in hand. "Ready for another Heineken?"

"Now did you really have to ask?" Piza answered with a wink. She had to be twenty years older than him, but an attractive woman was an attractive woman. She delivered a wry smile and left.

Morrow picked up the conversation. "And the street urchins? How are you coping with them?"

Piza paused, collecting his thoughts. "Interesting situation. As you know, I had every intention of keeping them at arm's length, if not farther. But I'm not so sure that's gonna fly anymore."

"And why is that? Going soft on me?"

"No, but I'm discovering you can't simply lump them into . . . how do I put this . . . like one faceless category, I guess. You know —'kids'. It's like it's impossible not to see them as individual little people, if that makes sense. I mean, one of the boys is dealing with being abandoned by an alcoholic father. Another one managed to scare the crap out of me by wandering off at the Museum of Natural History."

"Okay. But I'm not seeing the problem."

"The problem is that, after we got back from the museum, I was thinking about the lost kid and the lecture I'd given him on the error of his ways. And I realized I sounded exactly like Pop. I mean, is that what I am, some sort of surrogate parent? Is that how they see me? What the hell do I *do* with that?"

Morrow shoved an index finger toward his friend. "All right, that's it. What have you done with my roommate, you body-snatching dickwad?"

"No, listen to me," a grinning Piza said. "I'm serious. I think I may be having some sort of unintended effect on their lives. I think they're really miserable, and it's making me miserable. You know me. Mr. Personality. Mr. Center of Attention. Mr. Witty—"

"Mr. Humble. Don't forget him."

"Wiseass. The point is, my game plan may need some tweaking."

"So what are you gonna do, go into gung-ho teacher mode? How? I mean you're basically flying by the seat of your pants."

"I have no intention of doing that. This job is still a pit stop to . . . something. But as much as I hate to admit it, my initial sense of this whole thing was wrong. I can't be the Invisible Man.

It doesn't work. And as much as I may not wanna adopt these kids, I sure as hell don't wanna hurt them either."

"So?"

"So, I may not be a real teacher, but I know a lot of stuff and I know how to communicate. I guess I'll do what I can to make things more interesting, and see where it leads. God knows, it can't be much worse than it is now."

The waitress arrived with their beers.

"Thank God," Morrow said. "You have impeccable timing, madam."

"So I've been told, hon."

Morrow raised his bottle. "Well, T, a toast to your altered adventure. And with as much sincerity as I can legitimately conjure up in a bar, let me say good luck, and better you than me."

As they clinked bottlenecks, Piza was already thinking of how to handle the week ahead.

11

"Okay, let's see. Where exactly are we in this thing?" It was the Sunday after Piza's dinner with Morrow. Sitting in his bedroom, he was leafing through the history textbook he'd freed from his briefcase. "Ah yes. Henry the Eighth. A personal favorite."

The chapter seemed accurate, but the portrayal of Henry and his dealings with the Catholic Church was listless. "The man had six wives, for God's sake. How could you possibly manage to make him boring?"

He opened the door to his bedroom closet, got on his knees, and dragged out a large cardboard box containing many of the college textbooks he'd opted to hang on to. Rummaging through them, he found the world history volume from his freshman year, and blew the dust off.

"Now we're cookin'."

The next day, Piza arrived at school ten minutes earlier than usual. He sat with his feet up on his desk. The sunlight illuminating the room ebbed and flowed, subject to the whims of some meandering fair-weather clouds. It mirrored his mood—optimistic, with a touch of tentativeness.

He returned his feet to the ground when he heard the kids walking up the hall. The safety was barking at them to keep their lines straight. *Power-crazed little twit.*

As the class filed in, it was apparent the weekend hadn't done much to dispel their mood from the end of the previous week. Undaunted, he waited for them to settle in.

After the Pledge of Allegiance, he went to the corner of the room where the row of windows met the wall behind his desk. In one motion, he hoisted himself and sat on the waist-high, Formica-topped bookcase that ran the length of the classroom, beneath the windows. The children let out a collective gasp, followed by murmurs of confusion.

He motioned for them to relax. "Calm down, people, calm down. It's the least you should expect from a former Olympic gymnast." Nothing. "I'm kidding. Geez, you guys need to lighten up." They seemed as perplexed as before, so he decided to move on.

"I'd like you to take out your history books, and turn to Chapter Four."

Robert Giacobbi quickly raised his hand. "I don't mind reading, Mr. Piza."

"I'm sure you don't, Mr. Giacobbi, but we won't be reading from the textbook today."

"Oh," he answered, appearing surprised at the revelation. "Okay."

"The information in your textbook is all right," Piza continued, "but there's actually more to the story. I thought it might be more interesting if we looked at it from the characters' point of view."

Vacant looks.

"I don't think we know how to do that," Sukie said, raising her hand as an apparent afterthought. Others nodded in agreement.

"Actually, I'll do it," he stated. "You listen, and when I'm done we can discuss it." Overall approval wafted through the classroom. "You see, there are three main characters in this story. We have King Henry the Eighth, Anne Boleyn, and Pope Clement the Sixth."

"Henry the Eighth. Is that the Herman's Hermits guy?" Ralph Restivo asked. He launched into the British band's hit song, "I'm Henry the Eighth, I Am". The whole class broke out laughing, and even Piza couldn't stifle a grin.

"Actually, the *name* of the song is based on him, Mr. Restivo. But that's about it," Piza said as the laughter died down. "Anyway, I'm going to do all three roles."

An astonished-looking Majinsky blurted out, "Holy moly, Mr. Piza's gonna be a chick."

The classroom went deathly silent, and Majinsky's face paled. But if he'd gone too far, there was no sign of it in his teacher's expression. In a split second Piza had chosen not to view the boy's outburst as a threat to his status. Rather, he saw it for what it was—a kid talking before thinking.

"I'm not going to *be* a chick, Mr. Majinsky, I'm going to play one. There's a difference. Actually, a big difference, which I sincerely hope your parents will discuss with you at some point."

"Oh. Okay, Mr. Piza. Thanks." The color returned to his face.

"Anyway, it was the year 1533, and Henry the Eighth was king of England. Break into song again, Mr. Restivo, and I'll drop-kick you into the hall."

The class cracked up.

Piza continued. "Anyway, Henry was not a happy guy. He had a daughter, but no sons. And he wanted a male heir to take over as king when he died. His wife, Catherine, was getting up there in age, so it wasn't looking too good. So he decided he needed to do something about that." He acknowledged a raised hand.

"Why was that such a big deal?" Shirley Robinson asked. "They have queens in England, and they're obviously girls."

Piza liked this kid. She was bright and funny. Although small, her mini-afro made her seem a bit taller. "Well, that's true, Miss Robinson. In fact, Henry's daughter Mary eventually became the first officially recognized female ruler of England. Although, there's some dispute as to— Never mind, I'm getting off track. Anyway, if you were a king, you wanted a son to carry on the family name. You could have a daughter who was brilliant, and a son who was a complete numbskull, but the son always had the edge."

"Sounds like King Henry was a male chauvinist pig," a girl commented.

Silence again.

From day one Piza had been trying to figure out who this girl reminded him of. Now it came to him. With her granny glasses and long, straight hair parted down the middle, she looked like an eleven-year-old version of the well-known feminist, Gloria Steinem.

"Truth is, he *was* a male chauvinist pig, Miss Jablonski."

"Knew it," she responded. "Oh, and Mr. Piza, do you think you could call me Ms.?"

This kid's got guts, I'll say that. "Um, okay, if you'd like. Any of you other ladies want in on this?" No takers.

"Really?" Jablonski said, shaking her head. "Unbelievable."

Piza continued. "So, moving along, Henry had his eye on this young girl, Anne Boleyn. But how was he gonna ditch Catherine? So he talked to some of his trusted advisers—whose main job was to tell him whatever he wanted to hear—and they came up with the idea of having his marriage to Catherine annulled."

Majinsky raised his hand. "What's that mean?"

"Well, an annulment is the Church's legal way to get out of a marriage, unlike a divorce, which, as we all know, is a huge no-no. But, to get an annulment, you had to have a really good reason. And Henry was having trouble finding one."

"So then how was he gonna pull it off?" Kevin Davis asked. Twenty-six amazed faces gazed at him. The boy looked perturbed. "*What*? I ask questions sometimes."

With a hint of a smile, the teacher said, "The answer to your question, Mr. Davis, is that Henry had a brainstorm. You see, Catherine had been married to Henry's brother. But he died. Afterward, Henry decided *he* wanted to marry her. But to do that, he had to get special permission from the Church, which he finally got. But now that he wanted to dump her for Anne, he said that giving him permission back then had been a mistake. And since it was a mistake, technically there never should've been a marriage to begin with. So, he deserved an annulment."

"Was it a mistake?" Laura asked. "Giving him permission?"

"Probably not. But Henry didn't care. He was looking for any reason he could find."

Sukie followed up a loud sigh with, "This is very confusing. It sounds like one of my mother's soap operas."

"Well, just wait," Piza said, "it gets better. It turns out Henry could get what he wanted if he got the Pope's okay. A thumbs-up, and 'Bingo'! Bye, bye, Catherine. Except Pope Clement wasn't buying it. So one day, while Henry was lounging around the castle, eating popcorn and sharing a milkshake with Anne, he decides he's gonna call the Pope to try to convince him. So he picks up the royal phone and—"

"Um, excuse me, Mr. Piza," William Reilly interrupted, "but they didn't have telephones back then."

Groans.

"He's kidding, you weirdo," someone muttered.

"Hey, hey, watch the name-calling. It's called artistic license,

Mr. Reilly. It's kind of changing facts around to fit your story. So in this case—"

"Ohhh, like for dramatic effect. I get it now. Sorry about that, Mr. Piza."

"No problem. And I've gotta tell ya, I'm pretty impressed you know what dramatic effect is."

The child flashed a broad grin.

"Okay, so where were we? Oh yeah. Henry picks up the phone, and this is kind of how the conversation went." He put his fingers to his right ear, mimicking a phone, and switched hands as the speakers changed. He did Henry and Anne with an English accent, and the Pope with an Italian accent.

Henry: Hello there, Your Holiness, how's it going?

Pope: Eh, not so good. It's been pouring for three days. Very depressing.

Henry: I hear *that*. Rains here in London all the time. Anyway, I wanted to speak with you about this thing with Catherine. You and I go back a long way, and I simply can't understand why you won't cut me a bit of slack on this. Capisce?

Pope: Listen. Henry. Ask me for anything else, and it's yours. But I can't annul your marriage. I'd look like an idiot.

Henry: Well, certainly not in my book, but— Hold on, okay? Annie wants to talk to you.

Anne: Hello, Holy Father. I can't tell you what a thrill it is to be speaking with you.

Pope: *I* know. I have that effect on people.

Anne: Pope'y, dearest, won't you reconsider the annulment? Henry and I really, *really* love each other. And Catherine . . . well, she's a big meanie. Treats me horridly. I mean, Henry likes me better. Get over it, right? (She whispers) And, are you ready for this? She only takes a bath once a month. P.U.!

Pope: Wow. That's way more information than I needed. Anyway, you seem like a nice kid. But, I'm afraid I still have to say no.

Anne: Oh well. I'm going to go cry now, so I'll put Henry back on.

Henry: So no is your final answer, eh? Fine. Then you leave me no choice.

Pope: What's that mean, no choice?

Henry: Here's what's going to happen. I'm going to get the Archbishop of Canterbury to annul the marriage.

Pope: He'll never do it.

Henry: He will if he wants to continue breathing on a regular basis. And after that, I'm cutting off all ties with the Catholic Church.

Pope: Have you thought this through, big guy? You do that and I'll have to excommunicate you. You know that, right? Finito? Kaputski?

Henry: Hey, you've got to do what you've got to do. I understand completely. No hard feelings, old sport. Well— Oh, one other thing while I've got you on the phone. Since we may not be talking again for a while —or ever, actually—do you think you could send over more of that lasagna you shipped up last month? Huge hit at the last beheading party. The sauce had just a hint of—

Piza snapped his head in mock surprise.

Henry: He hung up on me!

The students had sat wide-eyed through the entire routine. They'd looked like they wanted to laugh but were suppressing it, apparently unsure how they were supposed to react. The Pope? Lasagna? Uncharted waters.

Suddenly, someone yelled, "All right, Mr. Piza!" And with that, the floodgates opened and the air exploded with appreciative applause. Piza hopped off the bookcase and bowed. Excitement inundated the room, with even the most hardened skeptics clapping. Except one.

From her office diagonally across from Piza's classroom, Mother John noticed her renegade employee sitting on the bookcase. "What's he doing now?" she murmured. She went to the window, arriving as he jumped off the bookcase and took his bow. And his students were applauding.

Has he finally lost his mind? Well, I guess it beats him sitting behind his desk like a sack of potatoes. And the children appear to be happy. No harm, I imagine.

"And then he had King Henry asking the Pope to send him lasagna. Do you believe it?" Robert Giacobbi Jr. was red-faced as he recounted the day's events to his parents.

As they sat at the ornate, cherry wood table that was the centerpiece of their opulent dining room, his mother remained passive during the tirade. But his father, from his perch at the head of the table, became more and more incensed as the story progressed. The Canadian Club that had been residing placidly in his cocktail glass now rippled, as the star-sapphire pinkie ring assaulted the fine crystal with increasing intensity.

"Something's gotta be done about this guy," the man said. "Talking about the Pope like that. It's— What's that word?"

"Sacrilegious?" his wife suggested.

“Right. I knew it, just couldn’t think of it for a second. Does Mother John know?”

The boy shrugged. “I’m not sure.”

“Well, I’m gonna change that, goddammit.”

“Bob, language. Please.”

“Zip it, Sandra. She’s getting a call first thing in the morning.”

12

It was the day after Piza's triumphant entry into the world of almost-giving-a-damn, and the positive mood in the classroom was as palpable as the day before. Not that he wasn't still winging it to a degree. There were limits to how much effort he was willing to expend. The difference was the presentation; his attitude. The tension that had been a daily presence was gone.

He'd been nearing the end of a late-morning geography lesson when nature called. Other than when he used the men's room in the teachers' lounge at lunchtime, his facility of choice was the boys' bathroom directly across the hall from his classroom.

Using the boys' room had initially been a little strange, what with the hushed comments and uncomfortable giggles from the lavatory's usual clientele. But, in time, his presence came to be accepted; sometimes even welcomed, if he chose to engage them in some sports talk.

Standing at a urinal, he was having a particularly animated discussion that morning when the bathroom door slammed open, rattling the mirrors lining the white tile wall ten feet behind him.

His shock intensified when he caught the image of Mother John in one of the mirrors, as she held the door open. Fortunately, the stalls between him and her blocked a direct view.

"What's all this commotion? Back to your classrooms. Now."

They instantly scurried to the exit. "Bye, Mr. Piza," one of them called out.

"Oh, Mr. Piza, I didn't realize you were in here," she said. "Just as well. I was coming to see you, anyway. Meet me in my office before the lunch break ends. I need to speak with you."

"Um, no problem. I'll be there." A darting glance at the mirror revealed she was no longer in view. Hearing the door click shut triggered a return to normal breathing and a release of the death grip asphyxiating his penis.

"She's a freakin' crazy woman! What the hell does she wanna see me about now?"

Piza's discomfort must have been evident. O'Brien, who'd recently started joining Bauer and him in the teachers' lounge for lunch, immediately asked what was wrong.

He looked around to assess the proximity of other diners. "Wrong? Wrong? What could possibly be wrong? I mean seriously, if I had a dollar for every time a nun barged into a bathroom while I was in mid-pee. . ."

"You are so full of it," O'Brien said.

"No way," Bauer added. "That's over the top even for you, pal."

"Full of it, am I?" Piza responded, his slightly quivering hands struggling to unwrap a veal parm hero. "Mother John. Boys' bathroom. Ten minutes ago. There I was, wazoo in hand— Crap. Sorry, Colleen."

"Nothing I haven't heard before." An impish grin was followed by, "No need to make a mountain out of a molehill."

"Very good, O'Brien," he conceded. "Clever little side door metaphor there. Of course, you have no idea how far off base you are, but—"

"Could you just continue with the story, please," a blushing Bauer insisted.

"Blame her, Jimbo. So anyway, there I was, and it's like she—"

"Wait a minute," O'Brien said. "Did she actually approach you while you were standin' there doin' your business?"

"No, thank God. She stayed by the door. But I caught a glimpse of her in the mirror. And if I could see *her*, then. . ." He shuddered.

Bauer shook his head. "Did she at least apologize? I mean, you can't tell me that wasn't awkward for her too."

"If she was uncomfortable, you could've fooled me. I don't get her. Sometimes she talks to me like an adult, and other times I really believe she thinks I'm ten."

O'Brien looked down her nose. "Well, the fact that you were in the little boys' room probably didn't help."

"Look, the teachers' lounge is across the building, and the boys' room is fifteen feet from my classroom. Do the math. Come on, back me up here, Bauer. Your classroom is as far from the teachers' lounge as mine. What do *you* do?"

Bauer grimaced. "Honestly, I hold it."

"Really? Needless suffering, if you ask me. But, anyway, more importantly, she said she needs to see me before the afternoon session starts. Either of you guys have any idea what she might want?"

"Not a clue," O'Brien said.

"Me either," from Bauer.

"Well, whatever it is, I guarantee it's not *good* news. I just hope—"

He stopped as he noticed Sister Theresa motioning to him from a few tables away. "Sister T seems to need something. Let me see what she wants, then I'll go meet the Grim Reaper. Might as well get it over with." A last bite of his sandwich, and he was off.

"Good luck," Bauer said.

"If she fires you, leave us a note," O'Brien added.

Piza flung a smirk. He caught up with Sister Theresa as she headed to an abandoned corner of the room.

With a muffled voice, she asked, "Mr. Piza, are you meeting with Mother John today?"

Despite his anxiety, the secretive tone amused him. He surveyed the room with feigned concern. "I am, indeed," he whispered back. "How'd you know?"

"Are you making fun of me?"

"Absolutely not."

"Oh, good. Because people who have a small piece of meat stuck in their pearly whites aren't really in a position to mock *anyone*."

Piza blushed and ran his tongue across his teeth, discovering the reluctant morsel and dislodging and swallowing it in a blink.

"There you go," she said. "Anyway, I was making copies in the office this morning. Mother got a call about one of your lessons. From what I could hear it had something to do with the Pope. But I don't have any details. She just told whoever it was she'd speak with you today. What exactly did you do?"

Piza looked deflated. "Tried to liven things up a bit with a little humor. New approach. New me. Apparently a mistake on my part."

"It's never a mistake to try to make learning more fun," she reassured him. "It'll be fine."

"Well, we'll see very shortly. I'm going to meet her now. Thanks for the heads-up, Sister."

"No problem. Let me know how you make out."

Sure, Tony, be a real teacher, he thought as he left. This is such bullshit.

By the time he reached Mother John's office, he'd riled himself into a state of acute resentment. *Chew me out for coloring outside the lines a little, eh lady? All I did was try to beef up your crappy textbook. Oooo. Mortal sin. I'm going to hell.*

"Ah, Mr. Piza. Have a seat."

"How can I help you, Mother?"

The abrupt tone didn't seem to faze her. "I got a call this morning from a parent of one of your students. This . . . individual had some concerns about a history lesson you taught yesterday. Is that what you were doing when you were sitting on the bookcase?"

Piza's brow furrowed.

"I can see your classroom from here," she said, pointing.

He turned. "Oh, so you can. Hmm. Uh, yes, that was the lesson I was doing. Who lodged the complaint?"

"Honestly, I'd rather not say."

"Don't I have the right to confront my accuser?"

She sighed. "Mr. Piza, you're not on trial here. I got a call, and I have an obligation to speak with you about it, that's all. The parent was concerned because supposedly what you were teaching wasn't in the textbook. He also said you were disparaging the Pope. Could you fill me in on exactly what happened?"

She said "he". One step closer to discovering the asshole's identity. "Sure. We'd reached the chapter in our history book about Henry the Eighth and the Church of England. If you recall from my résumé, I minored in history, and I felt the book kind of glossed over the relationship between Henry and Pope Clement. So I tried to augment it a bit. I also made believe Henry and the Pope were talking on the phone about the situation."

He was surprised by her reaction: a hint of a smile. "And the lasagna?"

Shit. "Well, since Henry felt he and Clement wouldn't be talking anymore, he asked Clement for more of the lasagna he'd sent up once before. A little humor."

Leaning back in her chair, the principal clasped her hands in front of her, the tips of her extended index fingers brushing her lower lip. "Mr. Piza, I realize our textbooks are dated. And I have no problem with your supplementing the material a bit. In fact, I'm impressed you went the extra mile, so to speak."

"Thank you."

"That said, however, you have to understand that this is a very traditional Catholic community. Not everybody's going to get your approach, or appreciate it, as seen by this phone call."

"The kids seemed to enjoy it."

"I saw that. And I was happy to see their reaction. It's not often you see that kind of enthusiasm from children. At least not in a classroom. But they don't make the rules."

He smirked. "Or the phone calls."

"Exactly. So in the future, don't push *too* far. If you think something could reasonably be seen as objectionable, steer clear. And 'reasonably' is the operative word. I don't want to completely tie your hands."

Piza was dumbfounded. He'd come into the office ready to spew volcanic ash. Now all he wanted to do was pet a kitten. "Um, thank you, Mother. I appreciate your understanding. And I'll keep tabs on the lessons."

"Okay then."

"And the irate parent?"

"I'll deal with that."

"Okay. Thanks."

As he left the office, he completely exhaled for the first time since the meeting began. *I can't believe she backed me up. I must be in an alternate universe.*

But he quickly shifted focus, for there was a traitor in the ranks.

13

As of the Friday after Piza's meeting with Mother John, he'd managed to walk the line between entertainment and blasphemy without any new complaints. But he was also no closer to finding the young Judas in his class.

He'd arrived earlier than usual, to draw a map of the area surrounding the Tigris and Euphrates rivers in Iraq—the next lesson in the geography book. He thought it might be interesting to tie this in with a recent religion lesson he'd taught, since this was the region where the Garden of Eden had supposedly existed.

The obligation to parrot religious dogma three times a week irked him. Occasionally, when his frustration level was topping out, he'd subtly stray from the rigid content of the textbook. It made for some interesting dialogue with the children, and hadn't sparked any negative repercussions. Mother John seemed to have no idea she'd unleashed an avowed skeptic on these unsuspecting youngsters. He figured she'd simply assumed he was a practicing Catholic, as she apparently had with Bauer.

As the children sauntered into the classroom, their overall mood seemed upbeat. He had the sense his relationship with them had improved during the week, probably because of the consistency of his new attitude.

After the obligatory early-morning housekeeping, he sat on the front of his desk. "Who remembers our discussion in religion about Adam and Eve?"

Virtually every student's hand went up. "Good. Now, does anyone know where the Garden of Eden was located?" Two hands this time. "Okay, Miss Robinson."

Before the girl could answer, the door at the back of the classroom opened. Mother John quietly entered the room and leaned against the middle of the back wall. Piza and the children immediately rose. The kids intoned the sing-song greeting they'd learned in kindergarten: "Good mooorning, Mother John, God bless *you*."

"Thank you, children. God bless you too. You can be seated."

Piza was a portrait of dismay. "Um, Mother John. Did you, uh, want to see me?"

"No, not at all, Mr. Piza. You can continue with your lesson."

"Because if you need something. . ."

"No. I'm fine. I try to do a spot evaluation of every teacher once or twice a year. I find it's more effective if it's unannounced. So please, carry on."

A million thoughts ran through his head, none of them remotely positive. The cascading doomsday scenarios ultimately boiled down to: *I'm screwed.*

"Mr. Piza?" the nun prompted.

"Oh, yes, Mother. Sorry about that." He sat down again. "So, anyway, the question was whether anyone knows where the Garden of Eden was located. And, um, Miss Robinson, you were about to give us an answer?"

To say the principal's presence had changed the atmosphere

would have ranked in the top tier of historical understatements. Without exception, the children were sitting ramrod straight, hands clasped on their desktops, unblinking eyes staring directly ahead. If Madame Tussauds was searching for a classroom exhibit for one of its wax museums, the quest could have ended right there.

"Miss Robinson? Your answer?" Piza gently pressed.

"Um, uh, ummm, I, I'm not really sure anymore, I think, Mr. Piza." Her lips were moving, but every other aspect of her expression screamed deer-in-the-headlights. Piza empathized, surmising he'd probably looked just like that moments before.

The teacher smiled. "Well, you must have been thinking of something. It doesn't matter if it's right or wrong, because it's not something we studied. I'm happy you're willing to give it a shot."

The girl seemed to relax just enough to comply. "Well, I was going to say heaven."

"That's an excellent answer, Miss Robinson, especially since we know it was God who talked to Adam and Eve in the garden. And when we think of God, we think of. . ." He made the slightest hand gesture.

"Heaven," they responded in unison.

"Exactly. But don't forget, God can go anywhere he wants, right? It's like he's got his own personal rocket ship that can take him anywhere in the universe in a split second."

No reaction from Mother John, so he figured he hadn't crossed the line.

He continued. "As it turns out, the Garden of Eden was actually here on Earth."

"Oh, that makes perfect sense," declared William Reilly. "They were the first man and woman, so they would *have* to be on Earth. I hadn't really thought of that."

"That's absolutely correct, Mr. Reilly. But as much as I appreciate your enthusiasm, please raise your hand next time, okay?"

He really didn't care, but he had to show the principal he was in control. "So, any other clues as to where the Garden of Eden might have been."

Vinny Pinto raised his hand.

"Yes, Mr. Pinto."

"I think it would have to be somewhere that had snakes, because of the serpent and all."

"Good, that helps us narrow it down. What else? Yes, Miss Perotta."

"I think it probably had to be someplace warm, because before Adam and Eve ate the apple, didn't they walk around without any—"

The possible impact of what she was about to say must have hit her, because she turned crimson. Most of the class tittered, and Piza even caught Mother John attempting to suppress a smile. He was tempted to toss in a clever quip, but one look at the child steered him in a different direction.

"Bravo, Miss Perotta," he said, lightly clapping his hands. "Excellent deduction. As it turns out, the Garden of Eden *was* in a warm climate." The child's face radiated thanks.

He acknowledged Robert Giacobbi's raised hand. "Does that map on the board have anything to do with it?"

"It does, indeed, Mr. Giacobbi. Good pick up." He rose from the desk and retrieved a pointer from the ledge at the bottom of the blackboard. "I-R-A-Q," he enunciated, pointing to the letters on the drawing. "Anyone know what that spells?" A few hands. "Miss Schaeffer?"

She pronounced it "I-rack".

"Good, Miss Schaeffer. Technically, it's pronounced 'i-rock', but the fact you came that close is very impressive. Good job."

He was being even more solicitous than the revised version of himself had been during the week, but he figured no harm in laying it on a little thicker, under the circumstances.

He pointed out the six countries that surround Iraq. When he got to Turkey he added, "If anyone has the urge to gobble, I suggest you save it for Thanksgiving." The children laughed. No reaction from Mother John. *I'm going down in flames.*

After explaining the current layout of the Middle East, he worked his way back to when the region was known as Mesopotamia. The children seemed genuinely interested. His revelation that the Garden of Eden was believed to have been where the Tigris and Euphrates rivers joined and emptied into the Persian Gulf, met with a question.

"So, Mr. Piza," Kevin Davis said as he simultaneously raised his hand, "if those rivers and all are still there, shouldn't the Garden of Eden still be there too?"

Davis's participation was so rare that the occasional question always surprised Piza. "Um, no, not anymore, Mr. Davis."

"How come?"

"Well, if you recall, after Adam and Eve disobeyed God and ate that apple, he punished them by making them mortal."

The boy nodded.

"But because of what they did, he also took away the Garden of Eden."

It was then he fell headlong into one of those moments that, for years to come, randomly jars you out of sleep, in a cold sweat. "So if Adam and Eve hadn't gotten the munchies all those years ago, maybe the Garden of Eden would still be there." He froze. *No, no, no! And on the eighth day God created potheads, you idiot?*

He felt the blood drain from his face, followed by a searing heat he thought might cause him to pass out. *What have you done, you unbelievable schmuck? That woman in the back now thinks she hired an absolute freaking stoner to mold these young, impressionable minds. Christ. I'm toast.*

Of course, all this self-loathing transpired in an instant, while he was still looking at Kevin Davis. The boy's mouth was agape, answering the question whether he'd picked up on the inadvertent marijuana reference.

But, as usual, Piza transitioned into crisis mode: virtual deep breath; will the mind and body to calm down. It never failed.

The first thing to do was assess the situation. Mother John's reaction would have the most immediate impact on life as he knew it, so he determined to get that out of the way. He raised his eyes and looked directly at her. Nothing. *Have I traumatized her into temporary paralysis?* But then there was a sign of life as her eyes conveyed a message that said, Why are you looking at *me*?

He joyously shifted his gaze from her as subtly as possible, and began surveying the rest of the room. Ah, Vinny Pinto—tongue in cheek, gazing at the ceiling, awkwardly shooting fleeting glances at his teacher. But other than the two boys, zippo. No discernible signs of surprise or discomfort. *Is this possible? Can the rest of them really be this innocent? Who cares? Wrap this baby up!*

"So, any more questions anyone? Hmm?" A fragmentary pause. "Okay then. I think we can move on to reading. Mother John, will you be staying for the next lesson?" *Please say no.*

"No, no, Mr. Piza. I've seen enough. I'll schedule a time for us to speak."

"Oh, um, okay." As much as he dreaded the possibility of a withering public assessment of his teaching skills, he needed some clue as to how he'd done.

She must have sensed it. "Overall, though, good lesson." With that, she was gone.

Relief washed over him. He'd realized from the start this visit was serious, but everything had moved so fast he hadn't fully processed the depth of its significance, both as to his employment status and his pride. He certainly didn't want to get fired, but it dawned on him that he also wanted to be seen as good at this job. Apparently, that had just happened.

The exhilaration hit him head-on, and without a thought to

appearances he pumped his right fist above his head and declared, "We did it!"

The children instantly echoed his enthusiasm, with applause, a healthy dose of woo-hoo's, and an epic "Yeah, baby" from Matt Majinsky.

Amid the revelry, Sukie turned to Laura, smiled, and said, "Told you he'd be a good teacher."

14

"Hmm. Why is Sister T sitting at our table?" Piza murmured as he breezed into the teachers' lounge at lunchtime. *Something's up.* But that didn't dull his mood. Life was good. A seemingly positive assessment from his principal that morning, and a baloney and Swiss hero, courtesy of the Casa Piza deli.

As he reached the table, he said, "Ah. Sister Theresa. What an unexpected pleasure. And may I say you're looking as lovely as ever?"

"No, you may not. I heard you were evaluated this morning, and I wanted to get the dirt first-hand. So spill it."

"Getting pushy in your old age, eh? Fine."

He recounted the morning's events in detail, including his inadvertent marijuana remark. "Yeah, so I looked at Mother John, and if she had any idea about what I'd said you could've fooled me, because she didn't flinch."

"That doesn't surprise me," Sister Theresa offered. "She's a very smart woman, but I don't think she's really in touch with the youth culture these days. I mean I'm sure she knows what marijuana is, but the term 'the munchies' probably doesn't mean anything to her."

Piza grinned. "And it does to you, Sister?"

"Would you be shocked if it did?"

"Shocked? Mmmm, no, not shocked. Let's say somewhat surprised."

"Well, don't be. I *have* had exposure to the outside world, you know"—she tugged at the sleeve of her habit—"before this. So, yes, I get the marijuana connection. Or would you prefer I call it pot, or weed, or grass, or— Shall I go on?"

Yikes. "No, no, that won't be necessary." He smiled. "Just out of curiosity though, did you become a nun as part of a juvenile delinquency plea deal or something?"

O'Brien and Bauer laughed. Sister Theresa, on the other hand, was stone-faced. "I beg your pardon? If you want to kid around, I'm fine with that, Mr. Piza. But certain topics are off limits, my holy vows being one of them. I assume you simply weren't thinking, but your little joke was totally inappropriate."

"God, I'm really, really sorry, Sister. If I thought for a second that— I mean I hope you know I wouldn't intentionally do anything to offend you like that."

The nun turned to the other two teachers, who now looked almost as anxious as Piza. "Think he's had enough?"

Their stunned expressions gave way to belly-laughs, which became contagious, as teachers at other tables looked at them and started laughing too.

Piza was perturbed, not used to being the butt of someone else's joke. But the beauty of the fake-out soon took hold, and he found himself laughing along with them. He wagged a reprimanding finger at her. "You have a bit of a cruel streak, Sister T, you know that? And here I thought you were a paragon of goodness."

Her hazel eyes flickered with mischief. "I am. Doesn't mean I can't have a little fun."

"Tell you what, Sister," he said. "I'm having my monthly Friday night card game at my parents' tonight. Young James here has once again politely declined my invitation; something about family responsibilities and such. But we've never had a female in the ranks before. And in light of your outstanding goof on me, I would like to formally invite you to sit in."

She smiled. "Unfortunately, I'll have to decline as well. As intriguing as it sounds, I'm pretty sure the order frowns on things like that. Sorry."

"Oh, well. I tried."

O'Brien arched an eyebrow. "So, your new nondiscrimination policy only applies to nuns? I see."

Sister Theresa picked up on the thread. "Yes, that doesn't seem fair at all. Why would you ask me and not her?"

Piza hadn't expected this. "Oh. Well, um, I kind of asked *you* because I knew you'd say no."

"Gosh, thank you for that."

Bauer chuckled. "Anyone else you'd like to alienate while you're at it?"

Struggling for an escape, Piza said, "I wasn't trying to alienate *anybody*. I mean if, ya know, if you'd really like to come, Colleen, then, uh, I guess it would be okay."

O'Brien mimicked a Southern drawl. "Well, aren't you just a sweet talker, you."

He rebounded. "No, I mean it. Seriously."

She pursed her lips. "You know what, if you'd asked me a couple of minutes ago, I'd have graciously declined, like my friends here. But I think we may have a women's rights issue on our hands. So tell me where and when, and I'll be there."

The gauntlet had been thrown. Piza squinted in response. "Done. Seven o'clock. I'll give you directions."

As O'Brien and Sister Theresa congratulated themselves on the coup, Bauer leaned in toward Piza. "Is it me, or does your mouth have a mind of its own?"

"Seems that way sometimes, doesn't it? What can I tell ya?" He winked. "But this should be quite an evening."

Sister Theresa poked her head into the principal's office. "You wanted to see me, Mother?"

"Yes, Sister. Come in. I wanted to talk to you about— I'm not keeping you from anything, am I? Because—"

"No, no, not at all."

"Oh, okay. Good. Um, Mr. Piza."

"Yes?"

"I did a classroom observation today."

"Yes, I heard about it at lunch. Seems to have gone well?"

"Actually it did. Let me ask you, do you know if he knew I was coming in today?"

"Gee, not that I heard. You don't usually tell anyone when you're going to do an evaluation." She smiled. "You've surprised me every time."

The principal returned the smile. "And you never disappoint, Sister. And, yes, the only place it's written is in my desk calendar, and only Mrs. Florino and I have access to it. I spoke to her, and she assured me she didn't let it slip."

"I'm not really sure what this is about, Mother. Why would you think he knew in advance?"

"How well do you know him?"

"Not that well. I mean, we teach the same grade, so of course we interact. But I've never really sat down with him and discussed his life, if that's what you mean. I'm— I'm still a little confused by—"

"Forgive me, Sister. I don't mean to sound so conspiratorial. I just wasn't expecting him to be quite so prepared. It made me a bit suspicious."

Sister Theresa paused in thought. "Well, for whatever it's

worth, I *have* noticed . . . how do I put this? From what I've seen, and from hearing him talk, it seems like he's enjoying this more. More engaged with the children I think."

"I've picked up on that too, to some degree. His classroom is across from here and—"

"Wow, you can look right in there," Sister Theresa acknowledged, straining a bit to see out the window.

"Exactly. I've noticed a certain energy that wasn't there before. Truth be told, there were times in the beginning of the semester when I was tempted to run over there and check his pulse."

Sister Theresa laughed, and Mother John made no effort to stifle a chuckle. "I'm serious," she said, smiling. "My impression is he sees himself as something of a scamp, so I'm never really sure where he's coming from or what to expect."

"Well—"

The principal held up her hand. "My point is that being animated doesn't necessarily translate into teaching. So I was surprised by the substance of his lesson today. And, don't get me wrong, if this is really who he's become, I'm thrilled. But I think you can understand why I'm a little skeptical." A nod invited a response.

"I do understand, Mother. Completely. And look, Anthony does have a kind of Peter Pan quality to him, but—"

"Anthony? I didn't realize you were on a first-name basis with him."

"Oh. I'm not really. It's just— I mean, it's his name. Did I do something wrong?"

"No, no, Sister," she replied, waving it off. "The informality took me by surprise, that's all. Please, finish your thought."

Reassurances notwithstanding, Sister Theresa was slightly unnerved. "Um, okay. Uh, what I was going to say is that I think the idea of not being good at something bothers him. And I think he's a performer at heart. Combine the two, and—"

"And we have the new and improved Mr. Piza."

"Exactly."

"I have to say, I'd be happier if the reason for his transformation was a deeper appreciation of the profession, rather than a fear of failure. But, under the circumstances, I guess I'll take what I can get. Very astute observations, Sister."

"Thank you for the compliment, Mother, but the truth is he kind of wears what he's about on his sleeve . . . despite what he may believe."

Mother John's lips formed a scant, yet pleasant, smile. "You like him."

What did she mean by that? I hope she doesn't think— Calm down, Theresa. "I do, Mother, I must admit. I realize he can come across as self-centered, and I guess in certain ways he is, but I have this sense that, underneath it all, he's a good person. Am I making any sense?"

"You are, Sister. And in the few years you've been here, I've come to trust your instincts. But do me a favor, if you get an inkling that he might be doing something . . . 'inappropriate' I guess is the word I'm looking for, let me know."

"I'm not really— What could he possibly do that—"

"To be perfectly honest, I'm not sure *I* even know what I'm looking for. And I'm not saying there's anything sinister, I certainly don't mean that. But he marches to his own beat, and I don't know if he realizes when he's crossing the line. That's all I'm saying."

"Of course, Mother. I understand. I'll keep an eye out."

"Thank you, Sister. I appreciate it. See you at dinner."

The young nun exited the office and quickly returned to her classroom, uncomfortable and confused.

15

Ever since lunch, Piza had been on edge about O'Brien attending the card game that evening. He wanted to believe that meddling with the "men only" tradition was the cause, but he knew it was more likely the prospect of seeing her outside the sheltered environment of OLPT. Either way, he vowed to get past it before seven o'clock.

He arrived home just in time to help his mother carry in groceries. "Ma, why would you possibly buy this many cans of peeled tomatoes?" He wrestled with the two unwieldy brown paper bags as he slogged into the kitchen. Setting them down on the table, he plopped onto a chair.

Mary continued unpacking her groceries. "If I told ya once I told ya a thousand times, Anthony, ya gotta grab 'em while they're on sale."

"I get that. But have you seen the downstairs pantry lately? You've got enough tomato cans down there to make spaghetti sauce for Congress. Not that they deserve it."

She turned to him, a head of lettuce in her right hand. "Very funny. You're such a comedian. But if there's a tomato shortage someday, then you'll be thankin' me. It's happenin' to gasoline, so. . ."

"I surrender," Piza said, raising his hands. "Oh, guess what? We're gonna have one extra for the game tonight. Another teacher from my school."

"That's great. What's his name?"

"It's not a he, it's a she."

Her eyes came alive. "Oh really? Is she Italian?"

Motioning for her to calm down, he replied, "She's a coworker, Ma. That's all. So please don't stand there fantasizing about grandchildren. And, no, she's not Italian. She's Irish."

"Oh. Well, they're nice too. Like Mrs. O'Malley, for example. Comes into the store every Wednesday, like clockwork. Always buys five pounds of ham and six pounds of baloney. Eight kids, you believe it? The woman's goin' straight to heaven. Do me a favor and put the rest of the food away. I gotta go back to the Acme."

"But you were just there. Why—"

"I forgot some stuff."

"Can't it wait?"

With a cursory wave, she hurried out of the kitchen. "Be right back. Keep an eye on Patty."

"Uh, okay. Be careful."

With the exception of Jack Morrow, Piza's closest friends were four guys he'd grown up with. They'd met in grammar school and remained a tight-knit group since. These were the Friday night card game regulars.

On arriving that evening, they exchanged the usual pleasantries with Mrs. Piza, then headed to the basement, a subterranean Shangri-La adorned in knotty-pine paneling and a cream-colored linoleum tile floor. As much as they enjoyed playing cards and shooting the breeze, the main reason for their perfect monthly attendance was the food. A card game at Piza's house was probably better catered than some weddings.

As they all lingered in the kitchen area, close to the basement steps, Piza informed his friends that a newcomer would be joining them. This immediately met with protests, until they learned it was a girl. None was more outwardly enthusiastic than Frankie Falco.

Frankie was Piza's best friend. The plumber in the group, a year of community college had confirmed what he already knew —school wasn't for him. He was pretty much set for life anyway, his father being an upper-level plumbers' union official.

He and Piza's bond had formed in fifth grade, when they discovered they had the same birthday. It was cemented when Frankie, always big for his age, bloodied the nose of an eighth-grader who'd pinned young Tony to a wall when he refused to relinquish his snack money.

Frankie had rarely had a relationship that lasted more than a few months. Piza was convinced he was gay. But Frankie had never hinted at it, and Piza felt it wasn't his place to push the issue with him, or let anyone else in on his personal notion.

Sal Amico, an electrician, demanded the female teacher's measurements, as his right hand patted a meticulously-crafted pompadour. The Dion and the Belmonts hairstyle symbolized his refusal to accept the passing of the doo-wop era. People mostly saw Sal as a stereotypical greaser, which was fine with him.

"Don't go there, okay?" was Piza's response to Sal's request.

"What, I'm just askin'. They don't have to be exact, like to an eighth of an inch or whatever. Just an estimate is all." He looked to the others for support that didn't materialize.

"She's very attractive," Piza stated. "But the only reason she's coming is because she all but dared me to invite her. It's a one-time thing, okay? And please try not to embarrass me."

Jeff Jennings adjusted his thick glasses. "Well, color me hurt."

Jeff was legally blind in his right eye, the result of an effort to pry open a jar of blackberry jam with a fork when he was five. He'd graduated from St. Peter's College in Jersey City in June, and was working in his father's hardware store while pursuing his dream of winning the Nobel prize for literature.

"Yeah, talk about being insulted," chimed in Joey "Strikes" Sabatini, an assistant manager at a local savings & loan. "Plus, you know, I'm married and all, so. . ." Joey was the only married one in the group, having wed his high school sweetheart, Megan, shortly after college graduation—he from Rutgers, she from William Paterson.

Joey had just finished his comment, when the doorbell rang.

"I've got it," Mary called out from the upstairs kitchen, a lilt in her voice.

Piza made a bee line for the stairs. "I can't have her making first contact. God only knows what she'll say."

As he reached the top of the steps, he could see his mother had a ten-foot lead on him. When he yelled "Ma, I'll get it", she doubled her pace. Game, set, match—Mrs. Piza.

Opening the door she said, "Well, hellooo, you must be— Wow, you're a tall one." Mary was 5'2". O'Brien was 5'8" in her stocking feet, and now had on black suede boots with two-inch heels.

The girl laughed. "Hi, Mrs. Piza, it's a pleasure to meet you," she said, crossing the threshold into the living room. "It's the boots. They make me look taller than I am. Oh, what a lovely home."

"Thank you, dear. Anthony look, your friend is here. And she's got boots."

Piza was too mesmerized to respond. He would eventually make it down to those boots, past the tight black denim jeans, but for now he was focused above the waist. An open black leather jacket framed a buttoned black suede vest and tight black cotton turtleneck.

He was used to her school outfits, mostly knee length skirts and loose blouses. Even that conservative attire couldn't completely mask her physical attributes. But this? This he wasn't expecting.

O'Brien tilted her head. "Hey there. Long time no see."

"Yeah, it uh . . . seems like ages." He tried to shake free of the spell. "Uh, c'mon, I'll show you downstairs."

O'Brien held up the paper bag in her left hand. "I brought some pretzels and chips."

Mary, often told by her son that she was a food snob, managed a plastic smile. "How nice of you. Give it to me and I'll take care of it." She took the bag and hurried it to the kitchen, as her son led O'Brien to the basement.

From her expression and the way she held the bag away from her body, you'd have thought she was escorting a sack of poo. She rolled her eyes as she set it on a countertop. "Pretzels and potato chips. On cards night."

Piza's friends were still loitering in the basement kitchen area as he and O'Brien descended the steps.

"Sweet Jesus," Sal muttered as he executed a rare *two-handed* pompadour pat.

Piza made the introductions, and if O'Brien was at all put off by the gawking, she handled it like a champ.

While this was going on downstairs, Mary knocked on the door of the master bedroom, to hurry her husband. Angelo had only gotten home from the store fifteen minutes before. He'd wanted to freshen up and change clothes before greeting his son's friends.

"Angelo, are ya decent?" She opened the door before the poor man could reply that he was in his underwear.

"Mary, why do you bother to knock if you're gonna come in anyways?"

"Oh please. Nothin' I ain't seen before. Listen, Anthony's got one of his friends from school here. Another teacher. A girl."

Angelo's head shot up. "Really? No kiddin'. Is she Italian?"

"No. Irish."

"Oh. Well, that's okay. They're nice too. Mrs. O'Malley from the store is Irish and—"

"Believe me, she ain't no Mrs. O'Malley. I think she may be a hippie. I dunno. Anyways, please finish gettin' dressed, and help me take the food downstairs."

"I'm done. See? I'm bucklin' my belt."

"Okay, good. And your hair looks like you stuck your finger in a socket, so. . ." Her voice trailed off as she walked out.

He ran his hands through the unruly shock of silver. "This woman, I swear to God."

When he entered the hall he knocked on Patty's bedroom door. "C'mon, kiddo. Cards night."

"Okay, Dad," she answered, scrambling to turn off her portable record player. She neatly stacked the 45-rpm records scattered on the floor. The thoughtful, almost tender, way she handled them left no doubt these were prized possessions.

In the kitchen, Mary handed out assignments for the initial delivery run. Angelo would lead the caravan with the obligatory Pyrex dish brimming with sausage and peppers. She would follow with the cold cut platter. Patty would bring up the rear with two plastic bowls and the unopened bags of pretzels and chips. Mary had been taught that when a guest brings food or drink, you put it out—no matter how senseless it might seem.

As the procession made its way down the stairs, the group of young people turned toward them. Angelo approached the base of the staircase, saw O'Brien, and missed the bottom step. Sal and Jeff saved him from showering the group with the piping hot food, while Frankie relieved Mary of the cold cuts.

Piza flashed a broad grin. "Whoa, you okay there, Pop? This getting old thing is really starting to hit home."

His father smiled back and made a fist. "I can still knock you into Rahway with one shot," he said, referring to a neighboring town.

"Pop, this is Colleen O'Brien. She teaches with me at OLPT. We decided to break the 'no chicks' rule for a night."

"Hello, Mr. Piza, it's so nice to meet you," O'Brien said, extending her hand.

Instead of shaking it, Angelo bent forward and kissed it, glancing at the target area on his way back up.

"Gosh, I feel like I'm in Europe," O'Brien declared.

Angelo blushed, shrugged, and grinned sheepishly. "What can I say?"

"Angelo, honey, can you help me bring a few more things down?" Mary asked.

Angelo, honey*? Shit, Pop's a dead man.* "You need help, Pop? Bringing the stuff down?"

"No, we're fine," his mother said, before his father could open his mouth.

As Mary and Angelo went upstairs, Patty moved front and center.

O'Brien bent down a bit. "And who do we have here?"

"I'm Patty Piza. You're pretty."

"Thank you. So are you."

"*I* know. My dad, Angelo Piza, tells me that all the time."

O'Brien laughed. Then, motioning toward Piza, "And how about this guy? Is he a good brother?"

A vigorous nod. "Yep. He's my number one pal. He calls me Peppermint Patty. But I tell him not to 'cause I'm not a candy bar. But he still does it." She shrugged.

"Well, I'm glad you're such good friends. Hey, why don't you give me those bags and I'll put them on the—"

"No, no, I'll get it," Piza said. "You're a guest. Relax."

"Don't be silly," O'Brien insisted. "I'll do it." She took the bowls and bags from Patty and brought them to the counter near the stove.

Patty turned to Piza's friends. "Hi, Frankie. Hi, Jeff. Hi, Sal. Hi, Strikes." She looked at them with raised eyebrows and a mouth slightly open.

"Hi, Peppermint Patty," they intoned in unison.

She grinned and placed her hands on her hips. "I am not a candy bar." Her laughter was punctuated by her clapping her hands and then slapping her thighs.

Meanwhile, Angelo and Mary were in the upstairs kitchen, where Angelo was watching his life pass before him.

16

"And then kissin' her hand? Are you insane? And you were starin' at her. How embarrassin'."

Angelo's basement interaction with Colleen O'Brien moments before had triggered a tirade from his wife, which he was doing his best to fend off. "She didn't look embarrassed."

"Not her. Me! *I* was embarrassed with whatever it was you thought you were doin'."

"I was tryin' to make her feel at home. That's all. And I wasn't starin' at her. I was admirin', ya know, her outfit. She looked very nice with her clothes on."

"*What?*"

"No, no, that didn't come out right," the harried man practically shouted. He took a deep breath and slowed his speech, emphasizing his words with hand gestures. "All's I'm sayin' is that her outfit was nice. Okay?"

"Nice? She looks like she's in a motorcycle gang."

Angelo threw up his arms. "What are you talkin', motorcycle gang? *Now* who's the crazy one? I got news for you, that's very popular today with, ya know, that combination thing with the vest and the chest and all."

"*Excuse me? Chest?*"

"What the hell are you talkin' about? I said vest. Vest! What 'chest'? I think you need a hearin' aid."

"*I* need a hearin' aid?" She looked to the heavens. "Give me strength, God, before I do somethin' that's gonna get me in big trouble, and then my beautiful kids are gonna be visitin' their mother in the slammer."

Angelo stretched to the full extent of his 5'7". "Enough! I'm the man of the house and I ain't gonna be accused by you like I'm some sorta criminal, just because I did somethin' nice. And that's it!"

A penetrating stare from Mary was followed by, "Fine. The subject is closed. Okay? Now please get the dish outta the oven, and I'll grab the bread."

Angelo held his pose a bit longer. "Fine." Were it not for the beads of perspiration dotting his forehead, he might have pulled it off.

When they brought the rest of the food down, O'Brien said, "Mrs. Piza, I can't believe the amount of food here. This is amazing."

There was a hint of intrigue in Mary's voice. "Well, that ain't all. I made somethin' just for you." With that, she removed the aluminum foil from the dish Angelo had placed on the stove. "Ta-da! Corned beef."

Piza's face twisted in horror. *That's what you went back to the store for? Stereotype on a platter? Oh my God.*

O'Brien clasped her hands in front of her. "I can't believe you went out of your way to cook this for me. Thank you so much." There wasn't a trace of sarcasm.

Mary held up both hands, palms out. "It was nothin', dear, really. I know how much you people enjoy it."

O'Brien bent down and hugged her. You could see it surprised Mary, but she reciprocated, albeit with less enthusiasm. Then, she sniffed. "Ooo, what's that you're wearin'? Smells so nice."

"Intimate. It's my favorite."

"I can imagine. How much did you pay for it?"

"Okay!" Piza said. "I think we've got it from here, Ma."

Mary looked momentarily confused. "Oh. Okay. Good. Uh, we'll be right upstairs if you need anythin'."

As usual with cards night, Piza had pushed the living area furniture out of the way, replacing it with a folding table and metal chairs from the eating space. That way they could simultaneously play cards, gorge themselves, and catch a game on television if they were interested.

Patty watched them play, while perched on a stool her brother had brought over from the small wet-bar. She'd already eaten dinner, but randomly snagged some of the cold cuts.

O'Brien fit right in, matching the guys wisecrack-for-wisecrack. She was accepted early on when Joey, who'd been needling her, asked if she was wondering how he'd gotten the nickname "Strikes".

"Actually," she replied, "I was wonderin' how you got the name Joey. I've never heard a male who was post-puberty called that before."

This elicited an "ohhhhhhhhh" from the others. "Eh, she's got chops, this one," Sal proclaimed, a compliment he handed out about as rarely as the arrival of Halley's Comet.

She did ultimately learn the name "Strikes" had been bestowed on Sabatini in junior year in high school when, as a member of the bowling team, he achieved a season average of 236.

O'Brien also gained favor by contributing a dollar to the Patty Piza Record Collection Fund, which was housed in a mayonnaise jar with a slit in the metal screw-on cap. Every profanity uttered during the game cost the offender a quarter. With each quarter deposited, the young girl issued a "Thank *you*!" and patted the jar. By evening's end, it was a-third full.

Around eleven they decided to wrap things up. By that time they'd put an appreciable dent in Mary's cooking, the cold cuts, and the Italian pastries served for dessert. Joey had won twelve dollars, O'Brien ten, and the rest were left to lick their wounds.

"God, all that food's made me tired," O'Brien mumbled through a yawn, as she closed her eyes and spread her arms back. She'd unbuttoned her vest during the course of the evening, and the stretch thrust her breasts front and center. Piza, Jeff, and Joey gulped; Sal made the sign of the cross. Fortunately, they regained their composure before the yawn came to an end.

Frankie hadn't reacted, but must have realized he'd missed a cue, because he immediately offered to drive her home. "Hey, if you're too tired to drive, I don't mind a ride to Brooklyn. I could pick you up tomorrow and drive you back here for your car. Maybe lunch in between? Whaddya say?"

"No, that's very sweet, Frankie, but I'm fine to drive. And I have plans for tomorrow anyway, but thank you. Patty, it was great to meet you. What are you gonna do with all those quarters?"

"Um, Ma makes them turn into money, and then we go to the record store."

O'Brien gave her a hug. "That sounds great. Guys, it was a pleasure. Sorry about takin' your cash. Well, not really. But maybe we can do it again."

Amid a chorus of "sure's" and "why-not's" Piza said, "C'mon, I'll walk you out."

When they got upstairs, he called out to his parents that O'Brien was leaving. Mary bolted from the lounge chair in the living room and rushed to the kitchen. She opened the refrigerator and removed four dishes wrapped in aluminum foil.

"Anthony, put these in a shoppin' bag for Colleen." Then, looking at the girl, "There was a lotta corned beef left, dear, so I thought maybe your family would enjoy it. Plus there's some sausage and peppers, cold cuts, and cannolis. Was the corned beef okay? It didn't look like you ate much. Didn't you like it?"

Piza jumped in like he was about to save an unsuspecting pedestrian from a careening bus. "Geez, Ma, how much tin foil did you put on these things? Whaddya have stock in the company?"

O'Brien looked unfazed. "The corned beef was delicious, Mrs. Piza. To tell you the truth, Tony raves about your cooking so much I had to try a little of everything. And, believe me, I'm glad I did, although I think I may have overdone it a bit." She patted a non-existent stomach. "And I really appreciate your packin' all this for me. Trust me, it won't go to waste."

"Oh, you're welcome. And is that true, Anthony? Do you go around blabbin' to everyone about my cookin'?"

"Hey, Ma, if you got it flaunt it. Am I right?"

Mary hit him lightly with a dishcloth. "Oh, you." She looked like she was about to levitate.

"Good night, Mr. Piza," O'Brien yelled.

"Oh, good night, young lady," Angelo shouted back from the living room. "Nice to meet you."

"Same here."

Other than helping bring down dessert, Angelo had wisely become one with his armchair for the remainder of the evening.

Piza carried the shopping bag as he walked O'Brien to her car. "Apologies for the corned beef, by the way. I hope you weren't insulted. I mean, she meant well, but sometimes. . ."

"Don't be ridiculous. I wasn't offended in the least. Besides, it was delicious. My parents will love it, although my brothers might actually enjoy the sausage and peppers even more."

"I didn't know you had brothers."

"Yeah, two. One older, one younger. A priest and a cop. Wanna talk stereotypes?" They both laughed. "No, really, your family's great. And your friends were very nice. A little obvious at times, but. . ."

He grinned. "Noticed that, did ya? I mean, you do look fantastic, for whatever it's worth."

"Thanks, Piza. Nice of you to say that."

"I hope Frankie didn't put you on the spot. You know, with the come-on and all."

"Nah. I'm a big girl. Plus, he's a little young for me. Anyway, I, um, don't think his heart was really in it."

"Whaddya mean?" Piza asked, although he had an idea where this was going.

O'Brien waved it off. "It's nothing. So, anyway, I go to the stop sign, make a left, then take a right at the second light? That takes me to the highway?"

"It does, but I'd like to know what you meant about Frankie."

"Look, I shouldn't have said anything. It's not my place, so—"

"You think he's gay."

She paused. "I do, yeah."

"How do you know?"

"I *don't.* Not for sure. Just a sense I had from talkin' to him. Apparently, you've been thinkin' along the same lines."

"Yeah, I have."

"Does it bother you?"

"No, not in the least. But I feel bad, ya know, because if he is, he's been living a lie his whole life."

O'Brien nodded. "I've gotta believe it doesn't help that he works in a kind of macho environment; the union and all. You have to wonder if he even sees truth as an option."

"So, any advice?"

"Well, if you really want my two cents, I got the impression you two are really close."

"He's my best friend."

"Okay. I'd say find a low-key way to reinforce with him that he can confide in you no matter what. Then, when he's ready, he's ready." She flashed a smile. "Of course, that means you'd have to learn the art of subtlety."

A playful smirk from Piza. "I happen to be a master of subtlety. The fact you haven't noticed proves just how ridiculously good at it I am."

"Adrift in a world of self-delusion, you are. Must be nice."

"It is at times, actually. Anyway, kidding aside, thanks for the input."

"Anytime."

"Okay, so drive carefully, and I'll see you Monday. And thanks for coming. It was fun. Even if you are a chick."

He waved as she drove off. Her take on Frankie provided a strained relief. It was reassuring having his opinion validated, but it only increased his concern for his friend's predicament.

Something else she'd mentioned nagged at him—her comment that Frankie was too young for her. *He's my age, O'Brien. Was that a polite way of telling me something?*

17

Piza spent the better part of the Sunday after the card game grading book reports, albeit with one eye on the television, watching his N.Y. Giants ruin the last weekend of October with their fifth consecutive loss.

He'd been tickled to find Esther Forbes's classic novel, *Johnny Tremain*, on the approved book list. Set in Boston at the beginning of the Revolutionary War, the story of the young silversmith's apprentice had been one of his grammar school favorites.

This was the first book report he'd assigned. Reading his students' efforts—set out within blue-covered booklets—reinforced his opinion that while, on the whole, they could memorize and retain facts, many fell short when it came to critical thinking skills. He believed reading comprehension and writing ability were crucial, and although he'd previously cut them some slack, he determined he was going to have to push the issue.

One pleasant surprise had been Kevin Davis's report. Although his grammar left something to be desired, he'd shown insight into how the surrounding circumstances had affected the young Bostonian. The effort earned him a B-plus, and Piza found himself looking forward to returning the paper to the boy.

Piza handed out the reports right before the lunch break on Monday. "Okay, people," he announced, "I know you're all salivating for that delectable cafeteria dining experience, but I have your book reports here."

He began distributing them up and down the aisles. "Most of them were okay. Some were actually pretty good. And there were a couple that led me to believe your little eyes managed to avoid everything about the book, except maybe the title. You'll know who you are by the gigantic red F adorning the inside cover."

He hadn't reached Davis at that point, but he'd been discreetly watching him. He could see the boy's head drop at the mention of failing grades. When he got to him, he nonchalantly dropped the booklet on his desk. Moving on, from the corner of his eye he could see the boy's hesitancy to look inside. *C'mon, kid. Open it.*

As he reached the front of the room he heard a resounding "Holy crap!" The entire class turned toward Davis. Piza hid his glee and tossed a scowl. "I'm sorry, Mr. Davis, what was that you said?"

"I'm, I'm really sorry, Mr. Piza," he answered, his expression a portrait of blissful shock. "I, I really didn't mean to say that, but — Is this right?" He held up the booklet.

With a look of feigned concern, Piza said, "Um, let me take a look." He walked to the boy's desk and took the booklet from him. "Appears to be. Why? You disappointed?"

"Disappointed? Are you kiddin' me?" He must have realized his gusto might be tarnishing his tough-guy image. "Uh, no. I'm not disappointed. Actually, it's, ya know, kind of what I expected. Just double-checkin'."

"No, that's fine," Piza responded. "Never hurts to double-check. Okay, folks, we're going to discuss these reports after lunch, so leave them on your desk and—" He was interrupted by the lunch bell, which was instantly followed by an eighth-grade safety appearing at the front classroom door to accompany the kids to the cafeteria. "Okay, enjoy your lunch. See you back here in an hour."

As they filed out, Robert Giacobbi glowered at his teacher.

Well, well. Seems someone's *not happy.*

"I've *never* gotten a B-minus before. This better be a mistake, and he better fix it."

"Oh, boo-hoo, Giacobbi," Ralph Restivo mocked from the other end of the twelve-foot-long cafeteria table.

"Yeah," Majinsky chimed in. "How's it feel to be like the rest of us poor . . . ya know, um. . ."

"Peasants," Laura Perotta said, not looking up from her book.

"Yeah, peasants. That's it."

No response from Giacobbi.

Sukie looked at Davis. "What'd you get, Kevin? You seemed happy."

Davis, who was seated across from Restivo, replied, "Uh, it was okay. No big deal."

Sukie wasn't letting go. "C'mon, Kevin. Tell us."

The boy blushed. "Um, B-plus?"

Giacobbi almost jumped out of his seat. "What? He gave you a B-plus?"

"Yeah, what of it?" Davis shot back.

A derisive laugh from Giacobbi segued into, "What a joke. How many times did you have to kiss his ass to get *that*?"

Davis was up and on him in seconds. Before Giacobbi could react, Davis yanked him off the bench seat and had him on the floor. "I never kissed anyone's ass in my life, you douchebag!"

Giacobbi was bigger, but overmatched. Davis straddled him, both hands clutching the previously unwrinkled starched shirt. Giacobbi struggled to free the grip as two lunch mothers pulled Davis off.

"Kevin Davis. Why am I not surprised?" declared one of the volunteers, Constance Baldino.

She helped Giacobbi up. "Are you all right, Robert?"

"I'm fine, Mrs. Baldino," he answered, straightening his tie.

"Thank God."

The other aide, Pam Rafferty, grabbed Davis's arm. "I'll take this one to the office, Connie."

"Okay, Pam. Now the rest of you kids—"

"What about *him*?" Davis shouted, pulling away from her and pointing at Giacobbi. "He said I kissed Mr. Piza's—"

"Watch it, young man," Rafferty commanded, gripping his arm again. "Let's go."

Sukie raised her hand. "Mrs. Rafferty, I really don't think this was Kevin's fault. Robert really did say what, um, Kevin said he said."

"This isn't your concern, Suzanne," the woman responded, pointing at the girl.

"But—"

"I said, enough! Now, all of you finish your lunch and head out to the playground." She led the boy away.

All eyes were on Giacobbi as he sat down. "What are you looking at *me* for? *He* attacked *me*. You saw it."

"Such an asshole," Vinny Pinto said.

The others at the table nodded.

After the children returned from lunch and began taking their seats, Piza said, "Okay, let's settle in and review these masterful book reports. I don't know if poor Johnny Tremain is ever going to recover from some— Hey, what's with the faces? And where's Mr. Davis?"

"He's in the office, sir," Shirley Robinson said.

"Why? What happened? Did he get hurt?"

"No. He's okay," the child continued. "He got into a fight with Robert in the cafeteria."

"What?"

Giacobbi's face reddened. "It wasn't my fault. He attacked me for no reason."

Karen Jablonski jumped up, planting her hands on her hips. "Whoa, that's not true and you know it. You were p.o.'d because he got a better grade than you, and you hassled him. Big time."

"Okay, okay. Thank you, Ms. Jablonski. You can sit down. All of you review your reports, and pay attention to the remarks I wrote in the margins. I'll be right back." With that, he strode out of the room.

When he got to the office, Davis was sitting in the waiting area. His face blanched when he saw his teacher. "I swear, Mr. Piza, this wasn't my fault. Giacobbi was pissed— I mean angry because I got a higher mark than him. And, and he said the only reason I got it was because I kissed your . . . ya know. And that's BS right, 'cause I got that grade fair and square. And— I did, didn't I?"

"You absolutely did. But, geez, what were you thinking? I mean, did you hit him? Why didn't you call one of the lunch ladies?"

"I didn't hit him. I just kinda pulled him off his seat and got him on the ground. And then Mrs. Baldino and Mrs. Rafferty pulled me off him, and—"

"Mr. Piza, what are you doing here? Who's watching your class?" Assistant-principal Florino glared at him from the doorway of her office.

"Um, they're studying on their own for a couple of minutes. I was concerned about—"

"Mr. Piza you're not permitted to leave your students unsupervised. Now please get back to your class. Mother John will deal with him as soon as she's back from her meeting."

"Is anyone gonna listen to his side of the story, or is he just presumed guilty?"

"I beg your pardon? How da—" She cleared her throat. "He'll be given every opportunity to explain his behavior, I can assure you. Mother will speak with him, as she will with Mrs. Rafferty, if necessary. Now *please* return to your classroom."

Piza was reluctant to surrender. But considering his class was unattended, he didn't have much choice. "Fine. But if there's a problem—"

"We know where to find you."

He turned to Davis. "You okay?"

"Yeah, I can handle this. No sweat." The white knuckles gripping the plastic arms of his chair said otherwise.

"Okay," Piza said, then left. "This kid can't buy a break," he muttered as he made his way back to the classroom.

Davis returned forty-five minutes later. He handed Piza a note and went to his seat. His sullen expression didn't invite conversation.

Piza glanced at the paper. Mother John had suspended the boy for two days.

He looked at Davis, who was staring blankly at his book report. *Yeah. Let's make sure the kid doesn't get more than five minutes to enjoy an accomplishment in his life, right, Mother? And why does* he *get suspended, but Giacobbi skates? Saying he kissed my ass is acceptable behavior? What am I missing here?*

18

"Welcome back, Mr. Davis. Nice to usher in November with you back in the nest. Miss us?"

"No," the boy answered with a goofy grin.

"You have no idea how sad that makes me. Anyone else sad that Mr. Davis didn't miss us?"

Most of the children thrust a hand in the air and laughed.

"See, Mr. Davis. See how many unhappy people there are in this classroom, all because of you?"

The boy rolled his eyes.

"Okay, people. As you know, we have parent-teacher meetings this evening. Just so I get some idea how long I'll be stuck here, how many of you have parents coming?" More than half raised their hands. "Really?"

"This is nuts. I have nineteen kids with one or both parents coming in. I thought this thing was supposed to be a few short conferences. I should've brought a pup tent and rations."

"Boy are you popular," O'Brien joked. "I only have nine comin'."

"You might wanna save some of that sandwich," Bauer said. "Midnight snack."

"And how many do you have, Mr. Helpful?"

"Ten."

"Seriously? I don't get it." Sister Theresa was sitting two tables away. He caught her attention and motioned for her to join them.

She obliged with a cheery, "And what can I do for you this fine day?"

Piza shook his head. "Aren't you ever depressed? I was wondering how many parents you're expecting tonight."

"Um, seven for certain. Eight, if one can get out of work early. Why?"

"Because I have nineteen."

"Wow. I'd have to check with Mrs. Florino, but that may be a school record. Congratulations."

"Very funny, Sister T. I'm serious here. Is this a good thing or a bad thing?"

She glanced at O'Brien. "Well," O'Brien answered, "in our experience parents don't normally come in to tell you how happy they are. They have concerns, for whatever reason. Although some just wanna know how their child is doin'. That's why nine or ten isn't unusual. A couple more sometimes."

"But not nineteen. Setting the 'school record' means I've got a problem on my hands, doesn't it?"

The nun winced. "I'm sorry I kidded you. I didn't realize how anxious you are about this."

"I'm not anxious," he said, body language to the contrary. "I'm only trying to figure out what to expect."

Bauer tilted his head. "Want my opinion?"

"Sure," came the deflated response.

"I think maybe some of these parents can't figure you out.

You're— I don't know, probably not what they're used to I guess is what I'm trying to say. And—"

"Wait, so I'm being penalized for not fitting into their perception of what a—"

"Jim's makin' a point," O'Brien interjected. "Let him finish for God's sake."

"You're right. Sorry, Jim."

"No problem. What I mean is that— Look, I haven't seen you teach. But from what you've told us, there's a degree of showmanship in your approach. And you interact with these kids in a way that didn't exist when you started out."

"Which I think is great," Sister Theresa added. Piza nodded a thank you.

"Plus," Bauer continued, "you've said you're making them do more writing. Reports, more essay questions than multiple choice on their tests. And there's probably a lot of parents who aren't used to seeing that. Do you have your kids writing more, Sister?"

"To a degree, but not nearly as much as Mr. Piza appears to be doing." She looked at Piza. "I'd be interested in seeing how your children adapt."

"I'll gladly trade notes with you at some point, Sister. But what do I do with these parents tonight?"

"Do you believe in the way you're doin' your job?" O'Brien asked.

"I do. Yeah."

"Then if that's what some of the parents wanna talk to you about, explain it."

"Exactly," Sister Theresa added. "Let them see what you see."

"Okay. I can do that."

"But bag the sarcasm," O'Brien warned. "You have a tendency to—"

"Moi? No, I get it. Less cynicism, more charm."

She smirked. "Well, *charm* may be settin' the bar a little high, but. . ."

Sister Theresa scrunched her face in mock disapproval.

O'Brien sighed. "Fine. I'll be good. Yes, Tony, by all means, be charming. Better?"

The nun smiled. "Much."

Piza clicked his tongue. "Thanks, all of you. I really appreciate the input. Hey, since the conferences don't start until five thirty, anyone wanna grab something to eat after school? Sister T, I know Jesus has dibs on you for dinner—"

She blushed.

"—but what about you guys?"

"Sounds like fun," Bauer replied, "but I'm only ten minutes from here. I think I'll get in a little family time and then come back."

Piza looked at O'Brien.

After a brief hesitation, she said, "Well, I was gonna grade some tests, but why not? I can spend the time calmin' you down and fillin' your head with positive thoughts."

"I don't need calming down. I'm perfectly capable of handling some inquisitive—albeit possibly irate—parents. In fact, I relish the challenge."

"Good for you," from Sister Theresa.

"Go get 'em," Bauer chimed in.

O'Brien puffed out a breath. "God, you people are killin' me. I'll meet you out front at quarter to four. I'll be the one carryin' the brown paper bag, in case you start hyperventilatin'."

Rocco's Pizzeria and Ristorante was a fixture in the neighborhood, and Piza had been meaning to try it for a while.

"I should go out and eat at four o'clock more often," O'Brien observed. "No lines, choice of table. . ."

An enthusiastic nod from Piza. "Good deal, huh? Hey, you might wanna try the Sicilian pizza. Best on Staten Island."

"You've been here before?"

"No."

"Then how do you know the Sicilian's the best on the island?"

"I just made it up."

With a knitted brow, she said, "There's something seriously wrong with you, Piza."

"I was working on my charm. For this evening. Like *you* said I should."

"Uh-huh. Work harder." She paused. "What are you so uptight about?"

A waiter brought water and menus.

When the man left, Piza issued a mischievous smile, and said, "In answer to your question, this *is* our first date. So I think a touch of apprehension's perfectly normal. Tell me you're not just the slightest bit nervous."

"Wow. You sure you didn't major in magic, 'cause you just made my appetite disappear."

He burst out laughing. "Okay, Round One to you."

"Seriously, though. You okay with these conferences?"

"Yeah, I'm fine, assuming some parent doesn't piss me off and my charm flies out the window." He took a sip of water. "So, let me ask you something. Back at lunch, when I was asking if having nineteen parents was bad, you kind of exchanged a look with Sister Theresa, and then you said 'in *our* opinion'. I didn't think she was teaching long enough to *have* an opinion. I mean, she's around my age, right?"

"Um, I don't think she'd mind my tellin' her age. She's twenty-nine."

"Get outta here. No way."

"Hand to God. She became a nun after college. The usual few years in the novitiate—you know, the place for nuns-in-training—then she took her vows. She's been teachin' five years."

"She looks like a kid."

"I know. Just like you."

"Har, har. Seriously, though? Five years?"

"Yep. And she's one of the best teachers I've ever seen. One of the most caring too."

"Well, I haven't seen her teach," he said. "But the caring part, yeah, that's kind of hard to miss. What else do you know about her?"

"Not a whole lot. She's kind of closed-mouth about her past. Why the interest?"

"No reason in particular," he answered, a bit defensively. "I guess— I dunno, she just seems too cool to be a nun."

"They're not mutually exclusive, bein' cool and bein' a nun."

"Oh, really? Other than Sister T, how many cool nuns do you know? Although Sister Joann seems pretty with it. I like her music classes."

"There you go. There's a couple more at school too. And there were plenty at BC."

He threw her a skeptical look. "If you say so."

The waiter came over to take their order.

"A slice of Sicilian for me," O'Brien said. She looked at Piza. "It *is* the best I've ever had, by the way."

"Do I have a gift, or what?"

A sigh and shake of her head was his answer.

They got back to OLPT at five fifteen. When Piza reached the second-floor hallway, there was already a line extending past his rear classroom door.

Jesus, people, what part of five thirty did you not understand? "Wow, if I'd known I was this popular, I'd have skipped dinner," he joked as he walked past them without making eye contact. He fished the key from his jacket pocket and, fumbling a bit, unlocked the front door.

Inside, someone had placed two faded-red, scratched plastic chairs next to his desk during his absence. He surmised the purpose was to avoid having the parents sit in the children's desks in front of him. The setup annoyed him; he'd anticipated a playing field that wasn't quite so level.

O'Brien had been right. There were concerns about too much homework, not enough homework, and why all the writing assignments. A couple of skeptics said he seemed too young to be a teacher. And some did just want to know how their kids were faring.

But there were scattered compliments too. Some of the parents said their children actually seemed to be enjoying school. Florence Schaefer had come in basically to say hello. In the school parking lot, after the museum trip, she'd told him he seemed to be a "natural" teacher. If she only knew, he'd thought.

"So, Mr. Piza, I just wanted to say hi and see how you were doing."

"I'm well, Mrs. Schaefer, but you didn't have to—"

"No, I know. And I see it's standing-room-only out there, but I wanted to share a quick story if that's okay?"

"Sure."

"Monday before last, Becky got sick that night."

"Right, right. I remember she was out for a day."

"Yeah, she had a hundred-and-one fever. Next morning I went in to check on her and . . . she's getting dressed for school. We had this big argument and I literally had to threaten to ground her if she didn't get back into bed." She shook her head. "I mean, how often does a child fight with you about *wanting* to go to school? Anyway, I thought you should know that, and I wanted to tell you I appreciate what you're doing. And now I'll get out of your hair."

Piza got up and shook her hand. "Thank you for that. It means a lot." He was sincere.

Two conferences stood out from the rest that evening. The first was with Shirley Robinson's parents, Charles and Darlene. The discussion was initially more or less in line with the others he'd had, and he only had good things to say about their daughter. But then the conversation took a turn he hadn't seen coming.

"Mr. Piza, this is Shirley's first year here," her father said. "We only moved here this past summer."

"Oh, that's great. How's it been going?"

"Good," Mrs. Robinson answered. "Traffic's kind of a nightmare. Well, for Charles at least. He commutes to work in Manhattan. Luckily for me, I can actually walk to work. I manage a small dress shop."

"Terrific."

Mr. Robinson ultimately broke an awkward pause. "Um, we chose Our Lady of Perpetual Tears because, by all accounts, it had an excellent academic reputation."

"Which was very important to us," his wife added.

Piza didn't know where this was going, but he felt himself getting defensive. "And are you saying you're not satisfied with—"

Mrs. Robinson interrupted him with a reassuring wave of her hands. "Oh, no, no, not at all. Shirley's really enjoying school. And I especially like that you have her doing more writing. She says she wants to be a writer someday, so she's in heaven with these assignments."

Mr. Robinson sighed. "Mr. Piza, there's no delicate way to get to this, so let me just say it. We know Shirley is the only black student in your class. And we just want to be sure she's being accepted. I mean, she hasn't said anything, but, in all honesty, I'm not sure she would."

Piza was obviously aware of the girl's race, but it had never occurred to him that it should, or would, be an issue. But he could see where her parents' perspective might be dramatically different from his.

"Honestly, I've never seen any indication that there's a problem," he reassured them. "She seems to have assimilated very well. To tell you the truth, with her personality and sense of humor, you'd be hard-pressed *not* to like her."

Mrs. Robinson audibly exhaled. "That's a relief. And, believe me, we're not looking to find a problem where there isn't one, but. . ."

"No, no, I get it," Piza responded. "And let me assure you that if I see or hear anything, it'll be addressed immediately."

"And you'll let us know?" Mrs. Robinson inquired.

"Absolutely."

The second memorable encounter was with Robert Giacobbi's parents. The boy's father had to be six-four easily, and had entered the room with an air of royalty. His arrival at Piza's desk was preceded by whatever cologne he'd doused himself with. He wore a crew cut and looked like he might have been athletic once. But a noticeable paunch and mildly bloated face signaled those days were likely permanently in his past.

His mother, on the other hand, was a knockout, with just the hint of an overbite that transformed pretty into sexy. She was trim, and tastefully dressed in slacks and a turtleneck. With her auburn hair pulled back in a ponytail, she looked younger than she probably was.

She'd come in behind her husband, taking the seat farther from the teacher. Not that she'd had a choice, her husband having commandeered the closer seat. Piza sensed she'd have taken the farther seat anyway.

He shook her hand first, both out of a sense of propriety and an immediate dislike of her spouse. Her smile was warm, but there was a sadness about her. When he segued to Mr. Giacobbi, his extended hand was ensnared in a vise. The man's face exhibited a barely perceptible sneer and a glint of challenge. Piza locked eyes with him, struggling not to reveal evidence of the growing pain in his hand.

"Let's get right to the point," the man commanded, releasing his grip and sitting. "I'm not happy."

"Is anyone truly happy, Mr. Giacobbi?" Piza said, not missing a beat. Giacobbi's eyes narrowed, and the teacher donned a saccharine smile. "A bit of humor to break the ice. What seems to be the problem?"

"It's about my son."

No shit, Sherlock. "Is something wrong with Robert? Is there anything I can do to help?"

"Yeah. You can start giving him better grades, how's that?"

"I can certainly do that . . . as soon as he starts earning them." Piza cut him off as he was starting to reply. "And just to set the record straight, for the most part his grades are excellent. He's a smart kid, but he has to understand that memorizing facts isn't all there is to learning. He needs to be able to analyze; to dig into the meaning of things and translate his thoughts into words. He can do it. He hasn't yet, for whatever reason."

Mrs. Giacobbi inched her chair closer. "I think our son's problem is that—"

"I'll handle this, Sandra," her husband spat out. She immediately backed off.

I'm gonna punch this bastard.

The bully folded his arms. "Do you know who I am, Piza?"

Of course I do. You're Zeus, down from Olympus for the upcoming holidays. The teacher smirked. "Is that a rhetorical—"

"I'm the president of the school board. I run this place."

"I'm not sure I'm getting your point, Mr. Giacobbi."

"If you like working here—"

"Bob, please. I don't think that's—"

A withering glare silenced her. "Another call to Mother John, and you're history."

"*Another* call? Is there something I'm— Ah, Henry the Eighth." *It was you, you son of a bitch. You and your kid.*

A smug look segued to, "Think about what I said."

Piza had to end this. He'd already been on the brink of verbally filleting this guy, and now this. "I'll certainly think about it. And please, *you* think about what I said as well. After all, we all have Robert's best interest at heart, right?" He forced a smile. "Now, if you don't mind, there are other parents waiting."

He stood without offering his hand. The president's mouth began to form a word, but faltered as a quizzical expression crossed his face, as if he was wondering if he'd been dismissed.

"Mrs. Giacobbi, it was nice to meet you."

"Same here, thank you." Her eyes apologized.

The rest of the evening wasn't nearly as interesting. As he drove home, he replayed the Giacobbi conference.

He talked aloud to himself. "Arrogant dipshit. And her. Warm, attractive. *Really* attractive. And totally submissive. Like his personal geisha. What the hell was that? '*I'm* the president of the school board.' Big friggin' whoop, dickwad. Explains why your kid gets the red-carpet treatment." A sudden concern jolted him. "Shit, can this jerk actually get me fired?"

19

The couple of weeks following the conferences passed in relative calm. To Piza's relief, there'd been no blowback from his muted confrontation with Giacobbi's father.

He'd done some asking around and learned the man owned a successful construction equipment business. Despite a reputation for being obnoxious, he'd been elected president of the school board the year before. This was more by default than anything else, since none of the other members wanted a job that often entailed butting heads with Monsignor Lombardo. Giacobbi apparently relished the battles. The result—two alpha males in a classic power struggle.

Piza's relationship with the kids continued to improve, their attitude becoming progressively upbeat. He was pretty confident this was his doing, although he had to concede their current level of good cheer might be partially due to the upcoming Thanksgiving holiday.

Something of note *had* occurred the Monday after the conferences. Kevin Davis's mother had sent a note in with her son, requesting a meeting that Wednesday, after school.

"Um, I guess I can do that, Mr. Davis," he'd told the boy. "Tell your mom three thirty works for me."

At exactly that time, Noreen Davis poked her head into the classroom.

"Mr. Piza?"

"Oh, hey, Mrs. Davis. Right on time. I could take punctuality lessons from you. Come on in."

"Thanks so much for seeing me. I promise I won't keep you long."

"Not at all."

He grabbed one of the plastic chairs from conference night, and placed it next to his desk.

She smiled. "Thank you. I had to work late the night of the conferences last week, but I needed to talk to you. I'm sorry if I'm—"

"It's fine, Mrs. Davis. Really."

"Oh, okay. Great. I, um, know what Kevin did was wrong. You know, when he got suspended for fighting. But I wanted to thank you for checking on him in the office."

"No problem."

She shifted in her seat, as if trying to get comfortable. "Mr. Piza, Kevin's had a rough go these past few years, what with—"

"His father?"

"Yes. He told me he told you about John—that's my husband—leaving us. And about his drinking."

"Uh-huh. When we were at the museum."

"I was surprised. He doesn't open up much. Did he say anything else?"

"Just that you and he were doing fine without his father in the picture. Although, to be honest, it wasn't too convincing."

"Well, that's the problem. He's not doing fine, Mr. Piza. Kevin was nine when John left. And when you're nine, your dad's your hero, ya know . . . despite his faults. Kevin fell apart."

"I don't doubt it. It's traumatic."

"He'd always been a good kid. A little sad, maybe, not that anybody but me'd probably notice. But when his father left, he changed. He became like— Like this tough guy. I mean not with me"—she put up her hands—"but with other kids. Always angry."

The teacher scoured his brain to find something positive to give the woman. "Um, well, it seems like he has some friends in class."

"Yeah, but not many, I don't think. There's only a few kids he mentions." She seemed momentarily lost in thought, then, "He was a pretty decent student too. Mostly B's. Couple of A's here and there. But when John left, his grades took a nosedive. I don't know if you know, but he had to repeat fourth grade. I moved him to OLPT so he could do it here. I was hoping a Catholic school might help him. Little more discipline, maybe."

"So technically he should be in seventh grade. Is he eleven or twelve?"

"Twelve."

"Okay. Is that why you wanted to see me? To give me some background?"

"Uh, partly, yeah." Her body noticeably tensed. "But also, um, that book report he wrote, the one he got a B-plus on?"

"Uh-huh."

"And look, I know I'm not a teacher—"

Yeah, me neither. Well, maybe.

"—but it looked like there were a lot of correction marks on the paper, and I was wondering. . ."

"You were wondering if the grade was too high."

"Well, yeah, kind of. I mean so many red marks and all. I guess I'm just trying to understand." She lowered her eyes.

"Mrs. Davis, the red marks were to correct grammar. What I was really interested in was seeing how the kids interpreted what they'd read; how they connected with the story, and whether they were able to express that in writing. You can memorize grammar.

Story analysis is a different ballgame. Kevin got it. It wasn't perfect, but he got it."

You could see the tension dissipate. "Okay, I understand now. That's really good news."

Without accusation in his tone, Piza asked, "Why would you think I'd give him a higher grade than he deserved?"

"To be honest, I thought maybe after he told you about his father that you— I thought maybe you felt sorry for him." She laughed. "And I gotta tell ya, I was a nervous wreck about asking you about this. But, Mr. Piza, as upset as Kevin was about being suspended, if you could've seen him dancing around the house with that report in his hand later that night, I— I guess I just needed to know it was real."

"Believe me, it was real, Mrs. Davis. And even though I was distressed by what Kevin told me about his father, I wouldn't be doing my job if I let that influence a grade."

"No, no, I understand. And I hope I didn't insult you or anything. But I needed to be sure he did this on his own. That maybe there's finally some hope that. . ." Her eyes welled, but she quickly wiped them and sat up straight. "I really appreciate you seeing me after school like this."

"Not at all. And he'll be fine. I really believe that."

She nodded, a glimmer of optimism in her eyes. After a brief pause, she stood and extended her hand. "Thanks, again."

Piza returned the gesture, adding a smile he hoped was comforting. "Anytime."

As she reached the door, she turned. "God bless you, Mr. Piza. Ya know, for your dedication and all."

Great. More guilt.

On the Monday morning after Thanksgiving, Piza's students seemed sluggish. He understood completely, having had to muster a considerable dose of willpower to pry *himself* out of bed.

Rather than dive into the normal schedule, he asked if anyone had any Thanksgiving stories they wanted to share. Several of the kids volunteered, and they spent the next hour listening to holiday accounts that ran the gamut from touching to comical.

He called on Karen Jablonski first, for a number of reasons. His initial thought was that she seemed the least likely kid in the class to share a personal experience, considering her overall seriousness and intensity, which sometimes bordered on confrontational. Also, the way she'd launched her arm into the air signaled she needed to say something.

They learned her maternal grandmother had suffered a debilitating stroke a month earlier, and was hospitalized, with no indication as to when—or whether—she'd be released. It was the first Thanksgiving dinner she'd ever missed with the family, so the girl and her mother had brought food to the hospital that evening. Piza found himself choking up as the child described sitting on the bed, feeding small spoonfuls of mashed potatoes to this woman she clearly idolized.

"I bet you didn't know she was a suffragette, Mr. Piza, did you?"

"I didn't, Ms. Jablonski. You must be very proud of her."

"What's a suffer— What is it again?" Majinsky asked.

The girl spoke before Piza could respond. "Suffragette. They're women who fought for a woman's right to be able to vote. And I *am* proud of her, Mr. Piza."

"As well you should be. She and others like her are real American heroes." *Now I know why you're such a little toughie.* "Maybe one of these days we'll take a break from the history book, and discuss women's rights. You could even bring in some pictures of your grandmother, if you'd like. Maybe tell us about her experiences."

"I *would* like that," the girl answered, a now slightly quavering voice her only concession to the emotions undoubtedly assaulting her.

On the other end of the anecdote spectrum was Ralph Restivo's recounting of the Battle of the Drumstick. After setting the scene of fifteen family members gathered around a dining room table, the boy launched into his narrative.

"So every year it's the same thing. The only people in my family who like turkey legs are my grandpa and my two older brothers, Jimmy and Carlo. Grandpa always gets one because he's Grandpa. But every year, Jimmy and Carlo argue about who's gonna get the other one. And every year they settle it by doin' rock, paper, scissors. Except, for the past three years in a row, Carlo won. So they do it and—"

"Let me guess," Piza interrupted. "Carlo won again."

"You got it, Mr. Piza. So, anyway, Jimmy says they should make it the best two outta three. But Carlo says, 'No way'. And then Jimmy says Carlo's cheatin'. And Carlo says, 'How can I be cheatin'? It's freakin' rock, paper, scissors!'"

He looked at his teacher, his expression asking whether he'd crossed a line. But Piza, who was ready to bust a gut, motioned for him to continue.

"So Jimmy says, 'I don't know how, I just know you're cheatin'.' And Carlo says, 'Yeah, right. Whaddya think I got, that ESP or somethin'?' Then he starts makin' ghost sounds and wigglin' his fingers in front of Jimmy's face, and so Jimmy knocks his hands away, and then they're all over each other. On the floor, rollin' into the living room, like two lunatics. If my cousin Sonny and my other cousin Sonny didn't break 'em up, they would've wrecked all of Ma's furniture. I swear, Mr. Piza."

Piza barely heard the last few words because the "other cousin Sonny" had launched him into uncontrollable laughter. The kids, who'd also been laughing, watched their teacher lose it, which caused them to laugh even harder. The rest of the morning progressed like there had never been a layoff.

In the teachers' lounge at lunch, Piza told O'Brien and Bauer about the morning's events. They were visibly touched by Karen Jablonski's story, and laughed out loud at his recounting of the drumstick debacle.

After some small-talk, his demeanor turned serious and he said, "You know, it occurred to me, after the kids left for lunch, that I hardly know anything about them, except for some things I found out at the parent conferences. But listening to their stories, they've got all this stuff going on in their lives, and they bring it to school every day, and I don't have a clue."

"What, and you think we *do*?" O'Brien asked.

"Well, kind of. I mean, you're both trained for this. Doesn't that give you some sort of insight?"

"Speaking for myself," Bauer offered, "I was taught to look for certain things. Little signs that maybe something's wrong. But, other than literally interrogating them, all you've got to work with is whatever may be in their school file, and what you see and hear every day."

"I agree," O'Brien said. "I know my psych background helps, but like Jim said, you can only work with the information you've got."

Piza shook his head. "It just doesn't seem like that's enough. I mean, look at everything Karen Jablonski's been going through with her grandmother. I could easily have mistaken something she did in class as her being surly, but instead, she could've been reacting to this tragedy in her life."

"I get that," Bauer said. "But you have to accept that there are limitations to what we can do. It's like anything else."

"You need to find a middle ground, Piza," O'Brien added. "I

mean, you started the year pretty much not carin' one ounce about these kids, and now you wanna *save* them all."

He was about to answer, but she cut him off. "I'm not tryin' to put you down. Really, I'm not. Even you know your attitude sucked. And what you're tryin' to do now is really admirable, but it's an unattainable goal. Listen, I don't hold a place in your life that entitles me to be disappointed in you or proud of you. Despite that, I'm proud of you anyway. You've done a complete one-eighty."

"Thanks. I'm trying."

"I know. But I don't wanna see you beat yourself up over this. The job's hard enough as it is. So keep doin' what you've been doin' and use what you learn to keep improvin'."

"Thanks, both of you. It's smart advice. But I'm not trying to *save* them all, Colleen. I'm just trying to get a better handle on what I'm dealing with. That's all. And as far as your status in my life, well"—wiggling his eyebrows—"we could work on changing that."

"You're beyond hope, Piza. And just because I paid you a compliment, don't think for a second this changes my opinion that you're a major pain in the ass."

He grinned. "Never crossed my mind."

"Hey, did you ever find out who got the other drumstick?" Bauer asked. "In the kid's story?"

"I was laughing so hard I forgot to ask, Jimbo. I'll find out this afternoon for you."

They were in mid-laugh when Sister Theresa came over to their table. "Looked like a very serious discussion there for a while. But it seems everything's okay now?"

"All good, Sister T," Piza replied. "Colleen thinks I'm the cat's pajamas as a teacher."

A roll of the eyes from O'Brien.

"Well, I'm glad everything's all right," the nun said. "'Cat's pajamas', eh? Is it me, or is someone stuck in the 1920s?"

Piza smiled. "Some expressions are timeless, Sister."

"That's true," she responded. "Unfortunately, I don't think 'cat's pajamas' is one of them."

Piza plucked an imaginary knife from his chest. "Cut to the quick by a nun."

She gave him a playfully condescending nod. "Somehow, I think you'll recover. Actually, the reason I came over was to see if you might want to have our classes do something together for the Christmas show. Strength in numbers and all that."

"Um, what Christmas show?"

20

The annual Christmas show was the highlight of the holiday season at OLPT. Typically a blend of religious and secular songs—traditionally, one song per class—it usually managed to strike a balance to satisfy the two faces of Christmas.

Piza had agreed to Sister Theresa's proposal, since his class was going to be involved one way or the other. To a degree, he resented the additional work. But that dissipated as the project awakened warm memories of high school musicals he'd participated in.

As much as he'd enjoyed performing, the more he got involved with the Christmas show the more he realized he was on the verge of attaining a new, more glorious status—producer.

"Am I wrong to wanna do something different?" he'd asked O'Brien and Bauer in the teachers' lounge, a few days after Sister Theresa's proposal.

"Let me be sure I understand this," Bauer said. "You don't want your kids to do just one song, you want them to do three. And you want it to be choreographed. Fifty-some-odd kids."

"Well, it's not three full songs. It's a medley. Look, from what

I can gather, every class does the same thing. The kids stand on the stage, they sing a song, they get off, the next class stands on the stage, they sing a song, blah, blah, blah. It's boring."

O'Brien looked incredulous. "I knew your mental status was iffy, Piza, but it's clear now you've completely lost your mind. What's Sister Theresa's take on all this?"

"She said, ya know, pretty much what you said. But I really think you guys are wrong. Why are you both looking at me like that? I'm not crazy."

It was Sister Joann, the music teacher, who ultimately brokered a peace. Mid-thirties, quick-witted and, like Sister Theresa, opting for the more modern modified habit and headpiece, Piza found her easy to get along with.

She'd met with the warring factions. "Okay, here's the deal. Sister Theresa, I'll prepare a simple arrangement for the three songs, which the children should be able to handle with no problem. In return for getting the medley, Mr. Piza, you have to deep-six the choreography."

Detente. Of course, they'd also disagreed on the song selection, since Piza preferred to exclude any religious numbers. But, once again, "compromise" was the word of the day. They'd do "O Holy Night", segue into "Carol of the Bells"—serious, but not overtly religious—and finish with "A Holly Jolly Christmas".

Coordinating this sixth-grade spectacular proved to be something more than Broadway Tony had anticipated. Each class had Music twice per week—but at different times. So they couldn't practice as a group.

"How are we going to get around this problem?" Sister Theresa asked him. "They absolutely have to practice together for *your* medley to work."

"*My* medley?"

She looked at him, eyebrows raised, lips scrunched.

"Fine. I'll own it. But stop worrying. Where there's a will, there's a way. The show must go on." No reaction from the nun. "Can I take it from your silence that I've calmed your fears?"

"No, you cannot. I was just trying to think of a suitable cliché to respond with."

"Little snippy today, I see."

"I won't let these children be embarrassed, Anthony. We've got to figure this out."

Wow, she called me Anthony. Glad to see she's finally loosening up.

The logistical dilemma was remedied by an agreement—which the kids enthusiastically approved—that they'd take two lunch periods per week to rehearse as a group. Sister Joann, who was also the resident pianist, graciously agreed to help.

A few revelations emerged from the practice sessions. Rebecca Schaeffer and Shirley Robinson from Piza's class, and Sean Malarkey—the recipient of Piza's five dollar bailout on museum day—had beautiful voices. The girls' singing was sweet and powerful, and if Malarkey had reached puberty it hadn't made its way to his larynx yet, because he sang with a crystal soprano tone.

On the downside, they discovered at least one thing Vinny Pinto wasn't good at. Compounding the fact he was obviously tone deaf, he attacked a song like a running back who would not be denied the end zone.

Piza ultimately resolved the problem, with a deft touch. Taking the boy aside, he said, "Listen, Mr. Pinto. Here's the thing. You have a powerful singing voice, which is great if you're doing a solo. Problem is, your voice is *so* strong it's drowning out some of the kids around you. Get my drift?"

"I get it, Mr. Piza. Tone down the volume a little, so you can hear *everybody*."

"Exactly. Actually, you might wanna tone it down even more than just a little. I don't think you realize how, um, *full-bodied* your voice is."

"Wow. Thanks. I never realized I was that good. Something to think about."

God help us.

The show was scheduled for the evening of Friday, December 21, the final day of school before the Christmas recess. By that week, Piza was reasonably certain everything was in place. He'd hovered over the production with the concern of an expectant father. Despite that preoccupation, he'd managed to conjure up a surprise ending for the show. All he had to do was convince Bauer to join him in a number he had no doubt would bring down the house.

"So here's what I'm thinking, Jimbo. Just when everyone thinks the show is over, we have Sister Theresa announce that there's a special surprise last act. And then you and I come out dressed as Santa's elves, and we do 'Rockin' Around the Christmas Tree'. Whaddya think?"

"Tell me you're joking."

"I never joke when it comes to show biz. It'll be hilarious."

"Oh, I'm sure it would be. But you have to understand something. I have stage fright."

Piza scrunched his face. "How can you have stage fright? You're a teacher."

"Um, there's a difference between standing in front of twenty-three seven-year-olds, and *five hundred adults*."

"But I'll be there with you."

"Forgive me if I take no comfort in that, whatsoever."

"Don't you think your kids would love it?"

"Probably, but that's not the point."

A sigh from Piza, a pause, then, "Actually, that's exactly the point. Twenty-five years or so from now, when one of *their* kids toddles over and says, 'Daddy—or Mommy—who was your favorite teacher?', don't you want the first words out of their mouth to be 'Oh, no doubt about it, that was Mr. Bauer'? How great would that be?"

"Gimme a break."

"Come on, Jimbo, this is important to me. And I can't do it without you."

"Why? Just do a solo."

"It won't be as funny. C'mon. I was really counting on you."

"I dunno, Tony. Besides, what would I do for a costume?"

Piza threw up his hands. "It's the gym, not the Metropolitan Opera. All you need is a pointy green cap and maybe something like, I dunno, maybe like a green vest. Just enough so they get the idea."

"Well, actually, my wife's pretty good with a sewing machine. I guess she could do it, but— Wait. What about music?"

"We'll have Sister Theresa stick Brenda Lee's recording on. We'll sing along with that."

Looking anything but convinced, Bauer said, "Okay. Fine. But I really hope I don't regret this."

"You won't. Thanks, buddy. It'll be a big hit. Trust me."

"Famous last words."

On the day of the show, Sister Joann had blocked out twenty-minute segments for each class to go to the gym, get their bearings on the stage, and practice one last time. When Piza learned early in the final week that the sixth-grade classes were the only ones to have teamed up for a performance, he was delighted. "No one to steal our thunder," he'd crowed to Sister Theresa.

After the final rehearsal, Sister Theresa appeared pleased. Piza, on the other hand, looked constipated. "I don't know, Sister T," he said. "Do you think we should have them intermingle, rather than girls in the middle and boys on the ends? I'm not sure it flows right the way it is."

"It looks fine. They sound fine. Do I need to say 'fine' again?"

"No, I suppose you're right. Yeah, you definitely are. It's good. We've done all we can. Now it's up to them to go out there and use what we taught them."

The nun's expression turned serious. She touched his arm. "You know, if you'd like, we can stop by the chapel. With a little help from Our Lord, every note they sing will be like a perfect prayer floating toward heaven."

With a vague look, he appeared about to speak, but she started laughing. "They're not doing brain surgery on the President, Anthony. It's a Christmas show. Lighten up and enjoy it. Please."

He delivered a deep sigh, followed by, "You win. Consider me lightened." *Kind of.*

21

Piza had opted to stay at school until show time. Of the two slices of pizza he'd ordered from Rocco's, one and a-half lay untouched on his desk. It wasn't his and Bauer's surprise number causing his diminished appetite, it was concern about the kids' performance.

The children had to report by six fifteen. He was in the gym by six to make sure he didn't miss any of them when they arrived. They'd have had no difficulty finding *him*. His all-black outfit—shoes, socks, slacks, open-collared shirt, and jacket—was a stark contrast to the bright-green and red in which most of the adults were decked out.

O'Brien and Sister Theresa were the only ones who knew about the evening's surprise performance. "I thought you were gonna be an elf for your mind-blowing finale tonight?" O'Brien had whispered to him at lunch. "Why are you dressed like Johnny Cash?"

"Did you expect me to dress like an elf all day?"

"No. Just seems like a weird outfit for a Christmas show, that's all."

"Consider it a fashion statement, okay? Hey, where's Jim?"

"I passed by his classroom on the way down, but he said he was gonna eat in today. Looked a little pale, but he said he felt okay."

Bauer was writing vocabulary words on the blackboard when Piza walked in, a few minutes before the lunch hour ended. "Missed you at lunch today, pal. What gives?"

"I decided to stay in. It's not a—"

"Whoa! Jimbo! Not for nothin', but your breath smells like a foot. Are you sick or something?"

"I'm a nervous wreck is what I am. My mouth feels like sandpaper. I'm not sure I can do this."

"Take it easy. You memorized the lyrics?"

"Of course I did."

"So, we're good to go. Plus, didn't you say your wife made you a costume?"

"Yeah, she did. Here, look." He pulled a satchel from under his desk and removed a green felt ensemble: pointed hat, vest with red buttons, and, elf shoes—the toes coming to a point and topped off with a jingle bell. "These fit right over my regular shoes."

Piza whistled. "Your wife's a sewing genius. This outfit's amazing. Are you really gonna let this go to waste?"

"I can't. I know that. And, believe me, I've been looking for any reasonable excuse to back out. The kids better enjoy this as much as you keep saying they will. And what about you? Are you ready? Why are you dressed like Johnny Cash?"

"What is that posted on a bulletin board somewhere? It's just an outfit. I'm ready. Costume's tucked away in my desk." He reached into his right jacket pocket and took out a box of lozenges. "And here, take these. They're good for your voice and, you know. . ." He held his nose.

"Gee, thanks for the encouragement."

When the show started, Piza sat with his class, in the student section. He noticed Mother John and Monsignor Lombardo sitting in the first row, and observed them occasionally during the performances. She seemed to be enjoying every minute; he looked like he'd rather be anywhere else. Giacobbi's parents were also in the front. He couldn't help but notice that the board president and the monsignor were separated by several seats, and that neither appeared to acknowledge the other.

As the last fifth-grade class made its way onto the stage, Piza felt the knot in his stomach tightening. Sister Theresa was serving as MC, so he quietly ushered both their classes along the left wall of the gym, past smiling audience members, up the stairs to backstage.

He gathered his class around him, and in a subdued voice said, "Okay, show of hands, how many of you guys are psyched?" Every hand went up. "That's what I like to see. You've practiced hard and you're ready. And if you happen to make a mistake, no biggie, right? Just keep on singing. Okay?" The children nodded, though some now appeared uncertain. *That's it, Tony. Plant the seed of failure in their heads, you idiot.* "Uh, not that you're gonna make any mistakes, of course, 'cause you've got this stuff down cold."

Sister Theresa, standing a few feet away as she made sure her students' white shirts and blouses were neatly tucked into their navy-blue pants and skirts, came over and stood next to Piza.

"What season is this?" she asked his students.

"Christmas," they all replied.

"And is Christmas a season of sorrow or joy?"

"Joy."

"And if we're joyful we're. . ."

"Happy!"

"So I think what Mr. Piza is trying to tell you is to go out there, be happy, and, most of all, have fun. Sound good?" Vigorous nods. "Okay, now all of you—my class too—move a little closer to the stage and watch the fifth-graders finish their song."

Piza sighed in relief. "Boy, did you save *my* butt. I mean save 'me', not my . . . you know. Um, anyway, I owe ya."

"You don't owe me anything, Anthony. I'm glad to help. Besides, saving sinners is part of what I do." She smiled and walked over to the children.

When it was their turn to perform, the kids did better than Piza could have hoped for. Rebecca, Shirley, and Sean's rendition of "O Holy Night" reaffirmed his opinion that the human voice is the most beautiful instrument ever conceived.

"Carol of the Bells" went off without a hitch, with Vinny Pinto and the other melodically-challenged students relegated to the occasional "ding" and "dong" in the background.

"Holly Jolly Christmas" proved to be the perfect song to end the medley with, as the kids built up steam down the home stretch, fueled by the crowd's clapping along to the music.

Exiting the stage, they ran to their teacher with variations of the same question: How was it? He stroked his chin in mock contemplation. "Um, let's see. The word 'fantastic' pops into my head." They could hardly contain themselves. "'Amazing' would seem to fit. 'Phenomenal' is another good one. I couldn't possibly be prouder of you guys." All of them wore grins he knew would remain etched in his memory.

As the second seventh-grade class finished performing, Piza found Bauer and took him aside. "Okay, here's the plan. When the last eighth-graders begin their number, you and I will go backstage. There's a bathroom in the wings, so you can go in and get changed. As soon as the kids leave the area, I'll give you the all-clear. Then, I'll change. Sister T will give a little spiel to stall for time, and then she'll announce us."

"Okay, got it. But I'm still a wreck."

"You'll be fine. And your breath smells like honey. Major improvement."

"I think I may have overdosed on these things," Bauer said, holding up the lozenges box. "I feel kind of woozy."

"Oh my God. Stop already. See ya in a bit."

Ten minutes later they were making their way backstage. As the curtain closed, the eighth-graders exited the stage area. When the last of them was out of sight, Piza knocked on the bathroom door to signal Bauer. He emerged with the look of a condemned man and shuffled the few feet to where Piza was standing.

"Holy crap, Jimbo, you look amazing. But you're walking like a duck."

"These elf feet are tough to get around in. They're kind of slippery."

"Don't worry about it. It'll be fine. I'm gonna change. Just take a minute."

Sister Theresa had already started her closing remarks, thanking various people and overseeing the gifting of flowers to Sister Joann for all her efforts. Within two minutes, Piza was back out. Bauer's jaw dropped. "Whaddya think?" Piza asked.

"What the— What the hell is *that*?" Bauer managed to wheeze. "Where's your elf outfit?"

Piza had tucked in his black shirt collar and attached a clergy mini-front to his neck—a black bib and white clerical collar combination. "Father Tony, at your service."

A crimson-faced Bauer managed to expel a guttural, "How could you do this to me?" He was clearly struggling to control the volume of his voice, as his extended arms convulsed. "How long have you been planning this? What the fuck, Piza!"

"I don't think I've ever heard you curse," Piza noted with

genuine shock. But then he eased into an impish grin. "Probably not a good idea in front of a priest, my son."

A scowl was the response.

"C'mon, calm down, Jimbo."

Bauer yanked off his cap. "I'm not doing this. No way."

"Geez, take a breath. What's the big deal? You look great."

"What's the big deal?" Bauer whispered at the top of his lungs. "*You're* a dignified man of God, and *I'm* a fat freakin' wood nymph. That's the big deal! I'm not doing it."

"Well, technically wood nymphs are female, so—"

"Oh, wait a minute, ladies and gentlemen," Sister Theresa announced. "I think I hear something backstage." She peeked through the crack in the curtain, then, sounding utterly surprised, said to the audience, "I don't believe it. It seems we have two very distinguished visitors this evening. James the Elf, directly from the North Pole, and Father Antonio Pizzeria from Fordham University."

Standing behind Piza, the overtly mortified Bauer hadn't been able to waddle into the nun's line of sight in time to stop her. His face was flushed. "She was in on this?"

"Uh, no. I kind of sprung the priest thing on her tonight. Listen, I'm sorry I didn't tell you, but I figured you might freak out. Kinda like you did. But it's a great idea. C'mon. For the kids."

Bauer glared, let go a prolonged exhale, and tottered forward. Piza pulled back the curtain opening, and as they walked onto the stage the audience broke into laughter. The children went berserk. "Mr. Bauer, Mr. Bauer!" his kids screamed, hands waving wildly. He waved back, tentatively at first, but then with increased enthusiasm.

Piza looked in the direction of his students. They were all standing, laughing, and applauding. He saw Matt Majinsky cup his hands around his mouth. "Hey, Father Antonio," he yelled, "you gonna be our new teacher?" More applause. Piza grinned and wagged a warning finger.

"I think we could use one more song to finish off the evening," Sister Theresa declared, looking out at the audience. "Whaddya say?"

Spirited applause. She hurried to the right front corner of the stage, where she'd earlier set up a record player. Brenda Lee's version of "Rockin' Around the Christmas Tree" was ready to go.

The duo launched into their rendition and, halfway through, Piza gestured to the audience to join in. They enthusiastically obliged. Bauer's stage fright must have gotten lost in the general exuberance, because he was singing as loudly as Piza and was every bit the ham.

At song's end, they received a standing ovation. Joining hands, they took a deep bow. Bauer's hat fell off on the way down, but he caught it in mid-flight and held it up like a trophy. When the cheering finally died down, they retreated behind the curtain. Sister Theresa thanked everyone for coming and announced there would be refreshments in the cafeteria.

Piza removed his clerical garb and freed his recessed shirt collar. Bauer opted to remain in costume, minus the shoe coverings. "I can't believe how much fun that was," he admitted.

"Told you so."

"I'm still gonna kill you for pulling that switcheroo on me, but I'm glad we did this. Did you see the kids? They went crazy."

"Right? How cool was that? Well, let's get down there and reap our richly-deserved accolades."

Piza had been so caught up in the excitement, he hadn't looked at any particular audience members, other than his kids, while he was onstage.

Had he observed the front row, he would have seen: Mother John lowering her head and rubbing her forehead; Robert

Giacobbi, Sr. shooting particle beam death rays out his eyes; and, Monsignor Lombardo contorting his face into a configuration that suggested demonic possession.

And there was no way he could have heard Colleen O'Brien mutter "Oh shit" under her breath.

22

As they hit the gym floor, Piza and Bauer were mobbed by their classes.

"Mr. Bauer, you were so funny," the first of his kids to reach him said. All her classmates chimed in.

"Where's your elf shoes, Mr. Bauer?" another asked.

"In my bag here."

"Could you put them on?"

"Oh, I don't know. They're—"

"Pleeeease?" another begged, the request instantly echoed.

"Okay. But just for a minute. If I try to walk in them I'm gonna land on my tush."

"What's a tush?" someone asked.

He pointed to his rear-end, which elicited a laugh.

Piza's kids were equally zealous in corralling their teacher, although they looked disappointed he'd abandoned the priesthood.

"Why'd you take your costume off, Mr. Piza?" a frowning Sukie asked.

"Because if I left it on, some poor unsuspecting parents might come along and ask me to hear their confession. How awkward would *that* be?" They laughed. "So, who's going in for cookies or whatever else they're serving in there?" They all raised their hands. "Okay, why don't you go round up your parents and such, and I'll meet you inside."

He'd barely finished the remark, when Giacobbi's father appeared. He didn't acknowledge Piza. "Come on, Robert. We're leaving."

"Oh, but Dad, can't we stay for a while? Everybody's gonna get—"

"I said we're going. Now."

Piza stepped in front of him, blocking him from the children. He spoke softly. "Can't you stay? Your son certainly wants to. And you *are* president of the school board."

The man's eyes narrowed. "Don't tell me what to do with my kid, especially after"—he glanced toward the stage—"*that* disgusting display." Stepping past Piza, he said, "Let's go, Robert."

The boy looked at his teacher as he passed him, his expression a mix of disappointment and embarrassment. "I have to go."

"I know. Merry Christmas, Mr. Giacobbi. See you in 1974."

The child nodded.

As the others dispersed to find their families, Piza made his way to the hall leading to the cafeteria. O'Brien sidled up to him. "Be prepared."

"That's cryptic even for you," he said. "Be prepared for what?"

"I don't think the 'powers that be' were too amused by your getup."

"The priest thing? You've gotta be kidding me. What was wrong with that? It was a costume."

"Don't you know these people by now?"

"Apparently not. It's not like I did anything blasphemous. We were doing 'Rockin' Around The Christmas Tree', not 'The Stripper', for God's sake. How'd you find out about this? Did Mother John say something?"

"No. But I saw her talkin' to Monsignor Lombardo and I eavesdropped, as best I could. It wasn't really her; it was him. I couldn't make out everything they were sayin', but they were definitely discussin' *you*. He was doin' most of the talking. I heard the word 'disgraceful'. More than once. It seemed like she was tryin' to calm him down."

"You think I'm in trouble?"

"Well, you may get an earful. I heard her say she'd speak to you. I don't know if that's gonna be tonight or— I dunno."

"Well, if she's gonna do it, I'd just as soon it be now. I don't wanna go through Christmas with this hanging over me."

She glanced behind him. "And, speak of the devil. . . Hello, Mother. Goin' in for some post-show treats?"

"In a bit. I need a word with Mr. Piza, if you don't mind, Miss O'Brien."

"Of course not. See you inside."

As O'Brien left, the principal stared at Piza, her look more perplexed than angry. He was about to break the suspense with some inane comment, but then she said, "When you and I spoke in my office, about not pushing things too far, and avoiding doing things that could be viewed as objectionable—"

"*Reasonably* objectionable is actually what you said."

She sighed. "What part of our discussion didn't you get? I told you this is a conservative community. And in case you haven't noticed, Monsignor Lombardo is as conservative as they come. Didn't it occur to you that he might see what you did as, well, appalling?"

Appalling? Cue the tap dance music. "Of course it didn't, Mother. If I thought for a second anyone would react even remotely negatively, I wouldn't have done it. In fact, Father Janicek—you know, from Fordham—actually suggested it," he lied, "when I mentioned I was performing in the show. He loaned me his clerical collar and all. So, I mean, if it was his idea. . ." He reasoned the good-natured priest—who'd reluctantly loaned him the collar—wouldn't mind being unjustly thrown under the bus for a worthy cause.

"Well, the Jesuits do march to a different beat. Monsignor thinks they should all be excommunicated."

"So how upset is he? And you."

"He was livid. Mad enough to suggest disciplining you. But I managed to convince him you meant no disrespect, because I don't believe you did."

He smiled with relief. "So you bought me a reprieve?"

After a pause, she said, "Mr. Piza, to be perfectly honest, I thought you and Mr. Bauer were very entertaining. The parents and the children loved it. Most parents, anyway. I don't think the school board president was amused."

"Um, yes. He made that clear a few minutes ago."

"Well, *that* man's a story for another day. But the point I'm trying to make is that, entertaining or not, what you did showed a lapse in judgment. Especially after our talk."

"First of all, Mother, let me say Jim didn't have a clue I was gonna do that. As far as he knew, I was gonna dress as an elf. I sprung it on him, literally when we were backstage."

"I don't have a problem with Mr. Bauer. And I don't want to belabor this. But you have to use your head."

"No, I get it, Mother. And I appreciate your coming to my defense. I'm still having some difficulty seeing how what I did was — Never mind. I understand."

"I hope so, Mr. Piza, for both our sakes. I don't need Monsignor's wrath added to all the other problems I have to deal with."

"Okay. And thanks again for your help. Are you heading to the cafeteria?"

"Shortly, yes. I just have to make sure there are no stragglers loitering in the gym."

O'Brien and Bauer had been waiting for him inside the cafeteria, lurking by the doors. As soon as he entered, they herded him into a corner.

O'Brien spoke first. "Still have a job?"

"Yes."

Bauer exhaled. "Okay, great. But are we in trouble?"

"We? Oh, no, young James. You're the *good* son. I, however, got a lecture on 'using my head'. Although, considering how pissed Lombardo supposedly was, the reprimand was relatively benign."

"So, how'd you leave it with Mother John?" O'Brien asked. "That was it? No other repercussions?"

"Not that she mentioned. Still seems like much ado about nothing, if you ask me."

"That may be," Bauer said, "but at least she went to bat for you."

"I guess. I think that—"

"Hey, Mr. Piza," Vinny Pinto yelled from across the room, waving his arms. "Hey, we're over here." The other kids started waving and calling out too.

"Your devoted fans await, Father Pizzeria," O'Brien proclaimed with a sweeping gesture.

A modest bow from Piza. "I hope you guys realize what a privilege it is to know me."

Bauer gave him a light kick in the behind.

Sister Theresa was chatting with some of her students' parents when she noticed Mother John motioning to her from near the cafeteria doors. She excused herself and walked over to her.

"Sister, a word please."

"Of course, Mother. What do you need?"

"Not here. In the hall." She opened one of the doors and followed the young nun out.

"Is everything okay, Mother?"

The principal's expression answered the question before she uttered a reply. "I assume you knew he was going to pull that stunt, seeing how you announced his and Mr. Bauer's performance."

"You mean the priest costume?" Mother John remained silent. "Uh, yes, I did. He told me right before the show started. You see, he was supposed to be an elf, like Mr. Bauer, but at the last minute—"

"And you didn't try to stop him?"

"As I said, Mother, the show was literally about to begin. I don't know what I could have done to—"

"You could have at least told me. I could have stopped it."

"Honestly, it never even dawned on me to tell you. It was last second, I was concerned with getting the show going and, well, it actually seemed pretty innocent."

"Well, not to Monsignor Lombardo. And since he's the head of the parish, his is the only opinion that counts when it comes to these types of matters. This is exactly what I was talking about when I asked you to keep an eye on Mr. Piza."

"Mother, no disrespect, but I wasn't really comfortable when you asked me to— I mean it almost felt like you were asking me to spy on him."

"Keeping tabs on him is not the same as spying. It was for his own good. And the school's."

"I understand what you're saying, but—"

"Listen, I'm not faulting you for what he did. And, truth be told, *I* didn't find it offensive. I realize it was all in fun. But my point is that I have to answer to Monsignor. And, ultimately, that's the bottom line."

Upset as she was, Sister Theresa's response was measured.

"So we have to live every second of our lives concerned whether something we do might offend our *pastor*? Don't we have a right to our own values? At least within reasonable limits?" She didn't know if she'd gone too far, but at that moment, she didn't care.

"Sister, please don't make this more than it is. This was a public event, and Monsignor felt that Mr. Piza's performance 'diminished OLPT'. His words. I think he also felt it made him look foolish, especially in the eyes of the school board president. As you've probably noticed, there's no love lost between them."

"I understand, Mother," she said, conceding defeat. "And perhaps I should have seen it possibly being a problem."

The principal paused. "I'm wondering, Sister, if you might have acted differently if it were someone else involved."

"I'm not sure what you mean."

"I'm just saying you seem to have a— How do I put this? A soft spot, I guess, when it comes to Mr. Piza."

The young nun struggled not to trip over her words. "I, I hope you're not suggesting there's anything other than a professional relationship between him and me."

Mother John appeared taken aback. "I wasn't suggesting that at all. What I meant was you seem to be protective of him. Why on earth would you think I meant something other than that?"

Sister Theresa felt herself trembling. "Well, when we last spoke in your office you— You told me I liked him. And now you're saying I have a 'soft spot'. I mean, how could I not think the implication was. . . I'm sorry, Mother. I obviously misunderstood what you were saying."

"No, no. It's my fault. I should have realized my words could be misinterpreted. I'm so sorry if I offended you, Sister. Truly I am."

"I'm not offended, Mother," she said, shaking her head. "I, I just don't want you to get the wrong idea. I do consider Mr. Piza a friend. But that's the extent of my—"

"You don't have to say anything else, Theresa. I know how

devoted you are to your calling. It's fine." She took the other nun's hands in hers. "And, again, I'm sorry if I embarrassed you." She reached for the cafeteria door. "Going back in?"

"Um, no. I was actually about to leave when you called me over."

It was her second lie in the last minute.

23

Christmas morning found Piza a bit subdued. He was certainly looking forward to the invasion of relatives that afternoon. But there was a lingering dismay from the previous Friday evening, with Sister Theresa's sudden, unexplained departure from the post-show party. He'd resigned himself to not getting an answer until after the holiday.

The good news was that Jack Morrow was joining them. His family had gone to visit relatives in Chicago, but he'd opted not to stray too far from his medical books.

Several of the day's expected guests had been there the previous evening to partake in Mary's traditional Christmas Eve fish-extravaganza—a smorgasbord of so much delectable sea life, a marine biologist would have been hard-pressed not to have an orgasm sitting at that dinner table.

Piza always marveled that anyone still managed to have an appetite the next day. But, here was Angelo, making pancakes and bacon. Mary was putting the finishing touches on two cold-antipasto platters, each a circular treasure trove of thinly sliced cold cuts, adorned with cured olives, marinated artichoke hearts, and roasted red peppers.

"You're an artist, Ma," Piza told her.

"Looks good, right?" she said, shoving an olive in his mouth.

At Piza's direction, Morrow arrived around noon, an hour before the other guests were scheduled to appear. That would give him time to catch up with Mary and Angelo. All he really needed was ten minutes, but with the kitchen transformed into Command Central, you had to fit in bits and pieces of conversation between Mary's orders.

"Patty, get the Christmas tree butter from the refrigerator downstairs. Jack, oh my God, it's so good to see you. Gimme a hug, sweetheart. How are— Anthony! Did you bring up the lasagna? If I don't get it in the oven right now, we're dead!"

The layout of Mary's dining room table was as much a Yuletide work of art as her food. The elegant red tablecloth, subtly checkered with fine lines of gold stitching, was a backdrop for place-settings of Christmas-tree-emblazoned china and gold-plated utensils. A green-trimmed, red cloth napkin topped things off.

Angelo and Jack placed Waterford-crystal water and wine glasses at each setting, except for two spots at the "kids" table, where grammar-school-age cousins would be sitting. With that accomplished, Mary placed sets of red and green Christmas candles on both tables. "Done," she declared with a nod of approval. "Who's ready for angel tips?"

"Don't have to ask me twice," Piza replied as he headed for the kitchen refrigerator. When he got back with the container of heavy cream, four shot glasses were lined up on the dining room table, and Angelo had a bottle of Creme de Cacao in hand. As he carefully filled each glass just shy of the top, his son followed with a splash of cream.

They raised their glasses, Patty joining in with a cup of alcohol-free eggnog.

"Well, Merry Christmas, everyone," Angelo said. "And, God willing, many more."

"Merry Christmas," the rest responded, clinking each other's glass.

Piza smacked his lips. "Boy, that never disappoints. Hey, Ma, shouldn't everyone be—"

The doorbell finished his sentence.

Angelo's sister, Rose, and her husband of eight years, Filippo—aka Flip—were the first guests to arrive. Rose was forty-eight; Filippo was just a few weeks away from seventy.

When Rose's fortieth birthday arrived to find her still single, the family's international matchmaking network had launched into action. She was an attractive woman, but had the worst case of halitosis imaginable, so much so that anyone who knew her would start breathing through their mouth as soon as she was within striking distance.

Angelo's cousin Filomena, who lived in Sicily, knew Filippo through a mutual friend. A widower, he was desperate for companionship—enough to even move to America if need be. Filomena had shown him a picture of Rose, and he was willing to fly her to Sicily so they could meet.

In a phone call with Filomena, Mary had expressed concerns about Rose's breath issues.

"What if she starts talkin' and he passes out? He might not pay to fly her back."

But Filomena had calmed her fears. "Get this. He hadda have surgery on his nose a couple a years ago. By the grace a God, the doctor screwed it up. Now he can't smell *nothin'*. It's perfect."

The botched rhinoplasty also caused an unrelenting post-nasal drip. Poor Flip's only relief was to occasionally hock up the accumulated secretion and spit it into a tissue. The prelude to the moment of discharge sounded like a cement mixer having a psychotic break. Compounding the discomfort to any bystanders was his insistence on holding the tissue several inches from his mouth when letting the mucus fly.

Arriving shortly after Rose and Flip were Mary's younger cousin Maria, her husband Phil, and their two small children, John and Janine. Maria was an office clerk with the longshoremen's union, and bore a resemblance to the Italian actress, Sophia Loren. But her looks were countered by a biting sarcasm, coupled with a penchant for spewing so many profanities even the most hardened dockworkers genuflected in her presence.

The dinner guest list was rounded out by Uncle Nunzio, Cheryl—his second wife—and Nunzio's daughter, Elizabeth, from his first marriage. Nunzio wasn't actually a relative, but he and Angelo had been friends forever, and he was Piza's godfather.

Nunzio had divorced his first wife seven years earlier, after discovering she was having an affair with the mailman. "Cheap bastard was probably lookin' for free stamps," Maria had observed on hearing the news. It had all worked out, though. Cheryl was infinitely nicer than her predecessor; she and Elizabeth, who was now a sophomore at Ramapo College, had bonded quickly; and, Nunzio finally seemed happy.

"Okay, everyone," Mary announced. "The antipasto's on the table. We got red and white wine, and Coke and ginger ale. There's a pitcher of water, for whoever wants it. The seeded bread's in one basket, and the plain's in the other. Mangia, everybody."

Angelo sat at the head of the table, with his son and then Morrow to his immediate right. There were multiple conversations going on at once.

"There's enough cold cuts here for ten meals," Morrow said.

"And I know there's more stuff cooking. How can anybody eat all this?"

Angelo assumed the task of enlightening him. "Let me explain how this works, Jack. You gotta space yourself."

"Like eat a little at a time, so you don't get too full."

"No. That's *pacin'*. Never works, because everythin' is too delicious. This is *spacin'*. You eat as much as you want, but then you wait before you eat as much as you want with the next course. There's a *space* in between. Capisce?"

"Makes sense, Mr. P, because there's no way I'm *pacing* myself with this antipasto."

"That's what I'm sayin', Jack. Smart kid. So we have the antipasto. Then we wait. Then the lasagna and meat in the gravy. Wait. Maybe play some cards. Then the fruit and nuts and candy. Wait again. Then dessert. Oh, and then later on, there's a turkey breast and glazed ham, potatoes, and breaded mushrooms to pick on."

Morrow laughed and threw his hands up. "I don't think the human body was built for this. I may need medical assistance by the end of the night."

It was toward the end of the lasagna course that Piza noticed it—the twitching nose. He tapped his father's arm and murmured, "It's coming. Pass it on." A few years before, he'd discovered that Uncle Flip had a "tell". His nose wriggled for about fifteen seconds before he released the dogs of war.

"Hold on to your soda," Mary whispered to Patty. "And don't say a word, or I'll bop ya." The girl giggled.

Everyone, including Morrow—who'd been forewarned—lowered their gaze. Don't look it directly in the eye, Piza thought, stifling a laugh.

The cataclysmic progression lasted five seconds: convulsive throat-clearing; tissue placement; mucus hurl; done. As often happened, the sheer force of the event caused Flip to bang his knees on the bottom of the table. When it was over, a quick survey revealed that an empty soda bottle had toppled. The only *human* casualty was four-year-old Janine, who'd begun to whimper at the blast. But she was quickly comforted by Phil, who'd opted to sit with his children and Elizabeth.

Maria, who was sitting next to Mary, leaned in toward her. "One a these days he's gonna blow a snot missile right through the fuckin' tissue."

Knowing Maria, she'd intentionally made her comment while her cousin was sipping wine. Mary somehow managed not to spit Chianti all over the table, but she was cough-laughing hard enough to excuse herself, slapping Maria in the head as she bolted past her.

After dessert, the group retired to the living room. Cheryl, who was sitting next to Patty, on a couch, nudged her. "You gonna give us a song this year, Patricia?"

That was all the prodding Patty needed. She practically dragged her father upstairs, and they soon returned with her record player and some 45's. Angelo plugged it in, and with remarkable dexterity, the girl had "Jingle Bell Rock" out of its jacket and on the turnstile in seconds. Her off-key rendition somehow made the performance more endearing, aided by her hand-clapping and gyrating dance moves.

Cries of "Encore! Encore!" elicited a radiant smile. This time, she commandeered Phil to join her.

"Hope you've been practicing, Phil," Elizabeth taunted with a playful smirk.

As it turned out, he needed as little prompting as Patty, and soon the two of them had their audience holding their sides.

Piza caught his roommate's eye and motioned for him to follow. When they reached the hall, Morrow asked, "Where are we going?"

"My room."

Morrow looked toward the ceiling. "Thank you, Santa."

"Dream on, ace," Piza said, laughing.

"Fine. But speaking of sex, any progress with that raven-haired, green-eyed goddess you were telling me about at O'Neals'? What was her name?"

"Colleen. O'Brien. Actually, it's kinda weird. The more I get to know her, the more I think of her as— I dunno, almost like a big sister. Strange. That ever happen to you?"

"God, no. And may I forever be spared from whatever horrifying psychological disorder you're suffering from."

Piza grinned. "I should try to get you guys together. She's a good five-ten in her leather boots. Perfect height for you."

"Leather? This just keeps getting better."

When they entered the bedroom, Piza removed a sheet of paper from a red accordion folder lying on his desk.

"And what have we here?" Morrow asked as he peeked inside the folder.

"Essays. The week before school let out, I asked the kids to write about what they were thankful for at Christmas, and how they'd like to see their lives change in the new year."

Morrow scrunched his face and said, "How they'd like to see their lives change? Isn't existential transformation kind of intense for sixth-graders?"

"Well, you're making it sound heavier than it really is. Besides, some of these kids are more introspective than you might think."

Morrow shrugged. "Okay."

"So listen. Do you remember at O'Neals', I mentioned the kid whose alcoholic father abandoned him and his mother?"

"Uh, yeah. Vaguely."

He held up the paper he'd removed. "This is what he writes about his life changing."

"I'd like my life to change by my father coming back to live with us again. But ONLY if he isn't still drinking so it won't make my Mom unhappy again. He's not so bad when he's not drinking."

Morrow winced. "Geez. Sad much? But I'm not sure what you need from me."

"What I *need* is some advice on how to address this with him. Even if his father stopped drinking, he's probably never coming back."

"Tony, I'm not unsympathetic to what this kid's going through. But you've gotta put the brakes on here. I mean, you seem to have gotten closer to these kids than you anticipated back in October. And I guess that's a good thing to some extent. But—"

"I know. Colleen said something about me trying to *save* them all. But like I told her, that's not what I'm trying to do. I just wanna understand what's going on, so I can deal with it better in the classroom. So what's your take on how—"

"Wait a minute. You just said you wanna understand what's going on, but a minute ago you said you wanted input on how to 'address' it with him. That implies taking some sort of action, and I don't know that that's such a great idea. You're his teacher, not his shrink."

"I know that. But the more he hopes for something that's not gonna happen, the worse it'll be when he finally realizes it's a pipe dream."

A skeptical look from Morrow preceded, "So now you're the self-appointed arbiter of how this kid lives his life? His personal reality check?"

There was a trace of desperation in Piza's voice. "Look. He seems to be finally building some self-esteem. Isn't talking to him a chance I should take if it saves him from being crushed down the road?"

"Thought you weren't trying to 'save' them."

"I said save him from being crushed, smartass."

"What's the difference?"

Piza mulled the question, but had no answer.

"I get what you're trying to do, T. But you're not a psychologist. You're not even a parent, for God's sake. And I don't think 'logic' is gonna make a dent in the emotional turmoil this kid's going through. Keep a sharp eye, obviously, but leave it to him to work out. I honestly think that's your best bet."

Piza paused. Then, with a sigh, "I hate it when you make sense. I have to think this through a little more, but you're probably right."

Morrow smiled. "I have my moments." He pointed to the folder. "Did you really read all of those already?"

"Yeah, over the weekend. Well, actually not all of them. I started reading this one kid's, and I thought I was gonna gag. Robert Giacobbi. Didn't like him from day one. He has that sense of entitlement that makes me nuts. Although I did feel kind of bad for him last Friday. His old man's got money, and he's president of the school board. Major dick. Probably where his son gets it from. But he wouldn't let the kid stay for the party after the Christmas show. He really looked disappointed."

"So what's the story with his paper?"

"Well, he's listing what he's thankful for, right? Stuff like his 'magnificent' house, his English Racer bike, and on and on. And then, get this, he says, his 'wardrobe'. Not his clothes, mind you —his wardrobe. What kid talks like that? I couldn't take anymore. Anyway, what say we rejoin the festivities."

"Sounds good."

Had Piza bothered to finish the boy's essay, he might not have been stunned by what happened when school reopened.

24

Considering how flat his students had been after the four-day Thanksgiving recess, Piza surmised they might be borderline catatonic returning after Christmas. To his surprise, they were remarkably upbeat.

Once they finished settling in, Sukie McDermott raised her hand. "So, Mr. Piza, did you miss us?"

"Hmm. Depends on what you mean by 'miss'. If you mean was I locked in my room every day, weeping while I clutched the class photo to my heart, then the answer would be no." Laughter. "If, however, you mean am I happy to see you guys, that would also be a no." His grin elicited another laugh.

A half-hour before lunch, he decided to let them take turns reading some stories he'd cut out of newspapers and magazines during the break. Current events wasn't part of the curriculum, but he'd occasionally incorporate it into the history lesson.

Several hands went up when he requested volunteers, but what struck him was that Robert Giacobbi's wasn't one of them. He couldn't recall that happening before. And the kid had seemed distracted all morning.

"Wanna give it a shot, Mr. Giacobbi?" No response. "Mr. Giacobbi?"

The girl behind him tapped his shoulder.

"Huh? I'm sorry, what?"

"I asked if you'd like to read a news story."

"Oh. Okay. If you want me to."

Piza handed him a magazine article on the launch of Skylab 4 in November. *Nothing like a little space travel to get the juices flowing.* Giacobbi's readings were usually an exercise in dramatic overreach. Today's performance was listless.

When the lunch bell rang, Piza dismissed the children. "Enjoy lunch. Mr. Giacobbi, if you could hang back a minute? You're not in trouble, I just wanted to speak with you about something."

As the last child exited, Piza sat at the front edge of his desk and pointed to the student desk in front of him. "Grab a seat, Mr. Giacobbi." He complied, his face expressionless. "So, what's going on? You seem as far out in space as Skylab, today."

"I'm okay. Just a little tired."

"You sure?"

"I'm really okay, Mr. Piza. I mean it."

This kid can't look at me. "I've gotta tell ya, that's not the impression I'm getting. If there's—"

"My mom's in the hospital, that's all."

"Oh, geez. I'm sorry to hear that. Is she okay? What the heck happened?"

The boy noticeably tensed. "Uh, she fell. She broke her arm. And hit her head." His eyes welled. "They, uh, said they had to put her in a coma? Because her brain was swelling up or something?"

"Oh my God. When did it happen? How?"

"Last Wednesday. She, uh, fell down the basement steps." Tears were now streaming.

Piza wasn't sure how to comfort him. "I'm so, so sorry, Robert. Is there anything—"

An angry shake of the head cut him off. "What a jerk I was to think my wish would actually come true."

"What wish?"

"My wish! In my stupid Christmas essay. For the new year. You know, when I said I wished my dad would treat my mom better." His agonized look pleaded for understanding.

A chill shot through Piza as the blood drained from his face. *Oh my God. How could I not have finished reading. . . Goddammit! Okay, Tony, slow down. Deal with your damn shortcomings later. If this kid's saying what I think he's saying, what do I do?*

The boy was sobbing; his head bowed.

"Robert, look at me. Robert." The child lifted his gaze. He looked lost. "Robert, are you telling me your father pushed your mother down those steps? Is that what happened?"

Piza took a handkerchief from his pocket and handed it to him. After wiping his eyes and blowing his nose, he attempted to hand it back.

The teacher forced a grin. "Oh, I think at this point that sucker's officially yours."

The boy managed a weak smile, which quickly faded. "I didn't actually see it happen. I know she was in the basement, doing laundry. He was at the top of the stairs, yelling at her. As usual. He treats her like garbage. But— But I mean, he's still my dad, ya know?"

"It's okay. I get it. Your dad is your dad. But tell me more about what happened."

"I was in my room. I try to stay out of the way when . . . they're like that." The tears came again. "Maybe if I'd gone out there; told him to just stop it. Stop picking on her! Maybe—"

"Hey. You listen to me. This isn't on you. There's no way this is your fault. You're a kid and they're your parents. This is not your responsibility. Do you understand me, Robert? It's important that you understand that."

The child nodded, composing himself. "I guess she came upstairs, 'cause I heard her say, 'Bob, please stop. You're hurting me.' Then I heard her scream and I could hear her falling." He grimaced, as if reliving the scene despite his best effort not to. "It was horrible. It sounded like someone had rolled a big box or something down the steps."

If Piza had the man in front of him, he'd have ripped him apart—size be damned. He sequestered his anger, and spoke calmly. "Has your dad ever hit your mom? Did you ever see that happen?"

"I'm not sure. Um, not that I remember."

"Okay. Anyway, what'd you do after you heard her fall?"

"I went running out, and my dad was at the bottom of the basement stairs. He had this crazy look. He said something like, 'Your mother fell, Robert. It was an accident. A terrible accident. Call 911.' So I did. The cops and an ambulance were there in a couple of minutes."

"And when the police came, did they talk to you?"

The boy cast his eyes down. "Yeah. But I— I didn't tell them the whole thing. I said I heard a noise, and when I went to check I saw my dad bending over her at the bottom of the steps. I told them he said she fell." He looked up at his teacher. "I, I know I should've said more, but he's my dad, Mr. Piza. I didn't wanna get him in trouble." He lowered his head again. "But my poor mom. My poor. . ."

Piza's heart was breaking. If ever a kid was torn. Day after day, emulating the arrogance of a father he obviously loved and despised. Out of what? Misplaced loyalty? The need for parental approval every child is cursed with? And now this? Guilt that in protecting his father he'd somehow betrayed his mother? Caused her to suffer by not confronting the bully he'd been taught to respect without question?

"I'll say it again, Robert. There's nothing you could have done to prevent this."

Anguish in his voice, the boy replied, "I could've stood up to him. Before this. But I'm a coward. My mom's the nicest person in the world, and now—"

"Listen to me. I've met your dad twice. And there's no doubt in my mind that if you'd confronted him, the only thing it would've done is piss him off. And he probably would've taken it out on her. Maybe even on you. Has he ever done that?"

"No. He never hit me. Yells at me once in a while. Tells me to 'grow up'. You know, 'be a man' and all." He paused. "But yeah, I think you're right. If I told him to lay off my mom, he'd probably get mad."

"Exactly. But you know what, as lousy as your father is to your mom, we may be jumping to conclusions here. I realize they were arguing, but it doesn't mean he pushed her. He may be telling the truth. This could've been an accident." *Maybe I can deflect some of this kid's guilt by lying to him.*

"I, I guess so. I just wish I knew for sure."

A brief pause, then Piza said, "Maybe when they wake your mom up, we'll find out more."

"Yeah, but if he actually did it, she won't say anything." He clenched his fists and blurted, "She's as big a coward as me. Why didn't *she* do something before? She could've—"

"Whoa. Hold on. This isn't her fault, either. She's a victim here, Robert. It doesn't matter that she's an adult. I— I think that no matter who you are, if you're overpowered long enough maybe . . . I dunno, maybe fighting back gets so hard you just give up. It doesn't mean she's weak. Just human."

An expression of puzzlement and dismay emerged as the boy said, "That was rotten of me. I shouldn't have blamed her. Why did I do that?"

"Listen. You're eleven, and you've been living with a weight on your shoulders no kid should have. Just remember, you didn't do anything wrong. Do you understand?"

"Okay" accompanied a nod.

"Good. If you want, you can stay here with me for the rest of the lunch period. I've got a pastrami sandwich I'll be happy to split with you for the very reasonable price of ten bucks."

The child's attempt at a smile fell short. "What am I gonna do? How do I handle this?"

Piza held his gaze. "There's nothing for you to handle. No matter what happened here, he's still your father. And I don't doubt that, in his own way, he loves you. So you go home. You go with him to visit your mom in the hospital. I read that even though people may be in a coma, they can still hear you. So talk to her. Tell her you love her. And when she wakes up, let's see what happens. Okay?"

"Okay."

"Now, what about that sandwich?"

"No. No thank you. I'd like to go to the cafeteria, if that's all right."

"Of course it is. And if anyone asks—which of course they will—tell them I wanted to personally compliment you on your Christmas essay." *You know, the one I didn't bother to finish.*

"Okay. Thanks, Mr. Piza."

"Anytime."

As Giacobbi left, Piza hoped the discussion had helped. But he realized this was far from over for the boy. And he vowed it wasn't over for him, either.

25

Bauer joined O'Brien at their usual table in the teachers' lounge. "Hey, welcome back to reality," he said.

"Same to you. How was Christmas?"

"Great. Yours?"

"Mayhem. But fun. I didn't realize how much I needed that week off."

"I hear ya. Now, if my eight-month-old would get on board with that concept, that would be great."

O'Brien chuckled. "Ah, the joys of parenthood."

"Indeed. Good news is it's Wednesday. Short week. Hey, where's Tony?" He looked around. "And Sister Theresa seems to be missing in action as well. Have you seen either of them? I was thinking about her during the holiday, what with her disappearing the night of the show."

"Sister Elena said she has the flu. Had it during the whole break, and she's still not a hundred percent."

"So she was sick. Explains her leaving so quickly. And the esteemed Father Pizzeria?"

"I caught a glimpse of him in the parking lot this morning.

But I haven't seen him since then. I assume he opted to stay in his classroom."

"Oh. Okay."

After mulling over the Giacobbi problem during the lunch break, Piza had made a decision. But now that the dismissal bell had rung, he wondered if he should take the evening to further assess the situation. *No, this can't wait.*

Mother John's door was open and she was at her desk, looking deeply committed to whatever she was writing. Piza wasn't sure whether he should disturb her, but determined that his problem had to be more important than whatever she was doing. He lightly knocked on the door frame. No response. He tried with a little more force.

Her head shot up. "Oh, Mr. Piza. You took me by surprise."

He smiled. "Stealth training from my occasional assignments for the CIA."

She laughed. "They appear to have taught you well. Come in. Take a seat. How was your Christmas?"

He pulled out a chair. "Very nice. Usual family craziness, but that's part of the fun. How about you?"

"Peaceful, actually. Not nearly long enough, though."

"I hear ya. Of course, personally, I was counting the minutes before I could get back here."

She laughed again. "I'm sure you were. So, what can I do for you?"

He shuffled in his seat. "I have a situation with one of my students, and I'm not quite sure what to do."

Her expression turned serious. "Situation?"

"Actually, it's not so much him as his family. The Giacobbis."

"The Giacobbis? What's the problem?"

"Well, Mrs. Giacobbi's in the hospital and—"

"Dear God. Is it serious? Does Robert need to take some time from school? Is that it?"

"Unfortunately, that's not it. But, yes, it is serious. She's in a coma. 'Induced' I think is the term they use. Because of brain swelling."

"That poor woman. What happened? Do you know?"

"She fell down the basement steps in her home. At least that's the official story."

The nun looked confused and concerned. "What do you mean, the 'official story'?"

"I had a long talk with Robert, in my classroom during lunch. He's a mess. I think there's a possibility Mr. Giacobbi may have pushed her."

She gasped. "What?"

Piza related the story as the boy had told it to him. Mother John paid rapt attention, displaying no emotion. When he finished, she rose and walked to the windows, staring out, motionless. "I knew the man was a bully, but the idea of him possibly doing this. . . And that child."

"But that's the problem," Piza said. "We're not positive he did it. I mean, it seems likely, but Robert didn't actually see it happen. If we pursue this, and they press Robert about what he heard or saw. . . I think being put in that situation would devastate him."

"No, no. I agree. And I have to tell you, Mr. Piza, I'm torn. I don't know what our role is here."

"I know. As much as I don't want to see Robert even more traumatized, what if that Neanderthal acts out again? Maybe on him. How do we risk that happening?"

Mother John puffed out a breath. "That's the dilemma."

"Isn't there something we can maybe do internally?"

"Like what?"

"I dunno. Maybe someone can talk to this guy in private and let him know we suspect what happened. Put the fear of God in him."

"And who would do that?"

"I'm not sure. Plus, now that I'm thinking it through, he'd probably figure out Robert was the source. That would only make things worse."

"True." She sat down. "Look, let me give this some thought. Have you told anyone else?"

"No."

"Okay. Let's keep it that way for now. I think the fewer people who know about this, the better."

"Agreed."

As he rose, she added, "And, Mr. Piza, thank you for trusting me with this."

He nodded.

Leaving for home, he felt his stomach churning. *This sucks.*

"Thank you for seeing me, Monsignor."

"Not at all, Mother," he replied, setting down his whiskey glass. He casually pointed to the bottle of Glenlivet resting a foot away. "Care for one?" There was the slightest slur to his speech.

"No, thank you."

He shrugged and put the bottle in a desk drawer. "I enjoy one now and then after dinner. Find it helps take the edge off."

Sounds like "the edge" was probably off about an hour ago. "I understand completely. Our work *is* stressful."

After an acknowledging nod, he said, "So, what's going on?"

"Well, we may have a problem, and I felt you should be aware of it."

"What kind of problem?"

"It involves Robert Giacobbi."

"Junior or senior?"

"Senior."

He visibly tensed, and took a sip. "So, tell me."

She repeated what Piza had told her. The deeper she got into the story, the more he seemed to relax.

When she finished, he said, "So this has nothing directly to do with the parish or the school board."

Mother John barely contained her disgust. *Have you no compassion at all?* "Directly? I guess not. But his poor wife. And his son."

He looked momentarily flustered. "No, no. Of course, of course. It's tragic. But, I'm not sure we have a role in this."

"I'm not either. That's why I'm here. I guess what I'm asking is whether we have some legal . . . or, at least, moral obligation to alert the authorities, considering the boy apparently left out the more damning parts when he spoke to the police."

Reclining back in his chair, he issued a muted, but demeaning, laugh. After downing the remaining half-inch of scotch, he said, "You want us to go to the police with this? Why on earth would you suggest that?"

She tried to ignore the condescending tone. "Because I think a crime may have been committed. Perhaps our lawyer could give us—"

He lurched forward. "We don't need to drag a lawyer into this. This isn't related to the church or the school, Mother. It's a domestic dispute. Pure and simple."

Her face reddened. "The woman's in a coma. I'd hardly characterize that as just a domestic—" She jumped as he slammed his right hand on the desktop.

"No. First of all, Mother, as *you yourself* said, we don't know what actually happened. If we went to the police, and it turns out he did nothing wrong, do you have any idea what he could do?"

"But surely—"

He stood as he cut her off. "Understand something. With money comes power. He's already a thorn in my side, and to have. . . No. This discussion ends here. This doesn't involve us, and you and your teacher are to keep this to yourselves. Clear?"

"With all due respect—"

"Thank you for stopping by, Mother."

"Yes. Thank you for your time, Monsignor."

Piza was fuming. "I don't understand why you had to tell him, Mother. Did you really think he was gonna help?" The nun had intercepted him Thursday morning as he walked by her office before the start of school.

"I really didn't have a choice."

"Why not?"

"Because I felt there might be implications that could make this a parish issue, if it even is an issue."

Piza's brow wrinkled. "If it even is? How's it not?"

"Because, like you said, we don't know for certain what happened. And as much as I was disappointed by Monsignor's response, some of what he said made sense. If we accuse Mr. Giacobbi of something he didn't do, there could be repercussions. Serious ones."

"Like a lawsuit."

"Possibly, yes."

"So we're at a dead end." He sighed. "Well, at least we tried. And I appreciate your efforts, Mother."

"I'm sorry I couldn't do more. And if there's anything we can do for Robert, please let me know."

"Will do."

"Oh, and as Monsignor said, please, not a word of this."

"Absolutely." *Yeah, right.*

Piza was already seated in the teachers' lounge when O'Brien and Bauer came in.

"This has to be a first," O'Brien remarked.

"I was especially hungry today, wiseguy."

"Great," Bauer said, shaking his head, "*no* one's food is safe. So, how was your Christmas?"

"Good. How about you guys?"

"Really good," Bauer answered. "Lot of fun."

"Same here," from O'Brien. "Everything okay? You were AWOL yesterday."

"Yeah, just needed to catch up on a few things."

She nodded. "Okay. Oh, and before you ask, Sister Theresa's out with the flu. Sister Elena said she had it really bad over Christmas."

"Well that sucks," Piza said. "Sometimes I think she tries to do too much. Even with *her* energy level, at some point it's gotta take a toll."

They ate in silence for a few minutes.

"You sure you're okay, Piza?" O'Brien asked.

"You look like you're in another world," Bauer chimed in.

"Yeah. I'm fine. Just contemplating ways to solve the world's problems, as usual."

"You're a good man, my friend," Bauer said, raising his milk carton in tribute.

"How true," Piza responded. His smile arrived a half-second late. "Um, Colleen, can I borrow you for a minute?"

"Uh, sure."

He looked at Bauer. "Be right back, okay?"

"Okay. But if you talk about me, I'll know. It's a gift."

"One of your many, Jimbo."

The two walked to the back of the room. "What's goin' on, Piza? Why so mysterious?"

"Listen. When we were at my house for the card game, you said one of your brothers is a cop, right?"

26

O'Brien had agreed to speak with her brother about the Giacobbis, but made it clear she wasn't certain he could help, or how long it might take if he could. Piza had gratefully accepted.

Friday morning, he learned from Robert Giacobbi that the doctors had reversed the induced coma, and his mother seemed to be on the road to recovery.

"That's terrific, Mr. Giacobbi," the teacher said. But the news didn't dissuade him from completing his mission.

Friday was also the day Sister Theresa returned. She was in the teachers' lounge at lunch. If she noticed Piza's entrance, she didn't acknowledge it. He looked her way a few times, without catching her eye.

O'Brien may have noticed, because she said, "So, have you had a chance to talk to Sister Theresa at all today?"

"Uh, what? Oh. No, not yet. Glad to see she's back, though."

"Yeah. She looks like her old self," Bauer observed. "Well, I've gotta get back to my classroom. A couple of things I need to get up on the board before the munchkins return. See you guys later."

O'Brien smiled a goodbye.

Piza gave a short wave. "Later."

When he left, O'Brien, who'd been sitting diagonally across from Piza, moved directly opposite him. "Listen, my brother got back to me. I'll meet you in your classroom after the final bell, okay?"

"Holy crap was that fast. This is great. Did he—"

"Talk to you later, Piza." She stood and left.

O'Brien appeared five minutes after the dismissal bell, closing the door behind her. She retrieved a plastic armchair from near the blackboard, and placed it next to Piza's desk. "Why do you have two chairs in here, and I have none?"

He shrugged. "Nobody ever took them away after the parent conferences. Clearly, I'm higher up on the pecking order than you."

"Highly doubtful, Piza. *Pecker* order, maybe, but. . ."

"Such dirty things from such a lovely mouth," he said with a smile.

"Yeah, whatever. So, here's the scoop. And I hope you appreciate this, because Patrick—that's my brother—put his ass on the line to dig into this guy. There was no active investigation for him to use as cover for snoopin' around."

"Of course I appreciate it. So, where are we?"

"Okay. Big Bob has no criminal record. But, the NYPD *was* lookin' at him for racketeering, about six years ago. Feds too, apparently. But nothing came of it."

"You're telling me this guy's in the mob? Holy shit."

"Patrick said it wasn't so much that he was in it; more like on the fringes. Like he had some dealings with them, but wasn't actually a member of the club."

"Okay, but what about this latest thing?"

She hesitated. "Unfortunately, it seems nothing can be done."

"Why not? This is such bullshit."

"Hey, this shouldn't come as a shock to you. There's no proof he did it."

"Well, what if his wife points the finger at him? What then?"

"I asked. Patrick said it certainly could make a difference, but it's still gonna be her word against his. And even if Robert says what he heard—which you and I agree is probably not a great idea—apparently it's still not a sure thing."

"Why, because he's a kid?"

"Yeah, partially. But it's more than that. He said a lot of the older cops have the attitude it's none of their business. It's a 'family' matter. He and most of the younger guys think that's crap. An assault is an assault. But they're outranked."

A sardonic look from Piza. "So this son of a bitch is gonna get away with it. Unbelievable."

"I'm sorry, Piza. I wish I had better news."

"No, no. Thanks for doing this for me. And thank your brother. Tell him I owe him a dinner."

"What're you gonna do?"

"What *can* I do? I'll keep an eye on Robert, and hope for the best. Frustrating as hell, though. The thought of that bastard. . . . Anyway, thanks again. I mean it."

"I know. And if you need anything, just say the word. This bothers the hell outta me too."

By his own assessment, Piza had too much time to think over the weekend. For the first time since September, there were no football games to offer a distraction. The Super Bowl wasn't until the following Sunday, January 13, and the Pro Bowl was the Sunday after that.

He'd come to terms with the reality of the Giacobbi

dilemma, albeit reluctantly. With that tucked away, he found himself thinking about Sister Theresa. It irked him that she hadn't made an effort to acknowledge him in the teachers' lounge.

But it went deeper than that. What really bothered him was that he felt like he had in junior year in high school, when his girlfriend of two years, Angie Belmonte, jettisoned him with no explanation. *Why would I possibly make that connection? I think I need professional help.*

Monday morning, Sister Theresa's class entered the school library as Piza's kids were coming down the hall, headed for the same destination. As he led them in, he noticed the nun pulling out a chair at a table at the farthest point in the back of the room. She was holding a book, which she started reading as soon as she sat.

He deposited his students with Mrs. Fitzsimmons, made his way through the book aisles, and stopped, not sure what to do. *She hasn't even picked her head up. Maybe I should— You know what?* He took a breath and ambled toward her table. As he drew closer, he could see her hands stiffen around the book.

What the hell could I have done to cause this kind of reaction? He put his right hand on the back of the chair next to hers, and in a subdued voice said, "Pardon me, madam, but is this chair spoken for?"

Her effort to look surprised was an epic failure. "Oh, Mr. Piza. Hello. I didn't see you come in."

He tapped the top of the chair.

"Oh. No, the chair is free."

You're killing me, Sister T. "So, word has it you were under the weather. Feeling better, I hope?"

"Oh, yes, much. Thanks. How was your Christmas?"

"Great. Yeah, really good. Ate enough to last me till Easter, of course."

A weak smile. "Yes, you're always saying what a good cook your mother is. Not surprising you maybe overdid it a bit." A few seconds passed, and she went back to her reading.

He'd never felt this awkward with her. *This is ridiculous.* "You know, my name is still Anthony."

She looked up. "I'm sorry, what?"

"Anthony. My name is still Anthony. When I came over you called me Mr. Piza. I thought we'd progressed past that, you and I."

"Oh, uh, right. It— It occurred to me that maybe that might be a little too informal. You know, for this environment. School and such."

"Really. Have I done something to offend you?"

"No, no, not at all. It's, it's just that, like I said—"

"Because if I have, just tell me. Something's off here, and I'd just really like our relationship to go back to where it was. So please, just tell me." He hadn't anticipated the intensity with which he'd delivered the words.

Her face flushed and she faintly gulped, her eyes on the brink of welling up. If he'd known how she felt about him, he wouldn't have misread her reaction. But he thought he'd hurt her feelings; possibly even frightened her.

"I'm sorry. I didn't mean for it to come out like that. It's just that it's important to me that—"

"It's fine, Anthony." The tension in her voice and body language was gone. "You're right. As long as I don't use your first name in front of the children, of course. As for anyone else, well, too bad. Although Mother might not be too keen on it."

"Listen, if you're really uptight about it. . ."

"No, no. Absolutely not. It's your *name*, right? I've been— I'm being foolish. Subject closed."

"You sure?"

"I am."

"Okay then," he said through a light, satisfied sigh.

She smiled. "So, for all these months we've known each other, we've never really talked. You know, 'talk' talked. How did you like Fordham? I was there a few times. Beautiful campus."

"It is indeed. And why, may I ask, were you visiting my beloved alma mater?"

"Actually, I went to some mixers there."

"Um, mixers? Like, beer and dancing with reckless abandon mixers? You?"

"Did you think I was born a nun?"

He laughed. "Uh, no. It's just that I'm having trouble visualizing this. No offense."

"I went to Marymount. Tarrytown, not Manhattan. We had a lot of mixers with Fordham."

"Oh sure. Marymount. Great location. Up the hill there, overlooking the Hudson. Um, so, you didn't become a nun until after college? Mind if I ask what led you to join?"

"My mom, actually. Well, indirectly. In my senior year, she got cancer."

"Geez, I'm so sorry. Look, if you'd rather not discuss it, that's fine."

"No. It's okay. She was in a Catholic hospital, and the nuns who took care of her were amazing. How they could remain so upbeat in the face of that kind of suffering is. . ."

"Are you sure you—"

"Yeah. It's fine. Anyway, they were an inspiration. And when Mom died, I guess that's when I got the calling. I knew I couldn't do what *they* did, but I wanted to be like them, in some fashion. I was already going to teach, so it was just a matter of finding the right fit. And here I am."

"That's incredible." A short pause, then he grinned. "I just realized, I'm probably not worthy to be in your presence."

"No argument from me."

"Apparently you didn't take a vow of humility." They both laughed. "What about your dad?"

"He eventually sold the house. Now he's living in one of those senior complexes, outside of Philly."

"You keep in touch?"

"We do. We were always close."

"I'm glad."

"Yeah, me too."

He adjusted himself in his chair. "So, I gotta tell ya, I'm still trying to wrap my head around you chugging a beer and rocking out to the Stones."

"Well, for the record, I didn't chug, I sipped. And I preferred the Kinks."

"Fair enough. So did you, uh, date at all?"

"What do *you* think?"

She seemed amused, but he was suddenly uneasy. He realized he didn't want to know about her college love life. "I guess so. Hey, listen, if you're uncomfortable speaking about it, I understand."

With a mischievous smile, she leaned in toward him slightly. "You started it."

She had moved only inches closer, but her eyes were alive, her breath sweet, and he pulled away as if he'd touched a flame.

She did likewise, clearly startled by his reaction. "Are you okay? I apologize if I— Is it my breath?" She put her hand to her mouth. "Um, I brushed really well this morning. You know, two minutes. Teeth. Tongue. I—"

"No, no. Not at all. Your breath is great. Terrific breath. I, uh. . ." *Help!* He reached for his left side. "You ever get one of those cramps in your side? Out of nowhere? You turn a little and then yowza!"

"Oh, yeah. Really hurts. You should rub it."

"Uh, yes, yes. Get out the kinks."

"The kinks. Very good. Quick-witted even in pain."

"Uh, thank you." *Should I tell her the pun was totally unintentional? I may have already telegraphed it. If she thinks I'm a phony—*

"Sister Theresa. Mr. Piza. Can I see you both for a minute?" Mrs. Fitzsimmons blared.

Oh, thank God. If I stepped on my tongue one more time, I swear. . . What the hell is wrong with me?

27

Murph's Pub was Piza's favorite hometown bar. The "h" in the neon sign was out more than it was lit, so the regulars called it Murp's. A stranger might easily have ranked it as one rung above a dive. But for Piza and his friends, it held the comfort of familiarity. And it was a trove of some of their most monumental revelations and decisions—whether truly historic or merely perceived that way through the haze of drink.

Sitting in a corner booth, Piza was nursing a cup of coffee. Frankie Falco sat opposite him. The encounter with Sister Theresa that morning had rattled him to the point where he needed a sounding board, and his friend was a good listener. Other than nodding occasionally, or uttering the random "Uh-huh", Frankie remained silent as Piza related what had happened.

When the story ended, the plumber brushed some pretzel crumbs off the table and took a slug from his second bottle of Bud. "So what you're telling me is you've got the hots for a nun."

Piza's face reddened and he slid to the end of the worn red-vinyl bench seat. Frankie laughed and grabbed his left arm before he could stand. "Hey, hey, relax, cowboy. I was just breaking your chops a little."

Piza glared at him.

Frankie looked confounded. "Seriously? When the hell did you get so sensitive?"

Piza maintained the scowl. "If I wanted my balls busted, I'd have called Sal."

Frankie gave a slight roll of the eyes and said, "Fine. Geez." Then, a deep sigh. "Look, I've known you almost all my life, and you're my best friend. So I know if you're this upset, there's something real going on here. But, Ton, you've gotta realize how weird this is."

"Of course I do. I mean, in a list of the top five things I never thought I'd hear myself say, 'I think I have feelings for a nun' would probably be number one."

"I hear *that*. Just for the hell of it, what would the other four be?"

Piza snickered.

"Okay, there we go. Close to a laugh. You want more coffee? Something stronger maybe?"

"No. I'm good."

"So, I have two questions. One, is the feeling mutual? And two, what are your options either way?"

Piza sipped his coffee and stared beyond his friend. He refocused. "Is the feeling mutual? I'm not sure. I mean, I kind of get this vibe from her sometimes. Like this morning, it almost felt like she was kind of teasing me. But is that what it really was? Or was she just being her ridiculously pleasant, playful self, and I flat out misread it. Seeing maybe what I wanted to see. Man, this is so messed up."

"Well, you said she'd been kind of distant lately. Any idea why?"

"None."

"I guess what I'm trying to say is—and this sounds

completely nuts considering she's a nun—but, do you think she was playing hard to get? Jesus, I feel like I should go to confession."

"I, I really don't think so. She's too genuine for that. God, I can't believe we're even discussing this. She's incredibly dedicated. I've seen her praying. She always looks like she's about to start glowing and ascend into heaven."

Frankie sat back in his seat. "I don't care how dedicated she is, she's still a woman. The Church may mess with your head, but I don't think they've figured out a way to control hormones."

A faint smile briefly interrupted Piza's empty stare at his coffee cup.

"Okay, Ton. Let's get past that. Bottom line. Whether it's mutual or not, what can you do about it? I see what this is doing to ya, and I'm hurting for you right now. But I gotta say it—to me this is an impossible situation. If you think I'm wrong, tell me. But I don't see a workable solution to this."

Piza lightly ran an index finger around the rim of the cup a few times. "That's because there is no workable solution. You're right. It's impossible. And I'm an idiot."

"You're not an idiot. I mean, hey, the heart wants what it wants."

A pained expression swept across Piza's face. "What? Jesus, Frankie, I feel crappy enough without you trying to make me puke. 'The heart wants what it wants'?"

His friend looked hurt. "What was wrong with *that*? I heard it somewhere. Or read it, maybe. I don't remember. But it's a nice saying."

"Maybe you should give up plumbing and work for a fortune cookie company," Piza scoffed.

Frankie's lip curled in a mock sneer. "Always *were* a snobby bastard." His ensuing laugh triggered the same from Piza.

After a couple of moments, "Seriously, though, Ton, whaddya gonna do?"

"Honestly? Not a clue."

In the course of a restless night, Piza decided how he would resolve the Sister Theresa problem. Do nothing. As he saw it, other than that he had two choices: keep his distance, or subtly convince her to leave the sisterhood.

The first would be difficult, considering they taught the same grade. And the second? Well, that was just ludicrous. *Hey, Sister. That roast beef on rye you had for lunch looked amazing. Speaking of which, how about leaving the order so I can ask you out?*

The next few days were uncomfortable for him, even though he only saw her in the teachers' lounge at lunch. Sitting with other nuns, as usual, she made eye contact with him each day when he came in, and modestly waved.

Despite his efforts at restraint, he'd glance in her direction a few times. Fortunately, she was always engaged in conversation, sparing him those awkward attempts to avert your eyes when someone you're staring at happens to look back.

By Friday, however, he changed course, concluding he needed to actively avoid her as best he could. He'd pined after Angie for months in high school. But after eventually succumbing to reality, he'd vowed never to waste another minute of his life sloshing around in dewy-eyed longing. It was a pledge to which he'd remained true, likely aided by the fact he hadn't allowed himself to get that emotionally attached to a girl again.

Sister Theresa was inherently unattainable. So why torture himself over something that could never be? Staying away from her would make it that much easier.

Friday morning also saw Robert Giacobbi enter the classroom

with a spring in his step. Piza motioned to him as he entered. "Can I take it from your ebullient demeanor you have some good news, Mr. Giacobbi?"

"Ebullient? I guess that means I look happy? 'Cause I am. My mom came home last night."

"Excellent. I'm really glad to hear that."

"Yeah. Everything's great. I can't believe how much I missed her." He leaned in. "And my dad's like a new person, Mr. Piza. He's treating her like a queen. I'm positive now it was an accident."

Piza hoped his smile was convincing. "That's terrific. Really great news. Okay, go settle in."

He opted to stay in the classroom for lunch, to start reading *The Hollow Hills*, by Mary Stewart, the legend of King Arthur being one of his favorite subjects. But being astutely self-aware, he knew this brief escape to the sixth century also would delay putting his new "ignore Sister Theresa" policy into action. *Probably a good idea to take the weekend to let it crystallize.*

Over the weekend, he decided to buy a box of chocolates and a get-well card for Mrs. Giacobbi. It was a sincere gesture, but not without an additional motive. He hadn't been able to completely let go of the Giacobbis' situation, and he saw this as a possible opportunity to intervene.

He handwrote a note and inserted it in the card, telling her how glad he was she was on the mend, and letting her know that if she wanted to discuss Robert, or anything else for that matter, his door was always open. He underlined "or anything else for that matter". It wasn't subtle, but, in his estimation, this wasn't a time for nuance.

On his arrival at school Monday morning, Piza stashed the card and candy in his desk. As the kids were filing out at the end of the day, he motioned to Giacobbi. "These are for your mom," he said, removing the items.

The boy's face lit up. "Wow. Thanks, Mr. Piza. She's gonna love this."

"Well, if anyone's earned a little comfort food, it's her. Tell her to enjoy it."

"Okay. Thanks again, Mr. Piza."

After school, Piza was talking to O'Brien in the parking lot. He mentioned what he'd done.

"God, you've really gotta let this go, Piza. You've done everything you possibly could. What's next, show up at her house?"

"Of course not. It just bugs the hell outta me that nothing's gonna come of this. That asshole's gonna skate without a care in the world."

"Let me ask you something, as a friend, and I need you to think about your answer. Are you doin' this out of concern for her and Robert, or your distaste for *him*?"

He paused a moment. "I get where you're coming from, but I don't think it's an either-or. Am I concerned for Robert and his mother? Of course I am. Do I think the father is a piece of crap? You bet. And if she takes the hint, maybe I can talk her into getting some help, including giving that bastard up to the cops."

"How are you gonna do that? What kind of help are you gonna get her? And what's gonna happen to her and her son if she does go to the police?"

"Well—"

"Hold on a sec. Let's assume your dream comes true and he's charged and convicted of assault. My brother said he's got no prior offenses. How long do you think they'd actually put him away for, if at all? And if they do, who's gonna support them in the meantime? You? Plus what's it gonna be like for them when he gets out?"

"Holy shit. You think this guy should slide on this? I can't—"

"Hold on. You know damn well if it were up to me they'd string that bastard up by his balls. But put aside your moral outrage and think about what I said. Do you have the answers to those questions? Have you thought this through?"

He lowered his eyebrows. "Don't you know me by now? Of course I have. They've got these places where abused women can go for counseling. I figured maybe I could put her in touch. And as far as him going to jail, there's probably plenty of money for her and Robert to live on."

"You know that for a fact?"

"No. But—"

"Look. Does Mrs. Giacobbi need counseling? Of course she does. Probably intensive therapy. Even if this is the first physical injury, you can bet he's been mentally abusin' her for a long time. But—"

"Well, you've got a masters in psych. Isn't there something you could do?"

Her frustration evident, she said, "Piza. Listen to me. It's not my place to intervene. Just like it's not yours. This is like the conversation we had a while back, about you tryin' to save the kids in your class."

"Which I said I *wasn't* trying to do, you may remember."

Through a sigh, she said, "Like I told you then, your heart's in the right place. But you've gotta get it through your head that our job is here, in this school. If we start gettin' involved in our students' private lives, we'll be crossin' a boundary we're not meant to cross. Believe me. I've been doin' this a lot longer than you."

He drew a breath and exhaled deeply. "Okay, fine. I have a lot of respect for you—as a person and a teacher. And as hard as it is for me to admit I don't know everything about everything, I'll follow your lead on this."

"Thank you."

"Question now is, what should I do if she takes me up on my offer, and wants to discuss it?"

"She won't."

"Why?"

"Because she probably believes this whole thing is her fault."

As he drove home, he replayed the day's events. The more he thought about O'Brien's advice, the more he realized she was right. It didn't make him feel better about Mrs. Giacobbi's and Robert's dilemma, but it did somewhat ease the angst from his inability to solve their problem.

He was hoping for a peaceful remainder of the week. But that was not to be.

28

Wednesday, January 16, marked the third day in a row Karen Jablonski was absent. Piza had been saddened to learn on Monday that her grandmother had passed away over the weekend. He knew she was a tough kid, but considering how close she and her suffragette heroine had been, he hoped she was doing all right.

A discussion of the French Revolution was on tap for the day, and Piza was looking forward to it. Six years of studying French in high school and college had generated an interest in the country's culture and history.

With an over-the-top French accent, he announced, "Today, we are going to study ze French Revolution."

"Um, Mr. Piza, are you gonna be teaching the whole lesson with that accent?" Sukie asked as she raised her hand.

"I was thinking about it, Miss McDermott. Why?"

She responded with a thumbs-down.

"No kidding? Geez, I thought I really nailed it. Anyone else agree with—"

A sea of south-facing thumbs appeared, followed by laughter.

"Okay, then. As unappreciated as I'm feeling at this moment, I'll attempt to soldier on—sans accent."

Ralph Restivo raised his hand. "My brother Carlo did a paper on that when he was a freshman last year. You remember Carlo, Mr. Piza, right?"

"Of course, Mr. Restivo. He of the Turkey Drumstick Wars. How could I forget?"

"Oh, okay. Anyway, he did this French Revolution paper, and he read it to us at dinner one night."

"And your point is?"

"Um, well, it was kinda boring. I almost fell asleep in my broccoli."

Laughter from all.

"Well, let me assure you, Mr. Restivo, my presentation will be positively scintillating. Edge of your seat excitement."

"Oh, okay. But then he said something about eating cake, and that made me think of dessert, and so then I was wide awake."

More laughs.

Shirley Robinson raised her hand.

"Yes, Miss Robinson."

"I think he's talking about when the French people were starving, and the queen . . . I don't remember her name, said something like 'Let them eat cake'. Right?"

"Very, very good, Miss Robinson. It was Queen Marie Antoinette, and she was married to King Louis the Sixteenth. Although there's some question as to whether she really said it."

She raised her hand again. "May I go to the girls' room?"

The teacher smiled. "I don't think Marie Antoinette said that either." The girl giggled. "Of course you can go."

Kevin Davis raised his hand. "Can I hit the bathroom too, Mr. Piza?"

"My God, we have the makings of an epidemic. Go ahead, Mr. Davis."

He was five minutes into the lesson when the back door of the classroom burst open and an anxious-looking Davis thrust his head in.

"Mr. Piza, you better get out here. I think there's a problem."

Piza snatched a piece of paper off his desk. "Mr. Giacobbi, write these definitions on the blackboard. And nobody move."

With that, he tore out of the front classroom door.

Davis intercepted him, pointing down the hall. "I was comin' out of the boys' room when I saw them. I was gonna go down there, but I figured I better get you."

Shirley Robinson was standing with her back against the right wall. Three older boys were around her.

"Good thinking, Mr. Davis. Okay, get back in the classroom. I'll take care of this." With that, he moved quickly down the hall.

"Hey, what's going on?" Piza said as he approached the group. "Back away from her." None of the boys moved. "I said back away. You have a hearing problem?"

As he came within a couple of yards, two of the kids moved. The third didn't budge. Piza positioned himself in front of the girl, going virtually nose-to-nose with the smirking boy. "Back up now."

The boy stepped back, the smug look still in place.

Piza turned to the girl. "You all right, Miss Robinson?"

She looked more angry than scared, but Piza could see her hands shaking. "I'm okay."

"Do you know these boys?"

She shook her head.

"What are your names?" No response. "I said what—"

"*His* name is Tommy DiGregorio."

Piza spun around as Davis pointed to the apparent ringleader. "Mr. Davis, I thought I told you— Never mind. Who else do we have here, since it appears they're all mute."

"The kid with the glasses is Richie Barone, and the other guy is Mike O'Leary. They're all eighth-graders."

"Did they do anything to you, Miss Robinson?"

She looked at DiGregorio. "He touched my hair. I told him to leave me alone, but—"

"It wasn't a big deal," DiGregorio interrupted. He grinned, stepped to the side, and pointed to her mini-afro. "We, uh, were just tryin' to figure out how you get a comb through that thing."

The other two boys started snickering, but stopped as soon as Piza spat out, "You think this is funny?"

DiGregorio's smirk returned. Piza was tempted to slam him against the wall. As disturbed as he was by the kid's insolence, that was an emotional blip compared to how he felt about what he'd done to Robinson. He forced himself to calm down. "Kinda young to be a bigot, aren't you, Mr. DiGregorio?"

"I don't think I know what that means."

"Really, ace? And you're in eighth grade? Sad commentary. Maybe your teacher— Whose class are you in?"

"Mrs. Kowalski," Davis said. DiGregorio briefly shifted his gaze to the boy. Davis held eye contact.

"Maybe when Mrs. Kowalski learns about this, she can explain it to you, along with anything else she decides to do." Barone and O'Leary looked nervous, but DiGregorio's expression didn't change. "And by the way, if I ever see any of you near my kids again—anywhere—Mrs. Kowalski's gonna be the least of your problems. Now get back to your classroom."

They left. When Piza felt they were a sufficient distance, he turned to Robinson and Davis. He was about to speak when he heard, "You should've left her alone, Tommy. We better not get in trouble 'cause of this." The tone was soft, but whoever said it probably hadn't accounted for the acoustics of an empty hall.

"*Are* they going to get in trouble, Mr. Piza?" Shirley asked.

"They are if I have anything to do with it. I'll talk to Mrs. Kowalski at lunchtime. And Mr. Davis, the next time I—"

"I know, I know. I better listen. But there were three of them and one of you so. . ."

"I appreciate the backup, Mr. Davis. I do. But trust me, I can handle myself." The boy nodded. "Okay, go back inside. Miss Robinson, stay here for a second."

When Davis entered the classroom, Piza dropped to a knee. "You sure you're okay?"

"Uh-huh. I was a *little* scared because they were so close to me. But mostly you kind of get used to kids like them."

He tensed. "Whaddya mean, 'get used to'? Has this happened to you before? Here? At school?"

"Oh, no. This was the first time here. But, you know, other places. The playground near my house. Nobody ever touched my hair or anything like that guy did. But kids say things. Mostly they just look at me and whisper. Sometimes I can hear them. They call me things like— Well, you know."

"Do you do anything when that happens?"

"My friends and I usually just walk away." She sighed. "Sometimes, though, Mr. Piza, I feel like I wanna punch them."

Her teacher smiled. "Might make you feel better." He immediately held his hands up in front of him. "I never said that."

She smiled back. "It's okay. My parents don't believe in violence, anyway. I mean, if someone hit me, I'd hit them back. But if it's only names. . . My dad says there'll always be ignorant people in the world, but you can't let that stand in your way." She stiffened her posture and deepened her voice. "Follow your dreams, Shirley Elizabeth. That's the way you'll win in the end."

Piza chuckled at the portrayal. "Your dad's a wise man."

"I think so too."

Standing up, Piza said, "Listen, I'll send a note home, to fill your parents in on all this."

"Okay. And thanks for helping me, Mr. Piza."

"Anytime. Besides, I'm pretty sure taking down punks is in my job description."

She laughed. "You're funny."

"I *know*, right?"

She laughed again.

That afternoon, as soon as he entered the teachers' lounge, he took Mrs. Kowalski aside and told her about the incident. "I would've done something myself, but you're their teacher and I didn't want to step on your toes, so to speak."

"No, it's fine, Mr. Piza. Richard and Michael aren't really bad kids, but they're immature. They seem drawn to this macho thing Thomas has going on. God forgive me for saying this about a child, but he's just a bad apple. Always has been."

"No, I understand completely. I couldn't believe the lack of respect . . . or fear. I'd have been scared to death at his age. And God forbid my parents found out."

"Well, that's the other problem. But we don't need to get into that. Anyway, I'm going to take this to the office. I think they should deal with it."

"Okay. Great. Whatever you think is best."

When he reached his table, he filled in O'Brien and Bauer.

"I can't believe it," Bauer said. "I mean, this is a Catholic school."

"Doesn't make a difference, Jim," O'Brien responded. "Catholic school, public school. Nice neat uniform or not. People are people. And children? As much as I understand the underlying dynamic, on a gut level their capacity to hurt each other sometimes scares the hell out of me."

"I know what you're saying," Piza concurred. "And Mrs. Kowalski implied this kid's home life wasn't a help. But she didn't go into details."

O'Brien chuckled. "The DiGregorio kid? Yeah, no kiddin'." With her index finger she pushed her pert nose to the side.

Piza grinned. "Are you attempting to say his old man's mobbed up?"

"Of course that's what I'm sayin', you dumb-ass." She pushed her nose harder. "Whaddya think *this* means?"

"Okay, okay. Calm down." He broke out laughing. "It's just that your nose is so small, I wasn't quite—" He was laughing too hard to finish.

Bauer was laughing as well, and joined in. "Maybe the guy's a really *low-level* mobster. Unworthy of a full-sized schnoz."

O'Brien gave them a "very funny" look. It took a minute for the two men to regain their composure.

"Boy, that was rich," Bauer declared, followed by a residual giggle. But then his expression changed. "Geez, Tony. If this is true, about the father, you think there's a chance that— Nah, that's ridiculous. Right?"

"Uh, yeah, I don't think I'd be overly concerned, Jimbo. I scolded the kid, I didn't break his kneecaps. Although if either of you would like to start my car after school. . ."

Piza's kids were in music class with Sister Joann for an hour that afternoon. He enjoyed her lessons, and often stayed to watch. But today he was using the time to compose a brief letter to Shirley Robinson's parents, informing them of what had happened, and inviting them to meet if they wished.

He was almost finished when he heard a knock at the front classroom door. He saw Assistant-principal Florino peering in through the door's small window. *Oh man. Mrs. Broomstick-up-her-butt. Now what?* He motioned for her to come in. *At least she knocked.*

"Hey there, Mrs. Florino. What's up?"

"Yes, Sister Joann said you'd be here."

"Well, Sister Joann always speaks the truth."

"I suppose. So, anyway, as you may know, Mother John is at an administrators' conference for two days."

"I didn't, but— Do you need my help with something?" She

arched an eyebrow. *Wow. She offended me without saying a word. She's good.*

"Actually, I wanted to bring you up to date on the DiGregorio matter. Remember? From this morning?"

Does she think I'm senile? "Yes, I remember. What's the latest?"

"Well, since Mother's not here, this fell into *my* lap. I spoke with Mrs. Kowalski and the boys involved."

"Okay. So you want to hear from me."

"No, not really."

"Oh, because I mean I was there. So—"

"I'm aware you were there. But it's not necessary. Thomas admitted what he did."

Piza almost did a double-take. "Well, color me surprised. I thought for sure he'd concoct some sort of story."

"He seemed to find it amusing. I'm not a doctor, but I think there may be something wrong with that young man. Impudent. But that's neither here nor there. His friends also confessed."

"So what's the bottom line?"

"I suspended Thomas for two days, and the other boys for one."

He looked shocked. "Wow. That's great. I was afraid they might get off with a reprimand or something."

With a look bordering on contempt, she said, "Don't you think we care enough about the welfare of our students to mete out appropriate punishment, Mr. Piza?"

"No, no. There was *never* any doubt about that. Whatsoever. I, uh, I wasn't sure what the protocol was, is all." *Please don't hurt me.*

"Ah. I see. So, any questions?"

"Nope. Not a one. Thanks for letting me know."

"Okay then. And don't forget, you have to get your children in ten minutes."

"Righto. Rest assured I'm on top of it."

"Good." She turned and left.

He couldn't contain his joy. *I can't believe she actually suspended them. And* two *days for that disrespectful little jerk. Hopefully, that ends that.*

He should have known better.

29

Shirley Robinson handed Piza a note the next day. It was from her mother, saying they appreciated being notified of the incident, and were happy with the way he'd handled it and the suspension handed down. Most importantly for him, she indicated Shirley seemed fine.

Later that morning he was laboring through a religion lesson. The topic was the catechism's definition of the two great commandments containing the whole law of God: thou shalt love the Lord thy God with thy whole heart, with thy whole soul, with thy whole mind, and with thy whole strength; and, thou shalt love thy neighbor as thyself.

Although the mandate to love God appeared first on the list, it made more sense to him to give the second commandment top billing. *Since we all live here on earth, shouldn't our priority be how we treat Ted and Louise across the street?* He didn't impart his assessment to his students, reasoning that relegating God to second-tier status could definitely imperil his job.

These types of situations contributed to an underlying frustration he felt each day. There were so many things he'd love to talk about with them. But either the subject matter was off limits, or a probing philosophical discussion would be above the head of some of them.

The front classroom door opened a crack, and Sister Elena poked her head in.

He walked over and stepped into the hall. "Hey, Sister. What's up?"

"Mrs. Florino asked me to get you. She's in the office with a parent. I'll watch your class while you're there."

"Which parent?"

"Sorry. No idea. What are you working on?"

"Um, the two great commandments. Did she say anything else?"

"No. Only what I told you. You'd better go. She didn't look happy. Although that's nothing un—" She coughed lightly and smiled. "I'm confident I can handle love God and love your neighbor."

Piza opened the door to allow her to enter, then inserted himself halfway in. "Listen up, you guys. I have to take care of something. Sister Elena's going to take over. Got it?" Not a sound. "Okay, Sister, they're all yours."

His heart raced as he hurried down the hall. *What's going on? Jesus, what if it's Mrs. Giacobbi?*

As soon as he arrived, Mrs. Florino motioned for him to come into her office. Seated in one of the two chairs in front of her desk was a balding, rumpled-looking man. He stood when Piza entered. He couldn't have been more than 5'6". His large frame, baggy gray sweatshirt, and sagging indigo jeans that almost completely covered mud-caked work boots, made him appear even shorter.

"Mr. Piza, this is Mr. DiGregorio. Thomas's father."

The man extended a calloused hand. "Eh, 'ow are ya? Joe DiGregorio."

As he shook the man's hand, he was astonished the grip was

so weak. *If this guy's a mobster, I'm Eleanor Roosevelt.* "Nice to meet you, Mr. DiGregorio."

"Please sit," the assistant principal ordered.

DiGregorio tugged lightly at the tattered, stained neckline of the sweatshirt. "Like I told this nice lady, excuse my appearance. I just come off the job. Took a early lunch."

Piza waved it off. "No problem. You're in construction I take it?"

"Yeah."

"Hard work."

"Eh, gotta make a livin'."

"I'd like to get to the business at hand, gentlemen, if you please," Mrs. Florino said. Both men turned toward her and straightened in their seats. "Mr. DiGregorio is here about Thomas's suspension. He tells me Thomas denied touching your student's hair, and— Did you push him, Mr. Piza?"

Piza's eyes bulged. "What?"

DiGregorio held out his hands and motioned for Piza to calm himself. "Look, I ain't sayin' it's true. If lyin' was a occupation, Tommy'd have a job for life. My other two kids are great. But Tommy? I think someone switched him at the hospital." He laughed. "But, he's still mine, so I gotta ask. Ya know, about the pushin'. You understand, right?"

Piza was beside himself. "I can assure you, Mr. DiGregorio, I didn't touch your son. But let me tell you something. If he were an adult, I might have. That's how disrespectful and arrogant he was. But hitting a child? That's—"

"Well, like this lady said, he said 'push'. Not 'hit'."

"Hit, push, what difference does it make? I wouldn't lay a hand on a kid. Period. Did he mention this yesterday, when you spoke to him, Mrs. Florino?"

"No."

DiGregorio sighed. "Okay. And this other thing wit' the colored girl. You sure *she* was tellin' the truth?"

Piza looked down his nose. "I'm sorry. *Colored* girl?"

"Yeah. You know. The little girl? In the hall?"

Piza all but sneered. "Yeah. I'm sure. If you'd seen how scared she was, you'd be sure too."

DiGregorio put his hands on his knees. "Okay, I'm good. I'll deal with Tommy on this. And I wanna thank both a you's for makin' time to talk to me." He got up; Piza and Mrs. Florino followed suit. "Goodbye, Miss. And . . . I'm sorry, I forget your name."

"Piza."

"Right. You wanna walk out wit' me?"

Um, no. "Sure."

When they reached the hall, DiGregorio stopped. "Look, I know my kid's got a attitude. I work a lotta hours, and I'm usually not home until late. And his mother, well. . . You're a paisan. Piza's Italian, right?"

"Uh-huh."

"You ever hear the expression 'Italian princess'? Well, whoever invented that probably thought it up after meetin' my wife." An expansive smile raised the curtain on a display of tobacco-stained teeth. "Don't get me wrong, she treats me good. Great cook. But disciplinin' Tommy ain't exactly high up on her *to-do* list."

Somebody save me. "Of course. I understand."

The man reached into his right pants pocket, extracted a smudged business card, and handed it to Piza. "Do me a favor. If my kid acts up again, call me direct. Save us all some time."

Piza looked at the card and read it aloud. "JTD Contracting, Inc. Joseph T. DiGregorio, President. Oh. So you have your own company. That's great. Whaddya do, home remodeling and stuff like that?"

"No, I'm buildin' a mall in Jersey, just over the bridge."

"A mall? Like, the whole thing?"

"Yeah. Me and my partners bought the land a couple a years

ago. Good price. We finally straightened out all the zoning and political bullshit—pardon my French—and now we're breakin' ground. Gonna be nice."

"Uh, great. Best of luck."

"Thanks." He extended his hand; Piza reciprocated. But now the man's grip strength had increased exponentially. As his grin widened, the light in his eyes dimmed. "And, just so we're clear, you sure you didn't maybe nudge Tommy or nothin' like that?"

Piza's gulp may have registered on the Richter scale. "You have my word, Mr. DiGregorio. One paisan to another." His attempt at a wink looked more like he had a tic.

"Okay. Just double-checkin'. You get it, right?"

Message received; bowels on the brink of total evacuation. "Yep. Completely."

"Good. Well, nice meetin' ya. Maybe I'll see ya around."

"Uh, yep. You bet."

Piza arrived back at his classroom as the lunch bell rang. He thanked Sister Elena, confirmed his students had behaved, and waited until the last of them was out the door before collapsing in his chair.

Those last minutes alone with DiGregorio had unnerved him. He realized concern was illogical; he hadn't done anything to the guy's son. But rational thought wasn't doing much to quell the churning in his stomach. He decided to stay in his room for lunch and let the quiet calm him. That plan went south when O'Brien and Bauer descended on his retreat.

"Heard you had some excitement this morning," O'Brien said, as Bauer retrieved the two plastic chairs from the corner.

"Jesus. You should work for the feds, O'Brien. They could use your intelligence-gathering skills."

"Just keepin' an ear to the ground, is all."

Bauer set the chairs next to Piza's desk. "So let's hear about it," he said. Then, with a grin, "Oh, and Colleen, please don't go trying to push your nose again. My ribs still hurt from yesterday."

She tossed him a playful curled lip as she sat. "Keep it up, Bauer." Resting her elbows on the desk, she cupped her hands under her chin. "Okay, so spill it. How was *Don* DiGregorio?"

"Well, let's see. He seemed harmless enough when I walked in. Kind of squat. Balding. Smelled a little like wet cement and perspiration. And he looked like he got dressed in a dirty-clothes hamper."

"How delightful," O'Brien said.

"I know. After your revelation about him, I guess I was expecting something else."

"Someone a little more dapper," Bauer offered.

"Yeah, maybe. But anyway, you ready for this? His kid told him I pushed him. You believe that? Boy was I pissed."

Bauer blanched. "That's terrible. Why would— I mean you didn't, right? Touch him or anything?"

"Of course not. You think I'd actually—"

"No, no. I'm sorry. I just remember you said the kid was really arrogant and disrespectful, and— No, I know you'd never do that. Stupid thing to say."

"Forget it. I *have* been known to get a little hot under the collar at times."

Through a smirk, O'Brien said, "Ya think? You hate bein' challenged more than anyone I've ever met."

"Hey, you have your moments too, toots," he shot back.

"Never said I didn't. And if you ever call me 'toots' again. . ."

He laughed. "I love it when you're sinister. Very sexy. Don't you think, Jimbo?"

Bauer held up his hands. "Oh, no. You're not dragging me into this. No way."

O'Brien patted him on the back. "Wise move. So, anyway, how'd it end up, with the pushin' his son thing?"

Piza shrugged. "I guess it's okay. He admitted the kid's lied before, so I think he believed me. But boy, you've heard of the apple not falling far from the tree? While we were discussing this whole thing, he referred to Shirley Robinson as 'the colored girl'."

Bauer looked stunned. "He said that? In front of Mrs. Florino?"

"Oh yeah. I don't know what was more disturbing—him saying it, or that he seemed totally oblivious to the fact it was offensive."

A curt laugh from O'Brien. "You kill me sometimes, Piza. You really do. What'd you think, the Civil Rights Act somehow magically made everything better? Poof! No more bigotry. Yay! And for our next trick . . . world peace! Woo-hoo!"

A wide-eyed Piza said, "Jesus, tiger, take it easy. I'm on your side, remember?"

"Yeah, I know. This stuff pisses me off, that's all."

"Me too," Bauer concurred. After a few seconds, his tone lighter, he said, "But, all in all, it sounds like the meeting went okay. The guy doesn't sound *that* bad. Other than being a racist, of course." He turned to O'Brien. "Maybe your info was wrong, Colleen."

Piza jumped in before she could answer. "I don't think so. When he and I were in the hall after leaving the office, he pretty much asked me to confirm I hadn't touched his kid. He was smiling when he said it, but you wanna talk about 'dead eyes'? I reassured him, although I was babbling like an idiot."

"Told ya," O'Brien said.

"Know what else was weird? Appearances to the contrary, I think he's really rich. He's building a mall. Not working on one, mind you, building one . . . that he *owns* with some partners."

"Yeah, he's loaded," O'Brien agreed. "Paid for three rows of pews in the church, and put in a new gym floor. Although, from what I hear, it was his wife's idea. Woman's something of a social climber. They rewarded him with the next available seat on the school board. I think she pressed him to take that, too. From what I understand, he hardly ever shows up."

Bauer whistled. "Church pews? Gym floor? Lotta money. So, anyway, how'd you leave it with him?"

"We shook hands, and he said maybe we'd see each other again."

O'Brien tilted her head. "See. You made a new friend. Maybe when the mall is done, you'll be invited to the grand opening."

"Yeah, right. If I'm not already part of the foundation."

Joe DiGregorio's office at the mall construction site was as disheveled as him. He dislodged a sheaf of papers on the folding table he used as a desk, found the phone, and pressed the intercom. "Charlene, get me Bob Giacobbi."

A few seconds later, "Got him, boss. Line two."

"Yeah, Bobby. How's it goin'? . . . Good. Listen. You know a teacher at OLPT, name's Piza? . . . No shit, your kid's got 'im? Let me ask ya, you ever hear anythin' about him roughin' kids up? Not like beatin' the crap out of 'em, but like, ya know, pushin', shovin', things like that. . .

"Yeah, somethin' happened wit' him and Tommy. He says he didn't do nothin', and I think he's probably tellin' the truth. I mean, you know Tommy. . . Oh, okay. Probably *was* tellin' the truth, then.

"You know anythin' else about 'im? . . . Yeah, I don't care if he's a pain in the ass, Bobby. Everybody's a pain in the ass. But do me a favor, if you ever hear anythin', just lemme know. . . Great. Thanks. . . No, it was just the one thing with Tommy. Guy rubbed me the wrong way, is all. Like he was better than me. . . Ha! Screw 'im is right.

"Hey, when's that new backhoe I ordered comin' in? . . . Oh? I was expectin' it sooner. Lean on 'em a little, okay? . . . Good. And say hi to Sandy for me. She completely back on 'er feet? . . . Eh, that's great. Really had us worried there for a while. . . Yeah, I will, thanks. She's been buggin' me for us to get together. . . Okay, sounds good. And like I said, if you hear anythin' on this mook. . ."

30

The ringing phone jolted Piza out of sleep. He lunged for it, knocking it to the floor. He fumbled for the switch on the small lamp atop the end table. The muted glow was just enough for him to get his bearings, as he leaned over the side of the bed. He caught 1:23 on his alarm clock on the way up.

"Uh, yeah, who is. . . Frankie? What the hell, it's almost one thirty. Are you okay? . . . Well don't you have triple-A? . . . How could you let it expire? God, you're unbelievable. Where are you? . . . Are you kidding? What the hell are you doing at the Lombardi rest stop? . . . Don't get pissy with *me*. You're the one who needs the favor. . . Yeah, fine, okay. . . No, don't wait outside. It's freezing. Just hang out inside somewhere; I'll find you. Just let me throw some clothes on. . . Yeah, yeah. Thank me later. I'll be there as fast as I can." He hung up.

Damn Frankie. He should've junked that piece of crap a long time ago. God knows, he can afford a new one.

He dressed, and shoved a stick of gum in his mouth. Thinking about the phone call, he was glad his friend's car wouldn't start; he thought he'd detected the slightest slur in his speech.

When he exited his room, his mother was standing in front of her bedroom, clutching the front of her turquoise housecoat to keep it closed. Her tone laced with concern, she said, "What's goin' on, Anthony? Who was that? I heard the phone, but when it stopped I figured it was a wrong number, till I heard you movin' arou—"

"It's fine, Ma. Go back to bed. It was just Frankie. His car broke down and he needs a lift home."

"What's he doin' out on a Thursday night at this hour? Don't he have work tomorrow? And what about triple-A? Or his parents? Or his brother?"

"His triple-A expired. And I don't know where his parents or Jimmy are. It'll be fine. Please, go back to bed."

"Okay. All right. But you have school, so don't—"

"Ma, please. It's fine. I'm twenty-two."

"I know how old you are, Anthony. Don't mean I can't worry."

He smiled. "I know." He kissed her cheek. "See you later."

"Be careful. And put a coat on. And a hat and gloves. It's cold out."

It took him a little over twenty minutes to drive the twenty-two miles up the New Jersey Turnpike to the Vince Lombardi Service Area—the highway's northern end, near the George Washington Bridge.

Even at two in the morning there was some activity in the place; truckers mostly, but others as well. Probably grabbing coffee or gas going to, or coming from, their odd-hour jobs. Or maybe taking a breather during an overnight journey to wherever.

There weren't enough cars in the expansive parking lot to avoid it looking barren. Piza parked as close to the rest area building entrance as he could. Walking to it, the ten-degree temperature and whipping wind slapped away any lingering drowsiness.

As he entered, he spotted Frankie waving to him from a coffee stand. One look confirmed his suspicion that his friend had been drinking.

"Hey, Ton," he called out, before Piza was anywhere near him. He raised his paper coffee cup. "Want one?"

Piza wasn't smiling when he reached him. "No, thanks."

"Man, you made it here in record time. You're a lifesaver."

"I made it in record time because the sooner I got here, the sooner I could get back to bed."

Frankie's face fell. "Geez, are you mad at me, Ton?"

"Of course I'm mad at you, you moron. How could you let your triple-A lapse? And I'm even madder now because you've obviously been drinking. Maybe it's lucky your car wouldn't start. That's all you need is a DWI on your already stellar driving record. Christ, Frankie."

"I haven't had that much to drink, I swear," he responded, raising his right hand.

"Oh, please. This is me you're talking to. And another thing, how'd you end up in *this* place? Where the hell were you drinking?"

"I, I was in the Village."

Piza lowered his eyebrows. "You were drinking in Greenwich Village, on a work night. By yourself?"

"Yeah. I felt like getting outta Jersey for a couple of hours. Jesus, Ton, I don't get why you're so pissed."

"Fine. Forget it. Let's just get outta here."

"Okay. Sorry you're pissed at me. But, ya know, you're my best friend and all, and—"

"Frankie, I'd go to the ends of the earth for you if you were in trouble. You know that."

The plumber cut loose a goofy grin. "But not the Lombardi rest stop?"

Piza gave him an exasperated shake of the head. "This whole thing is ridiculous. Let's go."

They exited the building, both instantly reeling from a blast of frigid air. Frankie hugged himself. "Holy crap is it cold. Anyway, I promise I'll be a good boy from now on, swear to—"

"Wait a minute," Piza said, stopping in his tracks. "You were on your way home from the Village. So why didn't you take the Holland Tunnel? What possessed you to drive north and cross the GW, just to go back south again? That makes no sense."

Frankie averted his eyes. "Look, Ton. I'm freezing my ass off. Can you save the cross-examination, please? I just wanna get home."

Piza was about to answer when a state trooper, parked along a curb a few feet from the entrance, stepped out of his car. Piza had seen him on his way into the building, but hadn't thought anything of it.

The trooper approached them and looked at Frankie. "This your ride home?" he said, pointing to Piza.

"Uh, yeah. Thanks, officer."

Piza was baffled. He looked at Frankie, who didn't make eye contact. "Uh, hi, officer. Yes, I'm giving him a lift home. Is there — Was there some sort of problem?"

The cop glanced at him. "Your friend here escaped a bullet tonight. Next time he may not be so lucky."

Piza looked at Frankie. "What's going—"

Frankie interrupted him. "Uh, the officer knows I was drinking a little. He's cutting me a break, long as I don't try to get the car started tonight."

The trooper's brow furrowed. "Well, that wasn't the only

bullet was it?" Frankie's lack of response elicited a slight shake of the head from the officer. "Anyway, Mr. . . What was it?"

"Falco," Frankie mumbled.

"Mr. Falco. If I ever see you and your friend up here again, this *will* end differently."

Piza was taken aback. "Um, not for anything, officer, but I'm only here to give him a ride home. No disrespect, but why are you including me in this? I don't think—"

"Not you. The other guy. Drive safely." He went back to his car, then turned before getting in. "I'll just hang around until I see you leave."

Piza's eyes were blazing as he quickly walked away.

Frankie grabbed his arm; his friend shook it off. "Hey, slow down, Ton. Let me explain."

"What 'guy', Frankie? And where's your car?"

"Over there," he answered, pointing to the farthest corner of the parking lot. "Jesus, Tony, what difference does it make?"

Piza surveyed the area Frankie was pointing to, then ordered, "Just get in."

"Why're you all p.o.'d about where my car's parked?" Frankie asked as he closed the door.

Piza started the car and headed for the exit. "Your car's not broken down, is it? And who's the guy the cop mentioned?"

"Look, I was having my coffee and, and this kid was asking around if anyone was going to Delaware. He was looking to hitch a ride. So I said I was heading down the turnpike and I could give him a lift to Exit 12. And we started talking. That's all. What's the big—"

"So then what's the other 'bullet' the trooper was talking about?"

"I dunno. Maybe, ya know, the DWI thing."

"No, Frankie. The DWI *thing* was the first bullet. What's the second?"

"I swear I don't know what—"

"Do you think I'm an idiot? Is that what you think?"

"No. Of course not. But I still don't get why—"

Piza slammed the steering wheel. "You park your car as far away in the lot as possible; no other cars anywhere near it. Under a light pole with a broken lamp. So don't tell me you don't know what the second bullet is."

Frankie stared at his friend; his eyes hard. "What're you sayin'?"

Piza calmed himself. For years he'd imagined this moment would come. But not like this; not here. He stared ahead. "You were having sex in your car with some guy you picked up at a rest stop. That's what I'm saying."

Frankie ran his fingers through his hair. His right leg began shaking as he rocked back and forth in his seat. "Oh Christ. Oh Christ." His head snapped to the left. "You think I'm a faggot?" he screamed. "That's what you think, you son of a bitch? I'm a fuckin' faggot?"

Piza wiped Frankie's spittle from his right cheek, and took a deep breath. "I think my best friend is a gay man, and that he's been wrestling with it for years."

Frankie stopped moving; his body rigid, his voice menacing. "My best friend. That's what you're supposed to be, right? And you've been lookin' at me like I was a queer? For *years,* you piece of shit?"

Clenching the steering wheel, Piza said, "Calm down. This changes *nothing* between us, don't you get it? I don't care if you're gay. You're my best friend and I love you, and I don't give a shit if you like men, women, or whatever. But, goddammit, it's time you came to grips with who you are and stop torturing yourself. I just wish you had enough trust in me to say something."

Frankie glowered at him. "Let's get something straight, me and you. I . . . am . . . not . . . a goddamn *queer*."

"Look, Frankie—"

"Let me outta the car."

"What? What the hell are—"

"I said let me outta this car. If you think I'm a goddamn fag, I don't wanna be in the same car with you. Let me out."

"Are you crazy? We're on the—"

"I don't give a shit where we are. Pull over and let me out, you son of a bitch." He reached for the door handle. "Pull over or I'm openin' the door."

"Are you insane? Let go of that."

Frankie was wild-eyed. "No! You gonna keep sayin' I'm a fag, then I'm openin' the door unless you pull over."

"Listen to me, you goddamn lunatic," Piza yelled. "I don't care if you were sittin' there wearin' a garter belt and tryin' to blow in my ear, I'm not droppin' you off on the fucking New Jersey Turnpike."

Frankie glared at him. And then he started laughing. He laughed to the point where he could barely catch his breath.

Piza had no idea what was going on, yet he couldn't help but laugh with him. "What the hell are you laughing at, you idiot?"

Frankie was practically gasping, getting words out as best he could. "Sittin' . . . oh shit, my side hurts. Sittin' wearin' a garter belt? And, and blowin' in your ear? . . . Oh, Christ, I think I'm havin' a heart attack." He calmed a bit, then started laughing again to the point of tears. "Oh, God. I mean— I mean, who thinks like that? I may be screwed up, but *you*. . ."

Piza was now laughing as hard as his friend.

It took a minute or so for them to compose themselves. Frankie looked out the passenger window and sighed. "You tell anyone?"

"Of course not." His card party conversation with O'Brien didn't count.

"No, I know. I shouldn't of even asked." After a pause, "Why didn't you ever say anything, Ton? To me."

"Number one, I wasn't a hundred percent positive. And if I'd mentioned it to you and I was wrong. . . I mean look at the way you reacted just now. You'd have gone *completely* bat-shit."

A snicker from Frankie. "Probably. Yeah."

"You okay?"

"I dunno. In a way, I'm kinda relieved. But I'm also scared to death."

"Well, hell, yeah. You've been carrying this around for so long. Honestly, I don't know how you've kept your sanity."

"It's funny, ya know? You rationalize. It's like if you don't actually say the word. . . I mean, how messed up is that? I've been having sex with guys since I'm nineteen, but I kept telling myself I wasn't gay. I was experimenting. I was this, I was that."

Piza winced. "Now I wish I'd said something."

"Nah, this is on me, Ton. I needed to pick the time. I think that's probably why I called *you* tonight; not my father or Jimmy. I do trust you, and I knew if anybody'd understand. . . How about you? You okay? I kinda lost it there for a while."

"I'm fine. But I'm worried about you. Getting it out is one thing, but now you've gotta figure out what to do about it. And this thing with picking up guys at rest stops, I mean, Jesus, Frankie."

"No, I know. And don't worry, by the way, I use rubbers and all, so. . ."

"Yeah, but that's not the point, is it? I mean, thank God you used protection, but—"

"No, I get it. I can't keep doing this. I've gotta get a handle on how to deal with what I am."

"God, Frankie, do you hear yourself? Deal with *what* I am? How're you gonna deal with anything unless you realize there's nothing wrong with you?"

"I— I didn't mean it like that."

"Look, have you considered therapy? A professional to talk to?"

"Therapy? Not really. Plus, how would I do that?"

"Whaddya mean? You get a referral for a good psychologist and—"

"No, you don't understand. I mean the money part."

"What are you talking about? You've got phenomenal insurance. You telling me they don't cover psychological treatment?"

"No, they do. But if I put it through the union, someone's gonna find out sooner or later. Maybe not the being gay part, but even if it gets out I'm seeing a shrink. Then what?"

"Then screw 'em, that's what. You can't get help because a few cretins might giggle behind your back?"

"I know, but—"

"And don't get me wrong. I know this won't be a walk in the park. But geez, Frankie, you can't back off because of that."

"And what about my parents? What's this gonna do to them?"

"You and Jimmy are their world. Whaddya think, they're gonna stop loving you? Banish you from the family? Come on."

"No, I guess not. But if my father or Jimmy start getting their balls busted over any of this. . . I, I don't wanna do that to them. It's not fair to put them—"

"Oh come on. Your father's one of the toughest guys I've ever met. And Jimmy's no slouch either. You've gotta talk to them. They have a right to know . . . if they don't already."

Frankie looked stunned. "Christ. You think that's possible? That they know?"

"Yeah, I do. Listen, what you wanna do with anybody else, that's something you've gotta work on. And I really believe therapy'll help you with that. But your parents and Jimmy? You owe them the truth. And I think they deserve to see you happy."

Frankie gazed out the side window. "I feel like a ton of bricks just fell on me, Ton. But I'm glad, if that makes any sense. I think it's gonna take me a while to sort through all this. But it has to get done, I know that."

"Good. So, where were you really? Before you went to the Lombardi."

"Murp's. Then, I dunno, I just found myself driving."

"Makes more sense, at least. But what I really wanna know is why that trooper didn't arrest you, when he caught you . . . ya know."

Frankie turned to his friend and grinned. "Ready for this? I probably found the one state trooper in Jersey who's got a gay brother."

"Get the hell outta here."

"Hand to God, Ton. That's why he let it slide this time."

"I swear, leave it to you. I can't believe he admitted it."

Through a shrug, Frankie said, "What can I tell ya?" A few moments later, he cleared his throat. "Listen, Ton, I don't know how to begin to—"

"Stop. You're my best friend. You don't ever have to thank me."

"Yeah, I do. Being able to talk to you about this. . . To, uh, to finally get this out. It, uh, it means more than. . ." He looked away again. A sob strained not to be heard.

The intensity of his friend's suffering struck Piza full force. Breathing became staccato bursts of air, heaving his chest and escaping his lips as testaments to his love for this man. Fighting tears, he searched for the right words, settling on, "Look, if you're gonna go all waterworks on me, I'll open the damn door for you myself . . . ya big fairy."

Gazing out the passenger window, Frankie laughed as he wiped his eyes.

31

"Seriously, Ton. I'm fine. And we can't mess up tradition. Super Bowl at your place; Pro Bowl here. No matter what."

Piza was a little surprised when Frankie called him that Saturday afternoon to confirm he was coming over for the Pro Bowl the next day. He hadn't contacted his friend since Thursday night's turbulence, figuring he might want time to let things settle in. He was relieved at the upbeat tone.

"You're right, Frankie. Nothing must ever impede our sacred rituals."

"There ya go. See ya tomorrow."

"It's a date. Not like a 'date' date. I don't want you getting your hopes up."

"Could you *possibly* be a bigger asshole?"

"With practice? Probably."

Lou and Chicki Falco were like second parents to Piza. Mary

often teased that he spent more time at their house than his own. The Falco men were die-hard union, and Frankie's dad had risen high up in the plumbers' local. He was tough and bright. A voracious reader, the lack of a college education rarely stopped him from being the smartest guy in the room.

Piza arrived at Frankie's on Sunday, carrying a plate of breaded veal cutlets and two loaves of Italian bread. His friend's older brother, Jimmy, answered the door. Handsome and blessed with an infectious smile, you'd be hard-pressed to find anyone who didn't like him.

Jimmy had spent two years in Vietnam, a situation Piza and his immediate group of friends hadn't encountered—Jeff because of his eye, the rest merely because their respective birthdays placed them toward the back of the draft lottery.

Unlike many others who made it back, Jimmy appeared to be none the worse for wear, except for the chain-smoking. Yet, his family and closest friends detected a melancholy that wasn't there before. If anyone could understand, it was Mr. Falco, who'd been wounded in World War II. Discussing Jimmy one day, he'd told Piza: "War robs you, Tony. It takes some of your light. And you never really get it back."

As they entered the kitchen, Jimmy announced, "Eh, Ma, look what the cat dragged in."

Mrs. Falco kissed Piza while relieving him of the food.

"You lost weight from when I saw you at Christmas, Mrs. Falco."

She struck a model's pose and ran her arms through the air, the length of her body. "I've been on a diet. Ta-da!"

"Well, you look amazing. Next time I come over I may need a magnifying glass to find you."

She blushed and waved off the compliment. "Okay, now take these pigs-in-a-blanket into the family room. Frankie and Lou are settin' things up. Jimmy, take these pizza rolls."

Lou Falco's face lit up when Piza entered. "Eh, there he is. What's cookin'?"

"Um, cocktail franks, pizza rolls, and veal cutlets, Mr. Falco."

"Always with the wisecracks. Never lose that sense of humor, Tony. It'll get you places."

Frankie grimaced. "God, don't encourage him, Dad. You don't have to see him as much as I do."

"Good to see you too, dipstick," said a grinning Piza.

Mr. Falco laughed. "You two, I swear. Never stops." He rubbed his hands together. "Okay, so who's everyone pickin', NFC or AFC?"

"I'm goin' AFC," Jimmy answered.

"Ditto," from Frankie.

Piza scrunched his face. "I'm gonna say NFC. True-blue Giants fan that I am—and thought you guys were, until now—I gotta stick with their conference. How about you, Mr. Falco?"

"Sorry, Tony. AFC."

Piza feigned distress. "I'm feeling a little abandoned here. But, ya know, crunch time is when you find out who your *real* friends are." He hadn't meant to reference anything other than the game, but Frankie gave him a faint nod.

The contest wasn't particularly exciting—the AFC won on five field goals—but something happened during the game that had Piza at the edge of his seat. Since the Pro Bowl is basically for show, hitting is rarely on a par with a game that counts. At one point, Jimmy's aggravation at the lack of intensity resulted in, "Why don't they just call it the Pansy Bowl?"

Piza cringed and looked for Frankie's reaction. His friend was laughing. *Frankie's putting up a great front. If they only knew.*

After the game, Frankie walked his friend to his car. "They know."

Piza stopped short. "What? How? Did you—"

"Yep. Last night."

"Holy shit."

"Turns out you were right. My parents knew. Jimmy said he'd never been sure, but he had an idea. He was actually pretty funny. After my parents went to bed, he said: 'All these years I figured you didn't have a steady girl 'cause you were butt ugly.' Then he gave me a noogie."

"Ah. The universal symbol of fraternal affection. But if he knows, then what was with the Pansy Bowl comment?"

Frankie shrugged. "It's Jimmy. Sometimes he just comes out with stuff. Plus he just doesn't associate the word 'pansy' with me. It probably never crossed his mind. I'm still the younger brother who can kick his ass."

"That's true. So, what was everyone's reaction when you actually came out and said it?"

"Well, my mom put her arms around me and kissed me. That's when she told me they already knew. Dad said he was glad I was finally comfortable sharing it with them."

"Did you mention your concerns? About work and all?"

"I did. Dad looked at me like I had three heads. He said to do what I had to do, and if anyone gave me a hard time, he and Jimmy'd be there to back me up."

"Honestly, I'd expect nothing less. Good people, your family."

"Yeah, they are." After a pause, "You know Dad's not really a touchy-feely kinda guy. But before he went to bed, he comes over to me and, and kisses me on the top of the head, and he says: 'I love ya, kid.'" His voice caught. "How lucky am I, ya know?"

Piza was gratified Frankie's revelation had gone so well. But, driving home, that joy gave way to the disquieting realization that Monday was sixth-grade library day. He'd be alone with Sister Theresa again.

Despite his recent efforts to purge any feelings for his co-worker, the knot in his stomach Monday morning evidenced his dismal failure. He'd managed to avoid any significant interaction with her since the last library session, their only encounters being the occasional "Hi" and a wave when passing in the halls, or in the teachers' lounge. But now, they'd be back where it started.

His class was the first to arrive at the library. He sat at a back table, opened his book, and read the same paragraph five times.

Sister Theresa's class arrived shortly after. He didn't look up. After a couple of minutes, a quick peek revealed she was talking to Mrs. Fitzsimmons. *Okay, maybe she's gonna stay up there. After last time, she probably realizes what a pathetic lap dog I am and doesn't wanna put me through agony again.*

She started walking toward the table.

Or not.

Pulling out the seat next to him, she said, "Um, pardon me, sir, but is this chair spoken for?"

Clever, using my own words against me. Touché, mademoiselle.

With a grin that would have scared The Joker, he stood. "Well, hello there, Sister. Seems like I haven't seen you in ages. Take a load off." *Take a load off? Classy, Tony.*

With an animated nod, she responded, "Seems like that for me too. Strange, isn't it?"

"Strange indeed."

She glanced at his open book. "What are you reading?"

"Um, *A Fairy Tale of New York*. It's a new book by J.P. Donleavy."

"Oh, sure. He wrote *The Ginger Man*. I read it in school. Terrific writer. Maybe I can borrow this when you're done?"

"Uh, yeah. Of course."

She brushed away the ever-present rebel strands of blonde hair from her forehead. "He had another book I've been meaning to read, if just for the title alone. *The Beastly Beatitudes of Balthazar B*. Gotta love it. Sometimes I wonder. . ."

She was still talking, but he was in another place. *She's amazing. And as out of reach as ever. Ha. Is it possible I have this God thing all wrong? Maybe he's up there ladling out some heavy-duty irony to punish the doubter. Kind of hoped if you* were *actively involved, you'd be more open-minded.*

". . .and so I'm resolving here and now to catch up on my reading. You're my witness."

"Yeah, uh, gotta make time for reading. Yep." He sighed.

There was an awkward pause, then she broke it. "So, are you and Mother John getting along better? Seems so. At least better than back when."

"Uh, yeah, if by 'back when' you mean a few weeks ago."

"Good."

"I mean, I'm not planning on sending her a birthday invitation this summer, but. . ."

She smiled. "Let me tell you something about Mother. For twenty-five years she taught third grade up in New York State somewhere. Excellent teacher, from what I understand. Tough, but fair."

A modified eye roll from Piza.

"Don't make faces, Anthony. Maybe she wasn't lovable, but she cared."

"So how'd she end up here?"

"She was directed to take the job by Mother Superior . . . you know, the head of the order. She didn't like it, but she had no choice."

"I don't buy that. There's always— I'm sorry. Go on."

"Anyhow, I get the feeling this job changed her. I mean, I know she still cares, but I think she's probably more cynical than before. And then, of course, Monsignor Lombardo came along and things got even— Know what, let me keep my mouth shut."

"No, no. I'd love to hear more about the Prince of OLPT."

"What I'm saying, wisenheimer, is cut her some slack. Okay?"

"Fine. Anything to make you happy."

Her eyes gleamed. "Remember you said that. I may just hold you to it."

He knew he was blushing and needed a distraction. Enter mock concern. "Now hold on a minute." He feigned giving it some thought. "Well, okay. But only if you promise not to go overboard with your requests. Even *my* largess has its limits, you know. Deal?"

"Deal." She extended her hand.

The gesture caught him off-guard, panic setting in at the thought of touching her. As he cautiously took her hand, he couldn't will away the desire and tenderness that raced through him, a euphoria tempered only by the fear his sweaty palm may have ruined the moment.

Her eyes never left his. "And, Anthony . . . we should talk more. I enjoy our conversations."

Screw keeping my distance. "Yeah. Me too."

"So what's with you and Sister Theresa?" O'Brien asked, pulling one of the student desks closer to Piza's, a few minutes after dismissal. It was exactly a month after that fateful library day.

"Whaddya mean?"

"I mean, it seems— Can you please take your feet off your desk, so I don't have to look around them to see your face?"

"I'm *comfortable*." He huffed and sat upright. "Happy now?"

"Delirious. Anyway, she used to sit with us at lunch maybe what, twice a month? But for the last few weeks, it's more like three or four times a week."

"So?"

"Listen, I love Sister Theresa. You know that. And I don't completely dislike you."

"Gee, thanks. What's your point?"

"My point is I sense something's goin' on."

He was getting annoyed. "Like what, exactly?"

"Don't get your panties in a bunch. I'm not accusin' you of anything."

"Doesn't sound like that."

"God, you're such a prima donna."

"Panties. Prima donna. I'm sensing my masculinity's under attack." He wasn't smiling.

"Quite the contrary. And I think that may be the problem."

He leaned forward, clasping his hands and resting them on the desk. "Of all the people I know, you're one of the least likely to beat around the bush. So why don't you just say what's on your mind."

"Okay. I'm pickin' up kind of a vibe between the two of you."

"That's your idea of a straight answer?"

"Fine. Do you have feelings for each other?"

He'd known the question was coming, as soon as the conversation started. It made no difference; he was flustered. "You mean like— Are you saying— Like 'feeling' feelings? Are you nuts? She's a nun."

O'Brien held eye contact. "Is that a no?"

"*Yeah,* that's a no. Jesus, she's a nun."

"I know. You said that already. She's also a woman."

"You know what, screw you, Colleen. Have you had this talk with her?"

"No. Because if I was wrong, she'd be embarrassed. More likely, distraught."

"What, and you assumed I wouldn't?"

"Certainly not like her."

He looked toward the windows. "Wow."

"Listen, I care about both of you. And if there's nothing there, okay. I apologize. But if there is, I'm just tellin' you to be careful. And I'm not talkin' about anything physical, I know both of you better than that. But emotionally . . . there's nothing good that could come of it. And I'd hate like hell to see that happen to you guys."

He continued looking out the windows. “Thanks for your unsolicited input.”

She got up. “I’m only tryin’ to help.” He didn’t respond. “Look, are we okay? You and I?”

Silence.

She walked out, but her words lingered in the vacated space.

32

You knew damn well O'Brien would find out. She's too smart; too observant. Piza glanced at the alarm clock for the umpteenth time since going to bed. 6:44. He hadn't slept all night. A glass of warm milk; reading about the magic of molds from a college biology textbook. No sleep-inducing maneuver had slowed the torrent of jangled thoughts zipping around in his brain.

Pulling back the covers, he swung his legs over the side of the bed. The effort seemed to exhaust him. He sat there, motionless, in his boxer shorts and t-shirt, hands resting on his knees. Staring at nothing.

After a few moments, life returned to his body. He slapped his thighs, vigorously massaged his scalp, and stood up. "Okay, stud, let's get this show on the road. One more day, then you've got the weekend to recuperate. You'll figure all this out. A quick shower, then some coffee. Strong and black. James Bond style."

Descending the stairs, he pinned his hopes on the coffee, the shower having done little to improve his condition. As he reached the bottom, he saw Angelo rummaging through the front hall closet.

"Morning, Pop. Aren't you late?"

"No. Manny's opening the store today. I can't find my spring jacket."

"Here, Pop, let me look. Why do you want it? It's February, remember? Ah, here it is."

"Thanks, Anthony. Uh, it's supposed to be sixty-something today."

"No kidding? I may skip a coat too. So, sounds like Manny's working out."

"Yeah. Good kid. Hard worker. His English is gettin' pretty good too. He's takin' night courses to improve. Plus, I'm pickin' up a little Spanish." He winked. "Pretty soon I'll be able to get a job at the U.N. See ya tonight."

Piza kissed his father. "Okay, Pop, see ya then."

"See ya tonight, Mary," Angelo called out.

She popped her head out of the kitchen. "Okay. Drive careful. And why are you wearin'—"

He was already out the door.

"Morning, Ma. Patty still sleeping?"

"You didn't hear her snorin' on your way down? Like a train whistle, that one. Want some eggs?"

"No, thanks. I promise I'll grab something at school. Ah, dammit."

"What?"

"I left my keys in my room. Do me a favor, Ma, stick some coffee in a thermos for me? Black, nothing in it." He headed toward the stairs.

"Okay. You sure you want it 'black' black? How about a little sugar at least?"

"Uh, okay, maybe a smidge."

"How much?"

"Um, I dunno. Four teaspoons? And maybe splash a little milk in there."

"I hope all of you wished George Washington a happy birthday this morning," Piza said when his class finished the Pledge of Allegiance.

Halfway down into his seat, Matt Majinsky raised his hand.

"What can I do ya for, Mr. Majinsky? You look confused."

"What else is new?" from Kevin Davis.

"Was that really necessary, Mr. Davis?"

The boy shrugged.

Majinsky glanced at Davis, then continued. "Anyway, if his birthday's today, shouldn't we have off?"

"We had Monday off for his birthday, Mr. Majinsky. How many days would you like?"

"Um, two?"

"Nice try. Plus, it was a 'rhetorical' question. Good vocabulary word for you guys to check out, by the way." He spelled it for them. "Okay, take out your science books. We're going to tackle gravity."

"Oh, Sir Isaac Newton," William Reilly blurted out.

"Correct, Mr. Reilly."

Ralph Restivo wore a wry smile. "Yeah, but mostly he's famous for cookies, right, Mr. Piza? Ya know, Fig Newtons?"

When the laughter died down, Davis muttered, "Ha, ha. You're so funny, Restivo."

Piza locked eyes with the boy. "Get up on the wrong side of the bed today, Mr. Davis? Lose the comments. Understood?"

The boy's expression revealed nothing.

"I said, *understood*?"

"Yeah."

"Excuse me?"

He made a face. "Yes, sir."

What the hell's going on?

A few minutes before the lunch bell, the loudspeaker crackled and Mrs. Florino's dulcet tones filled the air. "In light of today's temperate conditions, teachers will have the option of letting their students go outdoors after lunch. Again, this is optional. I repeat—optional. Thank you."

Okay, just so I'm clear on this, Mrs. Florino. . .

As he looked around the classroom, imprisoned eyes pleaded for parole. "Fine, you can go outside. Now stop staring at me. It's creepy."

"Sixty-degree warmth, and trees still barren of life. Almost surreal. I dunno. Maybe not."

Piza's observation came as he stood by a picnic table in the schoolyard at recess. Sister Theresa sat on the table, her feet resting on the bench, clasped hands nestled in her lap.

"If you hadn't hedged your bet there, I'd have thought you had the soul of a poet."

"I have the soul of a *skeptical* poet. Still counts."

She arched an eyebrow. "I'm not so—"

Shouts drew their attention to the basketball courts, and Piza saw Vinny Pinto running toward him. He moved to intercept the boy. "What's going—"

"You need to get over there, Mr. Piza. It's Davis and Giacobbi."

The teacher bolted to the courts, where his two students were wrestling on the macadam.

Amid the gasps—and some cheers—of the onlookers, Piza moved to separate them, almost catching an elbow to the face for his efforts.

Pinto looked like he was ready to jump in to help, and managed to catch his teacher's eye. Piza nodded. As soon as the opportunity presented itself, the boy grabbed Giacobbi under the arms and dragged him a few feet away. Piza did likewise with Davis.

In the interim, Sister Theresa and O'Brien had run over. The nun saw Giacobbi's nose was bloodied, and pulled some tissues out of her sleeve. "Good thing I carry these around," she murmured to no one in particular. "Sit up, Robert, and look at the sky. Hold these over your nose." He did as he was told, but kept glancing at Davis.

As soon as Piza let go of him, Davis got up. Dusting himself off, he shouted, "Better watch out, pretty boy. Your hair's messed up." He spat in Giacobbi's direction.

The teacher grabbed the boy's right arm and spun him toward him. "Have you lost your mind? What's gotten into you today?" Davis tried to pull away, but Piza wouldn't release his grip. "I'm not letting go until you calm down. Got it?" He kept the hold until he saw the boy's breathing slow a bit.

Giacobbi stood and wiped the remnants of blood. "Punk. Can't win without fouling, can ya?"

"Screw you," from a glaring Davis.

Piza moved between them. "Knock it off! Both of you." He turned to Sister Theresa and motioned with his chin toward Giacobbi. "He okay?"

"I think so. The bleeding's stopped. How he didn't get any on his clothes is beyond me."

O'Brien lightly touched Piza's arm. "Why don't you take them inside. Sister and I will watch the rest of your kids."

He held her gaze. "Okay. Thanks, Colleen." He hoped she realized he was telling her everything was all right between them. Her eyes and a nod said she did.

Piza walked the boys into the school, one combatant on each side of him. They were quiet, but still visibly seething. Two kids mixing it up didn't really bother him. It happens. What troubled him was the look in their eyes as they fought. It was primal. *Do these kids really hate each other that much?*

When they reached the classroom, both boys went to their usual seats, looking down, no eye contact. Piza paced in front of his desk. "Either of you wanna tell me what that was all about? Because that wasn't a fight out there, that was war."

Giacobbi suddenly became animated. "He hip-checked me while I was going in for a layup. Then he hit me in the face when I was taking a jump shot."

"That was an accident," Davis hurled back.

Piza stopped and glared at both of them. "Don't give me some story about who did what. I know you two have history, so let's get it straightened out now. Mr. Davis, you've been on edge all day. If it's got something to do with Mr. Giacobbi, then let's talk it out, so you guys can put this behind you."

The boy mumbled something Piza couldn't make out.

"I'm sorry, say again."

"I said 'it's nothing'."

"You know, Mr. Davis, I've tried to be as understanding with you as possible. I mean, even after that ridiculous tough-guy stunt you pulled on the first day of school. I'm trying to help here, and—"

"I don't need your damn help, okay? And stop tryin' to be my father."

"What are you talking—"

"I've already got a damn father, okay, and he sucks, so just— Just stop, okay?" His face had turned crimson, and he seemed on the verge of hyperventilating.

Christ, what the hell's going on here? He took a few steps toward the child. "Kevin. Listen to me. Calm down. Tell me what's going on." He realized whatever it was had to have occurred after school yesterday, because he'd been fine during class all day.

I've gotta get Giacobbi out of here. Davis'll never open up if he stays.

And what if all this is somehow supposed to be confidential? "Mr. Giacobbi, I'll speak with you later. But for now, I think maybe you should rejoin—"

"My father sucks too, Kevin."

Davis turned, quizzically eyeing the other boy. "What?"

"I said *my* dad sucks too."

Piza's head was spinning. He'd finally pushed Giacobbi's family problems to the back of his mind, and when he last spoke to the boy, things had supposedly improved. Clearly, something had happened. And now Davis, with whatever was going on with him. *I have no idea how the hell to handle this.*

But he had to make a decision. *If there'd be no problem with them discussing this between themselves outside of school, why should there be one here, right?*

He looked at Davis. "You look puzzled, Kevin."

Davis shifted his attention back to his teacher. "Uh, no. It's, uh, it's just that his"—facing Giacobbi again—"um, your father's loaded. I mean, I've passed your house. Your mom's got a Jag. How bad can it be?" There was no malice in his tone.

"He treats my mom like garbage. Wednesday night he shoved her against a wall. And he's been yelling at her for a while. Again."

The revelation dazed Piza. "Why didn't you say something, Robert? Maybe—" His privacy concern reemerged. "Um, I really think I should talk to you guys separately, so why don't—"

"I don't care if Kevin stays, Mr. Piza. It's fine. If he wants to." He looked at Davis, who nodded in response.

"I'm okay talking in front of Robert, too," Davis said.

I dunno. Maybe these kids can help each other. "All right. Uh, Robert, has your mom talked to anyone about this?"

"I don't think so." He shrugged. "Never has before, so. . . But she's been going out a couple of nights a week. I guess to get away from him. Some card club. Bridge, I think."

"How does your dad act when she's not there?"

"Okay. Mostly, he ignores me, so I stay in my room a lot. Half the time he falls asleep watching TV. I'll be all right, Mr. Piza. Don't worry."

Too late for that, kid. Piza took a student desk midway between the boys, reversed it, and sat. He motioned to Davis. "Kevin?"

The child took a deep breath. "So last night my old man shows up. After, I dunno, like three years? Just shows up. Around five thirty."

Piza smirked. "How'd your mom feel about that?"

"Are you kiddin'? She wouldn't let him in the house. I didn't go to the door right away, but I could hear them talkin'. My mom was really mad, and he kept tellin' her to calm down, which she wouldn't. So then *he* got mad and he said he wasn't there to see *her.* He wanted to take me to dinner. That's when I went to the door. I kind of stayed a little behind her, but I could see him and all." The child seemed to get lost in his thoughts.

Piza attempted to bring him back. "Then what?"

"Oh, yeah. So he gives me this big smile. And then he says—I guess he was kinda tellin' both of us—that he quit drinkin'."

"Was your mom buying that? Were you?"

"Well, he didn't *look* drunk. Not like I remember. And then, I'm not sure why, but I told my mom I wanted to go. She started to cry. Not a lot, just a little bit. I almost changed my mind. But she turned her back on him, and then she put her hand on my cheek, and just with her lips she said, 'Go'. It— It was kinda like she knew I needed to do it. So, anyway, she told him to bring me back in an hour, and that if it was a minute later she'd call the cops." He smiled. "She can be tough, my mom."

Piza smiled as well. "Yeah, moms are like that. So then what happened?"

The child's expression changed; a woeful anger. "He wanted to take me someplace fancy, but all I wanted was a burger. So we went to this diner I like, a couple of blocks from our house. He apologized like a zillion times for leavin'. Told me he'd—what'd he say? Oh, yeah—turned his life around, and was finally makin' money, which might've been true, 'cause he did have a pretty cool new car. Then he said he wanted to get back in my life; that he hoped I'd give him another chance. So I decided I would . . . like an idiot."

Giacobbi had been watching in silence, seemingly mesmerized by Davis's story. But now he jumped in. "Why were you an idiot? He, he wanted to be your father again. He cared. He came back."

Davis tossed a scowl at his classmate. "I was an idiot because on the way home we stopped for gas. He went in that little store they have, to buy cigarettes, and while he was inside I was pokin' around the new car. I opened the glove box. Wanna know what was in there, under a bunch of maps? A pint of vodka. Wanna know what it was sittin' on top of? A gun."

Giacobbi's jaw dropped, and Piza shot out of his chair. "What the hell? Are you okay? What'd you do?"

"Yeah, I'm good, Mr. Piza. There was a pay phone on the corner, so I called my mom." A mischievous grin. "Took the change outta his coin holder to call her."

Giacobbi got up and moved to a desk closer to Davis's. "What happened when your dad came out of the store?"

"Well, I mean, first he looked confused, when I wasn't in the car. Then when he finally saw me he ran up and asked me what was wrong and all. I told him to leave me alone, and that if he didn't I'd call the cops and tell 'em to look in his glove box. Can't believe the jerk left it unlocked. Anyway, that's when my mom came."

Giacobbi asked, "What'd he say to her?"

"Zip. As soon as she got there, he took off. Candy ass."

Piza sat down again. *Selfish, manipulative son of a bitch is more like it.* "Did you tell your mother what you saw?"

"Yeah. I wasn't gonna, but I figured this was too big not to tell her. She wanted to call the cops, but I convinced her not to. But I said if he ever showed up again, then. . ."

Giacobbi shook his head. "I think your dad may actually suck as bad as mine."

Piza broke the resulting silence. "I'm sorry, Kevin. Robert. I really am. You shouldn't have to deal with this kind of stuff." He wore his frustration. "I wish there was something I could do."

Both boys attempted to talk at once, then laughed at their jumbled effort. They looked at each other, and Giacobbi extended a hand toward his classmate.

"You did help," Davis said. "Most teachers would've just dragged us into the office. You let me— You let *us* talk, and I feel a little better. Doesn't mean my old man's not still a jerk, but, ya know. And I'm sorry for how I talked to you before. I didn't mean it."

"I know."

Giacobbi continued the dialogue. "Kevin's right, Mr. Piza. I know if I talk to you, you're gonna listen. And, I'm not trying to suck up here, okay, but I'm glad you're my teacher. I like coming to school." He shrugged. "Anyway, that's how I feel."

Davis nodded.

Wow. Wasn't expecting that. "Thanks. Both of you. That means a lot to me."

He could hear the faint sound of his class coming up the hall. "The troops are on their way back." He returned the desk to its original position, then waggled his index finger between the boys. "And you two, you good?"

They looked at each other.

"I'm good," Davis replied.

"Me too," from Giacobbi.

Still unsure whether he'd run afoul of some school protocol, Piza said, "I'd prefer this discussion stays here, all right? Whoever asks, just tell them you got a major chewing out."

"Sure," Giacobbi responded.

Davis gave a thumbs-up.

A satisfied nod from Piza accompanied, "Okay." He smiled. "Now, do your best to look repentant."

He would discuss this with O'Brien, about whether there was anything he could do. But he already knew what she'd say, just as he knew she'd be right once more. He only wished being right made things easier.

33

There were no repercussions from the schoolyard brawl. No notes from parents on either side; no mention of it from Mother John. But the incident had produced a camaraderie between Davis and Giacobbi, and that seemed to generate an even greater sense of harmony in the class.

Things stayed on an even keel through March: no major crises; no eye-popping revelations; no life-altering events, at least to his knowledge. He did vary the routine a little by allowing the kids to do a voluntary extra-credit project. They could research a topic, then present their findings to the class at the end of the month.

About half the students took advantage of the opportunity, some choosing to pair up. Ralph Restivo and Vinny Pinto gave a presentation on the comedians Abbott and Costello, and performed a hilarious version of their famous "Who's On First" routine.

Davis and Giacobbi spoke about basketball star Kareem Abdul-Jabbar, who'd grown up in nearby Manhattan. Shirley

Robinson discussed her favorite author, Judy Blume, and read some passages from her book *Are You There God? It's Me, Margaret.*

The most impressive presentation was Karen Jablonski's. Piza hadn't forgotten his post-Thanksgiving suggestion about doing a lesson on the women's rights movement. He felt this extra-credit exercise might be the perfect opportunity for her to showcase her grandmother's accomplishments—perhaps now more important to her than ever, what with the woman's recent passing.

Piza knew O'Brien had strong feelings on the issue, and had invited her to watch. He'd sensed his student's presentation was going to be special when she asked if she could have an overhead projector in the classroom.

She started with the Seneca Falls Convention of 1848—widely believed to be the first major women's rights conference—and followed the rights movement through the passage of the Nineteenth Amendment in 1920, prohibiting any U.S. citizen from being denied the right to vote based on their sex. Pictures of notable leaders and historical documents supplemented her narrative.

At the conclusion, she placed a black-and-white photograph on the glass platen of the projector. The frayed image appearing on the screen revealed a young girl wearing a dark, high-neckline dress adorned with a brooch at the throat. Dark hair loosely piled atop her head and knotted in place, she had large, vibrant eyes and wore the inception of a smile that reminded Piza of the *Mona Lisa.*

The child pointed to the screen. "This is my grandma. She was nineteen-years-old when this picture was taken. She was"—her voice caught—"so pretty. Don't ya think?"

Piza swallowed hard, then glanced at O'Brien, who was making no effort to hide the tears streaking her cheeks. The girl's classmates were reverently nodding in answer to her question.

The jarring lunch bell did little to dispel the solemnity of the setting. Piza lightly coughed, for no reason other than to compose himself. "Great, great presentation, Ms. Jablonski. Wonderful. Okay, people. Off to lunch. Ms. Jablonski, I'll help you gather your exhibits."

O'Brien touched his shoulder. "I'll leave you to it."

He nodded, then started toward the front of the room. As he neared the child he saw her remove the photo from the projector, kiss the tips of her fingers, and lightly press them to the picture.

He pivoted as subtly as possible and walked back a couple of feet, not wanting to intrude on the moment. A few seconds later he turned back, helped her pack up, and congratulated her again on a job well done.

"Thanks, Mr. Piza. And thanks for letting me do this. My mom and I got to go through Grandma's things together, preparing for this. It was really nice."

"You're very welcome. And I have no doubt your grandmother is very proud of you."

The girl smiled and left to join her classmates.

Piza joined his teachers' lounge crew, and sat next to O'Brien as she was telling Bauer and Sister Theresa about Jablonski's presentation. "Hey," she said to him. "I was fillin' them in on Karen Jablonski. You wanna—"

"No, not at all. You tell it. It's fine."

When she finished, Bauer said, "Sounds like the kid did an amazing job."

O'Brien nodded in mid-sip of her iced tea. "Let me tell ya. If she ever decides to go to grad school, she's got the basic research for a thesis practically done."

Piza put down his sandwich. "But that wasn't all. When I was going up there to help her, after you left, she kissed the picture of her grandmother, with her fingertips. I thought my heart was gonna break."

Sister Theresa said, "Are you okay?"

"I'm fine. The whole thing was just really moving."

O'Brien nudged him. "See, you're not so tough."

He blushed. "Tougher than you, ace. I thought I was gonna have to throw you a life preserver."

She stuck her tongue out at him, prompting a laugh from all.

Ten minutes before the lunch hour ended, Piza excused himself. "Sorry to eat and run, but I've gotta get that projector back to its official residence."

Sister Theresa stood as well. "Know what, I'll take a walk with you, if that's okay. Feel like stretching my legs a bit."

"Sure. Little company never hurts. See you guys later."

Watching them walk toward the door, O'Brien observed him say something that made the nun laugh. She also noticed two of the lay teachers watching them. One raised her eyebrows to the other, and O'Brien paled.

Bauer must have noticed the change in her, because he asked, "You okay, Colleen?"

"Uh, yeah, I'm fine. Just remembered something I need to take care of. Not a problem."

"Hey, got a sec?" An out of breath O'Brien was running toward Piza as he reached his car.

"For you? Always, my dear."

"Can we sit in your car? I'm freezin'."

A mischievous leer. "Front seat or back?"

"I'm serious, Tony."

"Oh. Okay. Of course." He held the passenger door open, waited until she was settled, then went around to the driver's side.

He was scarcely seated when he said, "What's going on? You all right?"

"Yeah, I'm fine. But I'm not so sure you are."

"Why aren't I fine? What's wrong?"

She grimaced. "Look, I don't want a replay of our little tiff in your classroom last month, okay? But you need to hear this."

"Just tell me already."

"Okay. When you and Sister Theresa were leavin' the teachers' lounge at lunch today, people noticed. Two people at least—Binetti and O'Rourke. You said something that made Sister laugh, and O'Rourke did that raised eyebrows thing to Binetti."

"That's it? Why is that a problem? O'Rourke's an old maid, who probably has nothing better to do than raise her eyebrows at stuff. And Binetti is the faculty busybody, who no one likes. So why would I care what *they* think?"

Her sigh was laced with frustration. "You know, for a smart guy, you can be incredibly dense. It's precisely because of who they are that you should care. They don't keep things to themselves. And as much as nobody may like them, *everybody* likes a juicy scandal. Or better yet, the hint of one. Anticipation is half the fun."

He peered down his nose at her. "Scandal. You're comparing my walking out of the teachers' lounge with Sister Theresa to a scandal. Seriously, Colleen? Don't you think you're being the slightest bit paranoid?"

"*I'm* not sayin' it's a scandal. I'm talkin' about perception. You two spend a lot of time together."

"Listen, I'm not gonna let 'perception' dictate how I spend my time or who I spend it with." His face was flushed; his breathing rapid. "And if a couple of jaded old biddies wanna see something sordid in my friendship with Sister Theresa, that's *their* problem."

"Calm down, okay? It's me here. But you talk about friendship. If the gossip starts, how's that gonna affect *her*, Tony?"

He stared straight ahead for a few seconds, then faced her. "You know the last thing I want is to bring any pain into her life. But what would you like me to do? Ignore her?"

"I'm not sayin' ignore her. Maybe just don't hang around with her as much at lunchtime, or if we're outside for recess. I dunno."

"That's fine for outside. But what about lunch? Am I supposed to tell her not to sit with us? *You* wanna tell her that?" He ran a hand through his hair. "And dammit, I don't want her to stop sitting with us."

She clicked her tongue. "Okay. Diplomacy obviously isn't workin' here, so let me lay this on the line for you, all right? I have absolutely no doubt you have feelings for her. And I think it's mutual."

"Look—"

"Let me finish. This . . . connection, or whatever you wanna call it, is a colossal mistake. And, again, I'm sayin' this as your friend. And hers. It can't work. It's a train to nowhere. You have to do something, Tony, before this gets any deeper."

Resignation and melancholy in his voice, he said, "It can't get any deeper, Colleen. Not for me, at least. I love her."

"Jesus, Tony. I had no idea it had reached— Have you told her?"

"*No*, I haven't told her. I couldn't possibly. Not under these circumstances. And don't think I haven't analyzed this a million times. When I first realized I had feelings for her, I tried to stop it. I literally did try to ignore her for a while. I just couldn't."

"Oh, man. What are you gonna do?"

He sighed. "Damned if I know. You're the psychologist, you tell *me*."

She let go a slight, cheerless laugh. "Well, I've already given you my clinical take on what you should do. I don't see where this can go. But what to do now is up to you . . . and her, if she's bein' honest with herself. She's a smart lady, and she had a life before the convent. She knows what she's feelin'. Whether it's love on her part, I have no idea. But there's definitely something there. She has as much of a choice to make as you."

Piza winced. "Honestly, I can't imagine discussing this with her. If she were a regular girl, then yeah, sure. But she's not."

"I know. I can't begin to imagine how awkward that would be."

He issued a feeble smile and winked. "What if you sat down with her and got a feel for where she's at? I mean, if she doesn't feel the same, then it would be easier for me to back away. I'd be heartbroken, but. . ."

She smiled back. "Sorry. For what it's worth, I did consider talkin' to her. But I don't think it's my place. We're friends, but not like that."

He shrugged. "Then I guess I'm stuck."

"Seems so. It's like you'll both be in kind of an emotional limbo. Of course, if the gossip mill gets goin', and word gets to Mother John. . ."

"Whaddya think she'd do if she found out?"

"Got me. You're talkin' uncharted territory, at least in this parish, that's for sure. I mean maybe the sisterhood has rules about this kind of thing, but . . . I dunno. And would Sister Theresa even admit to it?"

Piza exhaled his aggravation. "Ya know, it's only the end of March, but I feel like I've already had a year's worth of turmoil. It seems like I can't catch a— What?"

"I didn't say anything."

"No, but you're giving me your patented 'it's always about you, Piza' look."

She tilted her head.

Weariness in his voice, he said, "Listen, I know I'm not exactly Mr. Selfless, but I mean if I can't vent to *you*. . ."

She held his gaze. "I'm sorry. That wasn't fair of me."

"It's okay. It's just— I'd just like things to go smoothly for a while. I mean, shit's gonna happen. I get that. But. . ."

"But it'd be nice if it could be more evenly spaced out."

Piza turned his palms upward. "Exactly."

Flashing a grin, she said, "Well, here's hopin'."

But then April came.

34

"Are you shittin' me, Falco? If this is your idea of some kinda . . . like a joke or somethin', I am not amused." Sal Amico started raising and lowering his shirt collar, a nervous habit.

Sitting across the table from him, Frankie said, "If you flap that collar any faster, Sal, you're gonna start circling the room."

After more than two months of therapy, Frankie had decided to come out to the other members of the inner circle. And what better place than Murp's. He'd been noticeably anxious as he and Piza walked up the sidewalk toward the bar's entrance. "I'm still not sure they're gonna be okay with this."

His voice calm, Piza said, "Look, like I told you before, Sal might lose it, but I think Jeff and Strikes should be all right."

"I guess."

Jeff Jennings, as it turned out, wasn't surprised in the least. "Tell me something I *haven't* suspected for years."

Sal looked incensed. "So wait a minute, here. You and Tony knew, and nobody said anythin'? What a crock."

Jeff gave a casual shrug. "Sorry, Sal. First of all, I wasn't sure.

Second, even if I was, it wasn't my place. This was Frankie's business."

"What *he* said," Piza added, wiping beer foam from his upper lip.

Sal looked at Joey Sabatini. "And what about you, Strikes? How's about backin' me up here, with how pissed I am nobody said anythin'."

Strikes tossed him a sideward glance. "No big thing. I'm good."

Frankie clasped his hands on the table. "You can't even look me in the eye, Strikes."

With visible reluctance, the man turned to his friend. "No, it's not like that, Frankie. It's just that Megan— I mean, you know what a strict Catholic she is and all."

"What's your wife being a good Catholic gotta do with this?" Frankie asked, his voice measured.

Strikes squirmed in his seat. "It's like— It's just that I've kind of been going to church with her a couple of days a week. And some prayer groups. And I don't think it's right is all."

Frankie wasn't letting go. "Don't think *what's* right?"

"Gimme a break, Frankie. You know damn well what I mean." He looked around and lowered his voice. "Being a homosexual. It's a sin. At least that's what I believe."

Piza was incredulous. "Since when? All the years we've known each other—before and after you met Megan—you've never said that. I know you've always been more religious than the rest of us, but now, out of the blue, you become some kind of zealot?"

Strikes leaned toward Piza and, eyes narrowing, said, "Believing homosexuality is wrong makes me a zealot? Really?"

Piza replied, "Fine. Forget that. But what are you saying? This is Frankie we're talking about here." He swept the group with his hand. "Hell, this is *all* of us we're talking about. You gonna jeopardize—"

Strikes cut him off. "Don't lay this on me. I'm not the—" He glanced at Frankie, then turned back to Piza. "Shit, read the Bible, Tony. Okay? Oh, wait. I forgot. You don't believe in God anymore, right? But what about your parents? They're Catholic. How do they feel about it, huh? Do they even know? See how welcome he is in your house when they—"

Piza shot out of his seat, rattling the mugs on the table. Frankie grabbed his arm and eased him back down. The few other bar patrons went back to their drinks. But Piza's glare was unwavering. "Leave my parents out of this, you piece of shit."

Strikes, who'd momentarily jerked at Piza's move, now settled down and returned the stare. "I'm just saying."

Piza assumed an ominous calm. "I honestly don't know my parents' views on homosexuality. We've never discussed it. But whatever it may be, it's irrelevant to this conversation. Know why? Because, unlike you apparently, my parents actually *practice* benevolence. Every day. And if I'm certain of anything in this world, it's that they'd never turn their backs on Frankie over this. Never. Now why don't you get the fuck out of here."

Strikes laughed through a closed mouth. "Happy to. Sal, you coming?"

"Uh, I don't think so. I'm gonna hang back for a while."

"Suit yourself," as he left.

Frankie eyed Sal. "Sure you wanna stay?"

"Yeah, definitely. Whatever you got goin' on, you're still my friend. Shit, I can't even count how many times you saved my ass in a fight."

It was Jeff who broke the ensuing silence. "I can't believe what just happened. What the hell got into him? I don't ever remember him being like this. You know . . . homophobic."

"Me either," Frankie said. "I mean, we've all joked about it one time or another, even when we were kids. But if it was more than just kidding around to him, wouldn't we have picked up on that?"

Jeff nodded. "You'd think. But as much as I don't wanna believe this is something we flat out missed, I don't see how it could've just cropped up out of nowhere. Megan or no Megan. Makes no sense. How about you, Ton? You have any inkling this was roiling under the surface with him?"

Eyes locked on his beer mug, Piza answered, "Not a clue."

"Yeah, me too," Sal added. He drew a deep breath. "Look, what Strikes said sucked and all, but I gotta tell ya, I'm still havin' trouble wrappin' my head around this. I mean, how long you been like this, Frankie?"

"Seriously, Sal?" Frankie said, eyebrows raised.

The man blushed. "No, I meant like, how long've you known?"

"Deep down? As far back as I can remember."

"Even in high school?"

"Uh-huh."

Beads of perspiration formed on Sal's forehead. He extended his arms, palms out. "Okay, and don't take this the wrong way, all right . . . but when we were in the showers, after gym, did you ever like, ya know, sneak a peek? At me? No offense, okay?"

The plumber rubbed his chin, then leaned across the table, motioning with his index finger for Sal to come closer. "I did, actually. Once."

His friend scrunched his face. "Jesus, Frankie. Oh, man. Only once? Ya swear?"

Frankie placed his right hand on his heart, and raised his left. "Word of honor. Truth is, when I looked that one time, my pecker shriveled up. That was it for me."

The joke jolted Piza out of the doldrums, and he was laughing so hard he slammed a knee against the table. Jeff could barely catch his breath.

With a satisfied grin, Frankie sat back and interlaced his fingers behind his head.

Sal, who'd initially looked embarrassed, was now laughing

too. "Screw you, Frankie. But you got me, fair and square. Stupid jerk. That's worth a round on me."

That was their last drink of the evening. After saying goodbye to the others, Piza and Frankie shuffled toward Piza's car, in a corner of the bar's parking lot.

Jeff shouted from the other end, "Mark the calendar. Tuesday, April ninth, 1974, the date of the most mind-bending announcement in the history of Murp's."

Piza and Frankie both laughed, Frankie's accompanied by a benign middle finger. He raised the collar of his leather jacket against the damp chill. "So. Strikes."

Piza's response barely broke a whisper. "Yeah. Wasn't expecting that. Felt like a stranger was sitting at the table."

His friend bent down, picked up a small stone, and flung it across the mostly barren lot. "Honestly, I'm not really shocked. I dunno. I think anyone's capable of disappointing you at some point. Present company excepted, of course."

Piza lightly bumped his friend with his shoulder. "So, Jeff and Sal will keep their mouths shut. But what if Sabatini starts blabbing?"

"I don't think he will. Probably be too embarrassed, considering all the years we spent together. 'I was friends with a homo, oh nooooo!'" He stuffed his hands into his jacket pockets. "But if he does, he does. It's gonna get out sooner or later I imagine. I just feel bad, ya know? We've all been so close for so damn long. To lose that over something like this?"

With a shrug, Piza answered, "Listen, who knows? Maybe he'll come to his senses." His voice held little conviction.

Frankie surveyed the night sky, then stared straight ahead. "I don't think so."

"Well, let's see. Okay?"

"No. Things are changing, Ton."

It would be about two weeks before Piza learned how astute his friend's observation was.

35

"So here's what I'm thinking," Piza offered. "Sixth-grade day at a park. Maybe some Sunday."

Sister Theresa squinted in thought. "Are you talking about something school-sponsored? 'Cause we're only allowed one outing a year, and we already had our museum trip, so. . ."

Shaking his head, he said, "Nope, voluntary. We pick a park, and if the kids wanna show up, they show up. Let their parents drop them off. Would Mother John let you do something like that?"

"Um, I imagine. But what about additional chaperones?"

"We could ask Jim and Colleen if they'll help. And maybe some of the parents could pitch in. Could be fun."

"It does sound like fun. Which Sunday were you thinking?"

"Uh, today's the sixteenth. This Sunday's probably too soon to get it together. So maybe we do, let's see . . . the twenty-eighth?"

With an enthusiastic nod, she said, "Sounds like a plan. So, Sunday, April twenty-eighth."

"Done. I'll talk to Jim now. You wanna run it by Colleen?"

"Sure."

"Just be careful. Looks like her dodgeball game is pretty intense. Try not to get clocked in the head."

She smiled and got up from the schoolyard picnic table. "Okay, touch base with you later."

As Piza pulled up in front of the school, Sister Theresa was waiting by the curb. He exited and opened the door for her. "Where's your guitar?"

"Didn't feel like lugging it around today."

"You okay? You look a little down."

"No, I'm fine. Didn't get a great night's sleep. Then up early for mass."

"So why didn't you sleep well?"

She sighed. "I was up most of the night trying to figure out ways to stop people from asking other people why they didn't sleep well."

He smiled. "Apparently you were unsuccessful."

"So it would seem," she responded with a light laugh.

"So, any last minute hesitation on Mother John's part? About today?"

"Um, not that I know of. She's at a retreat this weekend."

"Okay then. Onward and upward to an afternoon of fun, frolic, and adventure."

She rolled her eyes. "Thank God this is only a five-minute ride."

The outing was supposed to be from one to four. Piza made the parking lot fifteen minutes early. O'Brien was already there.

"Piza. You're actually on time. Miracle of miracles. Hey, Sister, how are ya?"

"Good, Colleen."

O'Brien looked toward the sky. "We really lucked out with the weather. Low seventies, accordin' to the radio. Kind of breezy, but I guess—"

A blue 1968 Chevy Bel Air wagon interrupted her as it lumbered into the lot, a cacophony of engine noise and displaced gravel.

A beaming Bauer waved as he got out. "Hey, guys. I hope you don't mind, but I picked up a couple of hitchhikers on the way." He went to the passenger side, opened the door, and extended a hand inside. A diminutive young woman emerged; plainly dressed, but pretty, with chin-length chestnut hair and large brown eyes. She, in turn, opened the rear door and removed a sleeping child from a car seat.

"Everyone, this is my wife, Beth. And that slumbering bundle of curls is our daughter, Abby."

"Well isn't this a wonderful surprise," Sister Theresa said as she softly stroked the child's hair. "I'm Sister Theresa. It's so nice to finally meet you, Beth."

"Thank you, Sister. Likewise." She turned toward O'Brien. "And you must be Colleen?"

"Guilty, I'm afraid."

Piza moved in to shake Beth's hand. "This *is* a surprise. Jimbo, you never said you were married. I mean, after that insane night of bar-hopping we had last November. Who knew?"

They all laughed, and Beth said, "Well, if I had any doubt you were Tony, it was just dispelled. It's really nice to meet you."

"Same here. Hey, Jim, can you give me a hand getting the snacks out of my trunk?"

"Better get a move on," O'Brien suggested, pointing to the entrance to the lot, as cars began to stream in.

In all, thirty-two children came—fairly evenly divided

between the two classes. Seven parents also volunteered to stay, three from Piza's group: Darlene Robinson, Florence Schaeffer, and Matt Majinsky's mother, Anna.

They were standing together when Piza approached to greet them. "Hello, ladies. Mrs. Schaeffer, Mrs. Robinson, it's great to see you again. But I haven't had the pleasure. . ."

"Oh. Right. Hi. Anna Majinsky, Matthew's mom."

She appeared to be around 5'5", and by Piza's estimation couldn't have been more than a hundred pounds. *How could someone that skinny give birth to— I mean, talk about stretch marks.* "Well, thanks so much to all of you for doing this. What we figured we'd do is have the adults spread out among the kids. Should be pretty easy to keep an eye on them."

Although not that big, the park had decent accommodations. There were picnic tables, the standard array of playground fare, and three tennis courts contained within a fenced-in area.

A little before three, the adults gathered everyone for refreshments. When the children finished, and began abandoning the tables, Laura Perotta grabbed Sukie McDermott's arm. "Look. The tennis court on the left side there just opened up. Come on."

They took tennis rackets out of bags they'd brought. Before Piza realized what was happening, they took off. "Hey, wait a sec!" he hollered, a gust of wind blowing the words back in his face. "I've gotta get over there."

He noticed Matt Majinsky signaling to him. "Hey, Mr. Piza, you ready?"

"Oh man. I promised them I'd throw the football around. This is—"

Sister Theresa shooed him away. "Go. You can't break a promise. I'll keep an eye on the girls."

"You sure, I mean, they're not your kids. I don't wanna—"

"Stop. I like tennis, anyway. Now beat it." She started walking toward the tennis courts before he could respond.

When the nun arrived, the two girls were engaged in animated conversation. She opened the gate to the chain-link enclosure and approached them.

"Oh, hey, Sister Theresa," Sukie said. "Um, you here to keep an eye on us?"

"I am. Plus, I've always liked tennis. So, which of you is going to be Billie Jean King?"

The girls' eyes widened as they looked at each other, then back at the nun. "You know who Billie Jean King is?" Laura asked, the incredulous expression still in place.

"I do. Put that cheeky little Bobby Riggs in his place last September." As the girls' eyes widened more, she continued. "Watched the whole match on television. Made my day."

"That is so cool, Sister," from Sukie.

"Very cool," Laura concurred. She turned to her friend. "Do you wanna be Billie Jean?"

"Heck yeah. Uh, if you really don't mind."

"I don't mind at all. Question is, who should I be?"

"I'd say Chris Evert," the nun suggested. "Billie Jean's amazing, but I think Chrissie's the future."

Laura squinted and pursed her lips. "I like it, Sister. Being the future sounds good."

"Okay, then. Let's see you budding stars go at it."

With a voice hinting of insecurity, Sukie announced, "Oh, um, just so ya know, this is actually the first time we ever played."

With a flick of the wrist, the nun dismissed the child's concern. "Better still. I can say I was there when it all began."

As the grinning girls retreated to opposite sides of the net, the two men who'd been playing in the center court wrapped up their session, leaving only a man and woman at the far end of the courts.

He looked to be early-twenties and fit, with longish black hair he kept brushing away from his eyes. Wearing a white polo shirt and matching tennis shorts, he effortlessly returned the woman's weak volleys.

Every few minutes he'd lay down his racket and jog to her side of the court, speaking with her and sometimes standing directly behind her, their slender bodies almost touching as he guided her right arm back and forth in simulated swings.

Whenever he finished, he'd lightly touch her shoulder. Her reaction, consistent: a coy smile, a toss of her shoulder-length platinum hair, and a tug at the tennis skirt that even the most non-judgmental soul would have found too skimpy for someone who looked to be a weathered late-forties.

Sister Theresa, seated in the corner near the gate, on Laura's side of the net, seemed transfixed by the couple's ritual. *What on earth is that woman thinking? I mean I know what she's thinking, but—*

"Look out, Sister!" Sukie shouted.

The nun barely ducked under a yellow missile. A patently frustrated Laura dropped her racket, folded her arms, and stared at her friend. "Why do you keep doing that? It's bad enough we can hardly get the ball over the net hitting it easy. Then you try and kill it, and it winds up going all over the place."

Her point was well taken. Sukie had already launched three balls over the fence and whizzed two more to the other end of the courts. The young man had retrieved both for her, a smile accompanying his flipping them back with his racket.

His companion didn't seem to find it so amusing. Although neither errant shot had landed on her side, the first had elicited an eye roll; the second, a feral glare at Sister Theresa and a shouted: "Keep them on a leash, please!"

The unsmiling nun had waved an acknowledgment. "They're not dogs, lady," she'd murmured. "Suzanne, you need to tamp down the adrenaline, okay?"

The child had replied with a thumbs-up, but her efforts at

containment had the lifespan of a lit match, as evidenced by her now near-beheading of the teacher.

Sukie approached the net, a picture of heartfelt contriteness. "I'm really, really sorry, Laura. I swear I'll hit it easy from now on."

Her friend picked up her racket. "Fine. But one more time and I'm out of here."

"Promise. Oh, sorry about almost hitting you, Sister."

"It's fine, Suzanne. Pretty sure my heart's started up again."

Both girls laughed and resumed their positions on the court.

Ironically, it was Laura who triggered the incident that occurred five minutes later.

36

The blonde was in mid-serve when the wayward ball lightly caromed off her foot, the result of Laura Perotta's unsuccessful attempt at a backhand. The woman whiffed on the serve, causing her to stagger. By the time she righted herself, Laura was already retrieving the ball from the base of the fence.

"Sorry," the child offered, the delivery just shy of a yell, the tone laced with worry. She didn't make eye contact.

Three steps into the girl's escape, the woman threw down her racket and shouted, "Don't you move." Laura froze.

"Hey," Sister Theresa hollered, jumping up and running toward them. Sukie wasn't far behind.

Either oblivious to the rapidly approaching nun, or choosing to ignore her, the blonde strode the ten feet to the clearly petrified child, grabbed the front of her pink windbreaker, and slapped her hard across the left cheek. "I'm paying ten dollars an hour for these lessons, and I don't need you and your—"

She flew backward as Sister Theresa shoved her with her left hand, using her right to dislodge the woman's grip from Laura's jacket and then stash the sobbing child behind her.

The young instructor, who had leaped over the net seconds before, broke his student's fall. After she was upright, he attempted to keep a grip on her right arm. She pulled away as crimson displaced her dark-tan complexion. Looking both stunned and enraged, she managed a shrill, "You pushed me, you bitch."

"You're lucky that's all I did," the fiery-eyed nun shot back. "How dare you hit her. And from what I've seen, you're probably the *last* person to be calling someone else a bitch."

As soon as she'd seen the slap, Sukie had run to the gate and hollered for her teacher, her frantic motions leaving no doubt something was very wrong.

"Stay put!" Piza shouted to no one and everyone. Bolting toward the tennis courts, he tore through the open fence gate, grabbing the gate post to slow his momentum and then propel him in the direction Sukie was pointing.

"It's Laura and Sister," was all she managed to get out.

When he reached them, Laura was still behind Sister Theresa, whose gaze was locked on the bristling blonde. The nun's expression evidenced a contempt so intense and out of character, it jarred him. "What's going on?" he said.

"Are you in charge of . . . this?" the blonde asked, looking beyond Piza and sweeping her arm. He turned his head. Sukie was there and, despite his directive, several of his students. O'Brien was running toward him.

The raw arrogance emanating from the woman eradicated what sliver of impartiality Piza may have hoped to muster. "I'm one of the teachers."

She jutted her jaw in the nun's direction. "And her?"

"She's a teacher too. Like I said, you wanna tell me what the problem is?"

"What school?"

Piza didn't like the direction this was taking. "That's irrelevant. Now, I'll ask you again—"

"Our Lady of Perpetual Tears," William Reilly declared, stepping forward with ill-timed bravado.

Shit.

"Our Lady of Perpetual Tears. I see. Well, what's going on is that this"—turning to Sister Theresa—"*nun* threw me on the ground. I should call the police."

Sister Theresa broke her silence, never releasing her cold stare. "She slapped Laura."

"What?" Piza said, eyes widening then narrowing to slits. He moved to his right and dropped to a knee, so the child was in full view. She'd stopped crying, but dried tears lingered on her cheeks. So did a handprint. He curbed the escalating anger and placed his hands on her shoulders. "Are you okay, Laura? Are you in any pain or anything?"

She shook her head, then appeared about to speak; nothing came. Having seen this before, Piza knew what was happening. In times of stress, the girl always fought an internal battle between logic and emotion.

"Laura?" the teacher gently prodded.

"I was trying a backhand. And, and I messed it up. The ball wasn't supposed to hit her foot, Mr. Piza. I wouldn't. . ." Her voice caught, perplexity and hurt in her eyes. "I don't know why she hit me."

He was torn between hugging the child and launching this odious shrew into a different dimension.

While he was speaking with Laura, the blonde's companion touched the woman's shoulder. She didn't turn. "Not now, Bruce."

His jaw clenched and he practically shouted, "Yes, now, Marlene." He led her to the net.

"What?" she snapped.

"You've gotta back off. You hit that little girl. And you're talking about cops? Let's just get out of here, okay?"

"And what about that bitch who shoved me? I'm supposed to forget about that?"

"Jesus Christ, Marlene. She shoved you because you hit the kid and you were grabbing her jacket."

"You know what, Bruce? I didn't ask for your opinion. So shut up."

His head snapped back. "Shut up? Maybe it's time you got a new tennis instructor."

Her smirk reeked condescension. "Like you're not a dime a dozen."

He gave a curt laugh, and walked away; she returned to the others. A seething Piza was now standing.

Before he could speak, Marlene gestured toward Sister Theresa and said, "What are you gonna do about her? I might consider—"

"About *her*?" He gently moved Laura front and center. "What about this child? And *this*?" He pointed to the handprint.

The woman seemed knocked off-kilter by the bright-red mark. "That's, uh— That's ridiculous. She must've rubbed it. I didn't hit her that hard." A nervous laugh. "I see the game you're playing."

Piza stepped to within inches of her face. "Game? You smug—"

O'Brien lightly but purposefully took his arm. "Tony. Calm down. Let's go." Then, scowling dismissively at the woman, "She's not worth it."

Her voice now laden with anxiety, Sister Theresa added, "Yes, please. Let's just go."

Piza was reluctant to let it drop, but turned to the others and told them to go back to the park. After a lingering stare at the blonde, he joined them as they slowly made their way to the gate.

"If the nun apologizes, I'm willing to make believe this never happened. Otherwise, you'll be hearing from my lawyer."

O'Brien attempted to keep Piza moving, but he turned

anyway, wearing a thin, menacing smile. "You want *her* to apologize. You're not only arrogant, lady, you're delusional. Oh, and what's your name, by the way, in case *our* lawyer wants to make contact? Did I catch 'Marlene' before? What's your last name?"

No response. But as he started to walk he heard, "I don't respond to threats, junior."

He pivoted, fuming. "You just don't know when to keep your mouth shut, do you? One more word and you're gonna need a proctologist to remove my shoe from—"

"Piza, enough!" O'Brien hissed. "Don't make this worse."

Marlene's bug-eyed, open-mouthed expression told him he'd made his point.

The blonde gathered her things and left as soon as the tennis court cleared. O'Brien escorted an overtly distressed Sister Theresa to a picnic table, while Anna Majinsky—a nurse—checked Laura, after Piza gratefully accepted her offer to help. "The mark is gone, and there's no swelling," the woman reported. "She should be fine."

Relieved, Piza went to check on Sister Theresa. His efforts to comfort her were fruitless, and a look from O'Brien sent him to tend to the children.

Fifteen minutes later, the nun still sat at the table. O'Brien was seated next to her. "Sister, please. I don't know what else I can say to make you see you didn't do anything wrong. You've gotta stop beatin' yourself up."

"As opposed to beating up that woman?" the nun snapped. O'Brien's head jerked. "I'm— I'm sorry, Colleen. I didn't mean to talk to you like that."

"I know. But, for God's sake, you didn't beat her up. You saw a child in danger and you acted on your instinct to protect. What else were you supposed to do?"

"I don't know. Something. I didn't have to shove her like that. Who knows what would've happened if she hit the ground."

"Yeah, but she didn't. And even—"

"I appreciate what you're saying, Colleen. It's just that—"

"How are we doing?" Piza's sudden reappearance seemed to startle both women. "Sorry, didn't mean to scare you guys."

"She's gettin' there," O'Brien said. "I'm harassin' her into submission."

"Stop worrying about me. How's Laura?"

"Seems fine," Piza replied. "Not surprisingly, she was asking how you were. But I think she was a little reluctant to come over."

"I'll go talk to her. I have to apologize to her anyway for something I said."

Piza and O'Brien shared a puzzled look, but the nun continued before either of them could say anything. "What about the parents? Are they upset?"

"They're calmer now," Piza answered. "But if Lady Macbeth in tennis shoes hadn't torn out of here in her Eldorado, I think they'd have tarred-and-feathered her."

"No. I meant with me. Are they upset with me?"

"Are you kidding?" he said. "You're their hero. Same goes for the kids."

She looked down and shook her head. "No, no, no. That's the last thing I am. And I don't want the children to think that's the way to. . . This is a disaster."

Piza tried to contain his growing concern. "Listen to me. This will all be fine. So please, stop worrying." He forced a grin. "Your path to sainthood remains unencumbered. I guarantee it."

His attempt at humor was ill-placed, and her face transitioned to expressionless as she said, "Okay, I'm gonna talk to Laura now. Oh, and look, I don't know who's coming to get her, but if you want me to speak to them with you, I'll—"

"No. It's fine. I'll take care of it, don't worry."

"Are you sure?"

"Absolutely. Go talk to Laura. She'll feel better knowing you're okay."

"All right." She looked at her watch. "And we should probably start rounding everyone up. It's quarter to four."

"Good idea," Piza said.

When she left, he turned to O'Brien. "I'm really worried about her."

Bauer joined them. "Any luck?"

"Not really," from O'Brien. "I mean, she knows she had to do something. That's not the issue. I think what's eatin' her up is the intensity of her reaction; the loss of control. Like it's some sort of unforgivable character defect."

A couple of cars pulled into the parking lot. "Early parents," Bauer observed. "We should help the others get the kids together."

"So what did Laura's father say when you told him what happened?" The nun's question was in answer to Piza's third "Are you okay?" It was the first time she'd spoken since getting into the car.

"Ah, she speaks." He wasn't smiling. "Well, he was upset, obviously. I think Laura's reassurances and the fact she looked okay calmed him a bit. He said he'd speak with his wife to see if they wanted to file a police report. I doubt they will, though, because Laura seemed to panic at the idea."

"Was he—"

"Oh, not to cut you off, but he said to please thank you for what you did."

A derisive snicker led to, "Gee, everyone's just so proud of me."

He turned his head toward her, then back. "You know, cynicism doesn't really suit you."

"Oh, but it does. Spend enough time with me and—"

Her body lurched as the car swerved to the side of the road and Piza hit the brake pedal with the full force of his frustration. "You wanna tell me what the hell is going on?"

She was pale; visibly shaken. "I need to get back to the convent."

"Fine. But first you're gonna tell me why you're acting like you just committed a crime. You protected a child. What do I have to do to make you realize that's a *good* thing?"

"I wasn't supposed to go," was the barely audible reply.

"I don't— Whaddya mean?"

"She wouldn't give me permission. She told me no."

"Mother John? Why would she— Why didn't you say something? We could've canceled this. When did you find out?"

She gazed out the passenger window. "Friday night. I was nervous about telling her before then."

"Why? You said you didn't think it would be a problem."

"I know. Truth is I wasn't quite as sure as I made it sound. Wishful thinking maybe." She turned toward him. "It's just that it sounded like such a fun day, you know?"

"So, what was her reason?"

"She said it 'wouldn't be proper' for me to be there. I tried to reason with her, but she wouldn't budge. 'Wouldn't be proper'. How absurd is that? Later I found out she was going on the retreat all weekend. Temptation served up on a silver platter."

"Oh man. What about the other nuns? How did you—"

"I told Sister Joann I was going to the school to grade some tests and do some decorating for a few hours. Why would she doubt me, right? I betrayed her trust. And Mother's. And I didn't even blink."

He tried to fight off the anxiety enveloping him. "How much trouble are you in?"

She stared out the side window again. "Don't know."

"Okay, but listen. Maybe there's a chance Mother John won't find out."

"That's not gonna happen."

"Would you please stop staring out the window and look at me?" She faced him. "Thank you. Listen to me. I'm telling you she doesn't have to know about this. It was just our two classes, and we can tell the kids tomorrow morning not to discuss it with anyone. And I don't think that woman from the park is gonna do anything, considering she could be in trouble if she shows her face. We can do this."

"You're not being your logical self, Anthony." Then, with a smile that strained for relevance, "Although I do appreciate your gallant effort to save me."

His face flushed. "Don't patronize me."

Eyes widening, she said, "I'm not. Please believe me. I wouldn't do that to you. Our relationship means too— I just wouldn't."

"I— I'm sorry. But why won't my plan work? I'm telling you, we can do this."

A resigned shake of the head. "No. Word's probably started to spread already. Kids talk to other kids; parents to other parents. But even if they didn't, even if your plan was foolproof, it wouldn't matter, because *I'm* telling Mother. Tonight."

Piza stared at her in disbelief. "Why on earth would you do that? Whatever you think of my idea, at least it's a shot."

"I'm doing it because it's the right thing to do. I was wrong. And I think lying has come a little too easily to me this past year." She shifted in her seat, looking unsettled and confused. "I don't know what's wrong with me. Sometimes I just sit in my room and. . . I dunno."

"Listen, you have to stop being so hard on yourself. You're decent, and caring."

She answered with a listless shrug. "I try. But I have my flaws, like anyone else." Another smile, sad and more fleeting than the last. "Sorry to disappoint you."

He fought the urge to take her hand. "I'm not sure you *could* disappoint me, Theresa."

The tender words evoked a fierce glare and, "Have you heard anything I've said? I'm *human*. You don't think I could disappoint you? Are you that naive?"

He looked away, to conceal the depth of the hurt.

Her voice softer, she said, "Please don't hold me to a standard I can't possibly meet. It's cruel, Anthony, even though you don't mean it to be."

He made no effort to respond.

She broke the painful silence. "Anthony, look at me. Please."

He turned toward her, his expression a discordant mix of love and resentment.

Her visible affection for him eclipsed the melancholy in her voice. "If you care as much as you seem to . . . as much as I believe you do, then support me in this."

Her words steadied his roiling emotions, but he was far from convinced. "If you do this, and everything gets blown to bits, then what?"

"I wish I knew."

37

"So I guess You know what happened today. Odds are I'm in trouble. Or will be, at least. I'm not sure if anyone else knows what's going on. Nobody's said anything. Doesn't really matter. I'm gonna tell her later anyway. The outing. Pushing that woman. I had to protect Laura, but still. . . That uncontrolled anger. My language in front of the child. That's not me, right? Good old even-keeled Theresa? But I lashed out in the car too. Coming home. I dunno."

In the OLPT convent, Sister Theresa lay on the twin bed in her small, off-white room—the only adornment, a crucifix on the wall behind her.

Habit on, shoes off, hands clasped behind her head, she stared at the stucco ceiling. She prayed aloud when in her room; more of a personal touch, she liked to say.

"Anyway, You know it's not like me to disobey. But, no disrespect to Mother, I really think this was unfair. I mean, come on. A few hours at a park with the children on a Sunday? You'd think I asked permission to rob a bank. All these senseless rules. But that's no excuse. Bottom line is I was wrong. I just hope she understands. I'm worried, though. I mean, besides disobeying, everything else that went on.

"But there's more to it, and that's kind of the reason for this chat. The thing is, I'm not sure I'd have defied her if *he* wasn't going to be there today. But he was, and I did, and therein lies the problem. This . . . I don't wanna call it a 'hold' on me, that's a little melodramatic. But this attraction, this attachment to him. It's disorienting.

"Remember when I had feelings this strong once before? Sixteen. Geez, at that age I'm not even sure it counts. Funny though, this feels exactly the same as I remember it. Kind of the emotional equivalent of riding a bike. Little stab at humor there. You know how I get when I'm nervous.

"Anyway, I realize I should've talked to You about it sooner. In my defense though, at first I really didn't think it was a problem. Honestly. And when I finally realized it was becoming an issue, I figured I could work it out on my own. *Wrong*.

"But these past couple of months, I have no defense. Truth is I was enjoying it too much. I admit it. But I'm here now, and I hope any goodwill I may have built up through the years will offset Your disappointment. To some degree, anyway.

"I guess You'd probably like me to get to the point. Okay, here's what I'd like to do. Since it's now beyond obvious my emotions are a runaway train, I'd like to place this whole thing in Your hands and leave it to You to show me how to manage it. Assuming that's all right with You, of course. And, yes, I do realize this is a giant cop-out.

"So, like I said, I hope laying all this on You is okay, because frankly, Lord, I'm a mess. I've had bumps in the road before, but *this* one. . . So, whatever You can do, You know I'm grateful. As always."

"This is ridiculous," Piza muttered as he kicked off the bed covers. "I'm gonna be walking into walls."

Angst over Sunday's events had led to a sleepless night. He'd been so concerned about Sister Theresa's fate that he'd contemplated calling the convent to speak with her that evening. He'd scrapped the plan when no suitable excuse presented itself.

He arrived at school twenty minutes early, hoping to catch her alone in her classroom. Exiting his car, he was queasy, almost to the point of nausea. He headed directly to her room, opening the door with no pretense of subtlety. "Ah, you're here," he blurted out, relief instantly propping his spirits.

Her back to him, the nun turned, holding her heart. "Oh, Mr. Piza. You scared me half to death." A smile immediately followed.

"Sister Joann. I'm— I'm so sorry. I, um, thought you were Sister Theresa. From behind, you— I, uh, needed to speak with her about— Is she around?"

"No, she's—"

"Is she sick or something?"

"No, she's— Are you okay? You don't look well. Do you want some water?"

"No. Look, it's really important that I speak to her." He didn't care that he was being abrupt.

The nun looked more concerned than insulted. "Mr. Piza, she's gone. I'm not exactly sure what happened. All I know is she went back to the novitiate last evening. I'll be taking over her class for now, and we'll suspend music classes until we can get. . ."

He didn't hear whatever came after; he was already gone.

As he bolted into the office, Mother John's door was open, but she wasn't at her desk. Mrs. Florino was in, and just hanging up the phone.

"Mr. Piza, you're in unusually early."

"Uh, yes. I need to speak with Mother. Do you know when she'll be in?"

"She's here. In the chapel, I believe. Can I—"

"I'll see if I can catch her there."

"She doesn't like to be disturbed when she's praying, Mr. Piza. Why don't you—"

"No. It'll be fine. Thanks."

He hustled down the hall toward the chapel. Glancing at his watch, he calculated the time before the kids got there. *This gets resolved now.*

Through the small window on the left door of the chapel, he saw her in a front pew, alone. He pushed the door hard enough for it to bang against the wall.

The nun whirled around. "Mr. Piza. What are you—"

"You had to do it, didn't you?" He strode to the front. "How dare she defy a command from on high. Did you need to send a message to everyone? 'This is how we deal with defiance, no matter how stupid the order'?"

She'd made no effort to stop him, remaining expressionless through the rant. "I assume you're referring to Sister Theresa."

His face contorted in exasperation. "Of course I'm talking about Sister Theresa. Are you really gonna play coy right now?"

"I'm not being coy, Mr. Piza. I'm trying to give you a chance to calm yourself."

"I don't wanna calm myself, dammit."

Her look hardened. "Remember where you are. You want to vent, fine. We'll remove the 'principal' and 'teacher' labels for now. Just two adults talking. But remember where you are."

He looked chastened; it evaporated in an instant. "How—How could you just throw her out? Her, of all people. Did she explain what happened with that woman? How she did what she did to protect a little girl? Or is all that irrelevant. Just disobeying was enough to warrant shattering her life. That it?"

"Would you do me a favor and sit, please?"

"I don't wanna sit."

She held his gaze. "Please. I have to talk to you." Her tone held a sad resignation.

He sat in the pew across from hers, both of them hugging the aisle between them. "I was unhappy with Sister Theresa when she told me she went to the outing. I'm glad she was truthful with me, but we have rules for a reason, and I have to maintain control."

"Yes, but—"

She held up a hand. "Let me finish. The incident with Laura Perotta was disconcerting, and what that woman did was inexcusable. But Sister should have exercised better judgment. She should have intervened without pushing her, no matter how upset she was. Look, she's human—"

Yes, as she recently reminded me.

"—and, in all honesty, I'm not even sure how I'd have reacted. But I can't condone it."

The pleading tenor of Piza's voice softened his hostile air. "Even if she made a mistake, how does that— Has she ever done anything like this before? Rocked the boat?"

"No, never."

"Then how can you justify the punishment? She doesn't deserve to be banished, for God's sake. How can you not see that?"

"I didn't banish her, Mr. Piza. She left."

"Wh— What? Whaddya mean 'left'? How can— She's a nun. You can't just pick up and take off, right?"

"She asked for a leave of absence, and I agreed."

He tried to look impassive. "Did she say why?"

"We spoke for hours. She told me about the park, and then it was like a faucet opened. Things she'd kept bottled up; things that were gnawing at her."

His thumb and index finger massaged his forehead. "Like what?"

She hesitated, then said, "I really can't discuss it. That would be up to her to tell you."

He snickered. "How? She's gone, remember?"

The nun stared at him for a few moments. "I *will* say this, her relationship with you played a part in her decision."

Face ashen, his instinct was to go with miffed denial. "Whaddya mean 'relationship'? We don't have a relationship . . . other than being colleagues." He watched his contrived indignation fall flat.

"Mr. Piza, every word you've spoken since you came in here, every facial expression. . ." A barely audible sigh. "Your feelings for her are obvious. And she didn't attempt to conceal anything last evening. Her emotional connection to you. So let's be honest with each other, if for no other reason than respect for her."

He was done. Worn out. "Nothing happened. I hope you—"

A vigorous shake of the head accompanied her raised palm. "I know that. I know she wouldn't let that happen. Neither would you."

"Thank you for that." He was sincere.

She nodded, then stood, surprising him. "The children will be here soon. You need to get to your classroom."

He reflexively looked at his watch. "Oh. I didn't realize. Um, okay."

She lightly touched his shoulder as he started to leave. "And Mr. Piza, if you want to talk, my door is open."

"Thank you. I appreciate that." Doing his best not to sound desperate, he said, "Do you think she'll be back?"

"I really don't know. She has a lot to think about."

As he made his way to his classroom, each step seemed as labored as if he were walking in the surf.

I may never see her again.

38

"Why didn't you tell me sooner?" Bauer asked, sitting in a front-row desk in Piza's classroom. "Maybe I could've helped."

Piza had intercepted him right before lunch that Monday and asked him to come to his room. He'd also asked O'Brien.

"Sorry, Jim. I really didn't want anyone to know. Too bizarre. Too awkward. The only reason Colleen knows is because she sniffed it out and confronted me. More than once."

She winced. "Sorry for not sayin' anything, Jim, but I didn't think it was my place."

"No, it's okay, Colleen. I get it. But in hindsight, I should've seen it. Eating lunch with us more often; the way you and she joked with each other and all." A muted sigh came and left in an instant. "So, what are you gonna do now?"

With a weak shake of the head, Piza answered, "I have no idea. If there was just a way to talk to her. Maybe she'd come to her senses."

"There's no way they're gonna let that happen," O'Brien said. "Not under these circumstances. Plus—"

"I refuse to accept that. There's gotta be something."

She inched her plastic chair closer to his desk. "Listen. Trust me on this. There's not. And think about what you're sayin'. 'Maybe she'd come to her senses'. I know you mean well and, believe me, I know the hurt you're feelin'. But you have no idea what's best for her right now."

"I disagree."

Her exhale conveyed her frustration. "You said Mother John told you there were things eatin' at Sister Theresa. Things other than her relationship with you. Do you know what they are?"

"No. I told you, she wouldn't say."

"Exactly. And if you don't know what those issues are—the substance, the extent of them—how can you possibly know what she needs? None of us has those answers."

As important as logic was to him, at that moment he hated it.

Other than his discussion with O'Brien and Bauer, Piza hadn't told anyone what had happened. Of course, his malaise hadn't escaped his kids. They'd displayed a sprinkling of concern Monday; more so Tuesday. You okay, Mr. Piza? You look a little down, Mr. Piza. Did we do something, Mr. Piza?

He'd assured them everything was fine. A bit under the weather; nothing to worry about. And when they asked where Sister Theresa was, he'd told them she was up at the novitiate, taking care of some personal matters. That seemed to satisfy them. Besides, it was true.

Wednesday morning, his students were taking a science quiz. He was sitting on the bookcase—his favorite spot since the Henry VIII lesson—supposedly reviewing the history text, his mind elsewhere.

His windows provided a view of a portion of the parking lot, and movement there drew his attention. The hair on the back of his neck bristled as the Eldorado pulled into a space. *No. This isn't happening. Not now.* Marlene exited the car.

Time ground to a crawl as his attention shifted between the lot and the front door to his classroom. *How long is she gonna be in there? When will I be 'summoned'?* Twenty minutes later he had one answer, as the woman got into her car and drove off.

Ten minutes after that, Mrs. Florino simultaneously knocked on the door and opened it. The only words spoken: "Mother would like to see you. Immediately. I'll watch your class."

"What the hell is he doing here?" Piza murmured as he entered the waiting area and spotted Monsignor Lombardo seated at Mother John's desk. The priest glared at him from the second their eyes met. *Shit, this guy is pissed.*

Mother John was in one of the chairs across from the desk. He struggled to decipher her expression, without success.

The priest pointed to the second chair. "Take a seat."

What, no foreplay? "Monsignor. It's been a while." He nodded to the nun. "Mother."

"Mr. Piza," she acknowledged.

Crossing his arms, his raspy voice more sinister than usual, the monsignor said, "Do you know why we called you in here?"

"I'm guessing it has something to do with the blonde who left the parking lot a few minutes ago."

The priest unfolded his arms and rested clasped hands on the desk. "Mrs. Smith claims one of your students threw a tennis ball at her while you were on an outing on Sunday. An unsanctioned outing from what I understand. And—"

Piza interrupted him with, "It wasn't a school—"

"*I'm* talking now. You'll have your chance. She said that rather than disciplining the girl, you berated her—Mrs. Smith that is—and said things I wouldn't think of repeating." A look that oozed condemnation invited a response.

Piza wasn't going to let Laura take the fall for something she didn't do. But he was also reluctant to confess to what he'd said. Others had heard it, though, and he refused to put them on the spot. So, "Wow. Where to begin. First of all, that child didn't throw a ball at Mrs. Smith . . . if you actually believe that's her name."

Lombardo's tight-lipped mouth twitched.

"She miss-hit a ball, which *rolled* all the way across the tennis court and glanced off the woman's foot. Secondly, did she tell you she slapped the girl across the face?"

Lombardo looked uncomfortable. "She said the girl alleged she slapped her. But she denied doing it."

"Well, there was nothing 'alleged' about the handprint on Laura's cheek. And I'm not the only one who saw it."

Mother John stepped in. "I told Monsignor that Sister Theresa witnessed the slap."

Lombardo scowled at her. "Let's not get into that again, Mother. As far as I'm concerned, Sister Theresa has zero credibility, considering what she did. The only reason the woman's not pursuing the issue beyond reporting it to us is because we told her Sister Theresa is gone."

"And because we said we'd have to investigate the slapping allegation," the nun added. "That seemed to trouble her, Monsignor." The genial delivery couldn't quite conceal her obvious dislike for the man.

"Perhaps. But the bottom line is she won't be taking any legal action against us."

"Taking legal action?" Piza said. "For what? A teacher protecting a student? Seriously?"

A flick of the hand from Lombardo led to, "Save it, Mr. Piza. We need to move on to you. I think she may have been more angry with you than Sister Theresa. Your disrespect. Your foul mouth." His features hardening, he leaned forward. "Did you say what she said you did?"

Piza needed to put him on the defensive. "How can I answer that if I don't know what she told you? What exactly did she say?"

Lombardo leaned back and shifted in his chair. "I already told you I won't repeat it."

"Then, with all due respect, I can't answer your question, Monsignor. Try to see this from my perspective."

"Monsignor," Mother John said, her tone placating, "he has a point. And if you're worried about offending *me*, don't be. I already heard it from her, so. . ."

The priest puffed out the breath of a testy child. "Fine. She said— It, uh, had something to do with your foot and a part of her anatomy. I don't think I need to elaborate."

Piza weighed the value of pressing the man further, but saw no apparent benefit. "It wasn't quite as graphic as she seems to have made it sound." After a moment's hesitation, "I did make reference to my foot and a proctologist, but that was it."

Mother John cast her eyes downward.

The priest wore a self-satisfied look of conquest. "Anything to add?"

"Monsignor Lombardo, I realize what I did was . . . ill-considered. But I think if you were there, if you'd seen what she did to that child. And the arrogance and lack of remorse. . ." He was riling himself up. *Virtual deep breath, Tony. You know the drill.*

The pastor's response bordered on the theatrical. "Are you implying, Mr. Piza, *I'd* have said what *you* said? Is that what—"

"No, of course not. I'm just saying before you continue castigating me, please take into consideration the circumstances. The heat of the moment. That's all."

Lombardo got up and stood behind his chair, his forearms resting on the back. "Castigating you? Is that why you think you're here? For a scolding? Mr. Piza, you're here to be fired."

Piza was so shocked he didn't react when Mother John launched out of her chair. "What? You didn't say anything about firing him, Monsignor. You said *possibly* a week's suspension, if that. But terminating him? No, Monsignor, this is wrong."

The priest yanked his chair away from the desk and slammed his palms on the desktop. The menace in his voice matched the intensity of his stare. "Let me remind you of the hierarchy in this parish, Mother. You don't get to question my decisions. And besides that, you're the one who initially expressed doubt about his ability to do this job. Seems to me your concerns were justified."

The nun's face reddened. Piza couldn't disguise the feeling of betrayal, as Mother John's eyes darted between him and the priest. For the first time since he'd known her, he sensed panic.

"That's not fair, Monsignor. I told you that in confidence, back in September. Mr. Piza has done an about-face since then, and I consider him very competent. He may be unconventional, but the children are learning."

Lombardo tossed a dismissive look. "Well, that may be *your* assessment, but all I see is a growing list of complaints. Have you forgotten he mocked the Pope?"

The nun looked stunned. "I *never* mentioned that. How did you. . ."

Through a smug grin, he said, "I got a call from Giacobbi." The disdainful tone reappeared. "When he told me he'd already spoken to you, I assured him you'd know how to handle it. But maybe I misjudged your capabilities, Mother. Look at that disgraceful display at the Christmas show, and now this disaster." He motioned toward Piza. "You seem to have no control over him."

Piza's anger was fast approaching the level of his anxiety. "I didn't mock the Pope, and I explained what happened in the park, if you'd just—"

The priest cut him off, his face twisted in anger. "Yes, you explained it. By telling me if I'd been there I'd have reacted the same way you did."

"Whoa, that's not what I said, and you know it." The adrenalin of self-preservation had kicked in, and Piza was on his feet. "If you have a problem with me, fine. But at least be honest about it."

The man jabbed a finger at him. "You want honesty, Mr. Piza? As far as I'm concerned nobody as immature as you should be teaching here. You're a clown, plain and simple. And don't ever raise your voice to me again."

A smirk from the besieged teacher was followed by, "Or what? You'll fire me?"

Mother John intervened. "Monsignor. Respectfully. I realize you're upset, but consider the consequences of this. Mr. Piza is barely in his twenties. Firing him could ruin his chances of finding other employment. Plus, there's only two months of school left, so what's the harm in him finishing out the year? Please, Monsignor."

Lombardo didn't respond to the nun's plea, but from his expression it appeared it might have had an impact. He began pacing behind the desk.

What felt to Piza like an interminable silence really lasted only a minute or so, after which the pastor returned the chair to its proper location, and sat. Piza and Mother John, who'd both remained standing during the priest's deliberation, did likewise.

The man glanced at the teacher, then turned toward the principal. "You make a credible argument, Mother."

With an uncharacteristic timidity, she asked, "So he won't be fired?"

"No. I've—"

"Thank you, Monsignor," the clearly relieved nun said.

Piza joined in with, "I appreciate this, Monsignor. I can assure you that—"

The priest cut him off with a raised hand. "If you'd let me

finish. I've decided to give you the option of resigning, with my promise of a positive reference if a prospective employer requests it. We can say you left for personal reasons or some such thing."

The principal glowered at her superior, but his eyes were fixed on the young teacher.

Piza was a sea of emotions: anger at himself for just being duped by a hope born of desperation; gratitude to the nun sitting next to him for swallowing her pride to try to save him; but mostly, hopelessness—the kind that accompanies a total lack of power. "So that's it? I have no other options?"

Mother John was still locked in on Lombardo. "Actually, Mr. Piza, you do."

39

"I can't thank you guys enough for meeting me." Piza stood as Bauer and O'Brien joined him at a corner table at Rocco's. "I ordered us some appetizers. Figured we'd keep it light. I hope that's okay?"

An "Of course" from Bauer and a spirited nod from O'Brien.

Piza had briefed them on the morning's events, at the beginning of the lunch break. Once their shock subsided, he'd asked if they could meet at Rocco's after school to discuss it. "Anywhere but this place," he'd said, then went back to his classroom to spend the rest of the hour trying to calm himself.

"Okay, Colleen, so like I told you at lunch, Mother John said I have a right to appeal Lombardo's decision to the school board. You should've seen him, by the way. I swear, I thought he was gonna strangle her. So, do you guys have any idea how this works?"

O'Brien said, "Well, if it's anything like the procedure at their monthly meetings, people in the audience get to speak, then the board has a discussion, and then they vote. I assume this would be the same, although I can't swear to it. I don't think anyone's ever been fired from this place."

"And yet, here I am. So, the sixty-four-thousand-dollar question is whaddya think I should do?"

His friends looked at each other, as if they were sharing the same thought. O'Brien leaned forward. "Tony, we can't answer that. This is your—"

"I know, I know, it's my decision." He was bristling. *Calm down.* "Sorry. I guess what I'd like to do is maybe review the pros and cons."

"That's fine, but first off, what's your gut telling you?" Bauer asked.

"Hmm. My gut's telling me that, no matter what, I'm pretty much screwed. If I appeal and lose, Lombardo withdraws the offer to give me a reference. And really, what are the odds of me winning, with His Majesty Bob Giacobbi running the show? And if I resign, how do I know Lombardo's gonna keep his word? If he bails on it, what am I gonna do, sue him?"

O'Brien rested a hand on his arm. "There's one thing you haven't mentioned."

"I know, Colleen. The kids. Don't think I haven't thought about them. But this is my future."

"I understand that," she acknowledged with a tone free of judgment.

"I hope so. And no matter which route I take here, if it ends up with my leaving them with two months left, it's gonna eat me up. You know that, right?"

"I do."

Bauer squinted and rubbed his chin. "Boy oh boy. The way things stand, both choices stink. I have no idea what the answer to this is, Tony."

A dejected looking O'Brien added, "Me either."

Piza nodded. "That makes three of us. I feel like I'm playing a rigged game of Russian roulette."

That evening, over dessert, Piza told his family the story. Mary seemed to take it worse than he had. Pale, her voice scarcely above a whisper, she said, "No wonder you looked sick when you got home. I should'a never believed you when you said nothin' was wrong."

Concern replaced the blissful look Patty always wore when eating banana cream pie. "Tony's sick? What's wrong, Tony? You want to take your temperature?"

He did his best to find a comforting smile. "No, that's okay, sis. I'll be fine. Don't worry."

That seemed to satisfy her. "Okay. Can I have more, Ma?"

"Small piece," Mary replied, cutting a slice. "I, I don't understand why he would do this to you, Anthony. He's a priest. A *monsignor*."

Knowing his mother's religious devotion, Piza tempered his response. "Ma, you have to understand, not all priests are the same. I don't know, maybe Lombar— Monsignor Lombardo was different in the beginning. But for some reason, right now he's not a very nice person. And not just because of what he's doing to me. Believe me, if you knew the way he treated people. . . I'm really sorry."

There seemed as much disillusionment as understanding in her nod.

Angelo had remained quiet up to that point. Now, he said, "So, whaddya gonna do?"

Piza dropped what marginal pretense of objectivity he'd managed to muster. "I don't know, Pop. You know me. I need things to make sense. When they don't. . . I've been racking my brain all day to figure this whole thing out. Why it's happening; which one of the lousy choices I should. . . I dunno."

Angelo stared at his son for a few seconds. "I think I need to walk off a little of that pork roast. Keep me company, Anthony.

You don't mind, right, Mary, if we skip out on cleanin' the table tonight?"

His wife met his eyes with a sad, knowing smile. "No. 'Course not. You two take a walk. Me and Patty can do this. And put jackets on. It's chilly."

Piza turned up his collar. "Good call by Mom on the jackets."

Angelo drew a hefty breath and struck his chest. "It's good for ya. Wakes you up after a big meal."

His son gave his shoulder a nudge. "So, you have some words of wisdom for me, Pop?"

"What, I can't just ask ya to take a walk with me?"

Piza's skeptical look prompted a smile from his father. "Okay. You said inside you've been tryin' to figure this out all day, which don't surprise me. But just for a second, forget all that logic and other philosophy stuff ya learned in school. What are your insides tellin' ya?"

A frail laugh. "You're the second person to ask me that today. My instinct is telling me my best shot at saving myself is to resign, even if I don't trust Lombardo."

"And then what?"

"Go to law school in September, I guess, and hope when I get out this thing never comes up. Maybe three years from now nobody'll care what I did for a year after college."

Angelo didn't look convinced. "So, no more teachin'? You've been talkin' about your school more, last few months or so. You seemed happy."

"There's been a lot going on in my life, Pop. And maybe someday we'll talk about it. But, yes, I have been happy. And teaching's been a part of that. Certainly the kids. But no matter which way this goes, I'm not sure I could ever get another teaching job. Definitely not, if I'm fired. But even resigning, this close to school ending? It's gonna look fishy."

Angelo ran his fingers through his hair. "Okay, forget that for a second. Let me ask ya, you think you deserved to get fired for what you did?"

His son's eyes sparked. "No. No way. Listen, Pop, what I did was stupid. I admit it. I was angry, and I probably should've kept my mouth shut. But considering what that woman did to that little girl? Unh-unh. If Lombardo wanted to read me the riot act, fine. But not this. I didn't deserve *this*."

"So fight it."

"If I fight it I'm probably gonna lose. I really don't think it's a viable choice. Whaddya think I've been trying to tell you since dinner?"

The man stopped walking. "I think you're tellin' me you're afraid."

Jolted, his eyes reflecting hurt and anger, Piza said, "So you think I'm a coward? Gee, thanks. Great talk, Dad. I think I'll go back to the house now." He turned and took a step.

Angelo grabbed his arm. "Don't walk away from me, Anthony. It's disrespectful. We taught you better."

Piza stopped, but didn't look at his father.

The man released his son. "C'mon, let's sit in the park over there," he said, pointing to a small playground across the street.

"I don't— Fine."

They crossed the street and made their way to the nearest bench in the empty park. Angelo placed a hand on his son's knee. "Listen. I don't think you're a coward. That's not what I meant, and I never would think that. You know that."

Piza nodded. "I know."

"What I'm tryin' to say, Anthony, is that— Look, you think things to death. Before, you said your *instinct* was to resign. But I think that's still your head talkin'. You understand what I'm sayin'?"

"I dunno, Pop. Maybe it is." He got up and paced in front of the bench. "But what else is there? And please don't tell me to follow my heart, because that's always a recipe for disaster."

Angelo's eyes lit up. "See what ya just said? You just admitted your heart's tellin' ya somethin' different than your head is."

"I was speaking generally. It's got nothing to do with this."

"That's baloney, and you know it." He paused. "Here's the thing. Sometimes you can be like two different people. Once in a while, you can be a little selfish. But—"

"You think I don't know that?"

"Let me finish. I'm not sayin' that to hurt you. No one's perfect. And I couldn't love you more, no matter what. But even though what I said is true sometimes, when it comes to people you care about, there's nothin' you won't do for them. That's one of the best things about you, and it makes me proud.

"But my point is those kids mean as much to you as anythin' in your life right now. I can feel it. And if ya don't fight for them, then you're lettin' fear stop you from bein' who you are. And look, I ain't naive, Anthony. You never had this much on the line before. Have you?"

With a muted voice, he said, "No, not like this."

"But you're young and you're smart. If you fight this and lose, you'll find a way to bounce back. But if ya just give up? Let this guy get away with this? You do that and you're betrayin' those children . . . and yourself. The loyalty that makes you so special, some of that's gonna be gone. I know you, and *my* instinct's tellin' me if ya walk away, you're not gonna be able to completely let go of this. I ain't sayin' it's gonna ruin your life, but it'll always be in the back of your mind."

Piza continued pacing, making his way behind the bench. He placed his hands on his father's shoulders, bent down, and kissed the top of his head. "I appreciate your help, Pop. You've given me a lot to think about."

As he walked around to the front of the bench, his father stood. "So, how much time ya got to make up your mind?"

"Almost none. He wants my answer by tomorrow morning."

Angelo sighed as he shook his head. Then, he patted his son's cheek, wearing that expression every parent slips into when assuring their child there's nothing to worry about, even when there is. "Whatever you decide, it's gonna be okay."

"Thanks, Pop."

I just wish I could believe that.

"Morning, Ma. Pop. I think I heard Patty stirring around in her room. She'll probably be down in a bit." He hadn't looked directly at either of his parents, and his puffy eyes left no doubt he'd endured a long night.

Mary put out another plate. "You look terrible."

"Thanks, Ma. Uh, I'm not really hungry."

"Scrambled eggs are already in the pan. Toast and bacon are—"

"On the table, two feet from the cup of coffee sitting in front of me. I'm not *that* tired." He glanced at his father. "Manny opening up the store?"

"Yeah. I was, um, kinda anxious to see what you decided."

Standing by the stove, Mary said, "Your father told me about your talk, Anthony. Whatever ya decide to do, we're behind you. Hundred percent."

"I know, Ma."

She slid the eggs onto his plate, then sat. "So, whaddya gonna do?"

He took a sip of coffee, then placed his hands in his lap. With a pained expression, he said, "I— I've gotta do what's best for me. My future. I've, uh, decided to go with instinct."

Mary looked confused, her head rotating between the two men. "I don't understand. What's that mean, 'go with instinct'?"

"It means he's gonna resign," Angelo said. The disappointment painting his face instantly transitioned to a smile that fought not to look contrived. "Okay. Good. That's it then."

Looking at his father, Piza said, "Actually, it's not *my* instinct I'm following, Pop . . . it's yours." A mischievous grin appeared.

Mary threw up her hands. "Would somebody in this house please speak English and tell me what the hell is goin' on?"

Both men laughed.

A beaming Angelo declared, "He's gonna fight it, Mary." He turned to his son. "And you. Why didn't ya just say that to begin with? Everythin's always gotta be a production."

Piza wiggled his eyebrows. "Where's the fun without the drama?"

"I'll give ya fun, wiseguy," his father said, adding a teasing sneer. "So, you sure about this?"

"I am, Pop. I thought a lot about what you said. If I abandon these kids, I don't know that I'd be able to forgive myself. Plus, and this is the selfish part of me talking"—he placed a hand on his father's and winked—"if I do that, it's like admitting I'm not a good teacher. I couldn't live with that, either. No, this is what I've gotta do, and whatever happens, happens."

Mary got up. "Okay, good. It's settled. Who wants more coffee?"

40

On Wednesday, when the sky fell, Piza had done his best to hide his added distress from the kids. A few of them, lagging behind the others at dismissal, confirmed his doubts about how convincing he'd been.

"You okay, Mr. Piza?" Kevin Davis asked, head tilted, eyes wary.

"Yeah, I'm fine, Mr. Davis. All good."

"Are you sure?" Sukie said. "'Cause you look even worse than yesterday."

Through a forced smile, he answered, "I am *fine.*" The smile morphed into a silly grin. "See? Now go line up outside, before Mother John yells at me."

But on Thursday, his decision to appeal eclipsed the desire to keep his students at ease. He related the meeting with Lombardo and Mother John, without going into details.

When he told them about the pastor's decision to fire him, gasps and protests inundated the room. Laura Perotta turned ashen. She began trembling, almost imperceptibly. But he noticed.

"Okay, guys, calm down. Miss Perotta, it's gonna be fine."

An emphatic shake of her head was followed by, "This is because of me. You're getting fired because of me."

"No, that's not true. First of all, there's still a chance I won't be fired, which I'll get to in a minute. But this whole thing happened because of what that woman did, and how I reacted. She was dead wrong doing what she did to you, but I shouldn't have talked to her the way I did. This is on her and me. Not you. Not even close."

The girl straightened in her seat, and Piza could tell she was collecting her thoughts.

"I understand what you're saying, Mr. Piza, but don't you see? I'm the one who hit the ball across the court. I'm the one who, who made it hit her foot. That's what started everything. Don't you see that?" It was evident she was holding her composure intact by the thinnest strand of determination.

Piza struggled to find the best way to comfort this child, who reminded him so much of himself. "Miss Perotta, let me ask you something. Do you trust me?"

"I— Of course I do."

"Good. I trust you too. For example, I trust you to believe I wouldn't lie to you and that, as your teacher, I know more than you about certain things. Fair?"

A quizzical look. "Uh-huh."

"Okay. Then I'm going to say this one more time. I'm telling you this is not your fault. I know you, the way you constantly analyze things. But now I need you to just trust that I'm right about this. Can you do that for me?"

She paused, then nodded.

"Good. Thank you for that." He smiled. "Okay, people, I'm gonna need your help. Because there's a possibility we can beat this."

Most of Piza's kids were gathered in a corner of the schoolyard after lunch. Sukie had assumed command of the impromptu meeting. "Okay, you guys. I'm still not sure what this whole appeal thing's about, but it's up to us to get our parents to write letters, like Mr. Piza said."

Rebecca Schaeffer joined in. "Absolutely. And I think each of us should write a letter too. I mean, he's *our* teacher."

"Who's gonna care what a bunch of sixth-graders have to say?" Matt Majinsky said.

Rebecca pointed an accusing finger at him. "If you're too lazy to write one stupid letter, then don't write it."

"I'm not lazy! I don't know if it'll do any good is all's I'm sayin'. But if everyone else is gonna write one, I will too. I swear. I want Mr. Piza to stay as much as anybody else."

"We should picket the school." Everyone turned toward Karen Jablonski. "Make signs, then march with them when we get to school in the morning, and outside at lunch too. Just writing letters isn't enough. I mean, we should definitely still write them, but I think we need to do something more to show them we mean business."

Sukie looked doubtful. "Um, I have a feeling all that'd do would just get us all detention."

The young rebel threw her arms up. "So what? If we get detention, we get detention. C'mon people." Shrugs and murmurs relayed the lack of enthusiasm for her call to action. "I swear, sometimes I just don't get you guys."

"How about this?" William Reilly offered, pushing his glasses back up the bridge of his nose. "We write the letters, like Becky said. But, we get other kids to write letters too. A lot of the kids in Sister Theresa's class really like Mr. Piza. And some of us have brothers and sisters in other grades, and maybe they'll write some. Then the school board will *have* to pay attention."

"What a great idea," Laura said. "It'll be like *Miracle on Thirty-fourth Street*. Except instead of dumping a ton of Santa letters on the judge's desk, we dump our letters on, um, wherever the Board of Education people sit."

Robert Giacobbi spoke up. "Actually, they sit at a cafeteria table. My dad's always complaining that it's 'undignified'."

Sukie came alive. "Oh man, I forgot all about that. Isn't your dad the head of the whole thing? Maybe you could talk to him and, ya know, tell him we want Mr. Piza to stay."

The boy's discomfort was evident. "Um, I don't—"

"Robert can't do that, Sukie," Kevin Davis interjected, interceding on behalf of his friend.

Sukie glared at him. "That's ridiculous, Kevin. It's his dad. Tell him you can do it, Robert."

"No, Kevin's right," Giacobbi said. He shrugged. "I'm sorry, guys. My dad won't listen to me. It, uh— It could actually make things worse."

Sukie appeared about to respond, but an exasperated-looking Ralph Restivo piped in with a resounding, "This whole thing sucks. It's not fair and— And it just really, really sucks."

That set off a mass venting, expressions of frustration and anger colliding in mid-air.

"Listen, everybody, calm down, okay?" Davis commanded, moving to the front. When the unrest died down, he continued. "Let's just do what Mr. Piza told us, all right? We get our parents to write letters, and try to get them to show up at this appeal thing. We'll write letters too, and like William said, see if we can get anybody else to help. Okay?"

A drone of agreement settled the issue.

As Bauer entered Piza's classroom at lunchtime that Friday, he checked the hallway before closing the door. Once inside, he opened the coat closet, surveying the area.

"Okay, I give up, Jimbo. Are we supposed to know what

you're doing?" Piza was sitting at one of the student desks, legs draped over the writing area.

Bauer's eyes hinted at intrigue. "Well, since we've been having these covert meetings, I feel kind of like a saboteur. You know, plotting the defeat of King Bob and his minions. So I'm taking extra precautions in case we're being followed."

A smiling O'Brien was in Piza's chair. "Okay, Jim, you're officially nuts."

"That's great, Jimbo. I'm on the precipice of extinction, and *now* you develop a sense of humor?"

"Trying to lighten the mood, is all. And by the way, I've always had a sense of humor. It's just dry."

"That's what *everyone* with no sense of humor says," Piza replied.

Bauer tossed him a fake sneer. "Cynic. So, what's the latest?"

"Well," Piza said, "apparently they have to hold a hearing within fourteen days of the appeal being filed. So that gives me about two weeks. I handed in the letter yesterday, so fourteen days takes us to . . . May sixteenth. Hopefully, that'll give me enough time to round up some supportive parents, and get letters written."

"Well, maybe not," O'Brien observed. "*Within* fourteen days means it could be earlier."

Piza swung his legs off the desk. "Crap. You're right. How much sooner do you think they could do it?"

O'Brien turned her palms up. "Don't know. I mean they'd have to coordinate the board members' schedules. Their regular meeting is every second Tuesday. So that means they're scheduled for the fourteenth. Seems more feasible for them to do it then."

"Makes sense," Bauer said. "Gives you a *little* less time to get everything together, Tony, but still sounds doable."

"I guess. How about the school board members, Colleen. You find out anything?"

"I did. Two of them definitely don't like Giacobbi."

A curt laugh from Piza. "Only two?"

"That I know of. Of course, that doesn't mean they'll automatically vote against him."

"Not for anything," Bauer interjected, "but are you certain this Giacobbi guy is gonna go along with firing you? I mean, you said he and Monsignor Lombardo can't stand each other. If Lombardo wants you gone, maybe Giacobbi'll vote to keep you on, just to spite him."

Piza waved off the suggestion. "Doubtful, Jim. Giacobbi detests me. I think if he and Lombardo could find common ground on anything, it'd be me."

O'Brien continued. "Seems another board member is tight with Giacobbi. So that's not good. Supposedly, two others are kind of passive. Hard to say what they'd do."

"I assume this is majority rules?" Piza asked.

With a shrug, O'Brien answered, "It is for everything else, so I imagine it's the same."

"Okay," Piza said, "that's six people, from your tally. What about the seventh?"

She pursed her lips and arched her eyebrows. "Um, I'm afraid that would be your friendly neighborhood contractor, Joe DiGregorio."

Piza grimaced. "I forgot all about him. He might want payback for that problem with his kid and Shirley Robinson. Dammit."

"Not to rub salt in the wound," a rueful-looking O'Brien said, "but, if you remember, Giacobbi sells construction equipment."

A cryptic laugh from Piza segued into, "You've gotta be freakin' kidding me. He does business with DiGregorio."

She nodded.

Shaking his head and scowling, Bauer stated, "Well, that makes it more than likely he'll be in Giacobbi's corner. Which means King Bob only needs one more vote."

O'Brien raised an index finger. "Yes. But, remember what I told you a while back—DiGregorio misses a ton of meetings. With a little luck, he won't show up. So Giacobbi would have to snag *two* of the unknowns."

"That would definitely help," Piza responded, a hint of hope in his voice.

That fragment of optimism never would have materialized had they known just how much Bob Giacobbi hated leaving things to chance.

41

"Joe, I got Bob Giacobbi on line one. You wanna take it? He called before."

"Uh, ya know what, Charlene, tell 'im I'll get back to 'im. No, no, wait. I'll take it. He'll just keep callin'."

"You got it, boss."

Joe DiGregorio sighed, then poked the flashing button. "Hey, Bobby, what's up? We gotta make this fast, okay? I got a shitload a paperwork I gotta take care of."

"Yeah, no problem, Joe. Listen, did you get my message from earlier, about the Board of Ed meeting next Wednesday?"

"Um, hold on a sec, let me. . ." He cradled the phone on his shoulder as he sifted through a pile of pink message slips. "Okay, yeah, here it is. Yeah, Wednesday, the eighth. Wait, that ain't the regular meetin' date, right? Supposed to be the followin' Tuesday, ain't it?"

"Yeah. But this is a special meeting. And I know it's kinda last minute, but it has to do with—"

"Whoa, the message says four thirty? I can't be there at four thirty. I'm lucky I get outta here by seven most nights."

"I know it's an earlier time than usual, but—"

"I dunno. What's it about, anyways?"

"Ready for this? Lombardo canned Piza. Robert's teacher."

"The guy wit' the thing wit' Tommy?"

"That's him. And now he took an appeal. So it's up to us to decide if he stays or goes. I figured you might enjoy kicking his ass out the door."

DiGregorio's eyes narrowed. "Did he rough up a kid? 'Cause if he did, maybe Tommy wasn't bullshittin' back then."

"No, nothing like that. They were on a class trip at a park. Supposedly some broad playing tennis slapped one of the kids for hitting her with a tennis ball, and Piza threatened to stick his foot up her ass."

DiGregorio broke out laughing. "Hey, I may'a had this guy all wrong."

"Jesus, Joe. It's not funny. The lady was pissed. Threatened to sue the school."

The contractor's face turned serious again. "Where the hell does she get off hittin' a kid? Boy or girl?"

"I think it was a girl."

"A little girl? Even worse. If I was there my foot would'a *been* up 'er ass, never mind threatenin'."

"Look, it's not just that. At the Christmas show, this Piza dressed up like a priest. Big joke. And he even made fun of a pope once. You know I can't stand Lombardo, but this time I've gotta agree with him. He's gotta go."

DiGregorio picked up an unlit, half-smoked cigar from an ashtray on his desk, relit it, and leaned back in his chair.

"Joe, you still there? I—"

"What's in it for me?"

"What? Whaddya mean?"

"Whadda I get if I go along wit' this? Seems like gettin' rid a this guy is kinda important to you."

"C'mon, Joe. I mean, ya know, making fun of a pope?"

"Like I give a shit."

A few seconds pause. "Listen, what if I give you a discount on those jackhammers you're looking at?"

DiGregorio's expression hardened. "I thought ya always give me a discount."

"I do. Of course I do. I mean a bigger discount. Um, say, cost plus just a couple of bucks for me."

"Make it straight cost and ya got a deal."

"Geez, Joe, gimme a break. C'mon."

"Bobby, you obviously got a hard-on for this guy. Question is, how big?"

A frustration-tinged exhale ended with, "Fine, Joe. Cost."

"Good," the contractor said with a cold, satisfied smile. "You got enough other board people to make sure ya win?"

"With you, yeah. Sam Thompson's on my bowling team, and he does whatever I say, anyway. So, we got me, you, and him. I only need one more. Meg O'Leary hardly ever opens her mouth, but she's a real holy-roller. Practically lives in the church, from what I've been told. When she hears about the pope thing, there's no way she'll vote to keep him around."

"So that's everyone?"

"That I'm sure of. Old Lady Franklin and Vince Carbone hate my guts, as you may have noticed, so they're probably out. I've never been able to get a handle on Bill Santucci. Can't bank on him, but ya never know. Anyway, he'd just be gravy. It should be fine."

DiGregorio let go a weary yawn. "So, why can't ya do this thing at seven thirty, like all the rest? Why four thirty? It's a pain in the ass."

"Yeah, I know. And I really appreciate you doing this for me. But here's the thing—he's allowed to have people there. Kinda like witnesses. Not kids, but parents or whatever. Since we haven't heard any other complaints about him, I'm assuming anyone who'd show up would be on his side."

"I'm not followin'. What's that gotta do wit' the time?"

"I'm figuring a lot of these people work, or maybe they'd have to get someone to watch their kids while they were at the meeting. Be a lot harder for them to make it at four thirty than at night. Little extra precaution, just in case. The fewer people he has talking him up, the better."

The contractor emitted a low whistle. "I always knew you were a sneaky son of a bitch, Bobby." He smirked. "Maybe I gotta keep a closer eye on you."

A nervous laugh from Giacobbi. "Always gotta bust my balls, Joe. Right?" Silence. "So, you'll, uh, definitely be there?"

"Yeah, I'll be there."

The yellow legal pad lay barren as it rested on the small desk in Piza's bedroom, its lack of content made more conspicuous by the glare of the arched black desk lamp. He'd been stunned Monday morning to learn from a glum Mother John that Giacobbi had scheduled the appeal for Wednesday afternoon.

Now it was Tuesday evening, and untethered thoughts rambled around in his brain, unable to bond into a coherent defense of his status as a teacher. More than ever, he missed Theresa; the calming influence she had on him.

"It's that damn music in Patty's room. I can't concentrate."

He pushed away from his desk, took the few steps to the hall, and entered her room without knocking. His sister's momentary shock transitioned to a beaming, "Hi, big brother."

"Patty, you've gotta turn down this music," he said as he lowered the volume on her record player.

"Hey, that's my record."

"I know it's your record. But I'm doing something very important. And for now, you have to keep it down. Okay?" He forced a smile.

She nodded, looking confused.

Five minutes later the noise returned, amplified by Patty's off-key sing-a-long with the Ronettes' "Be My Baby".

Piza barged into the room, practically tore off the record player's arm, removed the 45, and flung it against a wall. "I said *enough*, dammit!"

Sitting on the floor, her legs crossed, the girl used her arms to back away. She looked terrified, a reaction so foreign to their relationship it startled him.

"Patty, I'm sorry. I, I have a lot on my mind and I just lost my temper. I didn't mean to scare you. Okay? All right?" As he moved toward her, she pushed herself farther away, floundered to get up and onto her bed, then buried her head in the pillow.

"Patty, please. I'm sorry. It'll never happen again. I swear. C'mon."

Within the muffled sobs, he made out, "You're not my brother. You're not my brother."

"What the hell's goin' on in here?" came from the hall.

Their mother appeared in the doorway. "What's all this— What's wrong with Patty?" she demanded, hurling a look at her son.

"I, I yelled at her. I'm sorry. I told her to turn the music down but she— I'm trying to write something for tomorrow and. . ." His dejection shrouded him.

Mary's expression softened. "I'll take care of this. You go. Write what ya gotta write. She'll be okay."

Piza went back to his room, closed the door, and sat at his desk. He stared at the blank pad for over a minute. Then, he spat out, "Fuck this. This is what you're turning me into? Some kind of scared, out-of-control asshole? You and your head games, Giacobbi? And you, Lombardo? You pompous ass. No. No way."

He finished his presentation in an hour.

On Wednesday, May 8, the pall that had hung over Piza's class Monday and Tuesday was even darker. He'd tried to project a positive attitude those days, with little success. Today he dropped all pretense of buoyancy, and conducted class with a resigned efficiency.

On the letter-writing campaign, each of the kids had written one, as had several students from other classes. A fair number of parents had contributed as well. But it was on the attendance front that Bob Giacobbi's gambit appeared to be working.

The short notice had proven to be a dagger to the heart of efforts to get parents to go to the meeting. As of Wednesday, only two were confirmed—Darlene Robinson and Florence Schaeffer. Noreen Davis had sent a note in with her son, promising she would do everything she could to try to get out of work for an hour. "Fingers crossed, Mr. Piza," the boy had said. "Fingers crossed, Mr. Davis."

When the dismissal bell rang, his students stood, but seemed reluctant to move. He was touched by the show of loyalty. "Come on, people. It's a meeting, not a firing squad."

Minus the grin that always accompanied his quips, Ralph Restivo observed, "It's a firing squad if they actually fire you."

"Okay, that's it, you guys. Gloom-and-doom is now officially forbidden. I need some good karma. Happy thoughts. In fact, add that to your homework assignment. Out into the hall with you. It'll be fine. Really."

Who am I kidding?

42

Piza sat at his desk, surveying the classroom; taking in details that had faded from awareness over the months. He knew it was maudlin, but he was invested in this space. If this was goodbye, he wanted to accord it the distinction it deserved.

At lunch, he'd filled in O'Brien and Bauer on the latest attendance status. "Two. That's it. And an 'if at all possible' from Mrs. Davis . . . which I know is sincere. I mean, don't get me wrong, I wasn't expecting a massive turnout, no matter when they had this thing. Most people don't wanna get involved. But I was sure as hell hoping for more than two, and I know there were others who'd have been here if they could. Goddamn Giacobbi."

They'd pressed to keep him company after school until the hearing started. But he'd fended them off, telling them with a manufactured smile that their likely overwrought efforts to bolster his spirits would just be depressing, and the whole thing would crumble into a forced-grin death watch.

At four twenty, he slipped into the jacket of his navy-blue pinstripe suit—attire he normally reserved for weddings and funerals—and, briefcase in hand, made his way to the cafeteria. Entering through the double doors, he was surprised to be greeted by semi-darkness. The lights were off in the back section of the room, where the doors were located, the front being the only lit area. The place looked desolate. The Board had barred attendance to all but those who would be speaking.

Despite his anxiety, as he walked to the front he almost laughed out loud at the symbolism. *I've got on my funeral suit, walking from the darkness into the light. I'm in a freaking Fellini film where heaven is hell and smells like this afternoon's meatloaf special.*

Approaching two small groupings of worn, metal folding chairs separated by a makeshift aisle, he spotted Bauer and O'Brien in the first row on the left. They'd been looking back when he entered, and he noticed O'Brien checking her watch.

Bauer made his way up the aisle to meet him. "Bride's side or groom's?"

"Cute, Jimbo. I'm not sure I like this new, moderately amusing side of you."

Bauer's nose had wrinkled during his friend's response, and now he reached into his pocket and fished out a packet of Sen-Sen mints. "Been buying these ever since you made fun of me the day of the Christmas show."

"Shit. Thanks. This isn't a good sign, buddy. I hardly ever get bad breath."

"Come on, let's go up," Bauer said, putting a hand on Piza's shoulder. "Apparently the accused gets the left side, considering Monsignor Lombardo's sitting over there." He gestured with his chin toward the right.

Lombardo was in the middle of the first row, separated from Mother John by three chairs. Neither of them looked at the other.

In the fifth row on the left, Darlene Robinson and Florence Schaeffer sat next to each other. Piza stopped to acknowledge and thank them, adding, "Why don't you move up? Closer to all the excitement."

The women looked at each other, and Schaeffer replied, "That's okay. We kind of just want to stay out of the way. Good luck. I hope we can help." Robinson crossed her fingers.

"Thanks. I'm sure you will."

Bauer took his seat to the left of O'Brien, while Piza sat on the aisle seat to her right.

"Cuttin' it kinda close, don't ya think?" she whispered, looking at her watch again.

Piza shrugged. "You know how I like to make an entrance. So, that's the Board, milling around by the table up there?"

"Yeah. They've been here for a while, except for—"

"Crap! That's DiGregorio."

"Uh-huh," O'Brien said. "He got here a couple of minutes before you. Didn't look too thrilled, either. Looks like he came right from a construction site."

With a shake of the head, Piza said, "Great. This just keeps getting better." He scanned the area. "There's no table for me to sit at. The Board gets a table. All I get is that microphone standing up there?"

O'Brien rolled her eyes. "Well, we tried to book the Supreme Court, but it was—"

The scraping sound of the metal chairs cut her off, as the board members took their seats. Some looked at Piza; others seemed to purposely avoid eye contact.

After the Pledge of Allegiance, Bob Giacobbi called the meeting to order and had the board secretary call the roll. That accomplished, he began his introductory remarks. "This is a special meeting of the Board of Education of Our Lady of Perpetual Tears school. We only have one item on the agenda—an appeal by a teacher, Anthony Piza, from a decision by our pastor, Monsignor Lombardo, to terminate his employment.

"From what I understand, this is the first time we've had

something like this for as long as anyone can remember, which says a lot about the quality of the teachers we've had here in the past. I can't stress enough how important this hearing is. The future well-being of our students could be at stake, depending on what we do today."

Oh, please. Could you possibly lay it on any thicker, you dipshit?

"Well, Bob, let's not forget the small matter of this *teacher's* future." There was no mistaking the scorn in board vice president, Vince Carbone's, comment.

Giacobbi appeared taken aback. "Well yeah, of course. Absolutely." He regrouped. "I assumed that was implied."

"You know what they say about assuming, Bob," the man responded with a smirk.

DiGregorio rapped his knuckles on the table. "Can we just move this along?"

"Sure, Joe," Giacobbi immediately answered. "Um, we received letters from some students and parents. Our board secretary made copies. You should have them in front of you. That was a courtesy, since I don't think they're relevant to what this teacher did or didn't do."

"Relevant or not, I wish we'd gotten them sooner," Margaret Franklin declared. "I'm skimming through some of them and —" Her eyes widened as she held up one of the letters. "Geez, this one is from your son, Mr. Giacobbi. Mr. Piza is his teacher?"

"Yeah, Piza's his teacher. What of it?"

Carbone looked incredulous. "What of it? Should you even be participating in this?"

Giacobbi's sly grin was a giveaway that he was prepared for the question. "Well, Vince, I thought of that, of course. Maryann checked the bylaws, and there's nothing in there that says I have to disqualify myself. Isn't that right, Maryann?"

"Not that I could find."

"That's ridiculous," Franklin protested. "It's common sense."

DiGregorio huffed. "Look, if you's gotta do somethin' wit' the bylaws, do it some other time, okay? We gotta get goin' here."

Looking resolute, Franklin said, "Oh, we'll be doing something all right. This is a major oversight." Settling herself, she picked up the letters. "At any rate, I'd have liked time to review these more thoroughly. But from what I can see, they seem to be very complimentary. Makes me wonder why we're even here."

Marry me, lady.

"Well, let's not jump the gun, Mrs. Franklin, okay?" Giacobbi said, looking peeved. "We haven't heard from anyone yet. So, let's get to it. Um, who starts, Maryann?"

"Oh. Uh, geez, I'm not sure," the board secretary answered. "We haven't really had something like this, so. . ." She began searching a thick binder. "I'm, uh, not . . . really . . . seeing anything off the bat here."

"Mr. Piza, you go first. It's your appeal," Giacobbi ordered.

"Actually, I'd rather go last, if that's okay. I think you should hear from Monsignor Lombardo exactly why he's letting me go, before you hear from me."

Giacobbi's expression hardened. "I'm running this meeting, and I say—"

"Would someone please just start talkin' already," DiGregorio pleaded, arms outstretched.

Monsignor Lombardo rose and approached the microphone. "I'll go, Mr. President. It's fine."

"Okay, Monsignor." Giacobbi hurled a scowl at Piza.

The priest laid out his case without going into great detail, although he did emphasize Piza's language when he confronted the blonde at the park outing. Regarding Sister Theresa's pushing the woman, he editorialized that his persuasive talk with the "victim" was the only thing that had averted a lawsuit. And when referencing Piza's "mocking" a pope, and dressing as a priest, he appeared to focus his attention almost exclusively on Meg

O'Leary, whose reaction to the revelations registered just shy of distraught.

Christ, the woman's holding rosary beads. This isn't looking good.

Mother John spoke next, her reluctance apparent. She related the underlying facts associated with the pastor's allegations, but didn't mirror his self-serving slant. Yes, Piza had facetiously referenced a pope in one of his lessons. Yes, he had dressed as a priest at the Christmas show. Yes, he made an unseemly remark to the woman on the tennis court. But she also made a point of saying that his occasionally unorthodox teaching methods hadn't had any adverse effect on the children. "On the contrary, I've noticed an enthusiasm from his students that you don't often see."

"Sounds like you should be testifying for *him*." The snarky comment came from Sam Thompson, Giacobbi's bowling buddy, who then glanced at the president, as if seeking approval.

The nun's normally narrow eyes were now slits. "Mr. Thompson, let's be clear. I'm not here to testify for *anyone*. I'm the principal of this school. My job today, as I see it, is to put everything being discussed here in perspective, and that's what I'm trying to do. And let me add something. As far as what happened in the park, that woman struck that child very hard, without provocation. So please keep that in mind when weighing Mr. Piza's response to what she did."

"With all due respect, Mother John, you weren't there," Giacobbi tossed out.

"No, I wasn't. But I've spoken to people who were."

Darlene Robinson stood. "I *was* there. So was Mrs. Schaeffer." She motioned to her. "Mother John is absolutely right."

"You'll have your turn, madam," was Giacobbi's surly response.

Her eyes locked on to his. "I'm aware of that, sir. I just wanted to set the record straight."

O'Brien lightly elbowed Piza. "Tough cookie."

Giacobbi looked at Monsignor Lombardo. "Anything else on your end, Monsignor?"

"No. That's it."

"Okay, then I guess we can move on. Mr. Piza, what do you have?"

DiGregorio stood up. "I gotta hit the john. Gimme a couple a minutes."

"Okay, let's take five minutes," Giacobbi declared.

Piza turned to the parents, offering a smile. A guilty-looking Darlene Robinson shrugged. "Sorry. Should've kept my big mouth shut."

"Not at all," Piza reassured her. "I'm glad you said it. It's fine."

Bauer tapped O'Brien and Piza, and motioned to an isolated spot. When they reached it, he said, "So, what do we think so far?"

O'Brien turned up her palms. "We already know which way Giacobbi and DiGregorio are goin'. Seems like that smarmy Thompson guy's definitely in Giacobbi's pocket. The others . . . I'm not sure."

"Seriously?" Piza said. "The lady clutching the rosary? She looked like she needed a grief counselor after Lombardo mentioned the pope thing and the priest outfit."

"Yeah, but that was before Mother John spoke," Bauer countered. "And they haven't heard from any of *us* yet. When it comes down to it, maybe she'll look past that other stuff and realize that letting you stay is just the right thing to do."

"I guess, Jimbo."

O'Brien took Piza by the shoulders and turned him directly toward her. "I don't know what you're plannin' to say, but listen to me. If any of those people are up in the air, the only way you're gonna move them is by bein' up-front with them. Anything else is gonna fall flat."

Piza sighed. "Actually, Colleen, that's exactly what I'm gonna do. I seriously considered bullshitting my way through this. I don't have as much faith in truth as you do. But I realized last night that that would make me as much a two-faced asshole as Giacobbi. If I'm gonna go down, at least I'll have my say."

She smiled. "Okay then. And remember"—lightly punching his arm—"be charming."

43

When the hearing resumed, Florence Schaeffer and Darlene Robinson gave their accounts of the incident at the park. Neither had seen Marlene slap Laura, but they both confirmed the handprint on her cheek, and how shaken she was when she left the tennis court.

Schaeffer told them the story of her tussle with her daughter to keep her out of school when she was ill. She concluded with, "Fighting me to go *into* school? With a hundred-one fever? How many teachers can inspire that? That's gotta tell you something, right?"

Robinson also sang Piza's praises, particularly how he'd handled the situation in the hall, when the eighth-graders harassed her daughter. She didn't mention DiGregorio's son by name, but Piza stole glances at the man to check for a reaction. If it bothered him, he didn't show it.

When it was Bauer's turn, he confirmed the parents' version of what happened in the park. He also mentioned the Christmas show costumes, saying how it was all in good fun and no disrespect was intended by either of them. When he returned to his seat, Piza leaned in and said, "Thanks for not mentioning how I completely blindsided you that day."

Bauer winked. "Don't think I wasn't tempted, pal."

Having been on the tennis court at the time of the ruckus, O'Brien was able to give a more detailed narrative. She emphasized Marlene's arrogance, even when confronted with the unmistakably traumatized child and the evidence of how hard she'd struck her. And she noted that as angry as Piza had been with the woman—justifiably in her opinion—that's how gentle he'd been with Laura. "I wish you could have seen how compassionate and comforting he was."

She stood there for a few moments, eyeing each of the board members. Then, in a voice rife with resentment and entreaty, she said, "He's a good teacher. Don't do this to him." With that, she turned and went back to her seat.

Giacobbi broke the ensuing silence. "Uh, yes. Well, I'm sure we all appreciate your opinion, Miss O'Brien. But we've got a job to do, and we'll make our decision based on facts, not sentimentality. Mr. Piza, do you have anyone else? If not, let's hear what you have to say."

Piza looked to the rear, checking to see if Noreen Davis had materialized, even though he knew she hadn't. *So be it.*

He reached into his briefcase and removed the yellow legal pad; then he hesitated. *I've reviewed this a hundred times. If I don't know what to say by now. . .* He put it away.

With a shallow exhale, he stood, buttoned his jacket, and approached the microphone. "Good evening. Well, technically, I guess it's still afternoon, so good afternoon." He tugged at the bottom of the jacket. "I've never experienced anything like I did last week, when Monsignor Lombardo told me he was firing me. Granted, I'm only twenty-two, and this is my first full-time job, but I've worked summer jobs and such since high school. Before last Wednesday, no one had ever told me my work wasn't satisfactory. Certainly never called me a *clown*."

A few of the board members shot looks at Lombardo: some quizzical; some disapproving.

"My initial reaction was shock. The fact that it was happening. The fact that someone would see me like that, especially since I didn't believe I deserved it. But then something else struck me. And, honestly, it scared me. How would this impact my future? To have this black mark on my record.

"Well, Monsignor must have been reading my mind, because he offered me an out. Resign, for personal reasons. Nice and neat. I leave voluntarily; no embarrassing termination on my record. And I've gotta tell you, as much as I felt what was happening was unfair, that offer sounded like it might be my best bet. Even with this appeal process available to me, I couldn't get past the possibility of this whole thing ruining my life. It took a talk with my dad to get my head straight.

"When I applied for this job, I had no formal background in education. But I mean, ya know, how hard could it be? You stand in front of some kids, spout out some facts from a textbook, answer any questions they might have, and, hopefully, they learn something." A clipped laugh. "I *hate* admitting I'm wrong, but boy was I off.

"Truth is, my attitude, and my understanding of what I was getting into, were pathetic. I had no clue how difficult teaching is, even on the best of days. Mother John tried to warn me during my interview. How you're not just dealing with a group, but really with individual personalities. And I don't doubt that after a week or two of my being here, she was probably wondering if she'd made a mistake. And I'll admit, she might have, if I was the same person now that I was then."

"So, you're a changed man, Mr. Piza?" Giacobbi scoffed. "Is *that* it? Touching. But what's any of that got to do with this hearing? With what you did?"

"Let him finish, Bob," Vince Carbone snapped.

"Fine. Just move it along."

Piza held eye contact with him. "In answer to your question, Mr. Giacobbi, how I changed has everything to do with why we're here today. And, frankly, it affects *you*, considering I teach your son. Just like it affects every one of my students"—turning to Robinson and Schaeffer—"and their families. Because eventually I learned that teaching's not about doling out information. It's about shaping lives. Not just *touching* lives; we all do that in some way. But actually shaping them.

"I mean, think about it. A job where, every day, what you do and say can influence the direction of a child's future; occasionally maybe impact how their lives turn out. And look, that's not gonna be the case with every student. But even if it's a few, or just one for that matter, how awesome and terrifying a responsibility is that?

"I didn't understand that in the beginning. But I was lucky. I had help from some really smart, dedicated people. Teachers I respect and . . . and, uh, care about. And I get it now. I won't pretend to be the teacher they are, but that doesn't mean I'm not capable. If I didn't believe that, we wouldn't be here today. But more importantly, I'm here because I owe it to my kids. I'm not leaving them. Not voluntarily. Not without a fight. Thank you."

Giacobbi maneuvered in his chair and looked like he was about to speak, but Bill Santucci spoke first. The man had remained passive throughout the hearing, and the teacher hadn't been able to get a read on him.

"Mr. Piza, I have to say I'm impressed with your take on teaching. My wife teaches in a public school, and I know what it's like for her. But even though Bob's comments to you before were a little sarcastic"—looking at Giacobbi—"he makes a valid point. We're really here because of a few specific incidents.

"Frankly, I'm not concerned with the priest costume at the Christmas show. I was there, and I didn't think it was disrespectful. It made me laugh, in fact. And as for the park, well, under the circumstances, I think we should cut you some slack. But

Monsignor's charge that you mocked the Pope concerns me. After all, this is a Catholic school. I realize Mother John seemed to think it was more 'facetious' than anything else, but I think the only way we can honestly judge the issue is if we know exactly what you said."

Piza explained the purpose of the Henry VIII lesson; how he'd used the concept of a phone call among Henry, Anne, and the Pope, and that his intention wasn't to be irreverent, but simply to inject a little humor and make it more entertaining for the kids. Finishing the narrative, he said, "When Henry realized he wasn't going to get his annulment, he knew he wouldn't be speaking with the Pope again. So he asked him if he could ship up more of the lasagna he'd sent once before. And the Pope hung up on him."

The reaction of the board members varied. Giacobbi and Thompson scowled. Santucci, Carbone, and Franklin smiled. Mrs. O'Leary stared down at the table and worked her beads. And DiGregorio? He unleashed a burst of laughter. "Sendin' 'im lasagna. I like that. That's funny stuff. Lasagna." He didn't seem to care that the other members were staring at him. He looked back at them, wearing an expansive grin. "Funny, right?"

Giacobbi quickly redirected the focus. "Anyhow, despite Mr. Santucci glossing over it, there's the park confrontation. It's bad enough one of our nuns pushed that woman, but—"

Piza cut him off. "What Sister Theresa did was what any decent person would've done. That woman had slapped one of our kids across the face, and was still latched onto her jacket. The child was terrified. Pushing her released her grip and protected the girl."

"Fine," Giacobbi responded. "My understanding is this nun's no longer at the school, anyway. But what about your mouth? The fact you almost got us sued?"

"What I said was wrong. For whatever it's worth, I never finished my thought when I was talking to Mrs. Smith, or whatever her name really was. I never mentioned . . . a part of her anatomy, contrary to Monsignor's implication. And, by the way, as I told him, I have no doubt whatsoever her threat to sue was a bluff, considering she assaulted a child.

"I don't know how many of you are parents, but think how you'd feel if your child had been on the receiving end of that woman's temper. I let my emotions get the best of me, and I apologize for that. Monsignor Lombardo reprimanding me for it, I get that. But firing me? I'm sorry, but I don't believe that's right. And I don't think it's fair to my students."

No one else said anything. Giacobbi looked up and down the table. "Anyone have any other questions?" No response. "Then I guess we can vote. Mr. Piza, you can take your seat." The teacher obliged. "Okay, let's—"

The secretary interrupted him. "Um, Bob, should we exclude the public from this part?"

"Oh. Well, we've got teachers. Other than them there's only the two women . . . and I'd like them to see this."

"If they want to stay, it's okay with me," Piza said. He looked back at Robinson and Schaeffer, who both nodded.

"Anybody else care?" Giacobbi asked. No one objected. "Okay, let's get on with this. A 'yes' vote means you agree with the appeal, and he stays. 'No' means his appeal's rejected. Maryann?"

Pen in hand, the secretary smoothed out the voting sheet resting on the table.

"Mrs. Franklin."

"Yes."

"Mr. Thompson."

"No."

"Mr. DiGregorio."

"Yes, he stays; no, he goes?"

"Correct."

"Okay, no."

"Mr. Carbone."

"Yes."

"Mr. Santucci."

"Yes."

"Mrs. O'Leary."

Fingers grasping her rosary, the woman looked tormented. She glanced at Piza, then turned away. "I, um— No. I'm voting no."

Piza's head dropped.

"Mr. Giacobbi."

"No. The appeal's denied."

O'Brien placed her hand on Piza's, as Bauer murmured, "I can't believe this."

Florence Schaeffer looked shocked, and Darlene Robinson uttered, "This isn't right."

"Well, I guess that's that," a smug Lombardo intoned. He looked toward Mother John and lowered his voice. "No thanks to you."

"I followed my conscience, Monsignor."

"Yes, yes, I'm sure you did. But he brought this on himself, so don't expect me to feel bad about—"

His attention shifted to the back of the cafeteria, as did everyone else's, drawn by the grating squeak of an opening door.

As the figure made its way through the darkened section of the room, Bauer squinted, then turned to Piza. "Mrs. Davis?"

Piza shook his head in disbelief. "Mrs. Giacobbi."

44

Sandra Giacobbi emerged from the dark, neatly dressed in a black skirt and white silk blouse, her hair down. It was a more purposeful look than the one she'd presented at the parent-teacher conference.

As she reached the microphone, DiGregorio grinned and gave a wave. "Hey, Sandy."

She smiled back. "Hi, Joe."

Her husband greeted her with a gruff, "What are you doing here, Sandra?"

Glancing past him, she looked at the other board members. "Um, I was hoping to say a few words. I hope I'm not too late, but there was a traffic jam, and—"

"The meeting's over," the scowling president said. "And there's no reason for you to be here anyway. Where's Robert?"

"He's with my sister. And there *is* a reason for me to be here, Bob. I don't want to see Mr. Piza fired."

"We've already voted to terminate him," he responded with a scant, twisted smile.

"Oh, no. I, I think that's a big mistake." She peered at the other members again. "I know I'm late, but can't I be allowed to say something?"

His face reddening, her husband fixed her with a glare. "No. How many times do I have to say it?"

"Wait a minute, Bob," Vince Carbone said, eyeing Giacobbi with unmistakable disgust. "What's the problem? I'd like to hear what she has to say. It's not her fault she got caught in traffic." Franklin, Santucci, and O'Leary nodded in approval.

DiGregorio looked baffled. "What's wrong wit' you, Bobby? It's Sandy. Let 'er talk."

The president made a show of sighing, then leaned back. "Fine."

Sandra lightly cleared her throat. "We have one child. Robert. Mr. Piza is his teacher." Her tone was soft but steady. "We've been fortunate. Bob makes a good living, and we've been able to give Robert anything he wants. Too much sometimes, I think."

Giacobbi sat up straighter, and his wife's eyes darted in his direction.

Clearing her throat again, she continued. "Our son's a smart boy. Always got good grades. But I'm not sure he ever really enjoyed school. He never had any close friends. Sometimes I think because we never said no to him, he felt he was . . . I don't know, maybe *above* other kids." You could hear her husband's pinky ring rapping the table. "But these past few months, his attitude's changed. He's made friends. He's a happier kid. And I think a lot of that is because of Mr. Piza. He's become kind of a role model, I guess, and—"

Giacobbi jumped up and planted his hands on the table, his face taut with barely controlled rage. "Okay, that's enough, Sandra. I think we've all heard enough. We'll discuss this when I get home." His unblinking eyes stayed locked on her. "Better yet, go visit your friends from that bridge club you're always going to. Maybe they wanna listen to you."

As the others in the room stared at him, his wife's demeanor shifted. Eyes smoldering and fists clenched at her sides, she said, "Discuss it when we get home, Bob? Like we discuss everything else? I try to talk; you tell me to shut up?" She was trembling. "Or maybe you mean the discussions where you bypass 'shut up' and throw me against a wall." The collective gasp quickly faded to stunned silence. "And it isn't a bridge club, Bob. It's a support group. For abused women."

Drained of color, her reeling husband felt his way back onto his seat. "Wh— What are you talking about? Support group? I— I never pushed you." His head pivoted from side to side, his frantic gaze taking in all those in the room. "I never pushed her. I swear. It's a lie." He pointed a quivering finger at her. "You're a damned liar." His bluster couldn't mask the fear; the desperation.

DiGregorio got up slowly and faced him. Piza recognized the dead eyes he'd seen in the hall when he first met the man. "You push her around? You hurt her?" He turned to Sandra. "How many times he done that, Sandy? More than— Oh, Jesus. When you was in the hospital, was that. . ."

She averted her eyes without answering.

The contractor radiated menace. "What kinda man does that to a woman like her? She's a sweetheart, you piece a scum. You mutt. We're done, me and you. Includin' my business."

A bug-eyed Giacobbi struggled to speak. "Wa-wait, Joe. Le-let's discuss this when you calm down. Okay? Okay? I know we—"

"Shut up," DiGregorio said, lip curled. "Ya sound like a girl." He started to sit, then stood again. "And one more thing. I changed my mind. I'm changin' my vote on this kid. Maybe he's a smartass, but I like 'im. He's funny. Wish I had a couple a funny teachers. I might'a stayed in school longer. So I vote he stays."

Giacobbi was now on his feet. "You can't do that. We, we already voted. That's not allowed, right, Maryann? It's in the rules, right?"

The secretary's voice dripped disdain. "I'm not aware of anything that says board members can't change their vote."

Giacobbi swung around toward DiGregorio. "You, you can't do this. We had a deal, dammit!" The words had scarcely escaped when his face registered the panic of awareness.

"What?" from Margaret Franklin. "A deal? What are you talking about? Mr. Giacobbi? Mr. DiGregorio?"

The contractor eyed the ensnared president. "Yeah, whaddya talkin' about? Durin' the bathroom break before, I told ya I was leanin' toward cannin' the kid, but I wanted to hear more. Since when's that a deal?"

His head bobbing, Giacobbi slumped onto his chair. "No, no, you're right, Joe. What I meant was that I thought it was a done deal. Ya know, on your part. That you'd made up your mind. That's all. I, I should've been clearer. Sorry. My fault."

After several moments of silence, as it became evident the visibly broken president wasn't moving to end the proceedings, Carbone asked, "Does anyone have anything to add?"

The board members all shook their heads, but Monsignor Lombardo approached the microphone. "Well, in light of these rather startling, disturbing revelations, I think there needs to be a discussion of Mr. Giacobbi's fitness to continue serving as board president . . . or in any capacity, for that matter."

That seemed to revive Giacobbi. "Wait a minute. This is her word against mine. She never pressed any charges against me. Uh, not that she could have because I, I never did anything. At the very least I'm entitled to a hearing."

"Well, this isn't only about whether you did these despicable things," the priest replied, unable to completely contain how much he was relishing this. "For a Catholic school like ours, perception is extremely important. Just the appearance of OLPT tolerating the behavior you're accused of could be devastating, both to the school and our community."

"Look," Carbone said, "as I understand it, the Board can

remove any member if a majority decide there's sufficient cause. We're all here. So why don't we just deal with it now and get it over with."

There were murmurs of approval, DiGregorio adding, "I gotta get back to the job. But I can stick around a little longer for this."

Carbone nodded. "Okay, so let's take a few minutes to clear our heads. Mr. Piza, you've won your appeal, so you're officially back in good standing. Now, I'd ask anyone who was here for the appeal, except Monsignor and Mother John, to please leave the room, so we can conduct this other meeting in private."

O'Brien squeezed Piza's arm; Bauer patted him on the back.

As the board members wandered from the table, DiGregorio approached Giacobbi, who was sitting with his hands in his lap, staring into space. The contractor put his hands on the back of the man's chair, and leaned forward. "I ain't sure what's gonna happen here now, Bobby. But I do know what's gonna happen if you lay a hand on her again."

Stepping away from Giacobbi, DiGregorio signaled Piza to join him.

Oh God. If he tells me I'm in his debt for the rest of my life, this time I'm definitely *gonna shit my pants.*

"So, you okay, kid?"

"I'm good, Mr. DiGregorio. And thank you for what you did. I appreciate it."

"Nah, it's nothin'. You believe that asshole, tellin' me I can't change my mind? Anyways, if he's still around after tonight—ya know, on the Board and all—and he ever tries bustin' your balls again, you call me. You still got my card?"

"Um, yep." He patted his back pocket. "Safe and sound in my wallet, as we speak."

"Okay, good. I like you, kid. That thing with the Pope and the lasagna? Hysterical. You're gonna go places, sense a humor like that. Anyways, good luck." They shook hands.

Piza bid goodbye to Mrs. Schaeffer and Mrs. Robinson, thanking them again for their support. As he went to rejoin O'Brien and Bauer, Mother John intercepted him.

"I hope you know how relieved I am," she said. "It shouldn't have come to this."

"I couldn't agree more. But at least it's over. And thanks for going to bat for me. Is this gonna make things more difficult for you with Monsignor?"

Her tiny eyes twinkled. "I don't think so. I get the impression Mr. Giacobbi may not be on the Board after this evening. He certainly won't be president. Either way, that's a bigger benefit than Monsignor could've ever hoped for when all this began. No offense, Mr. Piza, but you're a small fish compared to Bob Giacobbi when it comes to Monsignor's wish list."

Piza raised his hands, palms forward. "Believe me, I'm not offended in the least. This is one time I'm fine coming in second."

She sighed. "Okay, then. We'll see you tomorrow. I know some children who are going to be very happy."

As she returned to her seat, Piza approached O'Brien and Bauer, clapped his hands once and rubbed them together. "Okay, you two. My comrades-in-arms. Rocco's? On me."

"I'm in," from O'Brien.

"Wouldn't miss it," Bauer said. "Especially with you buying. I just wanna let Beth know what happened. She'll be thrilled you're staying."

"Great. Give her my best. I'll meet you guys in a couple of minutes, okay? I just wanna talk to Mrs. Giacobbi. Crap, she's leaving."

"Go," O'Brien told him. "Take whatever time you need."

Piza bolted up the aisle, catching the woman as she reached the cafeteria doors.

"Hey," he said, opening a door for her. They stepped into the hall. "I don't know how to begin to thank you for what you did tonight. I can't imagine what it must've been like for you to confront him like that."

She wore a look of tentative relief. "It's something I should've done a long time ago. Although I didn't mean for it to come out here . . . ya know, him pushing me and all. But that sarcastic mouth. It was like something inside me snapped. All I really wanted was to tell them about the difference you've made in my son's life. He's like a different boy. If you left now, it'd crush him."

"Well, truth is it would've torn me up too." After a slight hesitation, he said, "So, if you don't mind my asking, what are you gonna do now?"

Determination in her voice, she replied, "Bob and I have to talk. I needed help coming to grips with"—a humorless laugh—"well, pretty much everything. Still do. But he needs help too. A lot." She breathed a weary sigh. "To be honest, I'm not even sure he's capable of changing. Deep down. Or if he even wants to. I guess we'll see. All I know is I can't keep living like this. And neither can Robert." An expression fraught with the burden of guilt surfaced. "When I think of what that child's been through, because I didn't have the courage to. . ."

"Listen to me," Piza said, locking eyes with her. "Whatever the past, you've found the strength *now*. That's the important thing. And Robert? He's a tough kid. With a little support, he'll get through this. I truly believe that."

She managed a sad smile. "I can see why he likes you so much."

"Thank you," he responded, blushing. "Um, I know you said you guys need to talk, but considering what just happened. . ."

"No, don't worry. It won't be tonight. And when we do, it won't be alone. Actually, I spoke to my sister. Robert and I are gonna stay with her until things get sorted out. One way or another."

"Well, sounds like you've got some good people behind you."

"I do."

They stood there, silent, for a few seconds. Then she tilted her head and, with warmth in her voice, said, “So, are you gonna celebrate your victory?”

He answered with an engaging nod and, “I am, indeed.”

But first I’ve gotta get to a phone. I need to call my parents.

45

Piza's students marched in lockstep into the classroom, and lined the room's perimeter. He had no idea what was going on, but it was too interesting not to let it play out. When the last child was in place, Sukie approached the teacher. "Can I borrow this, Mr. Piza?" she asked, pointing to a pencil protruding from his desktop organizer.

"Sure," he replied, a pleasant wariness in his voice.

She plucked the yellow stick from the holder, then stood in front of his desk. Pencil in her right hand, she raised her arms and announced, "Okay, everybody. On the count of three. One, two, three."

The group broke into the "Hallelujah Chorus". Actually, it was the first line of the song, sung four times, after which Sukie lowered the makeshift baton, turned to the teacher, and bowed.

That triggered raucous applause and a mad rush to Piza's desk. They were all talking at once, but that was as much music to him as their take on the classical masterpiece.

Amid the turmoil, he caught Matt Majinsky's eye. "Well, Mr. Majinsky?"

The boy looked confused. Laura smiled and whispered in her friend's ear. He broke into a grin and discharged a massive "Oh yeah, baby!", which drew renewed applause.

As the hoopla subsided, Piza shooed the kids back to their desks. When they settled in, he said, "Thanks, you guys. If I wasn't afraid of tarnishing my image, I'd have wept at the sheer beauty of your collective voices raised in song. How long has that been in the works?"

"About ten minutes," William Reilly answered.

The teacher cast a skeptical look. "No way."

"No, it's true," Karen Jablonski said. "I mean, we couldn't plan it sooner, because we— Ya know . . . we didn't know if you were even gonna be here. Which would've made us super angry, by the way!"

Rebecca Schaeffer jumped in. "Shirley and I started making phone calls last night, after our moms got back from the meeting, so pretty much all of us knew what happened."

Piza felt a jolt of concern. "Did, uh, your moms tell you *everything* that happened?"

"My mom only said you won, and that you were still gonna be our teacher," Rebecca stated.

Shirley nodded. "Mine too."

Stupid of me to worry. I should've known they wouldn't go into details. "Got it. So, tell me more about this production number you just treated me to."

Vinny Pinto joined the conversation. "Yeah, so while we were in the parking lot this morning, waiting for the bell, Robert had the idea to do it."

Piza pointed at Giacobbi, who returned the gesture.

"We figured even we couldn't screw up marching in and standing around the classroom," Ralph Restivo said, drawing laughs.

"That was the only part of the song we knew," Laura added. "Sister Joann tried teaching it to us before Easter, but she kept shaking her head and then she just gave up." More laughter still.

"Well, thank you all again," Piza said. "For everything you did. The letters and— Well, just everything."

Kevin Davis nudged aside the resulting silence. "We're just glad you're back, Mr. Piza."

The teacher smiled. "Me too."

As he locked his classroom, about to head to the teachers' lounge for lunch, Piza spotted Mother John walking up the hall.

She quickened her pace and hailed him. "Ah, Mr. Piza. I was hoping I'd catch you."

"Hi, Mother. Everything okay?"

"Yes, yes," she said, slightly out of breath. "I just wanted a word in private. I thought your classroom might work better than the office."

Very cloak and dagger. "Um, of course." He unlocked the door, and as they entered said, "Would you like to sit at my desk? I'm happy to defer to rank."

She chuckled. "No. Not necessary."

He wanted to spare her from attempting to squeeze into a student desk, so he got the two plastic chairs from against the wall. "Equal footing at least," he said through a smile.

After they sat, she surveyed the classroom. "It looks cheery."

"Thanks. I'd love to take credit, but the kids kind of shamed me into it. A few of them stay after school occasionally and recycle some of the old stuff in the closet. Plus we put up some of their book reports and artwork."

"Well, it looks very nice. So, I wanted to fill you in on what happened after you left."

"Oh, great. I was actually gonna try to find you after lunch."

Her eyes widened. "It was quite exciting. Apparently, there

was a lot of bitterness among the members, and I think the revelations about Mr. Giacobbi gave everyone an excuse to vent. The bottom line is they voted him off the Board. The only vote he got was from Mr. Thompson."

"How was DiGregorio?"

"He was actually the most vocal about pushing him out. Between you and me, the man can be a little frightening. Those eyes."

Been there. "Yeah, I think it's fair to say he's a little rough around the edges. But, forgive me for saying this, if he laced into Giacobbi, that's fine with me. That guy didn't deserve to be in a position to make decisions about this school."

"Oh, I agree. I'm thrilled he's gone. Although I almost felt bad for him at the end. He looked so pathetic. But, you reap what you sow. I only hope Robert and his mother are going to be okay."

"Me too." With an uncertain smile, he said, "So, am I off the hook with Monsignor?"

She shrugged. "I'm not sure. This may rear its head again when it's time to renew your contract. But no need to concern ourselves with that now." He was about to respond, but she continued. "Um, there's something else."

Sensing her discomfort, he tensed. "Sister Theresa?"

"Yes. She requested a transfer to a school in another parish."

The possibility of her not returning had been a constant presence. But he'd found a degree of solace in her lingering indecision. Now, in the space of a sentence, hope abandoned him. A decisive and suffocating desertion.

The nun leaned forward. "Mr. Piza, are you all right?"

He fought to focus. "I'm uh— Yeah. Yes, I'm okay. I uh— Did, did this just happen?"

"Actually, over the weekend."

Heartache muted his response. "Why didn't you— You know how impor—"

"I didn't tell you because she asked me not to. With everything else going on, she didn't want to burden you with this."

He looked past her, attempting to collect his thoughts. After a few moments he asked, "Do you know where she'll be going? Someplace local?"

"No. A parish in Philadelphia. Her father lives just outside the city and—"

"Yeah, she, uh, told me about her dad. Philadelphia."

"Yes. She felt it would give her a chance to see him more often. One of the sisters from that parish will be coming here to take her place in September. In the meantime, Sister Joann will continue teaching her class until the end of the school year."

Struggling to conceal his growing desperation, he said, "I, um, I don't know what the protocol is, but is there a chance I could see her?"

With a wince she replied, "I'm so sorry, Mr. Piza, but she's already gone. Mother Superior approved her request on Tuesday, and she left last evening."

The jarring revelation elicited an anxiety laden, "Gone? But, but nobody's had a chance to say goodbye. I mean, I guess you and the other sisters, but what about her other friends? Colleen. Jim. How could she just. . ."

"Mr. Piza, I don't think you understand how difficult this has been for her. And she still has a lot of soul-searching to do. I can't say more than that, but you know she'd never intentionally hurt anyone. So please, give her the benefit of the doubt."

"I'm trying." He sat there. His face blank. "Thanks for letting me know, Mother."

"You're welcome. And again, I'm sorry." She stood. "Oh, and Sister asked me to tell you she's very happy you won the appeal, and also that she knows you'll do the right thing, although I'm not quite sure what she meant by that."

I am. She's telling me not to try to contact her.

"I've gotta go to the office and call a parent," Bauer announced, gathering the brown paper bag and empty milk carton remaining from lunch. He lowered his voice. "I'm sorry, Tony. About Sister Theresa."

"Thanks, Jim. I'll be okay." He managed a smile. "We Sicilians are very resilient."

Bauer squeezed his friend's shoulder. "I have no doubt. Okay, see you guys later."

"Later," O'Brien said. When he left, she turned to Piza. "You look like crap."

"Could we ease up on the candor a bit, Colleen?"

"I'm concerned, that's all."

"I know. God, I knew there was a possibility she wouldn't be back, but hearing it today, the finality of it. Knocked the wind out of me."

"Of course it did. How could it not?"

He looked lost in thought, then said, "You remember Monday after the outing, when we found out she'd left school, we were talking in my room?"

"Uh-huh."

"You said something to the effect that you knew the hurt I was feeling. What's the story with that?"

She ran her thumb gently along the handle of her coffee mug a few times. "I was, um, engaged a while back. It ended last year. February."

"Jesus, I had no idea." His eyes narrowed. "He broke it off?"

"No. I did."

"Oh. But then shouldn't he be the one who was hurt? Am I missing something?"

"I ended it because he cheated. Real cliché, huh?"

"He cheated? On you? What kind of a jerk would do that?"

A soft laugh. "That's very sweet of you." She took a sip, then smiled and added, "The good news is I just started seein' someone. Works with my brother."

A grinning Piza asked, "The priest or the cop?"

"Very funny, wiseguy. He's a detective in Patrick's precinct."

"That's great! When do I get to meet him?"

"Please, I don't wanna scare him away."

"Fine. Snub me."

"Pout all you want, it's not happenin'." After a pause, she touched his arm. "You're gonna be okay, Tony."

"I know. Doesn't make it suck any less."

"No. Not even close."

46

As Piza surveyed the platters of bagels, Bauer sidled up to him. "I need to talk to you for a sec."

"Hey there, Jimbo. Um, sure. Just let me make a decision here first. I'm leaning onion, but, I dunno, those lingering aftereffects. I'm not— Ya know what, screw it. Got any mints on you?"

"Never without them. Thanks again for making me paranoid, by the way." He reached into his pocket and removed the pack. "Take a few, just in case."

"Good man."

"I actually wanted to get Colleen in on this conversation," Bauer said, scanning the room. "Ah, there, by the cold-cut table. Walk over with me."

"Leave it to OLPT to wait until the last day of school to put out a spread like this," Piza observed. "Kind of weird, isn't it? School ending on a Tuesday? Seems disjointed. Should be a Friday." He chomped on the bagel.

Bauer shook his head. "You need help." His friend shrugged.

They reached O'Brien as she was ladling potato salad onto

the dish holding her ham and cheese sandwich. "More choices than last year, that's for sure," she said with an approving nod. "Wonder how they got this past Lombardo? Miser."

"I've got some news, Colleen," Bauer said. "Wanna sit?"

"Nothing bad, I hope."

"No, no," Bauer reassured as he scoured the rearranged teachers' lounge for an empty table. "There," he said, pointing, as a group abandoned a corner spot.

O'Brien glanced at Piza's bagel. "That all you're havin'?"

"No. Kind of an appetizer while I get the lay of the land. I got the onion just for you." He breathed on her.

Swatting the air, she said, "I'd say you're disgusting, but you'd probably take it as a compliment." As they sat, she turned to Bauer. "So, what's goin' on? Oh my God, is Beth pregnant?"

"No, no, no. At some point, maybe, but not right now. Um, I'm not coming back next year. I got a job at a public school in Queens."

His friends' jaws dropped. "When did this happen?" Piza asked.

"I only got confirmation after I got home yesterday afternoon. I didn't wanna say anything until I was certain."

O'Brien kissed him on the cheek. "That's fantastic, Jim. I'm really happy for you. Gonna miss ya, though."

Bauer blushed. "I'll miss you too. But I'd like to stay in touch . . . with both of you," he said, looking at Piza as well.

Piza gave him a thumbs-up. "Absolutely. Dinner at Rocco's every now and then. On you, of course, with your pay increase and all. This is great, Jimbo." With an impish smile, he added, "Plus, they won't care that you're Protestant."

"What?" from a confounded looking O'Brien.

"Really, Tony?" Bauer said, shaking his head.

Piza laughed. "Oh, c'mon. It's just Colleen. And the proverbial cat's already out of the bag, so. . ."

Bauer huffed. "Thanks to you. Look, I'm sorry I never told you about this, Colleen, but the truth is—"

"Wait, wait," Piza interrupted. "Let me tell it. So, first day of school, at mass, I'm standing behind Jim. Everyone's saying the Our Father, and when it's over, he tacks on the Protestant ending. Ya know, 'for thine is the kingdom', and so on. Fortunately for him, no one heard it but me."

Bauer playfully elbowed his friend. "Not that you let me forget it."

O'Brien unleashed a broad grin. "Why, James Bauer. You sneaky devil." A touch of melancholy crept into her voice. "It's gonna be weird next year. Sister Theresa gone. Now both of *you*."

It took a second for Bauer's face to register shock. "Both of us? What—"

"Crap. I'm sorry," O'Brien blurted out. She looked at Piza. "I'm so sorry, Tony. I thought you'd told him."

"It's okay." He turned to Bauer. "I'm leaving too, Jim. I was gonna tell you at some point during our farewell feast here. I only told Colleen yesterday afternoon, after dismissal. And Mother John. I looked for you, but you'd already left."

Bauer still looked flabbergasted. "I, I can't believe it. I mean, when you opted to take the appeal, and then everything you said at the hearing, I figured. . . When did you decide?"

"Ultimately? This past weekend. I'd been up in the air for a while though."

His words tinged with sadness, Bauer said, "So why?"

Piza leaned forward and clasped his hands on the table. "Well, like I told Colleen, I just don't think this is something I can do on a steady basis. Looking back, I think what made this year so special for me wasn't so much the teaching as it was this group of kids. And don't get me wrong, I enjoyed the intellectual give and take. But the thought of dealing with the same subject matter, year after year . . . I dunno."

"So you're saying the novelty wore off?" Bauer asked, his tone free of sarcasm.

Piza shrugged. "I didn't really think of it that way, but maybe, in some sense, yeah." He became more animated. "And that's just it, Jim. I meant every word I said at the hearing. And, thinking about what you said just now, teaching's too important to be someone's 'novelty'. You guys have a dedication I'll never have. I envy you."

There was a brief silence, then O'Brien said, "So, Jim, our friend here has decided to give law school a try."

Bauer perked up. "That's great. Oh, but isn't it kind of late to apply?"

"Actually, law school was on the menu before I landed at OLPT. The schools I was accepted at were willing to hold a place for me for a couple of years. All I have to do is send a letter."

"Oh, okay," Bauer said. "I had no idea. You never mentioned anything. Have you decided which one?"

"Fordham."

O'Brien wore a saccharine smile. "See, he wants to be close to us."

"Don't force me to breathe on you again, O'Brien," Piza said. "Actually, Jimbo, it was a toss-up between Fordham and Boston University until a few minutes ago. Your tacit agreement to pay for an occasional dinner at Rocco's tilted the scales."

Their laughter gave way to a wistful pause. Bauer looked around the room, then at his friends, and sighed. "Well, it was a heck of a year."

Piza popped a mint as he entered the office. A young man was sitting in the waiting area, reading. He lowered his book and nodded an acknowledgment.

"Hey," Piza said. "Are you here to see Mother John?" He motioned toward her closed door.

"Is she the principal? I'm waiting to see the principal."

"She is. Is she in with someone?"

"Um, not sure. The lady in the other office there told me to wait here, and she'd see if the principal could see me. I didn't have an appointment, so. . ."

"Oh. Okay. I'm just dropping something off. Only be a second." He took a few steps toward Mrs. Florino's room. Her door was open, but she was on the phone. Catching her eye, he gestured with his chin toward Mother John's office. The woman nodded.

Piza lightly knocked on the principal's door.

"Come in."

He entered, closing the door behind him. "Came by to return my keys," he said, smiling as he placed them on her desk.

"Ah, thank you. Sit a minute?" He obliged. She sat back in her chair. "So, this is it, then. Any second thoughts?"

"Well, actually, yes, Mother. I, uh, wasn't entirely truthful with you yesterday." Her now somber expression mirrored his. "The fact is, the only reason I'm leaving is to spare you from having to battle Monsignor Lombardo over renewing my contract. I don't want any thanks, just keep me in your prayers." The ensuing broad grin dispelled any notion of seriousness.

She laughed. "See, now that I'll miss."

"Not the aggravation though, I'll bet."

She looked down her nose at him. "I'd be lying if I said you didn't cause me more headaches than I care to remember." Then, with a smile, "But you certainly made the year interesting, no denying that. And in the end, you were a good teacher. That's what really counts. Do they know you're not coming back? The children? Not that you'd have had them again, but even so. . ."

"I didn't say anything this morning. But I'll be seeing them right after I leave you. Some of the parents decided a class pizza party might be a nice way to end the year, so I promised to meet them."

"That's terrific."

"So, do you know how many positions you're gonna have to fill next year?"

"As of now, only yours. One of the new sisters from the novitiate is ready, so she'll take Mr. Bauer's second grade."

"Oh, that's great." He shifted in his seat. "You know, I don't think I ever thanked you for the opportunity you gave me. It was an incredible experience, and I appreciate it."

"You're very welcome." She sighed and then stood. "So, best of luck in law school. I'm sure you'll do well."

"Thank you. I hope so."

As he reached the door, she said, "And stop by to say hello once in a while, if you get the chance."

"Thanks, I just might do that. Think of how crazy it'd make Monsignor if he knew I was anywhere near this place."

Her laughter accompanied him as he exited and closed the door. He was going to bid a quick goodbye to Mrs. Florino, but her door was now closed, and he opted to let the farewell slide. He smiled at the young man as he passed him.

"Um, excuse me," he heard. Turning, he saw the fellow was on his feet, hand extended. "My name's Paul," he said as Piza returned the gesture. "Do you work here?"

"Uh, no. Used to."

"Oh, okay. Would you happen to know if they have any teaching positions open?"

Piza paused, then said, "I'm Tony." He sat down and asked, "What're you reading?"

Paul sat as well. "*The Martian Chronicles*. Ray Bradbury?"

"Heard of it but never read it. Any good?"

"Yeah, actually." A crooked smile. "If things don't work out down here, I was thinking of trying my luck up there. Figured this might help."

Piza donned the look of someone about to deliver bad news. "Sorry to burst your bubble, but I hear it's nothing but a tourist trap."

"Really? Damn. Thanks for the heads-up though."

"Don't mention it," Piza said with a playful flick of the wrist. "So, you just graduate?"

"Uh-huh. Hofstra."

"Education major?"

"Psych, but I got my teaching certification."

"Got it. So, tell me if I'm wrong, but I'm guessing you can't find a job in a public school, so you're scouring the earth for anything available."

Paul blushed. "Kinda, yeah. I figured showing up in person, rather than just sending in a résumé, might give me a better shot. I thought about calling for an appointment, but I tried that with another school and they wouldn't give me one. So I decided to just roll the dice here."

"Seems like a logical approach to me." He looked toward Mrs. Florino's office. "Was *she* all warm and fuzzy?"

With a quick glance in that direction, Paul answered, "Honestly? Not really."

"Made you feel guilty about showing up out of the blue?"

"Made me feel guilty about existing."

Piza muffled a laugh. In the brief ensuing pause, his thoughts jumped back to his initial interview with Mother John. "Let me ask you something, Paul. When you were going for your teaching cert, did anyone ever suggest that you not smile . . . when you start the school year?"

The young man looked perplexed. "Huh? No. Why would— Who told you *that*?"

"Something I heard once. It's nothing."

Paul shrugged off the response with an "okay." Then, a glint in his eye, he added, "I couldn't pull that off, anyway. I'm too inherently charming."

Flashing a grin, Piza said, "Listen, there's an opening in sixth grade. But you didn't hear that from me."

"Not a word. But that'll help me gauge my pitch. Strong desire to teach older kids."

"Just don't oversell," Piza warned, nodding toward the principal's office. "Be straight with her, and she'll be straight with you."

"Got it. Set the dial between low and medium."

"Sounds about right. So, good luck."

"Thanks."

They both stood, then shook hands.

As Piza made his way down the abandoned hallway, a contented smile dawned. His pace unhurried, he ran his right hand along the faded wall tiles, removing it only when he reached the gray double doors crowned by a glimmering "Exit" sign.

THE END

THANK YOU AND GET FREE STORIES

Thanks so much for reading "Mr. Pizza". I sincerely hope you enjoyed it. (If you didn't, please feel free to lie to me. Yes, I'm that shallow.)

These days, reviews are critical to an author's success. So if you have a moment, I'd really appreciate it if you'd leave a review on the site from which you purchased the book. It doesn't have to be long. Just a few words would be great.

Be sure to visit my website at www.jfpandolfi.com to get FREE short stories, and to read my riveting interview with myself.

Thanks again, and be well.

J.F. Pandolfi

ACKNOWLEDGMENTS

Heartfelt thanks to my family for their support throughout this seemingly endless journey. (AJ, you're the ultimate beta reader.) And a collective fist-bump to my fellow writers group members. Your encouragement was a constant from day one, and your mince-no-words objectivity made me a better writer—with minimal emotional scarring.

Made in the USA
Middletown, DE
22 October 2018